S0-BTD-174

THE TOUR

THE TOUR SERIES - BOOK 1

JEAN GRAINGER

Copyright © 2022 Gold Harp Media

The rights of Jean Grainger to be identified as the author of this work have been
asserted by her in accordance with the Copyright, Designs and Patents Act, 1988.

www.jeangrainger.com

This book is sold subject to the condition that it shall not, by way of trade or otherwise,
be lent, resold, hired out or otherwise circulated without the author's prior consent in
any form of binding or cover other than that in which it is published and without a
similar condition, including this condition being imposed on the subsequent purchaser.

This is a work of fiction. Any resemblance to any person living or dead is entirely
coincidental.

❀ Created with Vellum

For my Family

CHAPTER 1

*C*onor O'Shea sat on the edge of the king-sized four-poster bed, trying to wake up. The heavy damask curtains hanging in the big bay window admitted not a single chink of light. It struck Conor, not for the first time, how odd it was to feel perfectly at home in any hotel, especially this vast edifice, but somehow he did.

He padded across the deep-pile taupe carpet to the bathroom. Twenty minutes later, power shower completed, he stood in front of the mirror, gazing ruefully at his reflection while he shaved. His silver hair had the effect of making him look older than his forty-five years, he mused, and although people told him it made him look distinguished, he wasn't quite so sure. As he dressed – black tailored trousers and a cream Ralph Lauren shirt, which contrasted sharply with his tanned skin – he mentally ran through his itinerary for the day ahead. He would have breakfast quickly, just some cereal and a cup of tea, and get the Mercedes mini-coach organised to pick up his passengers from Shannon Airport at seven o'clock.

Conor often wondered about the wisdom of his fellow coach drivers eating full cooked breakfasts every morning and then munching their way through scones and apple tarts all day during their numerous tour stops. Many of them were so overweight it made their job of loading and unloading heavy suitcases almost impossible. Conor liked to stay fit, and he was also careful not to get carried away with all the free food offered to him and the other coach drivers.

Today would be a nice easy day; it entailed nothing more than picking up his tour group at Shannon that morning and bringing them back to the Dunshane Castle Hotel. The tour operator, for whom Conor had worked as a driver-guide for nearly twenty years, had strong business links with the five-star castle. As a result, Conor stayed there almost once a week.

As he walked across the busy lobby towards the dining room, a haughty voice rang out. 'Mr O'Shea, your post,' said Ms O'Brien, the head receptionist, proffering several postcards and one letter. 'Although what gave you the impression that this was your office and that I and the reception staff are your personal secretaries, I cannot possibly imagine,' she added curtly.

Conor accepted the small bundle and smiled at Ms O'Brien in spite of her glare. 'I know that, Katherine. I'm an awful nuisance, and you are all so good to me here.'

The two young receptionists gaped at each other, seemingly amazed at Conor's use of Ms O'Brien's first name. No one else at the Dunshane would ever dare do such a thing.

'And I'm really sorry for the inconvenience,' Conor continued. 'But as you know, I'm kind of homeless during the tourist season, so I rely on your unending generosity in keeping my post and other things for me while I'm on the road. I really do appreciate it, though, Katherine.'

'Well, yes. I suppose we have no choice. By the way, Rosemary from your office booked in six more tours, so that means we have a whole summer of being your unpaid PAs ahead of us.' Ms O'Brien revealed just a hint of a smile.

Conor's twinkling blue eyes always seemed to have a melting effect on her frosty personality, something that was a source of amazement to the other staff. He knew her bark was much worse than her bite and that underneath it all, she actually liked him and appreciated that he didn't behave in the manner of some of the other coach drivers, who were always drinking and flirting with the waitresses. He was friendly and chatty but never disrespectful, and he genuinely did value all the extra little things the Dunshane staff did for him. Equally, however, he knew how important an asset he was to the hotel; his tour operator employers regularly sought his opinions on the accommodation used, and so it was in the hotel's best interest to keep him happy. It worked both ways. The hotel staff knew exactly how to cater to the clients he brought them and precisely what standards were expected of them, and they delivered accordingly. If things needed a little tweaking from time to time, Conor usually had a quiet word in the right ear and succeeded in solving the problem.

He continued into the dining room and was immediately greeted by Anastasia, one of the waitresses.

'Well, if it isn't my favourite communist!' he said with a big smile. When she didn't respond in her normal friendly fashion, Conor took a closer look and realised she had been crying. His first instinct was to ask her what was wrong, but he hesitated, in case it was something personal that she might not want to discuss with him. In any event, she had moved on and was busy taking an order from another table, so he took a seat and waited, wondering what, if anything, he should say. *Probably boyfriend trouble*, he thought to himself. *Best keep out of it.*

Among the Dunshane staff, the young Ukrainian was the person he had struck up the closest friendship with. His chats with Anastasia revealed that she, like so many of her countryfolk, had come to Ireland in search of a better life. Conor was surprised when she told him that she had, in fact, worked as a teacher in Kiev but the money she made waitressing in Ireland was twice what she could earn at home.

Two weeks earlier, in between departing and arriving tour groups, one of the receptionists had told him it was Anastasia's birthday, so he had taken her out for a meal to cheer her up; she had seemed a bit lonely for home. That evening, as they left the hotel grounds on their way to the restaurant, he had been acutely aware of the looks he attracted from the other drivers. Clearly, they believed there was something more going on between him and Anastasia. *Ah, what the hell*, he'd said to himself. *They always believe that about everyone.*

3

The female tour guides had an awful job coping with some of those drivers, much to Conor's embarrassment. For some, the idea that a man and a woman could remain just friends or colleagues was inconceivable. Only last week, Conor had caused a bit of a stir by telling Ollie Murphy to give it a rest as Ollie told one sexist joke after another to an eager audience of drivers whiling away the time in the airport car park as they waited for their passengers to arrive.

As if Anastasia would be interested in him anyhow, he mused. She was absolutely gorgeous and way too young for him – a mere twenty-five-year-old, he reminded himself. Although she actually looked a lot younger than that with her pixie-crop blond hair and enormous green eyes – reminiscent of Meg Ryan when she first became famous, he thought.

Anastasia's work uniform – a cream and gold fitted blouse and black skirt – was markedly different from her dress sense outside of work, which was quite bohemian, hippyish even. During one of their many long chats in recent months, she had explained to him that she loved to make her own clothes. Conor was well aware that they made an unusual pair – Anastasia's tiny five-foot frame beside Conor's six-foot-two muscular bulk. But they could gossip all they liked, the lot of them; he didn't give a hoot what they thought about any of it. He was far too interested in hearing her stories, and he loved to listen to her accent – a peculiar mix of Ukraine and West Clare. Her unique combination of inflections and idioms invariably made him smile.

'Hi, Conor.' She interrupted his reverie and stood beside the table, pen and notepad at the ready.

'Ah, Anastasia, are you all right?' he blurted. 'You seem a bit...eh... upset or something.'

The genuine concern on Conor's face seemed to have the effect of opening the floodgates. 'Oh, Conor, I am sorry. Is not your problem. Is just I get phone call this day from my brother. He tell me my mother is in the hospital, but he is cut off before he can tell me more. So now I am all day worried. I think maybe she is dead, or maybe she need me and...' Her voice broke.

Conor pulled out a chair and made her sit down, ignoring the disapproving glare from Carlos Manner, the restaurant manager. 'Ah, God love you...you poor thing. That's terrible. Listen, why can't you just call him or one of your other relations and find out what's happening? That's an awful worry to have going on in your head all day.'

'Well, yes, but there is no more a pay phone in the hotel, and my mobile plan don't let me make call to Ukraine. I must wait until after shift to go to internet place in Ennis.'

'Sure, that's no problem at all – use my phone. I use it to call the States for work all the time, so I'm sure it will manage a call to Ukraine too,' Conor said, relieved at being able to help his young friend in some practical way.

'Conor, you are so kind.' She smiled faintly. 'But even you cannot afford cost of calling Ukraine on mobile phone! No, is OK. I will call later in internet place.'

'Don't be ridiculous!' Conor said, handing her the phone. 'Sure I'm loaded! I'm only doing this job for the craic!' He was glad to see another hint of a smile creep across her tear-stained face. 'Now, go on over there to that quiet corner by the window and ring your brother. I'm sure everything will be grand. OK?'

Anastasia relented and took the phone. A few moments later, she was talking to someone and seemed, from her body language at any rate, to be reassured, although Conor had no clue what she was saying. Just then, he spotted the manager heading in her direction. As Carlos passed the table, Conor put out his hand to stop him. 'She just has something urgent that she needs to deal with at home in Ukraine,' Conor said quietly. 'She'll only be a minute.'

Carlos Manner was an imperious little man with slicked-down hair and perfectly manicured nails. Always immaculate in his appearance, he had the air of someone who slept in a straight line every night wearing a pair of perfectly ironed pyjamas. His clipped South African accent never ceased to grate on Conor's nerves.

'With all due respect, Conor, I think it is my concern if a member of my staff is attending to personal business on hotel time,' he intoned as he made to move towards Anastasia.

'Carlos,' said Conor quietly but firmly, 'just give her a chance to finish her call. I'm sure the place won't go up in flames without her for five minutes.'

Carlos winced at Conor's use of his first name but realised that he couldn't win against him. They both knew that if Carlos took it up with the general manager of the hotel, he would be overruled instantly. He would be told that Conor was a valued business associate of the chain and that he must be accommodated whenever possible. Carlos turned on his immaculately polished heel, seething with resentment.

A few moments later, Anastasia returned and handed Conor his phone. 'Thank you so much, Conor. You are so nice. My brother say she is OK, little pain in the heart. She must stay in the hospital for some more days, but it is not really serious. Oh, I am so better now! I would be all day worried if I could not call.' She smiled gratefully. Then, lowering her voice, she added, 'Is Mr Manner mad now?'

Conor knew the staff detested the prissy little man who found fault with everyone and everything. 'Not at all, no. He was just wondering if you were OK. I told him you were. Don't worry your head about it. Now I'm off to pick up my group, but we'll be back for dinner tonight, so I'll see you later. And I'm really glad your mam is all right.' Giving her an encouraging wink and a smile, he left the dining room, breakfastless but feeling none the worse for it.

As he walked towards the coach park, he reached into his pocket for the pile of post that Katherine O'Brien had handed him earlier. The postcards were from people who had been on his tours earlier in the season, thanking him for making their trip so enjoyable. A letter, postmarked Philadelphia, lay underneath a sheaf of postcards. Conor recognised the handwriting of the person who had scratched out his old home address and replaced it with the Dunshane Castle forwarding address. He stopped and stared hard at the envelope. There were only two people in America who would know his old home address in County Cork. Neither of those people had been in touch with him in well over twenty years. He ripped open the envelope, certain that the letter was from Sinead and not from his brother Gerry, who had appalling handwriting. Heart thumping, he read.

Dear Conor,

I know it must seem like a bolt out of the blue hearing from me after so long. I don't really know where to start. I'm sorry I didn't get in touch before, but maybe you've heard from Gerry. I don't know. I've not seen him in years. Things didn't work out with him, as you probably know. It all seems so long ago now, you and me and Gerry, in Passage West. Anyway, I'm writing to tell you that I'm coming home. Well, that is, we are coming home, young Conor and me, your nephew. He's seventeen. I know I should have told you when he was born, but anyway, here it is. I have a son, named after his uncle, and we are a one-parent family. Gerry knows about Conor. I did have his address at one point, and I wrote to him telling him he had a son, but apart from a postcard acknowledgement, I never heard from him again. I often think if I'd stayed in Ireland instead of coming to the States with your brother, things would have worked out better, but I guess that's all water under the bridge now. We had some fun times, though, didn't we?

Anyway, I'd love to get back in touch with you. My email address is sinead1234@aol.com. I'm sure Ireland has progressed into the age of technology by now!

Hopefully talk soon.

Lots of love,

Sinead xxxx

Conor sat in the coach. He had never expected to hear from her again. He had sent Christmas cards and things over the years but had never received a reply. Gerry was his only sibling, and their parents were long since dead. Despite Conor's best efforts, the two brothers had lost touch. The idea that maintaining contact between them might have achieved something positive caused Conor to feel even more guilt and pain. He had loved Sinead, more than he had ever loved anyone before or since, but she had chosen the better-looking brother, Gerry, and that was that. It was wrong to want your brother's girl, even if he had seen her first.

Gerry was always a bit wild, especially after their mother died, and Conor had become accustomed to taking care of him. Gerry had a reputation for being a useless layabout who felt the world owed him something, but Conor always believed that was because Gerry was orphaned at a young age. Conor's policy at the time Gerry took up with Sinead was to let on that he was thrilled. After all, it wasn't as if there had been any understanding between himself and Sinead. They had only gone out a few times.

Before Gerry and Sinead became an item, Conor had decided that she was the only woman for him; he had even confided in Gerry about his feelings. Gerry hadn't intended to hurt him – he knew that. It was just that Gerry always behaved like a child; if he saw something he wanted, he just took it. Conor knew that he should have declared his feelings to Sinead sooner. While he was dithering, waiting for the right time to tell her how he felt, Gerry had snuck in before him.

Conor had always believed Sinead was well aware of how he felt about her, yet she still picked Gerry. Maybe she thought she could make Gerry happy since no one else could. It seemed from the letter, though, that it all went wrong anyway. Did he want Sinead back in his life now, he wondered, after all this time? He really didn't know. A huge part of him was excited at the prospect of seeing her, having the chance to say...well, what? What could he say? What he should have said twenty years ago? And she had a son. That meant Conor had a nephew. It was a lot to take in.

CHAPTER 2

'*C*onor! You look well,' said Carolina Capelli, giving him a kiss on the cheek as she and her fellow tour guides waited for their groups in the arrivals area at Shannon Airport.

'Carolina! How are you? Who are you with this week?'

'Mad Mike Murphy.' She threw her eyes to the heavens. 'I'm over the moon.'

'Oh God help you! You'll have your work cut out for you so!' Conor chuckled.

'I think I sorted him out last week when he was *helping* me into the coach by grabbing my bottom. I told him I was going to speak to his wife, explain how *helpful* he always is to me the next time she came to drop him off. He nearly died.'

Conor laughed. Carolina and he had both had the misfortune to meet the scary, chain-smoking Mags Murphy. 'No more than he deserves,' Conor said. 'I reckon she'd murder him if she found out, though.'

Carolina was a twenty-eight-year-old Italian. Never in a million years would she be interested in Mad Mike, who was fat and fifty, had chronic halitosis and possessed a very cavalier attitude to personal hygiene.

'How many have you this week, Conor?' asked Carolina, sighing theatrically. 'Three? Five?'

'Nine,' Conor replied. 'I know, I *know*.' He smiled, reacting to her look of envy. 'The tour operator doesn't allow any more than ten people in my groups. It's a very expensive way of taking a tour around Ireland, but people seem to prefer it, plus the fact that we can get to places that the big coaches can't reach. I know how you feel, though. I served my time on the fifty-two-seaters back in the dark ages too, but I fell on my feet with this crowd. I'm my own boss, and it's great.'

'I won't pretend I'm not jealous, Conor! I've got forty-seven Italian dentists, so it's going to be a busy week. Oh look, here are some of mine now. I'd better look lively.'

Conor smiled at Carolina as she went to gather her group, who were beginning to trickle through the large glass doors. Soon, he himself was busy dealing with the first of his passengers, their faces registering relief as they spotted him holding aloft the welcome card bearing the tour operator's name and logo. He directed them to the toilets, the ATM and the newspaper stand, then instructed them to make their way out to the distinctive Mercedes coach in the car park, where he would join them as soon as he was sure everyone had arrived.

'Good morning and welcome to you all,' he said as he gathered his group of nine beside the coach. 'I'm sure you're all tired after the long flight, so I'll just get the bags loaded onto the coach and we'll be off to the hotel. You can freshen up or have a bit of a rest, and then we'll get together again later on for dinner and have a chat about the great time you are going to have for the next week.

'My name is Conor O'Shea, and for some sins that you have obviously committed, you are stuck with me driving and telling you all about our lovely country. If you have been here before and you suspect a bit of blarney on my part, there's a small "keep your mouth shut" fee available.'

The group laughed and immediately relaxed.

* * *

ELLEN O'DONOVAN'S sparkling blue eyes belied her eighty years. She was fit and healthy, and her hair was cut in a flatteringly soft style that framed her face. Observing her as she stood patiently waiting to board the coach, Conor noticed how fresh she looked for someone who had just arrived on an overnight flight from New York. She was dressed in an elegant pair of navy-blue tailored trousers and a beige silk blouse, and around her neck she wore a simple gold cross and chain.

Ellen walked slowly down the centre of the coach and chose a seat opposite a couple. She nodded and smiled politely and then closed her eyes and breathed deeply. She had made it, against all the odds and against the advice of everyone she knew. She was finally here. She leaned back against the plush leather seat, twice the width of the plane seat she had endured for the past six hours. This really was a lovely way to travel, she thought to herself.

The dark-green coach had large reclining seats facing each other. Between each set of four seats was a table, complete with power points and drink holders. The halogen reading lights overhead could be adjusted to suit individual passengers' requirements, and the large coach windows facilitated wonderfully panoramic views of the world outside. The entire interior of the coach was upholstered and carpeted in rich tones of green and gold. At the rear of the vehicle was a compact but perfectly functional bathroom. Under the dash at the front of the coach was a refrigerator, filled with complimentary water and soft drinks. Ellen had never been on a coach like it.

Her peace was interrupted by hushed yet urgent whispers from the couple on her left.

'Just turn it off, Elliot, please,' the woman muttered to her husband.

Without glancing up from his laptop, the small, dark-featured man with a distinctive New York accent said, 'OK, OK, I will. I just need to check something with LA. I'll only be a minute. Get the driver guy to hold on for me, OK? I'm going outside to get a better signal. The connection on this laptop dongle thing is terrible. I'm going to have to use my cell to call 'em.'

'We can't keep everyone waiting, Elliot,' she whispered anxiously.

Undeterred, Elliot left the coach and paced up and down on the footpath, talking animatedly into his mobile phone.

'He is very busy at work at the moment... His company is involved in investment projects. I'm Anna Heller,' the woman said to Ellen with an apologetic smile.

Ellen smiled warmly. Anna looked as if she was of German or Scandinavian extraction. She was tall, her blond hair was cut in a chic bob, and she had perfectly manicured nails. She was dressed in what to Ellen looked like designer gear, and she carried a handbag that Ellen guessed had cost an awful lot of money.

Ellen looked out the window. Anna Heller's husband was still pacing up and down outside. He too was dressed in what looked like very expensive clothes, his left wrist brandishing a Rolex Oyster. While he was handsome enough in a way, Ellen thought he was unusually short, an awful lot shorter than his much younger wife. Probably wife number two or number three, Ellen reckoned.

As she surveyed the assembled passengers, Ellen's attention was drawn to two women sitting in the front seats, both wearing what looked like hiking gear. Ellen judged them to be in their mid to late fifties. The one sitting nearest the window was tall and wiry, with sharp facial features and a cropped, utilitarian haircut. Her companion looked considerably more feminine, with a more rounded figure and a kind face. The sharp-looking woman was glaring at Elliot Heller with barely concealed fury.

'Have you been on a coach tour before?' she asked Anna Heller pointedly.

'Well, um, no... Uh, I mean, we have taken day trips when we were on vacation, but we, uh –'

Anna was interrupted mid-sentence by her interrogator. 'This is my twelfth trip with this tour operator. One of the reasons I travel with them so often is they have a policy of not waiting for latecomers. If a person cannot make it back to the coach at the prearranged time, well, then they just have to make their own arrangements. It's not fair to fellow travellers to make them wait for those who are too disorganised or too selfish to be on time.'

'Oh, that's a good policy, I guess,' Anna replied, her face betraying that she was acutely aware of the implication that Elliot was just such an individual.

'By the way, I am Dr Dorothy Crane, and this is my travelling companion, Juliet Steele. We are from Des Moines, Iowa.'

Juliet turned around and smiled bleakly at the rest of the group. 'Hi,' she said shyly.

The next passenger to board the coach was someone Ellen had noticed in the arrivals area. Like her, he too seemed to be travelling alone. He was, she thought, in his mid to late sixties, possibly older. He was small and fit and had longish grey hair that flopped onto his face and curled over his collar in a manner that Ellen considered somewhat bohemian for a man of his generation. His skin, leatherlike from seemingly lifelong exposure to strong sunlight, was offset by his large brown eyes that radiated warmth and intelligence. He was dressed in beige chinos and a dark-green shirt bearing a golf-and-country-club logo. He sat on the outside of a double seat, smiled and addressed the group in general. 'Hi, I'm Bert Cooper from Corpus Christi, Texas. Wow! It sure is fresh here, ain't it? I left ninety-six in the shade, so this is just great.'

Everyone except Dorothy Crane smiled and introduced themselves in turn.

Ellen looked up as the next two members of the group boarded the coach. One of them, a boy about sixteen or seventeen years old, had jet-black spikes of hair sticking out on one side of his head; the other side was shaved tight. His neck featured an elaborate spider's web tattoo, and his face was plastered in white make-up, his eyes lined in heavy kohl pencil. Piercings too numerous to count adorned his ears, nose, upper lip, eyebrows and chin. Hanging from his thin frame was a black leather jacket, decorated with a skull and bleeding eyes, and below that, black skintight jeans torn to shreds. To complete the look, he wore his trousers tucked into black Doc Martens, which were laced to the knee.

The woman following immediately behind him seemed to be travelling with him as, unprompted, the boy heaved her large 'Chanelle' bag onto the overhead luggage rack. Ellen saw Anna's face register the obvious fake.

'Just sit down there, Corlene,' the boy said in a surprisingly gentle voice, indicating the seat he had requisitioned. Corlene, however, had other plans.

'Well, isn't that just perfect,' she screeched in a high-pitched southern drawl, aiming for the seat beside Bert Cooper. 'I love a window seat, and you obviously want the aisle, so you and I are perfectly suited. I'll sit inside, and you can take the outside. I'm very flexible.' She batted her ridiculously long false eyelashes in what, presumably, she thought was a seductive manner, but in fact only succeeded in causing Bert to recoil in terror. His southern chivalry, however, prevented him from refusing her offer.

'Well, ma'am, I'd be honoured,' he replied, with an almost audible gulp of fear. 'The name's Bert.'

'I'm Corlene Holbrooke, originally from Ashton County, Alabama, but I'm a citizen of the world these days. I just love to travel and meet new folks, and y'all seem so nice. I think I'm going to have a really swell time here in Iceland.'

Her words seemed slightly slurred, and if she noticed her geographical error, she gave no indication. Ellen considered responding but then thought better of it. Most of the group seemed bemused by Corlene's antics, none more so than the teenager accompanying her, who was desperately trying to hide his embarrassment.

'*Ireland*, Mom, we're in *Ireland*, not Iceland,' he said through gritted teeth.

Corlene exuded a smell of bourbon, which intermingled with her nauseatingly strong perfume. Ellen thought she cut a less-than-stylish figure in her five-inch, leopard-print stilettos and matching leopard-print Lycra dress, which looked as if it had been spray-painted on her ample frame. To compound this disastrous look, it was impossible not to notice that her brassy-blond head of hair featured a good two inches of blackish-grey roots. She had possibly been good-looking fa few years ago, Ellen thought, but now she bore all the signs of a woman well and truly gone to seed.

'Ireland, sure, that's what I said,' she replied, returning her attention to Bert. 'This sure is a beautiful bus, isn't it, Bert? I've never seen one like it, but I guess I've never taken a tour before. I tend to do more sophisticated vacations, exotic beach locations, that sort of thing. I just spent a month at a friend's villa in the Caribbean. I sure do miss those mojitos.' She giggled, with even more exaggerated batting of her eyelashes.

'Yes, it really is quite something. It's nice to be able to stretch out,' Bert replied.

'Oh, I do love to *stretch* out too. Though you travelled first class, I noticed. I would have done also, but this trip was a last-minute decision and coach was all that was available. Still, now we're here, we can stretch out together.' Corlene flirted outrageously, running her red-taloned hand along Bert's arm.

Ellen caught Bert's terrified glance and tried not to smile.

Dorothy Crane decided to do a headcount. 'We seem to be missing someone,' she said in an imperious tone.

The coach suddenly seemed to list to one side, and all eyes were drawn to the enormous mountain of a man climbing on board, his face shining with perspiration, his green Hawaiian shirt sticking to his vast torso. He looked like he might be in his late fifties, Ellen thought, almost certainly of Irish origin. In his hair, which was short and greying, she could make out flecks of the original colour – unmistakeably red. He wore a sovereign ring on the little finger of his left hand.

'Well, you all just sit pretty here and leave the Paddies to do the donkey work. Me and Conor here had some job getting your luggage into this little bus. But we got it done, didn't we, Conor?' he said in a booming voice.

Conor climbed on board, looking mortified. 'No problem at all, folks,' he said, wishing with all his heart that Patrick O'Neill of the Boston Police Department would mind his own business. If there was one thing worse than tourists' ridiculously heavy suitcases, it was helpful but clueless tourists trying to assist the driver in loading them on board. Conor had perfected his own system, and he always preferred to be allowed to get on with it. Unfortunately, Patrick seemed determined to make friends with him. As he'd fired the bags into the boot in any old way at all, he told Conor his life story.

Conor had met so many Patricks in his career, he could almost predict their story before they started recounting it. In this Patrick's case, the salient details were: born in South Boston, a true 'Southie'; raised by a violent alcoholic father and a saintly mother, both of Irish origin; beneficiary of a Catholic education and a survivor of endless chastisement by two double-barrelled nuns, Sister Mary Margaret and Sister Bridget Bernadette; long-serving member of the Boston Police Department, where he had spent his career waging war against the organised crime perpetuated by erstwhile schoolmates, including the infamous Whitey Bulger, a neighbour's child.

Irish Americans like Patrick were Conor's least favourite tourists. They often considered themselves superior to others on the trip because they were 'Irish'. To most Irish people, these 'Plastic Paddies', as they were unflatteringly called, were no more Irish than the Dalai Lama, but they seemed to have a strong sense of belonging none-theless. The problem, or so Conor thought, was that the culture they were looking for simply didn't exist. Corned beef and cabbage was not the national dish, and you would very rarely hear 'Danny Boy' or 'When Irish Eyes Are Smiling' being sung at an Irish music session. It also seemed to be a mystery to these Irish Americans that most people in the Republic had a desire to find a peaceful settlement to the conflict in the North and did not burn with resentment towards England. Most reasonable people wanted to see a permanent solution to the hostilities, where both sides could be reasonably accom-modated.

Once he had everyone on board, Conor set off for the hotel, pointing out interesting landmarks to the group as they passed and giving them their itinerary for the rest of the day. 'After you've checked in, I'll be leaving you to get over your jet lag, get your body clock onto Irish time. You can eat in the hotel this evening, but there are also plenty of nice pubs and restaurants in Ennis, a short distance away by taxi. We'll be leaving tomorrow at 9:30 a.m. In the meantime, you might like to make a note of my room number – it's 409. Give me a call if you need anything.'

'Well, Conor, I'm sure we'll all be just fine, but it's so nice to know we are in your *capable* hands,' Corlene said breathlessly.

She virtually ignores all the women and fawns over the men, thought Conor as they drove through the gates of the hotel. Like Patrick, she was not unique. There was a perception that tours were full of wealthy old men and women, so gold-diggers of both genders were not uncommon.

As he and Patrick unloaded the last of the suitcases, Conor leaned over and said quietly, 'Thanks for all the help today, Patrick, but you relax in the morning and enjoy your breakfast. I'll get the porter lads here to help me load up. Sure they'll be glad of the few extra bob.'

The look on Patrick's face clearly indicated that he really would have preferred to lend a hand with loading the coach. On the other hand, it would be mean to begrudge the young lads the chance of making a bit of money.

CHAPTER 3

That evening, as Conor was coming back from the hotel pool, he saw Anastasia making her way down the corridor, looking distracted and more than a little pale and wan. He was practically beside her before she noticed him.

'Oh, so sorry, Conor, I did not see. You are not working now?'

'No, the group are on their own tonight, so I was a very good boy and did all my paperwork for the afternoon. I hate it, but it has to be done. I'm just back from a swim. How are you doing? You look very pale. Are you all right?'

'Yes. Just bit tired. I finish now only. Mr Manner make me stay behind to clean windows. I tell him it crazy to make cleaning of windows in raining weather, but he say he is the boss and he decide. Is easier, I think, to do it.' She sighed wearily as she examined her chapped hands.

'Ah, you poor thing. That seems a bit pointless right enough,' said Conor, thinking quietly that this must have been Carlos's way of punishing her for making the phone call in the dining room that morning. 'Will I run you home, or have you got a lift?'

'No, is OK. I have bicycle.'

'It's lashing rain, and there's no way you can cycle to your place now. Come on. I'll run you home. It'll only take a few minutes. Have you heard anything more from your brother?'

Anastasia gave another sigh. 'I spoke this evening with him, and he said she was OK, but people in her family, always they have problem with the heart. I am still worried. I think my brother do not tell me all of the full story because he knows there is nothing I can do from Ireland. I think maybe my mother tell him to not say to me, so I will not worry. It is hard, I think, for mothers – they want the best thing for their children, but also they want them to be close.'

Conor looked at the lines of worry etched on her face. 'I know, sure. My own mother had to manage without a man to support her, and even though it was tough with my brother and me to rear, she always thanked God that we didn't have to emigrate. So many boys and girls left Ireland over the years hoping to have a better future abroad. It's a wonder we Irish don't remember that when we're dealing with all the new people arriving into this country now. People have short memories, I think.'

'So your brother and you just stayed here for all of your life? Does he drive buses too?'

Conor was taken aback by the question. He almost never referred to Gerry. In fact, very few people even knew he had a brother. 'Em, no, he's in America. He did emigrate in the end, although he didn't have to. My mother was dead by that time. He's gone years.' Quickly changing the subject, he added, 'Are you whacked, or will we stop for a quick drink on the way home?'

Anastasia looked confused. 'Whacked? I don't know what is this word, but I think I need a drink if you have time.' She smiled.

'Righty-ho so. The lady has spoken.'

Conor observed Anastasia from the bar as he waited for their drinks. She had changed out of her uniform and was now wearing faded Levi's and a T-shirt with a smiley face. *God, she looks so vulnerable and childlike sometimes*, he thought.

As they sipped their drinks, Anastasia regaled him with stories of the dreadful Carlos and his stupid new rules, the latest being that even if there were no guests within earshot, the staff were to communicate only in English with each other. Conor hid his annoyance and reminded her that she didn't have to put up with harassment in the workplace.

'People are mostly nice here,' she replied, 'but it is a bit frightening, I think, for local people when they see so many of us foreigners coming to Ireland at one time maybe. Is funny, though – you know Betty who works in the laundry room?'

'I do indeed. She's a dote of a woman, washes my shirts for me every week – though the boss doesn't know anything about that, so keep it to yourself. She's real old stock Betty, so she is. A heart of gold.'

'Well, just yesterday, she said to me and Svetlana – remember I told you about her, she's my flatmate from Lithuania? When we were on our break and having a sandwich, Betty come in and say to us that she now eats only Polish bread. She say she buy it in Polski Sklep – she even say Polish word for shop! Svetlana and me laugh so much at this. She is so nice. The Irish bread she say make her say things many times. I don't know what she mean, but is funny to think an old Irish lady only eat Polish bread.' She smiled.

Conor burst out laughing. 'Did she say the bread repeats on her, by any chance?'

Anastasia looked at him blankly.

'In Ireland, when we say some kind of food repeats on a person, it doesn't mean they say things twice. It's more that the food doesn't make them feel too good. They get indigestion from it.'

Anastasia's face lit up. 'Ah yes! That is what she say. Ah, now it make sense. Svetlana and me don't know what she say most times, but she is very kind to us. She made Svetlana a cake for her birthday, and we all had it on our tea break until Mr Manner come in staff room and say is against safety and health! Then later he tell me and Svetlana we must look better. Her hair is too long and my false eyelashes are health hazard. I tell him my eyelash is real and not false at all, but he don't believe me. Everyone in my family have this long eyelash. I think he is a very mean man who is always grumpy and looking out for things to be wrong. Betty is only one who is not feared to be rude to him because she worked for many years in hotel and is friend of Mr

McCarthy. She tell him we on a break and he cannot harass us or she will speak to union. I think Mr Manner a bit feared of Betty.'

Conor laughed. 'Carlos better watch himself with Betty on your side, right enough. In a fight, my money would be on Betty every time. And you're right – I'm driving tours for twenty years, and Betty has been at the Dunshane for that long at least. She's known Tim McCarthy since he was a child, and he has great time for Betty. When old Tadhg McCarthy set up the hotel back in the fifties, Betty got a job there. I think she's the only member of the original staff still working there, so Mr Manner is right not to get in her way.'

Anastasia looked over at Conor. 'I think he is little bit feared of you too, Conor.' She smiled.

'Sure, myself and Betty are the old guard. That hotel is more like home to me, I stay there so often. Don't mind Carlos – he's just trying to make his presence felt.'

'Conor? Do you mind I ask you a question? Is kind of personal.'

'Ask away.'

'How old you are?'

'Forty-five. I suppose to someone of only twenty-five, that's ancient.'

'No, I think you don't look that much. But why do you live in hotel and have no home or wife or children? You are such a nice man and so kind – I wonder why you live such a life alone.'

Conor put down his drink and turned to face her. 'What brought this on?'

'I am sorry. It is not my business at all. I just was thinking about it and… Conor, I am sorry. I should not ask you about your life. It's just that…'

Conor smiled. 'It's just what?'

'Nothing. Is nothing.' She looked embarrassed to have crossed the boundary of their friendship.

'Well, Anastasia, to answer your question, I live in a hotel because I have no interest in going home. I do own a house, but it is just that, bricks and mortar. I work tours back to back because it's what I want to do. I take myself off during the winter months to Spain, where I own a small apartment, and I do crosswords and play a bit of golf. I don't have a wife because...' – he took a deep breath – 'because that side of things never really worked out for me. I've had a few relationships over the years but nothing too serious. I'm happy enough with my life. I have great friends, I love my job, and I've enough money to do what I want. Sometimes, sure, I look at people playing with their kids in the park or pushing them on a swing and wish I had that, but it wasn't meant to be. Does that answer your question?'

Anastasia looked at Conor with her big green eyes, smiled and nodded.

Conor wondered if he should tell her the latest developments and decided it would be good to have another perspective. 'In fact, it's funny you should ask about all that now. I did love a girl. Years and years ago. Anyway, she chose someone else – my brother, in fact. And well, off they went to America. I never said anything to either of them, but maybe I should have. Anyway, it's all done now. The thing is, though, I got a letter yesterday from the girl – her name is Sinead. The letter came out of the blue. We haven't been in touch with each other in almost twenty years. In the letter, she was saying she was coming back to Ireland and did I want to meet up. She has a son now, my nephew, but there's no sign of Gerry, my brother.'

Anastasia's face registered surprise.

'Ah no, he hasn't disappeared or anything like that. They broke up. Actually, he left her. I suppose he was never very reliable,' Conor added ruefully.

'What do you want to do? Do you want to see her again?'

Conor took a sip of his drink before replying. 'I don't honestly know, Anastasia. I really don't. There was a time when I would have given anything to have her back, but maybe too many years have passed now. I just don't know. On top of that, I don't even know if she'd be interested in me that way at all. Sure she could be coming back to Ireland for all sorts of reasons that I know nothing about.'

Anastasia seemed to be weighing up what to say next. 'Well, I suppose you must decide if she is still the only one you love. If she is, then maybe you must see her, and if she is not, then perhaps you can see her and just be friendly?'

Conor considered this for a few moments. 'I suppose you're right. I'll meet her either way. Maybe I'll have to see her in the flesh to know how I feel about her.'

Anastasia changed tack, seemingly sensing that Conor had said all he was going to say on the subject. 'I was asked to go back to school where I was teaching before as substitute in Kiev. I got letter from school manager. He offered me more wages and permanent job working with children with special needs if I go back in Ukraine. I think a lot, and now with my mother so sick and everything, I think maybe is best thing. I like Ireland and have made so many good friends here, but I don't think there is anything keeping me here. So neither do I know what to do, Conor. What do you think?' Her large green eyes held his, waiting for his response.

'Well, aren't we the right pair? Dithering and wondering and trying to decide. I don't know much about your situation, but I do know this. Anastasia, you are young and beautiful and bright and funny. You can do anything you want to do. Anything at all. What does your gut instinct tell you to do?'

Anastasia looked puzzled. 'I don't know this thing, gut instinct? What does it mean?'

'It means deep down, what do you want to do? What is your heart telling you?'

Anastasia sighed. 'My head tells me I must go back. There is nothing here for me really...' She hesitated.

'And your heart?'

'My heart tells me to stay here.'

Conor smiled. 'I think the best thing to do is follow your heart. And I'd miss you if you went back. Don't mind me, though – I'm an auld softie.'

CHAPTER 4

*C*onor had the bags loaded and all his charges safely on board. 'Good morning, everyone. I hope you all slept well and are fighting fit for the trip ahead of us. This morn –'

He was cut off by Patrick's booming voice. 'The fightin' Irish! Ha, ha! That's us, eh, Conor? We taught those Brits a thing or two in the soccer match on TV last night, didn't we? They never learn, do they? You can never beat the Irish!'

Patrick would have continued in this vein, pontificating on Irish history, if Conor had allowed him, but he didn't. The man's behaviour was too reminiscent of a particularly memorable occasion a few years before the Good Friday Agreement in 1998 involving the near annihilation of one James O'Leary of Chicago, Illinois, in the bar of the Europa Hotel in Belfast, 'the most bombed hotel in the world'. On that occasion, Conor overheard O'Leary expounding his version of the Troubles in Northern Ireland at the top of his voice and offering anyone who would listen his ill-informed and naive solutions. His behaviour would have been only barely tolerated in most Irish pubs in the south, but given that the main audience for this particular speech was the brother of the infamous Mikey 'Bulldog' Bull, noted loyalist terrorist, it was one sure-fire way of ending up face down in the River Lagan. It was only thanks to Conor's diplomatic skills, which were worthy of the most skilled United Nations negotiator, that James O'Leary of Chicago, Illinois, managed to escape from that bar alive.

'Yes indeed,' Conor answered Patrick. 'We had luck on our side, especially when you consider that soccer was invented in England. I must say I think it's really fantastic that Ireland and England can now play each other competitively without any fuss, year in, year out. At long last, thanks be to God, we seem to be managing to put the bitterness of the past behind us, once and for all. We can now truly say we're moving on, adopting a new way of doing things, no longer constrained by mindless hatred of our closest neighbour. I mean to say, I can't be blamed for what my grandfather did, so why should some poor Englishman be blamed for his grandfather's actions? Sure that'd make no sense altogether. Terrible things happened on both sides, I'll grant you, but living in the past is pointless. That gets no one anywhere, does it?'

Patrick, clearly taken aback by Conor's attitude, muttered a grudging, 'Eh, yeah, I guess so.' To dispute such worthy and seemingly innocent sentiments would have seemed churlish. Even though he didn't actually know any English people and had never even been to England, Patrick's Irish-American identity was bound up in hatred of all things English.

Conor could see his opinions were not what Patrick wanted or expected to hear from a 'fellow' Irishman. Plus, Conor knew from experience that Patrick wasn't at all sure how he would have defended his political views anyway – well, not in front of the other passengers, in any case – so maintaining a disgruntled silence was his best and only option for the moment.

* * *

Dr Ellen O'Donovan looked out at the scenery, wearing a wry smile. *Poor old Patrick*, she thought. He was typical of men she had known all her life in South Boston. She mentally addressed him. *Patrick, the Ireland you are looking for just doesn't exist any more, if indeed it ever did.* But what of the Ireland Ellen O'Donovan was looking for? Did that exist? she wondered. She knew a lot about the politics and history of this beautiful but turbulent island, both from her father and from her lifelong study of the Irish question. If only she knew as much about her own story, she mused for about the thousandth time. She had done a lot of research on the internet, but thus far, her efforts hadn't amounted to much. Apart from some general information and the census records, which told her a little about her Irish ancestry, she still faced many unanswered questions about her family background.

Ellen had spent her career teaching history at a tough Boston high school. She had a master's degree in Irish history and another on the history of the British Empire, and she had written her doctoral thesis on the international political and cultural role of the Irish diaspora. Her work had been published in numerous journals, and she was the author of two books. Throughout, her interest in Irish history remained personally motivated rather than something she pursued in order to advance her career. The world of academia had never interested her. She loved teaching teenagers, and despite the school's reputation as a mere holding centre for the state penitentiary, her students never treated her with anything other than the greatest respect. In fact, she had the peculiar honour of being the only member of the one-hundred-strong staff never to have been a victim of any kind of crime. She was known both personally or by reputation by all the likely perpetrators. They deemed her off limits, and so she lived happily and peacefully in one of the most disreputable neighbourhoods in the United States.

* * *

JULIET SAT BACK AND RELAXED, taking in the beautiful scenery. She was enjoying herself, although if she were being really honest, she would have to admit that she had been dreading the trip. Dorothy had kind of railroaded her into it, and Juliet found herself signed up and booked before she knew what hit her. What had started out as an innocent conversation after church on Sunday, about how she had been looking at a friend's holiday photos of Ireland, had somehow ended up with her agreeing to accompany Dorothy on a trip there.

Since the death of her husband, Larry, the previous year, Juliet had found herself tearful and quite incapable of dealing with any kind of confrontation. Dorothy had somehow decided that what Juliet needed was someone to take the lead. In everything. It wasn't as if she even knew Dorothy all that well. They attended the same Episcopalian church and they knew each other enough to make small talk at the odd social event, but that was about it. Juliet recalled her friend Monica, who served with her on the church flower-arranging committee, telling her that she needed to be careful, that she shouldn't allow Dorothy to take advantage.

On the one and only occasion that Juliet had actually been invited inside the front door of Dorothy's house, she had been quite horrified at the lack of photographs, paintings or anything even vaguely personal or homely about the place. 'Clinical' was the term that came to mind. The only evidence of Dorothy's hobbies or interests was three large glass cabinets displaying dead butterflies, each one labelled with its correct Latin name, and a fourth cabinet filled with different species of fungi, also correctly labelled with their full Latin names.

Juliet contrasted Dorothy's sterile house with her lovely home in the leafy suburb of Carlisle, outside Des Moines. The house that she and Larry had bought as a young couple was still her home. She loved the area for its lovely walks, green open spaces, friendliness and relaxed pace of life. She and Larry had planned to move somewhere bigger when they had a family, but since they had never been lucky enough to have children, they stayed put in their cosy, three-bedroom bungalow. Juliet loved interior decorating, and she worked hard to make the house a happy haven for them both. Chintz-covered sofas and easy chairs filled her sunny living room, the walls of which were covered with photographs of nieces, nephews, friends and dogs. Juliet knew that she and Dorothy were a mismatched pair, to say the least.

She missed Larry desperately. He would have loved Ireland,

looking at all the old castles and ruins in this green country. Her life would never be the same again; her loneliness was profound and seemingly endless. She felt so vulnerable and alone. Logic told her that running away on a vacation wouldn't mean a vacation from her grief, but foolishly, she continued to hope that it might. She was facing retirement soon and was quite at a loss to know what to do with her life. Larry's brother, Joe, and his wife, Lainie, had bought a condo in Florida and had asked her if she would consider moving down there too. The winters would be easier to take certainly, but she just couldn't summon up the energy to do it. Maybe if they'd had children, she thought, things wouldn't seem quite so hard, so pointless.

* * *

DOROTHY CRANE SIGHED HEAVILY as Conor joked about the prolific love life of some long-dead chieftain. Honestly, did the man think she had paid good money for some kind of stand-up comedy routine? The rest of the group were laughing like drains, which showed just how inane they were. She glanced at Juliet, who seemed lost in thought, probably mooning about the departed Larry again for God's sake. She would speak to Juliet later, tell her that it wasn't fair to keep going on about him as if he were some kind of saint. Dorothy could barely remember the man, other than as a kind of do-gooder type, always collecting for some charity or other. She was glad she had never married. She never understood people's need to have others stuck in their business.

Dorothy's father, a pathologist, had died but she didn't mope around the place like it was the end of the world, did she? A severe man who did not believe in showing affection to anyone, including his only child, he had been widowed at an early age, when Dorothy was not yet four years old. While Dorothy was growing up, he ensured that his dead wife's name was never, *ever* mentioned, and as far as Dorothy was aware, there were no known photographs of her in existence. He had resisted all efforts from his wife's family to maintain contact with Dorothy, and eventually, after several thwarted attempts, they gave up. He sent Dorothy away at the age of five to be educated at an exclusive girls' boarding school, but despite spending twelve years there, she made no real friends. Occasionally, a kind teacher would try to break through her forbidding coldness and self-containment, but never with any success.

Dorothy excelled at her studies and graduated first in her class. She went on to Radcliffe and again excelled academically but did not engage socially. Neither her father nor anyone else turned up for her graduation ceremony four years later. When he died in Florida a few years ago, just months into his retirement, she sent a cheque to cover the cost of the cremation expenses but did not attend his funeral service. Dorothy remembered the look of surprise on Juliet's face when she recounted this particular detail, but what Juliet, and others, failed to understand was that Dorothy's father simply disliked fuss of any kind. So what purpose would have been served by a showy funeral?

* * *

ANNA HELLER LOOKED at her husband's sleeping face. She wished he would wake up so that he could see the scenery and hear Conor's entertaining commentary. He had been up most of the night working, she conceded. Perhaps this trip had been a really bad idea after all. Her sister Gemma had advised her to just call it a day with Elliot. She said he was boorish, selfish and obsessed with his work. But Gemma had it all wrong, and anyway, there was one big problem – Anna loved him.

Elliot had been married to a wealthy New York socialite for seven years when Anna came to work for him as his PA. They had an affair within weeks of meeting. Looking back, Anna had to admit that the affair had not been torrid, as they were called in novels. *He* had a distracted affair, she thought grimly. One day, a few weeks into the relationship, Elliot announced that he was leaving his wife. Anna was stunned. She had never expected the handsome Elliot Heller ever to be really hers. In one of their frank exchanges, Gemma had told her the only reason he had married her was because she was such a good PA, whereas his first wife had done nothing to help Elliot's precious business. Anna knew otherwise. Elliot had married her because he loved her. While she had to admit that he had never actually said those words as such, she believed deep down that he really did.

Elliot's mother, now dead, had been harsh and unloving. Elliot had gone straight from living at home with her to living with his first wife, who had never understood him, he claimed. Anna lavished love and affection on Elliot; she adored him, organised his life. Elliot almost never concerned himself with the minutiae of daily living, how his suits managed to get dry-cleaned, who cooked dinner for the important clients he entertained at home. Anna took care of everything, including the arrangements for this particular vacation, which had also been her idea from start to finish. The booking, made at the last minute, was therefore non-refundable. Elliot had reluctantly agreed to come, as the prospect of losing money – any money, *ever* – was abhorrent to him. Besides, he told her the night before they left New York, he was thinking about expanding the business and maybe Ireland was a location worth investigating.

Anna, who was the youngest of three sisters, had grown up in a loving family in Kansas. Her parents were the kind of people who believed in God and America and were still in love after forty years of marriage. Her father did everything he could to please his wife, and she in turn supported him in every way possible. Anna's two older sisters, Gemma and Claire, were both married to wonderful guys, and they all lived in the same neighbourhood. Her brothers-in-law, Matt and Steve, regularly played tennis together, and between the pair of them, they took care of all the household maintenance jobs that her father was physically unable to manage any more. Her sisters brought their kids around to Grandma's for barbecues at weekends, and the whole clan seemed to genuinely like and enjoy each other's company.

She thought back to the disastrous weekend she brought Elliot home to meet the family for the first time. It was shortly after she and

Elliot returned from their three-day honeymoon on Long Island. The disaster began to unfold when they missed their flight from JFK to Kansas because Elliot was delayed at a meeting. As a result, the big homecoming party that her mother and sisters had spent the entire day preparing was wasted. And as if that weren't bad enough, Anna's young nieces and nephews had spent hours making an enormous banner declaring 'Welcome, Uncle Eliot', which they hauled into the airport's arrivals hall the following morning. When Elliot saw it, his first words to eight-year-old Katie, who was holding the banner aloft, were, 'My name is misspelled. There are two Ls in Elliot.'

A mortified Anna caught her two older sisters' horrified expressions. They just needed to understand, she said by way of apology, that Elliot had never had any dealings with children and had no nephews and nieces of his own. That was why he was always a bit awkward around kids. He really had no idea how to deal with them, the poor man.

The rest of the weekend was horrendous. Elliot refused to take part in a prearranged tennis match and spent most of the time on the phone because, he explained, it was a particularly busy time for the business. He then compounded his unpopularity by suggesting that Anna's parents sell their house and invest the proceeds in some mineral exploration company in Mongolia in which he was involved. Anna would never forget the expression on Gemma's face when Elliot added that the house probably wasn't worth much as it was so old-fashioned, but the site it was built on was probably reasonably valuable, even considering that this was Kansas and not New York.

Later that same weekend, Elliot recounted to Anna that he had overheard Gemma and Steve joking about how short he was. Elliot wasn't short, Anna said. He was five feet four in his shoes, and anyway, that sort of thing didn't matter when you loved someone, she reassured him. She tried to talk him around to seeing all the positive aspects of her family, but he hated them and they really, *really* didn't like him. Elliot was quintessentially New York and her family were not. That was the root of the problem as she saw it.

* * *

DYLAN HOLBROOKE PLAYED his handheld computer game as the coach
made its way south. He could not believe how early these people had
wanted to get up that morning. He had spent most of the night on the
hotel's computer emailing his friends and the guys in the band about the
situation he found himself in. He had only been asleep for about an hour
when he got the wake-up call from the hotel reception desk. *Still*, he'd
thought, *I can sleep on the coach. I mean, it's not like I'm missing anything,
what with that old guy driving and talking about some dead king or whatever,
and field after field of green.* Dylan wished with all his heart that instead of
being stuck in this godforsaken hole, he could be in California with the
band. He didn't trust them not to get signed to some big label in his
absence and leave him out of the frame. His mother had prevented him
bringing his guitar with him on the trip. As a result, he was now falling
behind with his practice. The band, which included four guys he had
met at a club a few months ago, was called the Screaming Cadavers; they
played goth metal, a blend of death-doom and aggressive heavy metal,
he had explained to his totally disinterested mother.

Jeez, Dylan thought as he gazed bleary-eyed out the window of the
coach, *what do people do all day in this country?* His mother had spent
the night at the hotel bar, trying to chat up some man, as ever. He had
noticed her eyeing up the old Texan guy, Bert, the minute the group
had assembled at Shannon Airport. She was on the lookout for
husband number five and had read a magazine article about tours
being full of wealthy widowers and divorcees, so here they were in
Ireland. He knew Corlene had blown a lot of cash on this trip. When
he'd questioned whether it was a smart thing to do, she'd just snapped,
'You've gotta speculate to accumulate.'

Dylan knew that no matter how much he hated the idea of a tour
like this, he had no option but to oblige and come with her. Aside
from all that, she was kind of desperate these days. He didn't know
the exact details, but he guessed that she had somehow overestimated
the proceeds of her most recent divorce settlement. The judge had

called her a fortune hunter in court and had awarded her a tiny fraction of what she was expecting. Later that night, she had announced to Dylan that there would be no more divorces for her. 'No way,' she had declared. 'It's death or nothing now.'

He tried hard to suppress his sense of frustration with his mother. He badly wanted to cut her loose, focus on his fledgling music career, but without him to rein her in, even a little, the mess she could get herself into was unthinkable.

* * *

BERT WAS REALLY ENJOYING HIMSELF. Ireland was such a magnificent country, and from the little bit of it that he had seen, it felt as if the Irish had got things the right way around. From what he'd noticed thus far, there were no billboards blocking out views of the countryside, no graffiti and no litter. People seemed really friendly. The lady on the hotel reception desk had been so kind when he asked her for a plug adaptor for his laptop charger.

Bert had recently watched a TV show about tracing your ancestors, and although he had no Irish blood, this was a country he really liked the look of. It was one of the reasons he had chosen it for his next project – the details of which were known only to himself and three other people on the planet.

Bert's parents were part German, part English, and Bert had been forced to grow up quickly when his father died suddenly at the age of forty. He trained as a plumber and went on to build up a large construction business. He had met Abilene on a construction site one day when she defiantly approached a bunch of block layers, one of whom had shouted, 'Hey, baby, how about we go somewhere quiet and get to know each other?'

Bert had watched, mesmerised, as this gorgeous girl walked up to the guy, calmly removed the can of Coke from his hand and poured the entire contents all over his head. As the last drops trickled down his nose, she addressed the now-humiliated offender. 'Sorry, but I never date outside my species.' Then she confidently strode down the street as if nothing had happened.

Bert knew that someone who could handle herself as well as that was the very one for him, and so he pursued her relentlessly. Eventually, his courteous manner and ways managed to break through Miss Abilene Tallarico's tough exterior, and she agreed to become Mrs Abilene Cooper. They had enjoyed forty-one years of happy marriage and had five children, all of whom still lived in Texas. Abilene had died two years ago, and her loss was something Bert felt deeply.

After retirement from his very successful construction company, he had time to indulge his love of travel. It was because of the many diverse places he had been in recent years that he became involved in the project. Ireland wasn't the most obvious place to choose as his next project location, but life experience had shown him that the obvious choice was often the wrong choice. He had built his business from nothing and believed in himself and his instincts.

'Cooeee! Bert!'

As he crossed the street of a charming little town where the tour had stopped for a break, on his way to buy a newspaper, he heard someone calling his name loud and clear. Turning around, he found himself facing the woman travelling with the weird-looking boy wearing make-up. As she kissed him on both cheeks, she gushed, 'Well, I know we aren't in France, but I just love these European customs, don't you? Such passionate people, not like us buttoned-up Americans, eh? I was going to take a little stroll around, but I don't have anyone to accompany me, and when you're a stranger, especially a single woman, well, you can't be too careful, can you?'

Bert was nonplussed. The woman seemed a little unhinged and was enveloped in a cloud of alcohol fumes and perfume. He quickly tried to regain his composure. 'Well, Miss Holbrooke...?' He raised his eyebrows.

'Corlene,' the woman replied, in an accent that Bert couldn't quite place. It was definitely southern, but hard to tell exactly where. 'Please, call me Corlene. I'm so glad to meet you properly.'

'Likewise, Miss Corlene,' Bert managed to reply.

'Perhaps you would like to accompany me?' she asked, frantically batting her eyelashes.

Bert thought quickly. 'Well, Miss Corlene, what a kind invitation, and normally I'd enjoy a walk. But just right now I have some urgent errands to run, so maybe another time?'

Having made sure there was no danger of falling into the clutches of the dreadful Corlene, he dove into the nearby SPAR store.

CHAPTER 5

'OK, folks,' Conor said over the speaker system on the coach. 'This is the famous Blarney Castle. You have a few hours to spend here at your own pace. I'll park the coach here, and you can just walk across the road there and make your way up to the castle. Even if the steps all the way up to the stone are a bit too much for you, go and have a walk around the grounds. If you're going to kiss the stone and get the gift of gab, make sure to hold on to any parts of yourself not naturally attached, shall we say? I have had enough of trying to reinstate glasses, hats, teeth, hair and so on that fell off when our visitors were leaning back. Don't worry about falling to your death, though. They never drop anyone on a Tuesday – it's the caretaker's day off.'

Conor's jokes and good humour were catching. The group were all smiling and laughing as they left the coach.

'I'll see you all back here at four, OK?' Conor said. 'And then we'll head straight to the hotel.'

The group dispersed, mostly in the direction of the castle. Ellen took her time walking. Even though she was physically fit, she was aware of the importance of keeping herself safe, not wishing to be a burden on anyone. She always got where she needed to go, but these days it just took a little bit longer.

'Hey there, Ellen,' Bert said as he walked alongside her. 'I know what it's like to get stuck with someone on one of these trips when you want to be alone, so if you would rather that, just say so and I'll make myself scarce. But if not, mind if I tag along with you?'

Ellen looked into his face. He had kind eyes and a mischievous grin. 'Sure,' she said. 'But I must warn you I'm kind of slow. I don't think I'll try to make it to the top of the castle, but I'd be happy for you to join me in a stroll around the grounds if you'd like.'

'I would be honoured, ma'am.'

As they walked through the gardens, they fell into easy conversation. Bert told Ellen all about Abilene and said that while they'd had a great marriage, he was now grateful for the opportunity to travel alone. Ellen told him about her long teaching career and her family in Boston. He seemed surprised that she had never married.

Ellen looked at Bert, fixing him with a piercing stare. 'Well, not yet I haven't, but you never know.'

Bert was lost for words. He had sought out Ellen precisely because she seemed non-predatory, unlike the busty Corlene, and with sudden fear in his voice, he stammered, 'W-w-well, Ellen, that's sure true. And I am certain there are lots of great guys out there who would be only too delighted to meet someone as...um...great as...um...'

Ellen's peals of laughter stopped him in his tracks. 'Bert! I was only pulling your leg. I have absolutely no interest whatsoever in a man at this stage of my life. But it was worth saying it just to see your face. You have nothing to worry about with me, Mr Cooper. However, just between you and me, I think *one particular lady* on our trip might have some plans in your direction.'

Bert's southern chivalry wouldn't allow him to admit to having noticed such a thing. *How astute Ellen is*, he thought. 'Well,' he replied, 'my grandma always told the girls to go for the older guys. Her motto was, "Better be an old man's darling than a young man's slave". Maybe I'm the one who'll strike gold on this trip,' he added with a chuckle.

'That's the thing, Bert. I think gold is *exactly* what Miss Corlene is expecting to strike too,' Ellen replied wryly.

Weak sunshine struggled against an overcast sky, causing Bert and

Ellen to smile at all the Irish people around them who insisted on removing as many of their clothes as possible the moment the sun appeared at all. Ellen and Bert, although from different parts of the United States, were nonetheless used to temperatures of ninety degrees plus, and the sight of the Irish sunbathing in a 'cool' sixty degrees fascinated and amused them.

'At this temperature in Corpus Christi, they'd be wearing their coats,' Bert joked.

The pair found a seat under a tree and licked the mysteriously named '99' ice cream cones they had bought from a nearby van.

'It sure is a lovely country,' he continued. 'Nice people, beautiful scenery and great food. It's hard to believe it's the same place we heard about in the news for so long, with the bombings and the killings and whatnot. I never took too much notice of it, to be honest, never imagined for a second I would ever get to come here, but now listening to Conor telling us all those stories, it seems so hard to reconcile the two images of Ireland. How long did the fighting go on, did he say? Since the 1960s?'

'Eight hundred years,' Ellen replied slowly. 'The English occupied and subjugated Ireland for 800 years, and the peace that is being enjoyed now is the work of so many thousands of Irish men and women who made it their life's work – and of course many also sacrificed their lives – to free this beautiful island.'

Bert glanced at Ellen. *Hmm,* he thought, *I'm certainly not dealing with some harmless little old lady enjoying a bus trip.* Clearly, there was a lot more to Ellen O'Donovan than met the eye. 'What brought you here, Miss Ellen?'

'It's a long story.'

'I've got a week,' Bert replied with a smile.

* * *

DYLAN WALKED around the village of Blarney despondently. Three hours to kill. All the stores sold lame crap with shamrocks and sheep plastered all over it. Stuff he wouldn't be seen dead with. Even the one music store only sold stupid CDs of old-timers playing violins and accordions. *No one listens to proper music in this dump*, he thought, wondering bleakly how he was going to survive a whole week here. His mom still hadn't given up on that guy from Texas who looked about a hundred years old. Seriously, she was so embarrassing.

All his life Dylan had wished he could have a normal mother who baked cakes and went to PTA meetings, but no such luck. Corlene should never have had kids; she had even admitted to him that he had been a mistake and that if she didn't have him hanging onto her, costing her money, she would be living the high life by now. Mind you, she only said stuff like that when she was drunk. Most of the time she just ignored him, and at least his new look meant that she had stopped using him as bait to lure guys. It was a giant pain to get made up and everything every day; the temporary tattoos looked real but took ages to get right. But they did scare people off, which was exactly what he wanted.

As he passed an old church just outside the village, he heard music. It wasn't like the church music at home; in fact, it wasn't like anything he had ever heard anywhere. Intrigued, he moved closer. The doors were open, and inside, a wedding was in progress. Dylan wasn't sure what kind of church it was, but he assumed it was Christian. Neither he nor Corlene was religious, and although his grandmother had been an Episcopalian and had often taken him to church when he was little, for some reason, he always felt a bit intimidated in a church environment.

The sounds that were emanating from near the altar were not being created by strings or by a wind instrument, he thought as he stood on the porch listening and trying to get a glimpse of the musician. The music stopped and the preacher continued. Dylan edged in from the porch to get a better view. At the top of the church, he could make out three musicians holding a guitar, a violin and some instrument that Dylan had never seen before. As he gazed at the trio, the ceremony came to an end, and after signing the register, the bride and groom proceeded down the aisle, followed eventually by the assembled wedding guests.

The three musicians struck up again. To Dylan's ears, the unique sound of the strange instrument, whatever it was, soared high above the other two. The music was loud, like a battle march or something, and it made him smile – the first smile he had managed since his arrival in Ireland, or indeed in several months. As he listened, entranced, he suddenly realised that, unawares, he had been making his way up the side aisle of the church as the wedding guests filtered out. He caught the eye of the man playing the strange instrument. The man smiled at him and Dylan smiled back.

The crowd were now almost out of the church, chatting and taking photos of the happy couple. When the music stopped, the band members began talking and joking. Impulsively, Dylan approached them.

'Howareya?' the man with the strange instrument said.

Dylan didn't know what that meant; maybe the guy was speaking Gaelic. He replied, 'Hi. Um…what is that thing you were playing?'

'Pipes,' the man replied, seemingly unfazed by Dylan's appearance. 'The uilleann pipes. They're an old Irish instrument, a bit like the Scottish bagpipes but you don't blow into them with your mouth. Would you like to have a look?'

'Sure – I mean, yes, please. I've never seen anything like them before.'

It seemed to Dylan that this thing wasn't just a single instrument as such; it had various different parts. The man had a leather strap around his waist and another around his arm. A third piece went under his arm. Dylan was intrigued. It looked like one of those things people used to blow air into fires to get them going in old movies. The fourth piece consisted of a bag covered in green velvet with yellow trim, which the man placed under his left arm; it expanded when he squeezed the bag-like thing under his right arm. Across one leg lay a series of wooden pipes with keys attached somehow to the rest of the instrument, which the man seemed to be constantly adjusting. In his hands, he held another pipe, a bit like a flute. It was the most compli-cated instrument Dylan had ever seen.

'This is a love song,' the man said. 'It's about 300 years old, written by a very famous Irish composer called Turlough O'Carolan. It's called "Bridget Cruise".'

The sound that emerged completely transfixed Dylan. It was slow and plaintive and transported him to another place, where only he and this mesmeric sound existed. A surfeit of images crowded his imagination – glens, mist and an ethereal woman, a girl with long dark hair, sitting alone on a rock. When the music ended, Dylan couldn't speak.

'So where are you from?' the man asked.

'Um...America. I'm here on vacation. I...um... Thanks for playing that for me. It's really awesome. Did it take you long to learn to play like that? I mean, how do you learn that? It seems really complicated.'

'Well...what's your name?'

'Dylan Holbrooke.'

'Well, Dylan, my name's Diarmuid. I've been playing now for about thirty-four or thirty-five years. I learned from my brother to start with, I suppose, and when I got a bit better, I went to a pipe master, who taught me. I suppose, though, you never stop learning. Do you play an instrument yourself?'

'Kind of.' Dylan felt so intimidated by the skill of this musician that he felt stupid talking about his own efforts at electric guitar. 'I play a bit of guitar with some friends back home, but I'm just a beginner so I'm not that good yet.'

'Would you like to have a go at these?' Diarmuid asked. 'But I must warn you, most people can't even get a sound out of them at the start,' he added with a smile.

'Can I?' Dylan asked in amazement, unable to believe that this stranger would be so trusting.

Diarmuid began by giving Dylan the leather strap to tie around his waist, attached to which were the bellows. He strapped a buckle onto Dylan's upper arm, then attached the bag to the bellows, placed the body of the pipes across Dylan's knees and placed the chanter into his hands.

'Now, Dylan, pump the bellows with your right arm – that provides air for the bag. When you've got the bag full, apply pressure under your left elbow and we'll try to get some air to the chanter – that's the part you're holding in your hands. First, we have to cover the holes on the chanter. Now put your fingers like this and keep the chanter on your knee. Now start filling the bag with air from the bellows and see what sounds come out.'

Dylan did as he was instructed, and to his great delight and surprise, a raw but clear bright sound came forth.

'That's good,' Diarmuid said. 'Now try lifting this finger.'

After a few minutes making various sounds, Dylan was able to play several different notes.

'Well, I've often had students take weeks to get to that stage, Dylan. So you have a knack for them all right.'

'Wow! That's so awesome!' Dylan exclaimed. 'I never did anything like that before. Thanks so much for letting me try them.'

'No bother,' Diarmuid replied with a smile.

Dylan had no idea how to pronounce the man's name. It had sounded like 'deer' and 'mud' stuck together but that probably wasn't right, so he decided against trying to say it.

'Where are you off to next?' Diarmuid asked.

'Um…we're on a bus tour, so I think we're staying in Kinsale tonight.'

'Well, Dylan, we're playing a session tonight at the Armada in Kinsale if you want to hear more. We start about half nine, so maybe I'll see you then. If not, enjoy the rest of your holiday in Ireland and keep on playing that guitar.'

Dylan walked back to the coach feeling happier than he had in as long as he could remember. He was definitely going to that session, which must be an Irish word for gig. *Yes*, he thought, *things are definitely looking up.*

CHAPTER 6

*A*nna had spent a delightful afternoon in the shops in Blarney, buying presents for her friends and family. It would have been nice if Elliot had been able to come with her, but he had discovered that the hotel next door to Blarney Woollen Mills had a business centre, so he spent the three hours in there, checking his emails and talking on the phone.

He had promised, however, that that night he would leave his phone in the room and take her out to dinner in one of the lovely little restaurants on the waterfront that she had found on the internet while she was researching their trip.

Now, as she lay back in the bath in her room in Kinsale's luxury boutique hotel, the Blue Haven, deciding what she would wear that night, she smiled to herself. Their vacation could really begin now. Everything was OK in the office – Elliot had said so earlier – so hopefully that meant he would now concentrate on her and on their relationship.

As she emerged from the bath, Elliot called through the bathroom door. 'I'm just going down to the bar for a pre-dinner cocktail. Come and join me when you're ready.'

Anna smiled. She was always happier when left to dress alone, as she was a perfectionist who never wanted Elliot to see her until she had completed her look. 'You're so considerate,' she replied. 'I won't be long.'

While initially Elliot had been dead set against the trip, in the week before they left New York, he had warmed to the idea. He knew a lot about the Irish economy it seemed, and she had even overheard him talking to Conor about Irish planning regulations and land prices. It touched Anna that he took such an interest in a country that she had chosen for their vacation. As she heard the bedroom door shut behind him, she emerged from the bath and looked critically at her reflection in the full-length mirror. Gemma might be right; she was getting too thin. On the other hand, Elliot hated fat women, and he always commented when she put on a pound or two. Maybe tonight she could treat herself to an appetiser *and* a main course, but not a dessert – she hadn't eaten one of those for four years.

As she made her way across the foyer wearing a black sleeveless Donna Karan minidress, fuchsia-pink Manolo Blahnik mules and a matching silk wrap, heads turned. Elliot was sitting at the bar, deep in conversation with someone.

'Hello, darling,' she said as she approached him.

'Oh, hi,' Elliot replied and continued talking to his companion.

'Well, this must be the lovely Mrs Heller. You're a lucky man, Elliot. What can I get you to drink, Mrs Heller?'

'Anna, please,' she replied. 'I'd like a sparkling water.'

Elliot never chats with people. He must be really relaxing at last, she thought.

'Ah now, Anna, if that's what you really want, then thy will be done, but since we're celebrating, maybe I could tempt you to something a bit more cheerful?'

'What are we celebrating?' Anna asked, raising an eyebrow at Elliot. 'I'm sorry, I don't know your name, Mr...'

'Tony, Tony Walsh. I'm sorry, Anna, I thought Elliot had mentioned me. Obviously he was so preoccupied with your beauty and your charm that a big eejit like myself didn't come up in conversation. Frankly, I don't blame him. If I were lucky enough to be married to you, I wouldn't be talking business either,' Tony said smoothly.

'Business?' Anna said, surprised. 'I didn't know you knew anyone in Ireland, Elliot? What sort of business?'

'It's nothing,' Elliot replied briskly. 'Tony and I have been talking for the past few weeks, just bouncing a few ideas around about a bit of potential real estate development over here. Nothing for you to worry about, Anna,' he added dismissively. He turned his attention back to his companion. 'So where are we going for dinner? I'm starving.'

'Well, I told the architect and the planning rep to meet us in Jean-Claude's at eight if that suits you both? It's French, but the portions are Irish. So you won't be going for chips afterwards! Righty-ho, will we go so?'

Tony stood up and drained his pint, Elliot finished his whiskey, and as Anna never actually got her drink, she simply stood, and they walked out of the bar.

* * *

PATRICK WAS ENJOYING HIMSELF, and he walked into town with a pronounced spring in his step. The late-afternoon sun reflected off the water in the harbour, and the clinking of masts on the dozens of boats moored there provided a pleasant soundtrack to this colourful and cheery little place. He felt truly at home.

He had done some family research before his departure. He had visited an aunt-in-law in New York, who told him that she thought his great-great-grandfather had come from County Cork, but as he emigrated in the 1870s, there was nobody still alive who could provide any more detail. Patrick would have loved to hear all about a long Irish lineage, and maybe even meet up with some cousins here, but based on the little information he had acquired to date, that seemed impossible. Strolling along a side street, he caught a waft of garlic coming from a nearby pub. He'd only had a light lunch, so maybe an early dinner mightn't be a bad idea.

He found himself a corner table and made himself comfortable. A thin waitress with unnaturally black hair and a very pointy nose appeared and, in heavily accented English, asked him what he would like to order.

'Well, miss, what would you recommend for a returning Irishman?' he asked jovially.

'Specials are on board. Everything else is on menu. It is all good,' she replied brusquely, clearly impatient to take the order.

A bit chastened by her attitude, he asked for fish and chips and a pint of Guinness. Patrick had hoped to be served by an Irish colleen, all freckles and smiles, not this vicious-looking creature from behind the Iron Curtain. But hell, he was determined not to let anything – certainly not that sour broad – spoil his vision of his homeland.

The pub began to fill quickly, and soon there wasn't a single free table to be had. As he was tucking into his beer-battered fried fish, he heard a voice say, 'Excuse me, I wonder would you mind awfully if I sat here? There don't appear to be any more free tables.'

Patrick looked up to see a tall, bizarrely dressed woman with wild hair smiling down at him.

'Of course,' he responded enthusiastically. 'I can recommend the fish too – it's really great.'

'Well, I might just order that then,' she replied, 'though I usually have a salad. My name is Cynthia Jeffers, by the way, and *you* are?' She stared at him, one hairy eyebrow raised inquisitively.

'Patrick O'Neill, Boston, USA, at your service, ma'am. Delighted to make your acquaintance,' he added with a flourish. 'I'm here on a tour of the old country. My folks came from Ireland, so I'm settling in just fine here. Are you on vacation too?'

'Gracious no! I wish I was. I live here – well, not here exactly, further east, County Waterford. Do you know it?' Without waiting for an answer, she continued. 'My aged uncle died recently, and as he had no children of his own, I'm rather afraid that dealing with his affairs and sorting through his impedimenta seems to have fallen to me. Old Uncle Herbert was a nice but totally dotty old goat. Daddy and Mummy despaired of him, forever chasing the stable hands and trying to goose the maids, but of course, fairly harmless really. His house is just outside the town here. I've been working on his stuff all day, so I really deserve a nice meal and a glass of wine! God knows the last time anyone cooked anything in his kitchen. An ancient local woman came in once a week, but apparently he was being a bit frisky even with her. I think she used to just look in, check that he wasn't dead and then leave again. The place really is in the most *dreadful* state. The vicar's wife called around earlier – a mousy little thing, but she means well, one supposes – with a pot of rhubarb preserve. But I felt I deserved something a bit more substantial to eat. So *here I am.*'

She had a tinkling, girlish laugh, which belied her odd appearance and her age, which Patrick guessed was mid-forties or thereabouts. He examined her closely as she spoke to the scary waitress. She was wearing what appeared to be men's shoes, albeit in a small size, purple woollen pantyhose with several holes and a caftan dress of the type favoured by hippies in the 1970s. Her hair was a tawny blond colour but seemed badly in need of a comb.

When she had finished placing her order, Patrick said, 'Wow, Cynthia, you sound like you've had a busy day. By the way, did you say you grew up here?' He was confused. Her accent sounded English – like one of the royal family if the truth be told – but she had said, or had implied, that she was Irish.

'Oh yes, we live at Kilgerran, near Dungarvan. Daddy wouldn't ever leave, but Mummy has never missed a season in London. She dragged me along a few times, but in the end, she just gave up. She claimed the reason I never made a good match was because Daddy insisted on confining my social life to the local fellows. I do rather enjoy going back to the mainland occasionally, catching up with school chums and so on, but not to live – gracious no! The hunting is gone for a start. In addition, England now is so full of dreadful jumped-up types with lots of money. But I mean to say, who are they? An old school pal of mine had to sell their seat to a used car dealer! His ghastly wife is buying up everything she can find in Laura Ashley. The woman is obsessed with chintz. Mummy nearly choked when she heard. Oaklands had been in the Gore-Patten family since Agincourt.'

Patrick was mystified. Although Cynthia spoke English, he had absolutely no idea what she was on about. Still, something about her made him want her to keep talking. He tried again. 'So you went to school in England?'

'Naturally. I mean, it's what one does, isn't it? Though thankfully Daddy lost a packet at Ascot the year I was to go to that finishing school in Switzerland – saved me from that *horror* due to lack of funds. One can only imagine how *ghastly* that would have been. Arranging flowers and designing interesting table settings...dear me, no, definitely not for me! Though that's another reason Mummy claims I didn't manage to make a good match. No, after that I came home, and a jolly good thing too! Honestly, Mummy and Daddy are simply hopeless. So I took over the estate. It's doing well now. I have a frightfully clever chap over from New Zealand of all places, a genius with the geldings! Oh, hark at me blathering on... I'm so sorry. I haven't spoken to a single human being all day!'

Patrick just gazed at her, mesmerised. He was sure of one thing: Never in his fifty-six years had he met anyone like Cynthia. She might as well have been speaking Arabic for all he understood, but God she was highly entertaining.

As they enjoyed their meal and ordered more drinks, the conversation flowed. Her tales of her Uncle Herbert and a DNA test for paternity had him wiping his eyes in mirth. The loveliest thing about her, he thought, was the fact that her humour and chatter were effortless. He was amazed when he checked the time to discover that the pub was about to close.

When they were ordered to move outside by the Stalinist waitress who was busy mopping the floor, he had a brainwave. 'Y'know, Cynthia, our group is staying here again tomorrow night. We're supposed to visit a fort tomorrow, but I'd be happy to skip the tour and come and help you sort out your uncle's house if that would help. It doesn't seem right you having to do it all on your own. And you know, I'm a member of the Boston Police Department, so you're quite safe.' He wasn't quite sure what he was doing, but he knew he really wanted to spend some more time with this bizarre but compelling woman.

'Well, Patrick, that is really extraordinarily kind of you. If you're sure I wouldn't be imposing on your holiday, I'd be delighted with the help. Though I hope you aren't squeamish. It is in rather a state.'

'After thirty years in the Boston PD, I think I've seen it all.'

He walked Cynthia back to her very dirty and battered Volvo station wagon. They shook hands and arranged to meet the following morning.

CHAPTER 7

*J*uliet Steele was unpacking her bag and taking in her surroundings when Dorothy's voice interrupted her thoughts.

'It says here that you can avail of an early bird special in the Fish-market Restaurant if you order before six thirty. I have booked us a table for six fifteen.'

Juliet groaned inwardly; they had only eaten lunch at three, and she wasn't remotely hungry. On the other hand, she knew better than to argue with Dorothy when she was in money-saving mode, which was all of the time. Juliet thought she had never met such a penny-pincher as Dorothy in her entire life. She would have much preferred to wait until eight o'clock and have something small in one of the local pubs and maybe absorb some of the atmosphere of this charming seaside town. The prospect of an empty hotel dining room with only the sound of a ticking clock to break the silence filled her with dread.

She thought again how much Larry would have enjoyed being here in Ireland. Being from landlocked Iowa, he was fascinated by the ocean. What she wouldn't do right now just to be able to sit on the terrace of one of the local hotels overlooking the harbour, order a glass of wine and have a leisurely chat with her dear late husband. She had never admitted to anyone that she spoke to Larry every day in case they thought she was crazy.

Suddenly, a new sensation washed over her, and she heard herself say, 'Actually, Dorothy, I'm not really hungry. I think I'll pass on dinner if you don't mind. I might just go for a walk to stretch my legs after that long bus ride today. I'll see you later.'

Her heart was pounding as she reached for her jacket, but she made the fatal mistake of making eye contact with her travelling companion.

'Don't be ridiculous, Juliet,' Dorothy said with weary disdain. 'You can't just go wandering off on your own. Anyway, Ireland is a very expensive country. If we don't eat here and avail of the special offer, we will probably be ripped off in some fancy spot up the street.'

Reluctantly, Juliet placed her jacket back on the bed. 'I'm sure you're right, Dorothy.'

'Well then, let's go down now. And remember, we must stock up at all the included meals, take anything portable, so that we can have snacks in the evenings when meals are not included. That way we can eat in the room and we won't overspend.'

The pair left the hotel and headed for the restaurant.

As they took their seats in the empty dining room, a waiter approached with the wine list. 'Good evening, ladies. Can I get you a drink while you browse the menu?'

'Um, yes pl –' said Juliet.

'No thank you, just a jug of water please. Not mineral water now – tap water is fine.' Dorothy dismissed the young man peremptorily. 'You didn't want a drink, did you? It's probably swill sold at Grand Reserve prices anyway. Better stick with the water. Oh look, they do a starter platter for two – let's order that.'

Juliet looked at the menu. The starter platter was all shellfish, which she didn't like, but since she wasn't hungry anyway, she figured why not.

The dinner progressed in silence, as Dorothy ate and Juliet picked at the food on her plate, the only interjections coming from Dorothy, who criticised the hotel, the staff, the bus, Conor, generally finding fault with just about everything. This latest stream of complaints grated on Juliet even more than usual. Fortunately, no one else could hear them, so at least she was spared that embarrassment.

While Dorothy rattled on, Juliet recalled one of her friends from church telling her a story about how Dorothy had managed to wangle a free holiday by way of compensation for the litany of complaints she had lodged with one particular tour operator. Juliet wished she had the nerve to stand up to Dorothy and be allowed to do her own thing, but the prospect of confronting her and speaking her mind was just too daunting. She knew that at the first sign of conflict, she would dissolve into floods of tears.

En route to the room after their dreary dinner, Juliet gave herself a pep talk. *Come on, Juliet, you're a grown woman, and* she *is not in charge. Just be* assertive. As Dorothy was putting the key in the door – Juliet was never allowed to take the key in case she lost it – she heard herself say, 'I'm just going downstairs for a little while, Dorothy. I need some fresh air.' Before Dorothy could object, she took off down the corridor, all the while fighting the urge to giggle at her audacity. 'I don't know what's gotten into me!' she said to herself delightedly.

Deciding to make the most of her temporary freedom, she headed to the hotel bar and ordered a glass of wine. Glancing across the bar, she spotted Conor sipping a coffee, frowning slightly as he concentrated on a newspaper crossword. She didn't know whether she should interrupt him or not. Maybe he was trying to unwind; on the other hand, she didn't want to appear rude.

'Hi, Conor. I won't disturb you, but I just wanted to say how much I'm enjoying your commentary on the coach. It's really interesting, all the history and everything. I don't know how you manage to remember it all.'

Conor looked up from his paper. 'Ah, Juliet! No Dorothy with you, I see.'

Conor had seen women caught up in this type of arrangement many times before. As ever, he was mystified as to why a nice woman like Juliet would be friends with an old battleaxe like Dorothy. But, as he reminded himself, his job was to drive the coach and keep them happy, not enquire too deeply about what was going on.

'Um, no… She…she's in the room. I just came out for a walk and thought I might just have one glass of wine since I'm on vacation…' Juliet's voice trailed off.

Conor smiled. 'Of course you did. You *are* in Ireland after all. Do you want to join me or would you rather some peace and quiet? I won't be insulted if you want to be on your own?'

'Well, if you're sure you don't mind, I would be happy to join you.'

Juliet moved to a seat next to Conor's.

'So have you and Dorothy been friends for long?'

'Well, yes and no, I suppose. I know her through our church, and when my husband died, she suggested that we take a trip together. And so, I guess, here we are.'

'You must get on great so, to say you went on holidays together,' Conor prompted. He was intrigued by this woman who, when away from her companion, wasn't nearly as mousy as he had originally thought.

Juliet smiled sardonically. 'I guess so. Though to be honest, I sometimes wonder what, if anything, we have in common. Dorothy is very well travelled and well read. She's actually a university professor in some kind of science, but to be honest, I'm not sure exactly what. So she's kind of hard to please, I guess. She's very definite about what she does and doesn't want and usually gets her own way in the end. I tend to go with the flow a bit more.'

Conor considered the various aspects of Juliet's predicament. 'Well, Juliet, I'll tell you something I've observed in my amateur studies of human behaviour – well, on my coach tours anyhow – for the past twenty years. You can please some of the people some of the time, but not all of the people all of the time. To my mind, people decide either they are going to have a great time or a miserable time, and there's very little anyone can do to change it once they have decided on that. I hope you decide you are going to have a great time and that you don't give a damn what anyone else thinks.'

Juliet smiled. 'Do you know, Conor, I think you're right. That's exactly what I'm going to do,' she said with a grin.

For the next hour, a very pleasant hour, they spent the time talking about Larry and about her life in Des Moines. She told him she was thinking of buying a condo in Florida, and about her life as a librarian. Conor was so easy to talk to, she even confessed to him about her daily chats with Larry.

'I guess you get all kinds of fruitcakes on these trips, so one who talks to a dead guy every day isn't all that amazing.'

Conor smiled. 'Do you know something, Juliet? I think you are a very lucky woman to have known such happiness as you had with your husband all those years. I do believe we go somewhere when we die, and that we'll all meet again, so why shouldn't you keep in touch with Larry? He's probably looking down at you right now, hoping you have a great holiday, that you splash out on a nice steak and a bottle of wine tomorrow night and that you forget about having anything to do with the tap water and the early bird seafood platter.'

Juliet felt guilty about revealing all that stuff about Dorothy, but it felt good to let off some steam. Somehow, she knew that Conor O'Shea was the soul of discretion. She finished her third glass of wine and stood up. 'Thank you for a lovely chat, Conor. I really enjoyed talking to you.'

'And I enjoyed talking to you too. See you in the morning, Juliet. *Codhladh sámh.*' Noting her confused expression, he said, 'It's the Irish for goodnight. It means I wish you a peaceful sleep.'

'Well, "colla sawve" to you too,' she replied, and went back to face the wrath of Dorothy Crane with a lighter heart – the first time she had felt lighthearted since she left Des Moines the previous week.

CHAPTER 8

*A*fter the informative tour of Charles Fort the following morning, the group sat outside a café, taking in the spectacular harbour view. Bert was entertaining the group with stories of the funeral party he had stumbled across the night before.

'I walked up to the bar and this real old-timer was sitting there, just a few teeth, you know? And he asked me where I was from. I guessed the guy was a little deaf, so I said loudly, "I'm from Texas, in the United States of America." I tell you, this guy looked like he hadn't moved off that stool in fifty years. Then he said, "Well, I only was in Texas once, but I spent four years in Butte, Montana, and my brother lives in McCool Junction, Nebraska." You could have knocked me down with a feather. I was trying to find out more about him, why he went there and why he came back to Ireland, but *no way*, he wasn't one for sharing! He wanted to know what I had for breakfast, but I didn't even manage to find out his name! Man, that was some party. I think when I die, this is the right place to have a funeral shindig. You know what they told me? The only difference between an Irish funeral and an Irish wedding is that there's one less drunk.'

The group laughed at Bert's story.

'Of course, the Irish have always had a weakness for alcohol. It's probably due to an innate inability to face reality,' Dorothy interjected.

Conor noted the embarrassed looks on the faces of the other group members at this obvious slight against his compatriots. Quick as a flash, he piped up. 'Do you know why God invented whiskey?'

There was relief on the faces around the table, as he was obviously going to save the situation.

'I have a feeling you're gonna tell us, Conor.' Bert laughed.

'Well,' Conor replied, 'they say that the good Lord invented whiskey to stop the Irish taking over the world.'

There was laughter all around the table, and Dorothy's withering remark was instantly forgotten.

The skinny latte that Anna Heller had bought for her husband sat cooling on the table. He had walked away to take a call on his mobile phone twenty minutes earlier in the middle of the fort tour and had not reappeared since. Anna tried not to look like anything was amiss, but she was acutely aware of how antisocial her husband was being. Ellen, who was seated on her right, sensed this and said, 'So, Anna, what did you and Elliot get up to last night?'

'Oh, we...um...' she seemed awkward being put on the spot, 'we went for a meal with some business associates of Elliot's. He's looking at some investments over here, so it was nice.'

Nobody had anything to say about that, so there was a moment of silence.

Dylan addressed the group for the first time. They gazed at him, looking a bit surprised that he had decided to involve himself in the conversation. Bert couldn't be exactly sure, but he thought Dylan was wearing lipstick, which was a mystery to him as he had remarked to Ellen earlier. Ellen had replied that she wasn't remotely shocked by Dylan's appearance. She had seen many students over the years experimenting with a variety of different images; it was all part of growing up.

'I went to a gig,' Dylan said quietly. No one responded to this conversational offering.

Ellen noticed colour beginning to creep up the young boy's neck, so she asked, 'What kind of music was it?'

The group looked even more bemused at the notion of this strange young man discussing music with an elderly lady.

'Irish music, like traditional kinda stuff,' he replied, grateful that someone in this group seemed capable of having a normal discussion. 'I heard these guys playing music in a church yesterday, when you were all at that castle place, and so I just got talking to them.'

The group exchanged looks as if the idea of Dylan spontaneously starting a conversation with anyone was unlikely, to say the least. Ellen smiled encouragingly at the boy, so he continued. 'They said they were playing a session last night in a bar downtown, so they said I could come along. A session is what they call it when a bunch of musicians just all show up to the same bar at the same time and just start playing. It was awesome!' His eyes shone with enthusiasm. 'There is this thing like a bagpipe, but it's not, and it makes the most incredible sound, like...I dunno – I can't describe it.'

He suddenly became aware that everyone at the table was looking at him, and he stopped talking, embarrassed once again.

'Were they uilleann pipes, I wonder?' asked Conor. 'Was the fella squeezing them with one arm and covering holes on the pipes with his fingers?'

'Yeah,' Dylan replied, but much quieter this time. 'That's it – that's the name. There were some other guys playing violins and guitars too.'

'Lord save us, Dylan, don't leave the fella with the violin hear you! In this country that's called a fiddle.'

'Oh, OK, I'll try to remember that,' Dylan replied, smiling for the first time since the conversation had begun.

'My son is a very talented musician,' Corlene announced to the table. 'I mean to say, he would have to be – my whole family is very creative. My niece won the beautiful baby contest at our state fair three years running. I myself of course am no stranger to the catwalks either...' She smiled coquettishly at Bert. 'I have done some photo shoots as well. Swimwear, lingerie, that sort of thing. If anyone wants to see them, I could bring them on the coach tomorrow – the photos, I mean, not the lingerie! Hahahahahahaha,' she finished raucously.

The faces regarding her display were a mixture of disapproval and horror. Some of the group gave their coffee their undivided attention to avoid looking at the long false eyelash that had escaped from her overly made-up eyes. It had already slipped halfway down one cheek and looked set to progress even further.

'So, Conor,' said Ellen, anxious to distract them all from the disaster, 'are you from around here?'

'I am actually, Ellen,' Conor replied. 'I was born here in County Cork, about twenty miles from Kinsale.'

'And do you get home much?'

'Not much during the season, to be honest. I work tours back to back from around March to November.'

'And is there a Mrs Conor?' Bert asked with a wink.

Conor smiled. 'No, I'm not married.'

Corlene cast another lingering glance at Conor. He was very attractive, she thought, no doubt about that. He obviously worked out. His colouring didn't look Irish. His particular combination of tanned skin, blue eyes, shock of silver hair and tall, muscular frame made him quite unusual looking, and he attracted attention. She was a keen people watcher and had registered that he never seemed to notice the admiring glances he received, especially from women. He was a bit on the young side, she would prefer someone closer to their demise, plus he was only a bus driver, so he wouldn't make enough to keep her. With regret, she dismissed the idea of a potential conquest.

* * *

CONOR ARRANGED for them all to meet for dinner that evening in the hotel. In the meantime, as he had a few hours to himself, he drove to the town of Passage West. While manoeuvring the coach down the main street, he was hit with that familiar feeling of wanting to get out of there as fast as he could.

The village consisted of one street, which split in two around a public square. On a hill overlooking the town sat a Catholic church, with a Protestant one tucked behind it. The defunct St Mary's girls' primary school with boarded-up windows dominated the main street. It had been replaced by a newer, more modern building outside the town. There was one small shop, a children's playground and five pubs. Although he had grown up there, it didn't feel like home to him. His father, Jamsie, like many of his generation, had left to find work in England just before Conor's eighth birthday. From that day on, he never returned once to visit his wife and two young sons. Conor had heard rumours years ago that his father had remarried in Dagenham and had a family there, but the gossip never really affected him. At the age of almost nine, he assumed the role of man of the house. His mother, Lily, was a quiet kind of woman, slight and dark, good-looking in an understated way. Everyone said his brother, Gerry, was the image of his mother, whereas Conor was tall and broad with reddish-brown hair, just like his father.

Lily was inoffensive in every way. He supposed she had to be, because even though it was not in any way her fault that her husband upped and left one day, it was regarded with shame in the area. She looked after her two boys, went to Mass, kept her house clean and lived out what must have been a lonely kind of existence, Conor thought. For women in her position, remarriage or even a friendship with another man was utterly out of the question – a fact that had made Conor sad for her, since he would have really liked his mam to have met someone nice.

Passage West was his father's home place, and despite the fact that his mam came from a village nine miles away, she was always considered a blow-in. She died as she lived, quietly and without fuss, when Conor was sixteen and Gerry was twelve. It was decided by the all-powerful village triumvirate – the headmaster, parish priest and local sergeant – that Conor should get an apprenticeship as a mechanic and Gerry should go into care, as there were no relatives willing to take the boys on and all attempts to contact their father in England had failed.

Conor knew the word 'care' had very little to do with how children who ended up in industrial schools were actually treated in the Ireland of the 1970s, and he was determined to keep his brother out of one of those institutions. With the help of his mother's only real friend and neighbour, Mary Harrington, he fought long and hard to win a reprieve. Eventually, it was agreed that Conor could continue to live in his mother's house, get a job and look after Gerry.

As he parked the coach, memories of his past came flooding back. Gerry had always been spoiled. He had no recollection of his father, and by way of compensation or something, he had been indulged throughout his childhood by his endlessly uncritical mother. Conor remembered the last time he saw him: dark hair combed back in a Teddy-boy style, trousers so tight Conor wondered how he could manage to walk in them, his feet clad in a pair of winkle-pickers and a gold ring on his little finger.

Gerry left school at the age of sixteen, the year after he spectacularly failed his Intermediate Certificate. What he lacked in academic prowess, he equally lacked in ambition and the desire to work. Conor managed to talk Matt Sheehan, the owner of the local hardware shop, into giving Gerry a job. Matt had great time for Conor, so it was with a heavy heart he came into the garage where Conor was working as a mechanic two months later to say he would have to let Gerry go. He had caught him stealing from the till, and, he told a horrified Conor, Gerry had only laughed when confronted with the accusation. Matt assured Conor that there would be no question of involving the Guards or anything like that, but under no circumstances was Gerry to show his face in Sheehan's Hardware ever again.

Conor arrived home that evening to find Gerry lying on the sofa watching cartoons. Gerry wore the same smug expression he always wore – as if he were laughing at the world. He did not acknowledge his brother's presence; Conor might as well have been invisible. Conor flipped.

'Do you have any idea how hard it was for me to stop them taking you to that industrial school? And then you do this to me?'

Gerry remained motionless, glued to the television, unfazed by his brother's outburst. Incensed at his attitude, Conor pounced on him, dragged him outside to the backyard and punched him in the face. As blood began to pour out of his mouth, Conor stopped and stared in horror, imagining his mam looking down on him.

'Oh God! I'm sorry, Gerry. I shouldn't have hit you... It's just...'

Still wearing more or less the same smug expression, Gerry walked back into the house, lay down on the sofa and continued watching TV while holding a tea towel to his bleeding mouth.

After Sheehan's Hardware, there were several more jobs, but none lasted more than a few months. Either he was fired or he got bored and stopped turning up for work. Eventually, Conor resigned himself to supplementing Gerry's weekly dole money out of his slim earnings. The strange thing about Gerry was that, outside the house, he was considered by his peers to be a great fellow, full of fun and devilment, a great hit with the girls. Along with his dark, Brylcreemed hair and startling blue eyes, Gerry O'Shea had charm and style – all far too exotic for Passage West. He listened to Jerry Lee Louis and Elvis Presley – the glam rock of the 70s didn't interest him at all. He made retro seem so cool. He was an expert in all things American and was frequently heard saying that the minute he got a chance, he'd be out of Passage West and off to the States, never to return. In the meantime, the local girls fought for his attention, and the younger lads wished they had his sex appeal. Everyone else in the village considered Gerry O'Shea very bad news indeed.

Conor was seen as the opposite of his younger brother, hard-working and decent. When his boss, Joe Kelly, got arthritis, Conor kept the business going. Joe had long since been the father figure in Conor's life, allowing him to tinker around the garage when he was young, never losing his temper with him, no matter what the circumstances. Conor knew that someday he would make Joe an offer for the business, and he worked hard so that he could save enough to get a loan from the bank. Joe and his wife felt very protective of the young apprentice, and Joe even had hopes that their daughter and only child Noreen would catch his eye. But while Conor was always friendly to Noreen, he never thought of her in any romantic way. He even drove her and her father to the church the morning she married Tom Butler, the butcher from the next parish.

Conor pulled up outside what had once been Kelly's garage. These days, Mary Harrington had told him, someone was renting it as a lock-up. His mother's old friend was the only person from Passage West with whom he kept in touch. Joe and Eileen were both dead now. He didn't go to either funeral because he was away travelling on both occasions, but he sent flowers and wrote to Noreen expressing his sadness at her loss.

He was glad he didn't recognise the two girls crossing the street and, therefore, wouldn't have to make conversation with them. Once again, he thought about how much he hated coming back here, how he dreaded making conversation with old neighbours. The village itself was fine and the people very nice and friendly, but the place held nothing but bad memories for him. If it weren't for Mary, he thought as he stood there waiting for her to answer the door, he would never again bother with this godforsaken place.

'Conor!' Mary exclaimed. 'Why didn't you ring me? I'd have made a few scones or something.'

Conor gave her a hug, noting how thin and old she had become even in the few months since he'd last seen her. 'Spur of the moment thing,' he replied. 'It's great to see you. I have a group over in Kinsale, so I just thought I'd call in to see how you are.'

'Ah sure, you know how it is, Conor. Dragging the divil by the tail the whole time. I had a Mass said for your mam last week, for her anniversary. Hard to believe it's twenty-nine years, isn't it?'

'Indeed it is,' Conor agreed. 'A lot of water under the bridge since then.'

'Actually I'm glad you called. That young couple renting your place wanted to know if they could put up gates to make the garden secure for the little one. I told them that would probably be fine but I'd check with you,' Mary said as she filled the kettle. 'There's a pile of post there for you, but something came a few weeks ago marked urgent and personal, so I sent it on to the Dunshane. Did you get it?'

Conor looked up from the pile of mostly junk mail that she had handed him. 'Oh yeah. I did. Thanks for that.'

He knew better than to mention Sinead's name to Mary. She had felt at the time that Conor was wrong to say nothing when she went off with Gerry. Mary had also said that if Sinead were any kind of a girl at all, she would realise that Conor was the better man by far. It didn't say much for her that she couldn't see that. The last thing Conor wanted to hear was Mary's opinions about the feckless Sinead. Mary didn't understand, not really.

Conor took a piece of paper from his pocket and put it on the table. 'Here's a voucher for a travel agent in town. Now I'm not going to argue with you about it, so just go in and book a flight. Go to see Joanne, all right? It's all covered, and I don't want to hear another word about it.'

'Ah, Conor, there's no need,' Mary argued.

'There's every need, but we're not having that debate, right? I owe you so much that I could never repay you. We both know it. You're going to New York to visit your daughter and I'm paying for it, and that's the end of it. And before you say another word, here's a few bob to spend too. I get dollars as tips and it's not worth my while changing them, so you're going to take those too.'

Mary opened the envelope. 'Jesus almighty, there must be hundreds in here! I'm not taking that off you.'

'It's $1500 and you *are* taking it. Now where's my tea?' he said with a big smile.

He chatted with Mary for another half an hour before announcing that he had to get back to the group. 'Sure I'll call again in a few weeks or so,' he said as he left.

Both of them knew it would be more like a matter of months before he would return to Passage West, and that once Mary died, he would never go back again.

CHAPTER 9

'Conor!' Patrick said with obvious pride. 'I would like you to meet my friend Cynthia Jeffers.'

Conor had been passing through the bar on the way to his room after dinner. Patrick had not joined the group, but he'd assumed the Boston man was otherwise engaged. It seems he was right.

'Well, how are you, Cynthia? Patrick was telling me you have a lot on your plate at the moment, sorting out your late uncle's house?'

'Oh gracious, yes,' she replied. 'Though without the invaluable help of Patrick here, I should imagine I would never have emerged from that dratted pile! Uncle Herbert – did you know him?' she asked, raising an enquiring eyebrow. 'He was whipper-in for the Weston Hunt for many years. Large fellow, handlebar moustache. He won a prize for his marrows at Chelsea several times.'

'Em, no, Cynthia,' said Conor, suppressing a smile. 'I can't say I do...em, did.'

'Well, never mind,' Cynthia continued, unperturbed. 'Anyway, as I was saying, Patrick here really was wonderful. Therefore, I simply *must* buy him a drink to say thank you. You *will* join us, Conor. What will you have?'

'Well, just the one,' Conor replied, fascinated by this friendship between Cynthia and Patrick.

She turned heads as she swept ahead of the two men following her into the bar. It wasn't just that she was tall; it was also the way her hair seemed to sit on her head like an enormous nest – hair that looked as if it hadn't been combed for many, *many* years. She was wearing what appeared to be a long knitted purple tube affair, which stretched from under her arms to just above her knees. Over that, she wore a short, pillar-box-red woollen cape.

'Cynthia was telling me all about the history of her uncle's house today,' Patrick recounted as they sat awaiting her return from the bar. 'I never knew about the way all those beautiful houses got burned during the independence struggle here. You should see this place, Conor. I mean, sure, it's run-down now, but it must have been spectacular in its day. And the way all the people who lived around here worked on the estate or in the house. Y'know, when you think about it, those rich people were just trying to live their lives too. I mean, they got here just by an accident of birth, the same as the rest of us. Some of them were bastards for sure, but I guess most of them were just ordinary people trying to keep going.'

Conor suppressed another smile. Was this the same man who had been spouting all that anti-English propaganda on the bus the other day? Amazing what a woman could do.

'That's exactly it, Patrick. You're right when you say some of those landlords behaved very badly towards their Irish tenants. God knows they paid a high price for that when the time came, and rightly so, but the thing to remember is that even though we always saw the gentry as kind of English, if you know what I mean, they thought of themselves as Irish, a lot of them. There aren't many left nowadays – most of them went back to England during the Troubles – but the ones who stayed seem to have got on well enough. It's sad all the same, I always think, to see all the old Protestant churches sold off, turned into houses and restaurants and the divil knows what. Still, I suppose there's no way to keep them going, no congregation and no clergy. Most of the ones that are still operating around here only have a service once every few weeks because the vicars have to go from church to church since there aren't enough Protestants in any one place to warrant a full-time clergyman.'

'Do you think Cynthia's a Protestant?' Patrick asked in amazement. The idea that the Irish were anything but Catholic hadn't occurred to him.

Before Conor had time to answer, she was back.

'Oh, there you are, chaps!' cried Cynthia, expertly balancing three creamy pints of stout.

Patrick looked at Conor as Cynthia downed the first third of her pint in one go and then proceeded to wipe her mouth with the back of her hand.

'So, Cynthia, you aren't from around here, are you?'

'No, no, not at all. I grew up in Waterford, near Dungarvan. My parents, frightfully elderly and doddery now, of course, still live there. But for how much longer, one simply can't tell. The upkeep of those draughty old places is simply crippling, as you know.'

Conor nodded in agreement and smiled at the idea that his childhood terraced house in Passage West would have given him any experience of the travails of running a big Georgian house and estate.

'We have most of the rooms closed now, of course,' she continued. 'I'm simply confounded as to why my ancestors felt the need for such enormous houses in the first place. These days, we live between the stables and the kitchen mostly. A local woman, Mrs Mooney, comes in to do for us. She and her family have worked at Kilgerran forever. Her husband takes care of the grounds. Mind you, Mr and Mrs Mooney are as ancient as my parents, so it's a rather poorly run establishment,' she concluded with a tinkly laugh.

The conversation flowed easily, and Conor excused himself as soon as was polite, leaving Patrick and Cynthia alone. When eventually the barman began calling time, Patrick was reluctant to leave. 'Well, Cynthia, can I just say what a great time I've had...'

Despite his usual chat and bluster, he wasn't finding it easy to say the right thing. He knew he didn't want this extraordinary woman to walk out of his life forever, but he couldn't think of how to say that without sounding like some kind of a creep or a stalker.

'Oh, Patrick, so have I, my dear,' Cynthia trilled. 'It does seem rather a pity that you have to go so soon...' Cynthia, it seemed, was as tongue-tied as Patrick.

As they walked to her filthy Volvo, there was an awkward moment when neither of them could decide whether to kiss on the cheek or shake hands. The result was a sort of ungainly mutual stabbing of stomachs and half a hug.

Cynthia got into her car. 'Enjoy the rest of your holiday, Patrick, and thank you again so much for all your help,' she said. She closed the door, wound down the car window and thrust a business card at him. 'In case you are ever in the area,' she said hesitantly. She drove away erratically to the sound of the exhaust backfiring and much grinding of gears as Patrick stood in the hotel car park and waved forlornly.

* * *

THE FOLLOWING MORNING, the group gathered outside to board the coach.

'So, everyone, what should we do about seats? Should we rotate the front seat, or does anyone have any preferences?' Bert asked pleasantly.

Anna and Corlene had discussed earlier at breakfast how tiresome it was that Dorothy always grabbed the front seat.

Dorothy was furious. She always engineered it so that she got to the coach before anyone else every morning. 'If you were as familiar with taking tours with this company as I am, you would realise that it's always operated on a first-come, first-served basis,' she replied with barely concealed contempt.

'Well, I only asked,' Bert replied, 'because I've got myself a bad knee and I sure would appreciate it if I could have an aisle seat so I can stretch out my leg – if no one minds, that is.'

He had hoped to sit beside Ellen today. He'd enjoyed himself walking around with her in Blarney and Kinsale. She was a very relaxing person to be with, and she had some interesting opinions on lots of subjects that she always delivered in a soft, gentle voice. Despite their easy companionship, however, he never even toyed with the idea of telling her about his project. In some ways, he found it hard to imagine her in front of a class of teenagers before she had retired. As he got to know her, he knew that they must have liked and respected her, and so she probably rarely raised her voice. The way she spoke to Dylan was an example of how well she related to young and old alike.

Juliet boarded the coach and deliberately chose a seat in the middle, half hoping that she could sit with someone else today. Buoyed by her successful escape two nights ago, she had promised herself that from now on she would be more assertive and would not accede to Dorothy's every demand. She was mortified by her travel companion's attitude and the way she treated people, and was now trying to distance herself from her as much as possible. While she was putting her jacket on the overhead luggage rack, the voice she had come to dread rang out impatiently. 'Juliet, you are in the wrong seat. Our seat is here. Sit inside this morning, will you? I prefer to look out the front window. The roads in this country are terrible. I feel ill if I don't keep the horizon in my line of vision at all times.'

Juliet dithered and was about to insist on staying where she was when Dorothy said in exasperation, as if dealing with a pouting toddler, 'Quickly, Juliet, you're blocking the aisle.'

Juliet turned to see Dylan waiting for her to move. Sheepishly, she picked up her handbag and slipped into the inside front seat with an air of weary resignation.

Dylan headed for the back seat, hoping to make himself invisible in the corner, where he could listen to his music uninterrupted. He had bought all the CDs the traditional music group were selling at the gig and was looking forward to a day of reacquainting himself with the tunes that had enthralled him so much. He believed some kind of chemical reaction took place in his brain every time he listened to the fast rhythmic tunes or the haunting, slow airs. According to the sleeve notes, between them, the various members of the group played a whole range of instruments. Dylan really hoped that the music he had discovered was to be found in other towns that the coach would be visiting over the next few days. If he could manage to immerse himself in the music, maybe this trip would be halfway bearable after all. Diarmuid, the piper, had told him lots of interesting things about the traditional music they played, and where it had originated. He gave Dylan some names to look out for, bands that would be playing later in the week in Killarney if Dylan wanted to come along. Dylan decided there and then that no matter where Corlene and the rest of the tour were going, he was going to the gig, come hell or high water.

He had noticed a strange thing at the first traditional music session he went to in Kinsale. Whereas in America different age groups each had their own kind of music, here there were at least fifteen musicians, from guys and girls his own age and younger to real old-timers. Initially, it had struck him as weird, teenagers and pensioners all playing music and chatting away together, but then he realised that was how the tunes got passed on. People didn't seem to have lessons as such; they simply learned from listening to each other. The way that Diarmuid had been so helpful and open when they met in the church seemed a bit odd at first, but now that Dylan saw exactly how a session worked, Diarmuid's attitude made perfect sense. It was as if everyone owned the music, and therefore, sharing it willingly was one of the things that made it so powerful. If you were a part of that world, you had a duty to share it with everyone else.

God, how much he would love to be a part of that world! But of course, he would never be able to play anything like the guys in the pub. Besides, he wasn't even Irish. It was just a dream, he was aware of that, but it helped him to block out the shameful antics of his mother, whose displays of desperation were growing worse by the day. He knew she was broke and badly needed to find another meal ticket, but somehow he had to stop her making a total fool of herself.

CHAPTER 10

Their journey took them out of County Cork and into County Kerry. As they made their way around the Ring of Kerry, Conor recounted legends from Celtic times, his patter interspersed with facts about the geology and archaeology of the area. The group gazed in awe at stone circles and ring forts dating back thousands of years.

One stop was at a sheep farm where the surprisingly debonair farmer explained the complicated process of training Border collies to herd sheep in the high mountains of the peninsula. The dogs endeared themselves to the tourists with their eagerness to do their jobs. When the talk was over and they had seen a variety of different sheep, Conor led them to the nearby pub. Leaving the group to enjoy their Irish coffee, Conor returned to the coach to wait. This morning he wasn't in the humour for meeting the other drivers and tour guides. He needed some time to think. The prospect of having Sinead back in his life again was gradually sinking in. She was the only person he'd ever really loved enough to want to marry. So much time had passed, however; they were both so much older now. He knew he couldn't just ignore the letter, even if he wanted to. Reaching for his BlackBerry, he wrote:

Hello Sinead,

Thanks for your letter. It certainly was a surprise to hear from you. No, I haven't heard from Gerry in many years either. I'm sorry to hear it didn't work out. I don't live in Passage West any longer, but I have my post forwarded. It's as easy to contact me by email if you wish to.

Best wishes,

Conor

He reread the email three times. It still didn't sound right, but he didn't know what else to say, so he just pressed send. As he did so, his phone beeped, indicating an incoming text message.

Hi Conor, Betty tell Mr Manner he is 'jumped-up little eejit'. He nearly explode! Hope tour going good. See you soon, Ana x

Conor smiled. He could just picture the scene. He was about to text back when he noticed Juliet at the door of the coach.

Conor pressed the button to open the door. 'Juliet!' he said. 'Everything OK?'

'Conor, I'm really sorry to interrupt your break, but I wonder if I could just ask you something...in private.' Juliet looked even more timid than usual.

'Come on in and sit down there. What can I do for you?' Conor replied, intrigued but at the same time certain it had something to do with that lighting devil poor Juliet was landed with.

'Thank you,' Juliet replied. 'It's... Well, I'll get right to the point. You see...the thing is that, well...'

'C'mon now,' said Conor, smiling, 'spit it out.'

Juliet gave a wan smile in return. 'The thing is, I was wondering if – and if it's a problem, just say so – but I was thinking, I was hoping really, that when we get to our next hotel in Killarney, I could get a room of my own. I mean, I will pay of course, but it's just that I'm finding sharing – well, let's just say it's a bit difficult.'

'I'd say that's a bit of an understatement,' Conor replied wryly. 'I'll see what I can do for you, Juliet, and if it's possible at all, I'll swing it for you. Now, would I be right in guessing that it would be easier if the reason for this change was presented as a miscommunication between the travel agent and the hotel as opposed to a response to a request from anyone?'

Juliet sighed with relief and gave Conor a grateful smile. 'Thanks so much, Conor. That would be wonderful.'

* * *

CORLENE LOOKED with distaste at the sheep. Her interest in anything agricultural had come to a swift end around the time of the debacle of the Montana widower. She nearly had him in the bag, until his interfering daughter turned up, flinging unsavoury and totally ridiculous accusations at Corlene. That had all ended very badly. The problem was that the pressure was on now; she needed to find a replacement because the cost of living was so expensive these days, and well... something would have to be done. Dylan was really getting in the way on this trip, and he was doing nothing to attract any potential suitors for her. He had told her he was going to make sure she didn't make any more stupid mistakes. Who the hell did that kid think he was? She had been taking care of herself for a few years now, and what she most definitely did *not need* was some sanctimonious teenager telling her what to do.

She wandered away from the sheep-shearing demonstration and headed to the bar attached. Conor had said the group were to go there after the talk anyhow. She was badly in need of a drink. Things were not working out as well as she had hoped with the old Texan, Bert or Bart or whatever he was called. He was obviously a bit shrewder than she had first thought. Anyway, she appeared to have some competition from that old fossil Ellen. Incredible!

A handsome young barman interrupted her reverie. 'What can I get you?' he asked with a broad smile.

Corlene smiled back. *Hmm,* she thought. *He's cute. What the hell. He's broke for sure, but he will do for a bit of fun.* A Mr Right Now while she continued trying to locate Mr Right. She fluttered her eyelashes at him.

'Are you all right there, missus?' he asked in a strong Irish accent. 'Have ya somethin' in yer eye?'

'No...um...no, not at all,' Corlene replied. 'I'll have a Manhattan please.'

The barman looked at her and then surveyed the old-fashioned pub with a grin and said, 'I don't know if you noticed, missus, but there wouldn't be much call for fancy cocktails in this place. It's more of a pints and drops of whiskey sort of establishment, if you know what I mean. Having said all that, my mam always told me to try and help people out if I could, so if you tell me what goes into a Manhattan, then I'll see what I can do for ya.'

Corlene eyed him up and down. He was no more than seventeen or eighteen years old and had a really fit body and a kind of innocent charm.

'Aiden!' roared a voice from the end of the bar. A middle-aged man was reading the paper and seemed to be only halfway through his pint. 'Throw on another pint there for me, will ya? Herself is gone into Killorglin, so I have half an hour. If she rings, though, I'm not here. I'm supposed to be cleaning her mother's headstone. I swear she's only trying to think of jobs for me to do. And no doubt that self-same auld cow is looking down laughin' at me! The sight of a man relaxing over a pint seems to send my wan wild altogether, heh, heh. It'll be all picture and no sound and me dinner in the dog if she catches me in here.'

'Coming up, Paddy,' Aiden responded good-naturedly. Aiden turned his attention back to Corlene.

'Well, Aiden.' She luxuriated over his name. 'I guess a Manhattan is just the wrong kind of drink for here. When in Rome... What do *you* think I would like then?' She gave her best kittenish smile and a little wink so that he would be left in no doubt about her flirting. She didn't want him to feel intimidated by her. She thought she must seem very sophisticated and glamorous to someone like him. Maybe she would let him visit her that evening in the hotel. Her reverie was interrupted by his response to her question about what drink he thought she would like.

'Well, I'm not too sure what you'd like. I know that when my mam and my aunties go out, they have a glass of sherry. And my nan usually has a glass of Guinness. Would that be OK?'

Corlene hid her horror. The cheek of him! Comparing her to his mother and, worse still, to his grandmother!

Aiden waited innocently for her to make up her mind.

'Just give me a strong cup of coffee,' she replied flatly.

* * *

BACK ON BOARD THE COACH, Conor continued his banter. Most of the group were delighted by his knowledge and his stories; however, Dylan was much too caught up in the music he was listening to with earphones to have heard a single word that Conor said, Corlene was still smarting from her treatment at the hands of the innocent Aiden, and Elliot Heller's eyes never left his phone screen.

Anna gazed out the window. She had never seen such glorious scenery. The wild landscape of rugged cliffs and rolling ocean, green mountains with those sheep everywhere simply wandering around, all combined to have the most relaxing effect on her. She allowed herself to think about the whole situation with Elliot. The thing was that no one really understood him like Anna. She knew that people thought he treated her shabbily, but that was just his way – he didn't *mean* it. Still, she was hoping to find the right time to tell him what she had known for a few weeks now. She was pregnant. She could barely conceal her excitement, and she just knew this was going to change everything. Elliot had so much love to give, but he found it hard to open up. When he held his own baby in his arms, Anna felt sure it would be just the thing that was needed to open the floodgates.

She knew he had said he could never see himself as a father, but that was in the abstract, right? Maybe somewhere out here would be a good place to tell him. That way, when the baby was grown up, Elliot would have a great story to tell, of how he had heard the most wonderful news in the most stunning place in the world. Maybe they would choose one of those beautiful Irish names for the baby. The prospect of all these possibilities made Anna almost cry with happiness.

Conor was in the midst of describing an upcoming photo opportunity at a place called Ladies View, something to do with a visit by Queen Victoria, she thought Conor had said. Nudging Elliot, she said, 'Come on, honey, let's get off and take a walk around here.'

Elliot didn't look up from his screen. 'You go,' he answered distractedly. 'I'm doing an email to Jim Schwartz. I gotta nail this before the share price drops.'

'Please, Elliot, just five minutes?' she pleaded. 'You haven't looked at anything today.'

'Sure I have. All I've seen all day is hills and rocks and water. Don't tell me there's anything out there that isn't just more hills and rocks and water,' he said, smiling at his wit. Eventually, he looked up at her and raised a hand in submission. 'OK, OK, OK, just this one? One photo, then you give me some peace. Deal?'

'Deal.' She smiled.

They walked onto a slight headland; below them, the Black Valley opened up to reveal the majestic Lakes of Killarney. Anna led Elliot away from the rest of the group, who were busy snapping and admiring. She carefully chose a spot of uneven ground so that she could stand below him and he wouldn't have to look up at her. He hated that she was taller than he was. She knew she had to keep everything perfect. Gazing up into his eyes, her heart pounding with anticipation, she said, 'Elliot, I have some news for you – well, us really. The thing is...'

Just as she was about to make her announcement, she realised he was not paying attention. He was checking his backup phone for messages.

'Go on. I'm listening,' he said, phone stuck to one ear.

'I'm pregnant,' she blurted. 'We're going to have a baby. I can't believe it myself! It's just so exci –' The look on his face stopped her mid-sentence.

'Please tell me this is a joke,' Elliot said in a slow, measured tone. 'You did *not* just tell me you're pregnant.' His voice was like ice.

'No...no joke. I really am... Aren't you pleased?' Anna's voice trembled now.

Elliot walked a few feet away, his back to her as he looked down on the lakes and the valley below. There was a long silence.

'Pleased?' he finally spat. 'What the hell would I be pleased about? No, Anna, I'm not *pleased*. I told you I don't want kids – I never have and I never will. If you thought you could go off, get yourself pregnant and expect me to just go along with it, well, you don't know me as well as you think you do. I don't *want* a kid, now or in the future, so you'd better sort this mess out. I suppose this is going to cost me more money? Jesus, Anna! What were you *thinking?*'

'What do you mean, sort this mess out? Do you want me to...' – her voice dropped to an anguished whisper – 'have an *abortion?* Is that what you're saying?'

Anna waited for his answer with fear in her heart, blood pumping quickly now, her temples throbbing. Every fibre of her being wanted him to take her in his arms and say, 'Of course not! It's just a bit sudden.' She stared in horror at her husband as all her dreams drained away. His look said it all.

The sound of Conor's voice calling everyone to get back on board seemed incongruous in the circumstances, but as she watched Elliot walk off, she realised her fairy tale was over. This was it. She was on her own. She walked slowly towards the coach and climbed on board. He was back on his laptop again. She slipped into the seat and stared straight ahead. She needed to be alone, to think, to decide.

CHAPTER 11

*D*orothy was disgruntled; Juliet was behaving in a most irritating fashion. If it hadn't been for her, Juliet would never have had a proper, interesting vacation. The height of her cultural experience would be a trip to Florida for God's sake! But no, instead of gratitude for ensuring that she got out of her little cocoon and saw the world, she was deliberately going against Dorothy's decisions one by one. Since that first night in Kinsale, Juliet seemed to use every opportunity to head off on her own somewhere. She was usually such a mouse, but honestly, at the moment she was being completely ridiculous, chatting to Conor and that dreadful Patrick. Sometimes Dorothy wondered if Juliet was a bit mentally slow. She was useless at saving money and could easily be taken in by any gangster who wanted to rip her off. *Well,* Dorothy thought, *from now on she can fend for herself. See how long she lasts.*

* * *

JULIET'S HEART was racing as the coach pulled up to the front door of Hotel Killarney. The five-star hotel sat peacefully on the lake shore, surrounded by mountains. Conor got off first, asking everyone else to hold tight for a few minutes until he got the rooming list. Dorothy was gathering up her belongings and exuded impatience from every pore. She always wanted to be first off the coach, but for what reason, Juliet had absolutely no idea.

Conor reappeared. 'OK, folks. Bert, you're in 102, Ellen, 103, Dylan, 104, Corlene, 105, Patrick, 106, and Anna and Elliot, 107.'

Dorothy was just about to interrupt him to say they had not been allocated a room when Conor smiled at her.

'Dorothy and Juliet, if you two could just hold on for a second, I need to explain a small adjustment to the rooming list. Nothing to worry about,' he added, giving one of his infectious grins.

They followed him into the hotel lobby, where Conor explained the itinerary for the following day to all of the group. Dorothy stood beside Juliet wearing a face like thunder and muttering out loud, 'I don't know what kind of stunt he's going to pull, but I will not pay one extra cent for a second room. That's for certain.'

'Well, I'm sure there is nothing to worry about, Dorothy,' Juliet said. 'I mean, Conor knows what he's doing.'

Dorothy glared at her and snapped, 'Don't be so ridiculous, Juliet. These people are always looking for the angle. Well, he is not dealing with an amateur pushover here. When he comes back, just leave the talking to me. You would end up agreeing to anything just to be nice.'

As she watched the porter removing the suitcases from the boot of the coach, Juliet had what felt like ice cubes churning around her stomach. She needn't have worried, however; Conor dealt with the situation perfectly.

'Well, ladies,' he began, 'I didn't want to be explaining this in front of everyone in case they all started asking for it, but I want to let you know that Orion Travel has offered a room upgrade to you, Dorothy, by way of recognition for your loyalty to the company all these years. They have assigned you a junior suite on the top floor. For the duration of your stay here, you will have that suite at no extra cost. Room service is also included.'

For once, Dorothy's face showed something other than disdain. 'Well, I'm sure Orion appreciates my continued business. I *have* taken many tours with them, so I'm probably one of their most important clients,' she said smugly.

'That was certainly the impression I got from the message they left for me,' Conor agreed. 'Now, Juliet, I have to tell you that, like myself, you are in an ordinary room with no obvious perks.' Handing her the key, he gave her an almost imperceptible wink.

'Oh, she'll be fine,' Dorothy replied. 'Any hotel room is a treat for Juliet. Isn't that right, dear?'

Juliet chuckled inwardly at the condescension, so relieved at having finally made the break from this monstrous woman.

'Oh yes, Dorothy,' she said, trying to conceal her glee. 'I'll be fine. See you in the morning!'

Before Dorothy had time to suggest that they meet for dinner, Juliet was gone. She caught up with Conor on the stairs while Dorothy was being ushered to her suite by the manager.

'Conor, I don't know how you did it. I can't thank you enough,' Juliet gushed once Dorothy was clearly out of range. 'I know the suite is probably much more expensive, but just tell me the cost and I'll take care of it immediately. Honestly, you've no idea how relieved I am...'

Conor turned and put his big hands on Juliet's shoulders. 'Now you listen here to me. I want you to relax and enjoy the trip. The others are a nice bunch, and they'll be happy to have you join them as they go around, so long as herself is out of the picture. As for the room, it won't cost you a penny.'

Juliet began to protest. 'But I can't expect –'

Conor interrupted her in mock-stern tones. 'You can and you will. The manager here is a pal of mine, and the suite was empty anyhow. I won a few bob off him a few weeks back at poker, and he's looking after Dorothy for me as a kind of alternative payment arrangement, shall we say.' Conor gave her a wink. 'Consider it my good deed for the day, OK? Now, not another word on the subject, right, or my reputation as a hard man will be in tatters.'

Juliet's eyes filled with tears. 'You are one of the kindest men I have ever met. I just don't know what to say.'

Conor blushed and gave an embarrassed smile. 'Go away out of that,' he replied, and headed for his room.

As Juliet put the key in the lock, she heard a noise coming from further down the corridor. 'Psst! Are you alone?' a voice asked in a stage whisper.

Juliet saw the face of Patrick O'Neill emerge from around the door of the room across the corridor.

'Um, yes... Dorothy has another room on the top floor, so I...' Juliet was shy around the big police officer.

'Well, get yourself down here, girl. We're having a little cocktail hour.'

Juliet threw her bag on the bed and crossed the corridor. In Room 105, she found Bert and Ellen sitting at a table in the bay window.

'We're actually drinking to save Bert!' Patrick laughed. 'Corlene has set her sights on him, so it's not safe for him to be out alone.'

'She sure does believe in the institution of matrimony,' Bert said. 'She is a pretty lady, but I guess I'm just too old for chasing skirts any more. A nice scotch on the rocks and an early night are my idea of excitement these days.'

'Now, Juliet, what's your poison? We got whiskey, beer and wine – take your pick.'

'A glass of wine would be just lovely,' Juliet replied. 'You really are very kind to invite me.'

'Nonsense!' cried Patrick. 'We've just been waiting for you to ditch old iron drawers.'

Juliet broke into peals of laughter at the perfect description of her travelling companion.

Patrick took a long slug of beer from the neck of the bottle and said, 'Y'know, Juliet, we've been feeling really sorry for you. How in hell's name did you get stuck with that whining old bat?'

'Oh, Patrick,' Juliet replied. 'I know, I know. I mean, I don't like to speak badly of her, but it's been so embarrassing. I never wanted you all to think she was speaking for both of us. Talk about the ugly American. She gives the rest of us such a bad name.'

'Hey, Ellen!' Patrick said. 'What about Anna? We should call her room and see if she wants to join us, right?'

Ellen and Juliet had both noticed the heated conversation between Anna and Elliot earlier on, and it was obvious when she arrived back to the coach after the stop at Ladies View that things were anything but right.

'Her room is just beside mine, and I just might have a little bottle of something to add to the party down here, so I'll bring her back with me if she wants to join us,' Ellen said as she headed out the door.

Stopping off at her room, she collected the six-pack of Guinness she had bought on impulse that afternoon. If only her family and friends could see her now. One week in Ireland, and she'd taken to the drink!

She knocked gently on Anna's door, and when it opened slightly, Ellen could see that the younger woman had been crying.

'Oh, Ellen, I'm sorry... I was just...something...' Anna began incoherently.

Anna had been hoping that Elliot would realise his reaction was crazy by the time they had booked into the hotel, but instead he had just dumped his bags and stalked off in the direction of the town. He hadn't reappeared since. Anna had been sitting on the bed, stunned, horrified and trying to assimilate the impact of the crisis, when Ellen knocked at the door.

Ellen moved towards the little table by the window. 'You can tell me to mind my own business if you like, but sometimes it does help to talk.'

Anna looked at this kind old lady and felt that if she was going to confide in anyone, then Ellen was as good a bet as she was likely to get. Slowly, and in between sniffles and gulps, Anna explained her situation. When she finished, she looked plaintively at Ellen. 'So now what do I do? I don't have a job. My family thinks I was crazy to have anything to do with Elliot in the first place. I don't have a house. I mean, how can I give this child anything it needs?'

Years later, Anna would replay this scene in her head, and every time she did, she told herself how fortunate it was that the person who heard her story that night was Ellen O'Donovan. Someone else might have railed against Elliot, or told her that in this day and age, women had choices. They might even have berated her for being so stupid that she couldn't see what was perfectly clear to everyone else.

But Ellen fixed Anna with her clear blue eyes. 'All any child needs is love. My father raised me on his own in a strange country where he had no support. It wasn't easy and I'm sure there were lonely times, but he loved me with all his heart. And I loved him. Neither of us regretted a second of it, and it will be just the same for you, my dear. Congratulations.'

As Anna dried her tears, she realised that her world had not just come to an end.

Ellen announced, 'I don't know about you, but I could use a drink! There's a little cocktail party going on in Patrick's room, and I've been sent to fetch you. So how about we both touch up our make-up first, eh?'

CHAPTER 12

espite spending an hour in Patrick's room, where everyone
had been so kind, Anna still felt exhausted and miserable.
She was slowly acknowledging that she had made too many excuses
for Elliot, but she still couldn't bring herself to believe that he
wouldn't come around to the idea of the baby. The night wore on and
there was still no sign of him, so Anna undressed and got into bed.
She awoke at four in the morning, still alone. As she made a cup of
coffee and watched the sunrise, she placed her hands on her still-flat
stomach and spoke to her child directly for the first time.

'Your father is a cold-hearted shit. Everyone tried to tell me, but I
wouldn't listen. But your mommy loves you enough for two. Don't
worry, sweetheart. I'll take care of you. I don't know how exactly yet,
but everything is going to be fine.'

* * *

As SHE BOARDED THE COACH, Dorothy asked in her usual acerbic
manner, 'I suppose we all have to wait for your husband yet again?
This really is getting most tiresome.'

The normally apologetic Anna turned and looked her straight in the face. 'No, *Dorothy*,' she replied, emphasising the older woman's name. 'I think we have all waited long enough for Elliot, don't you? Some things will never change, no matter how much you may want them to.' Then turning to Conor, she said, 'I don't think Elliot is going to continue with the trip. I'm sorry, but it would be best if we just moved on.' Despite being on the brink of tears, she remained composed.

Ellen moved into the window seat and offered the other seat to Anna. Anna smiled gratefully.

'Ireland is a magnificent country, isn't it? I'm really enjoying the trip so far,' Ellen proffered. Her gentle voice had a soothing effect on Anna. She knew that Anna was fragile and that light rhetorical conversation was exactly what she needed.

'Today is a very special day on our trip,' Conor began. 'We will be touring the Dingle Peninsula, which is just spectacular. We will be visiting some Celtic and early Christian sites, and of course, we'll be in the heart of the Irish-speaking part of the county. So I know you'll really enjoy it. As well as that, we're going to visit the Blasket Islands, which is a rare treat. The weather out there can be very unpredictable, and life on the island was hard for those who lived there. But despite all that, such a wealth of writing and art has been created there – it's remarkable. There are no permanent residents there now, of course. They have all either emigrated or have come to live on the mainland.'

Patrick was confused. He'd come to Ireland expecting lots of things, but most importantly, he wanted to feel like an Irishman. He remembered all the family get-togethers he had attended as a child – events that filled the young Patrick with patriotism for 'the old country'. He'd listened to his uncle singing 'Danny Boy', and to his father and his friends telling stories of the 'boys' and their noble struggle for freedom in the fight against the English. As a young police officer, he began to make regular contributions from his meagre salary to NORAID, the organisation that supported the families of republican prisoners, a subject he had hoped to raise during his conversations with people in pubs while he was on vacation here. If he were honest with himself, he wanted a little bit of gratitude, or if not that, at least a sense that he'd earned his badge as an Irishman and could take his place at the bar with his fellow countrymen as one of them. He wanted to be identified as culturally and socially different from the others on the coach. They seemed like nice people, but they weren't Irish. They were just tourists.

So far, however, this vacation had been less than satisfactory. Conor appeared to have no animosity at all towards the British oppression and occupation of Ireland and seemed, very subtly, to have been able to get Patrick to agree with his calm and reasoned opinions. Outside the tour group, the only other person he had managed to have a proper conversation with in the past few days was Cynthia.

She was something else. She seemed kind of quirky, and her background was strange, to say the least. She had said she was Irish, lived here all her life, but was educated in England and appeared to identify with the age-old enemy more than she did with her own country. All her talk of horses and big houses had Patrick totally confused. On top of that, it seemed she was a Protestant. The whole thing was a mystery, but since he had kind of set himself up as an authority on all things Irish, he couldn't ask anyone.

* * *

CORLENE DECIDED that if she couldn't get Bert into some kind of romantic clinch today, then there was no hope. Granted, he was an old guy, but hey, he was on this tour, which meant he was rich, so he wouldn't be the worst person to get stuck with. Corlene wasn't too keen on dusty Texas, but beggars couldn't be choosers, she reasoned. She had dressed with particular care that morning. Her leopard-print wraparound dress left nothing to the imagination; it would be a waste not to put the boobs paid for by husband number three to some practical use, she reckoned. Her vertiginous sandals caused the ever-diplomatic Conor to express some concern about her safety during the day ahead. Apparently, this Blasket Island place was 'a bit rough', whatever that meant! She wasn't going to put on sneakers for anyone. They would look ridiculous, and most unflattering, with her dress.

That Conor doesn't know who he's dealing with, she thought with a smug grin. She had been homecoming queen three years in a row, admittedly quite a few years ago, so she was used to walking in high heels.

She had managed to wangle her way into sitting beside Bert on the coach today, but not before she noticed him trying to chat up that old relic Ellen yet again.

Her thoughts were interrupted by Bert's Texan drawl. 'Excuse me, Miss Corlene, would you like some candy?' he asked, offering her a paper bag containing a variety of sweets.

Corlene turned on her brightest smile; her scarlet collagen-enhanced lips – funded by husband number four – contorted into what she thought was a combination of coquettish charm and suggestive allure. Maybe all was not lost. 'Why, Bert, that's really kind of you, but I'm sweet enough. Thank you for thinking of me, though.' She fluttered her eyelashes. 'Are you enjoying the trip, Bert?'

'I most certainly am, ma'am. It's real pretty, and the people seem great.'

Corlene deliberately let her leg rest against Bert's and applied some pressure as she spoke. 'Oh yes, it's lovely, but I get so lonely sometimes. You must be the same, travelling alone...'

Bert realised this was his opportunity, and if he didn't take it now, he could find himself in real trouble with this woman. 'Well, y'know, Miss Corlene, I'm real lucky like that. I don't ever get lonely. I was very happily married for forty-one years. My kids and grandkids are wonderful. I got enough money to keep me comfortable, and I've handed over the running of the company to my son and daughter. I thought, what's the point of holding on to stuff when I don't need it? I'm sure you feel the same. It's all for the kids in the end anyhow, so now I've just got a small pension, and I live in a one-bedroom apartment, take the bus everywhere. And as I said, I have things just the way I want them. Nice and simple and easy. I've no interest – and no point – in changing my life at this late stage.'

Bert's innocent brown eyes looked straight at Corlene. While his speech seemed innocuous enough, Corlene realised for the first time that Bert was a tough guy, and he'd made it clear he wasn't going to be taken for a fool. He knew her game, and in a gentlemanly and diplomatic way, he was telling her in no uncertain terms that she was wasting her time.

Recovering her composure, she replied, 'Well, Bert, it seems like you got life all figured out.'

I'm no quitter, she added silently. *That old Texan might be off the list, but there are plenty more fish in the sea.*

The day passed pleasantly as the group continued to bond under Conor's unobtrusive but effective guidance. They visited wonderfully atmospheric Celtic ruins and early Christian churches, and strolled through the Gaeltacht village of Ballyferriter. A Gaeltacht was an area of the country where Irish was spoken, Conor explained while they shopped for their picnic lunch on the island.

Walking back to the coach, Conor joined in the conversation between Patrick and Bert.

'I'm tellin' you, Bert, one guy came into the little store there and said "dig a ditch" and the guy behind the counter answered him by saying, "dig a squirrel ditch"!'

Bert laughed out loud. 'What the hell is a squirrel ditch? And why would you need to dig it?'

Conor guffawed. 'What those fellas were saying is an Irish greeting, our form of hello, if you like. It means God be with you, and the reply is, "God and Mary be with you. *Dia Dhuit agus Dia is Muire agat"*. Nothing at all to do with squirrels, I'm afraid!'

'Well, I dunno about that, Conor. It sure sounded like "squirrel ditch" to me.'

The trip out to the island fulfilled all their expectations, and they marvelled at how people had managed to live in such an isolated place in harsh winter conditions. The weather was glorious, and it seemed to most of the group that they were as close to heaven as it was possible to get. As they spread their picnic on the grass, Conor told them stories of the writers and poets who had come from the island, and he read them poems and stories, including a short extract from some famous book in the Irish language. While the words sounded strange to their ears, there was a wonderful musical quality to the language.

As they lay on the grass, curlews and gulls circling overhead and the wild Atlantic pounding the cliffs relentlessly below them, each member of the group was lost in his or her own thoughts. When eventually Conor insisted that they make their way back to the pier to get the boat to the mainland, it was with great reluctance that they gathered up their belongings.

Dylan fell into step with Conor and Ellen.

'Thank you so much, Conor,' Ellen said. 'What a wonderful experience you have given us. You know, there are expensive spas and wellness centres all over the world, but I think sitting there on the grass, listening to you read us those poems and stories, well, no money could ever pay for that.'

'When the weather cooperates here, which is hardly ever, I might add, it's the most special place on this earth, and it makes my job very easy.'

Dylan liked Ellen and Conor the best of the group, so he had the confidence to contribute his own opinions. 'This country is totally awesome,' he said with enthusiasm. 'When my mom said we were coming to this island place, I was like, totally bummed out, but especially today, I can, like, hear where the music comes from. There's this tune called 'The Lonely Sailor' or something, and it's like the sound of the sea, with birds and everything. It's awesome.'

Conor smiled at Dylan's turnaround. 'Would that tune be called 'The Lonesome Boatman' maybe? It's usually played on a tin whistle.'

Dylan clicked his fingers. 'Yeah, dude, that's it!' He marvelled at the older man. 'Is there anything you don't know?'

'God, Dylan, there's so much I don't know about everything. You just got me on a good day.'

* * *

BACK AT THE HOTEL, Conor checked his BlackBerry. He deliberately hadn't looked for a reply to his email because he still wasn't sure what he wanted to hear. As he opened his messages, he instantly spotted Sinead's name among the long stream.

Hi Conor,

Great to hear from you! I was worried when I didn't hear back. I didn't know if you just didn't receive my letter, or worse, you received it and didn't want to get in touch. As I said in the letter, I'm coming home with my son, Conor. We're arriving this weekend into Shannon. Conor is really excited. I've been telling him all about Ireland and about his Uncle Conor, so he can't wait to meet you. I don't really have a plan as such, as it depends on some things.

There's no easy way to say this, dear Conor, but I have cancer and it's not looking good. I just need to be at home. I don't know how things are going to go, but I do know that the happiest I have ever been was all those years ago in Passage West. My family and I haven't spoken for years. They hated Gerry, as you know, and well, that's all water under the bridge now. They did try to see young Conor, but we don't need them or their 'I told you so'.

Anyway, I'll hopefully see you soon!

Lots and lots of love,

Sinead xxx

CHAPTER 13

The more Ellen got to know their driver and guide, the better she liked him. She realised how much work he did behind the scenes, trying to help each of them in different ways, and all the while he maintained his constant good humour. He seemed to have a great knack for allowing the group to do their own thing. He never got in the way but seemed to be instantly available if he was needed. He was relaxing in the lobby of the hotel with a cup of coffee and *The Irish Times* after the group had dispersed for dinner when she approached him.

'Excuse me, Conor. I'm really sorry for interrupting you. I'll only keep you a minute, if that's all right?'

'No problem, Ellen, sit down. Can I get you a coffee? There's plenty in the pot. I can just ask for another cup.'

'Well, if you are sure, that would be lovely. Thank you.'

Conor gestured to the young waitress, who produced another cup almost instantaneously.

'I'll get right to the point, Conor. There's a free day tomorrow, and I have something I need to do alone. I will meet you all back in the hotel in the evening. It's just that I didn't want you to worry about me...put me on a missing list.'

Despite her soft voice and equally gentle approach, Ellen tended to present things in a way that indicated the matter was already decided. But that didn't mean she didn't expect objections and questions about whatever it was she was presenting. She was very pleasantly surprised when Conor replied, 'Righty-ho, Ellen, that's perfect. Thanks for letting me know. The next couple of days are relaxed ones anyway. Is there anything I can do to help you, or have you it all under control?'

'Well, actually, I was going to ask the front desk, but maybe you could suggest someone. You see, I need a car and driver for the day. Do you know of a local taxi firm or chauffeur service that I could use?'

Conor thought for a second. 'Well, Ellen, I'm sure I can sort something out. If you could tell me where it is you want to go, I could maybe organise a price for you too. It would be cheaper, I'd say, to do it that way. Cheaper than per mile on a taxi meter anyway. But if you would rather keep the destination details to yourself, well then, that's fine too. Whatever suits you.'

'I guess I want to go to... Well, this might sound crazy, but I am not that sure. It's a long story, and I'm sure you don't have time to –'

'Ellen, I have all night. I was going to go into town to a nice quiet little pub I know and have a bite of dinner, maybe even a pint, and do the crossword. If you would like to join me and tell me some, none or all of your story, then I would be delighted with the company.'

Ellen's face broke into a radiant smile. 'Well, Mr O'Shea' – she laughed – 'if you are sure I'm not intruding on your private time, a dinner and a pint sound like just what I need.'

'I can see I have a hardened drinker on my hands so. Mind you, with a name like yours, it couldn't have been any other way, Ms O'Donovan,' he said, standing up and offering her his arm and embarking on what was to become a most extraordinary evening.

* * *

SETTLED in the corner seats of Murphy's Pub and Restaurant, Ellen sipped on a glass of stout. 'This really is a good drink. I'm not much of a drinker, but I could develop a taste for this.'

Conor took a gulp of his pint. 'Well, actually, it's probably just as well you never had it at home. The breweries export this all over the world. I don't know what they do with it when it gets there, but they seem to make a right pig's ear out of it. Maybe it's the water or something. Whatever, the thing about stout outside of Ireland is that it's something that shouldn't be inflicted on anyone.'

Ellen smiled. 'Then I guess it's right that I should have waited till I got to Ireland to consume my first pint of Guinness.'

They ordered bacon and cabbage with potatoes, and as they waited for their food, they chatted generally about the trip. Conor was careful not to discuss any individuals – a policy that had served him well for many years.

'So,' Ellen began, 'are you sure you want to hear this?'

'Fire away. I'm all ears.'

'OK then. I was born on December 18, 1920. My name is a West Cork one, I know, so no prizes for guessing my Irish connections. What might surprise you, though, is that I was born in the parish of Inchigeelagh in County Cork.'

'I know it well,' said Conor.

'My father brought me to America when I was a few weeks old, after my mother died – in childbirth, I believe. He remarried a few years later, and they had a son, my stepbrother, but that marriage broke up. I stayed in touch with my brother and his mother, but she passed away from breast cancer in her early fifties. I think she really did love my father, but it was never going to work really. It seems my dad could never fully commit to the marriage. I remember Diane – that was her name – saying years ago that he must have loved my mother so much he couldn't let her memory go. He would never talk about it or about his life before coming to America. I tried asking him many times about my mother and his family back in Ireland, but all he ever said was that we were Americans now and the only way to get on in America was to be American and leave the past behind.'

Conor nodded encouragingly.

'My father avoided anything to do with Irish organisations, and even when discussions started about Irish neutrality during the Second World War, or the Troubles in the North, he would never engage. Despite that, I found the subject fascinating, and my whole career was spent researching and teaching the story of this little island. He was always encouraging and supportive of me, but he never offered an opinion or asked me anything about it. I didn't even know if he ever read my books until after he passed away. Then I found one I wrote about the Easter Rising in 1916, and it was so well thumbed it was almost falling apart. Yet never a word to me about it. I...' Ellen's voice faltered.

'It seems that there was some correspondence between him and his Irish family over the years, though, but he never mentioned it to me. When he died, I found a pile of letters and Christmas cards in a box in his apartment. The address on the letters was Inchigeelagh, County Cork, and they were from Sean, my father's brother. The letters were just newsy ones, announcing births and deaths in the parish and things like that. I'd really hoped, when I found them, they would tell me more. I know my father had an older brother – I think he was called Michael. I remember one time when my stepbrother and I were playing with an old coat we had found in a wardrobe, my father came in and told us we should find something else to play with because that coat was special. He told us that my Uncle Michael had given it to me to keep me warm on the way over from Ireland. I remember saying to my father, "We don't have an Uncle Michael," to which he replied, "Yes, you do, but he lives back in Ireland, and he can't come to visit because it's too far away to come without a coat."'

Ellen smiled at the memory, and her eyes welled up. 'I don't want you to get the impression my dad was a cold man, far from it, but something must have happened here, perhaps the death of my mother, that made it so painful for him to recollect. He was such a good and loving father to me and my brother. He did everything for me. I often think what it must have been like for him, with a baby, all on his own in a foreign country. I don't know why, but I feel like there's something I don't know about the story. I just want to go there, maybe see if I can find my mother's grave. I've been thinking about it for years – ever since he died, to be honest. But I've never felt really ready until now.'

'Well, Ellen, what a story. Your dad sounds like he was a remarkable man, to bring you up alone like that, so far from all his family. I'm not sure I could do that now, and those times were so different. Fathers had very little to do with their children, leaving it all to the women. I have vague memories of my own father boasting how he had never pushed a pram, but then my father and yours sound poles apart. Anyway, where do we go from here? I'm happy to help in whatever way I can.'

'Thanks, Conor. I want to try to find the house, maybe see if anybody knows anything about my family there. My father's younger brother, the one who wrote the letters, was a young child when we left. I think he lost touch sometime in the 1950s. I realise it's probably a wild goose chase, but I'd like to try. Even just to be in the village they came from.'

'I am not a genealogist, Ellen, but tomorrow is my day off and I'd be happy to drive you there if that would help. I'm at a bit of a loose end anyhow.'

Tears welled up in Ellen's eyes again. 'Conor, that would be just wonderful. I was thinking how on earth I would ever find the place on my own. I insist on paying you for your time and the fuel and so on...'

'Indeed, and you will not. It's no problem whatsoever. In fact, it would be a pleasure. Do y'know what, Ellen? This is turning out to be a very interesting tour altogether.'

CHAPTER 14

*D*ylan was totally hooked. The trouble was he didn't know what to do next. He sat at the back of the large pub crammed with Irish people and tourists and listened to Diarmuid and the others as they played their music. Tonight was different to the atmosphere in the pub in Kinsale, more of a concert than a session, but still amazing. The songs were sometimes wild, other times funny. One song in particular completely transported Dylan to another place.

He had never enjoyed anything about school, least of all history, which he regarded as a litany of just one boring thing after another. But when he heard the song 'Kilkelly', it made him want to cry. It was based on a true story, the singer said. It seemed to be a conversation in the form of letters between a father in Ireland and his son in America, all a long time ago. Dylan remembered Conor mentioning something about there being a famine in Ireland, so he guessed the song referred to events around that time. The father wrote long letters telling the son all of the news about the family and all the people that the son would have known from home. The son wrote back and sent pictures of his wife and kids but never returned to Ireland. The song ended with the last letter from the man's brother, telling him that their father had died.

Dylan wondered what it would have been like to have a father who cared so much that he wrote every month even though he hadn't laid eyes on his child for years. Dylan's own father hadn't stuck around when he discovered that Corlene was pregnant. In fact, Corlene wasn't too sure who Dylan's father was. It seemed the guy she tried to pin the pregnancy on could not have been the father for medical reasons, so Dylan had no clue who his father was.

He used to fantasise when he was a kid that his dad would show up, having found out about the existence of his son, and that he would take him away from Corlene and bring Dylan to live with him. In Dylan's fantasy, his father was a shopkeeper who had a nice wife and lots of kids who welcomed Dylan into the family. But as Dylan grew older, he realised that the family of his dreams didn't exist anywhere outside of his imagination, and he eventually gave up on the idea. Grandma was the closest he came to having a family, but Corlene didn't really get along with her mother, and she only ever went back home to visit when things were very bad in her own life. Every time things got rough, Dylan wished he could up sticks and go stay with his grandma, but Corlene always moved them on to wherever she could manage to scrounge enough money.

Something was happening here in this little place in Ireland. He could feel it. He really wanted to be part of this world, but he felt that he might as well be a Martian; he had so little in common with these people.

There was a break in the music, and the musicians were chatting to a group of people sitting together near the stage. Dylan remained in his seat, feeling ridiculous. Everyone else here seemed to be with someone, and he had never felt so out of place. As he looked into his glass, he heard Diarmuid say, 'Dylan! How are things? Are you on your own? Come over here and meet some people.'

Dylan smiled and gratefully followed the piper.

'This is my wife, Siobhán, and one of our daughters, Laoise, and my cousin Sean and his wife, Kate. These here are a variety of relations, all on the way back from a funeral in Kerry of an old lady we knew.'

Everyone in the group smiled and said hello. Slightly thrown by such attention, Dylan blushed. 'Uh...hi, guys,' he managed to stutter.

They looked like nice people. Diarmuid's wife was younger than him and kind of hippyish, but she had a very friendly smile.

'If you're sitting up there on your own, why don't you join us?' Siobhán asked, nudging the teenage girl sitting beside her. 'Push up there, Laoise, and make some room.'

Diarmuid's daughter moved over, creating just enough space for Dylan to squeeze in. She was about seventeen and dressed in black from head to toe. Not exactly his image of an Irish colleen, but he was nonetheless fascinated by her.

'So,' she said, then sipped her drink, 'you're American?'

Dylan nodded.

'We went to Savannah, Georgia, last year. Dad and the lads were playing there for St Patrick's Day. It was brilliant. We had such craic...' Registering the look of surprise on Dylan's face, she laughed and explained. 'Not crack as in cocaine! It's an Irish word – it means having a good time. It was so much fun compared with being in Ireland for Paddy's Day. It's always feckin' raining for a start. My dad said you were at the gig in the church the other day, and that you went to the session in Kinsale too.' Laoise seemed very confident and very scary.

'Well, your dad said it would be OK... I didn't get in the way, I hope. I mean...' Dylan felt himself blushing again.

'Nah,' Laoise replied. 'It's just I was expecting you to be different. Dad said you might come tonight. I think he thought I could talk to you, being your age and all that. Anyway, I dunno what I was expecting, but you're not it anyway.' She laughed.

Dylan froze, but then quickly realised she was only kidding him, so he laughed too. She was amazing-looking, he thought. She had really short raven-black hair with streaks of fluorescent pink. Her tiny frame was dressed in a mixture of black denim and leather, and her tongue was pierced. On her neck, she had a small tattoo of a treble clef.

'Cool tattoo,' Dylan ventured.

Laoise beamed. 'Yeah, it's deadly, I know, but my mam and dad went mental when I got it done. You're supposed to be eighteen to get it done, but I have a fake ID. Dad is getting used to it now, but for ages I had to wear a scarf 'cause every time he saw it, he went off on one. You'd swear he was a saint all his life the way he went on at me. I mean, like, it's my neck, right?'

'I think your dad is awesome. I've never heard anyone play like him,' Dylan replied, thrilled to be talking to this incredible girl.

'Yeah, he's grand. I suppose he'd want to be good by now. He's been doing it, like, forever. I've been listening to it all my life, so I suppose you get a bit immune to it, you know what I mean?' Laoise took a sip of her Coke.

'How do you spell your name?' These Irish names were a total mystery to him.

'L-A-O-I-S-E, but pronounced "Lee-sha",' she said, her mouth full of potato crisps.

It was the most beautiful name Dylan had ever heard.

The band had restarted, and the singer was calling someone to the stage. It suddenly dawned on Dylan that it was Laoise they were looking for. With a sigh, she got up, shuffled past Dylan and headed for the stage. Without a hint of nervousness, she took the microphone and began singing in a language Dylan couldn't understand. Diarmuid accompanied her on the tin whistle, her mesmeric voice stilling all conversation in the pub. When the last sad plaintive notes rang out, the crowd erupted with whoops and cheers and calls for more. Laoise said something to her father, took up a small blue electric fiddle, nodded to the other band members and began to play a furious and frantic tune. As the music reached a crescendo, the whooping and cheering erupted all over again, but this time the crowd were on their feet yelling and applauding. Laoise handed the fiddle player his instrument, smiled her thanks for the applause and sauntered off the stage, cool as a breeze. She made for the front door and, as she did so, gestured to Dylan to follow.

The cool air that greeted them was a welcome contrast to the hot and sticky pub.

Laoise lit a cigarette and offered Dylan one. They stood smoking in silence for a few moments. 'That was amazing,' Dylan finally managed to say.

'What was? Oh, the tune? Thanks.' As ever, Laoise was unfazed. 'It gives the lads in the band a chance to have a pint.' She took another long drag. 'My mam goes mad over me smoking, though, says it will wreck my voice.'

'So are you, like, professional now?'

Laoise burst into peals of laughter. 'Yeah, right! Me and all the other 50,000 Irish girls who can carry a tune. Nah, I've just done my Leaving Cert and finished school. I just sing a bit with my dad at home and an odd time at something like this. It's a tough way to earn a living, music, even if you are out of the ordinary, which I'm not. My folks want me to go to college and all that. I suppose I will, but I really just want to do music.'

'I think you could totally be, like, famous. That fiddle you were playing was amazing,' Dylan said, really proud of himself that he hadn't made the mistake of calling it a violin.

'Thanks, but you are a session virgin.' Laoise laughed. 'I'm OK, but there are hundreds like me. If you went up to Milltown for the Willie Clancy Summer School in July, you'd see what I mean.'

Dylan looked at her, astonished that he could feel relaxed around someone as cool as Laoise. 'Well, I know I don't know much about it. Hell, I was calling that thing you were playing a violin until yesterday! But if I could play like that, man, I sure would be happy,' he said with a grin.

'Why don't you learn?' Laoise asked as if it were the most logical thing in the world. 'I'm doing a beginner's course on the Irish harp, starting next Monday in Cork. I always wanted to play it, but my mam says the house is coming down with musical instruments and we're not buying any more. But my dad got around her, so I start Monday. I can't wait. They have all kinds of courses there – fiddle, banjo, box, anything really. You should check it out.' Stamping out her cigarette, Laoise continued. 'The teachers are really good there. There's a guy called Ger Murphy teaching box – they call him the "Ceili King" – and a fiddle player called Vince Milne – the guy is a total legend. You could learn to play better no bother. My dad's best friend – he's the singer and the guitarist in the band, and he's called Tim – would give you any help you needed if you want to carry on with the guitar. All the lads are really sound, and they love to see young lads and girls playing.'

Dylan loved the sound of her voice, as well as the fact that she made it all sound so easy. If he hadn't seen a session for real, he wouldn't have believed her. He knew one got nothing for nothing in this world. But in this music scene, here in Ireland, the same rules just didn't seem to apply.

As the band was loading up the sound equipment into the back of a white van, Diarmuid suddenly appeared behind them. 'I sincerely hope that wasn't cigarette smoke I saw a second ago.'

'Nah, Dad, you're just getting fuzzy eyes in your old age.'

'Well, better not have been, miss. Your mother could well pull the plug on the harp thing if she thinks you're acting the maggot, d'you hear me?' As he turned towards Dylan, Laoise stuck her tongue out behind his back.

'Well, Dylan,' Diarmuid said, 'we're off now. I hope you had a good night and that my daughter didn't try to lead you astray.'

'Definitely not,' Dylan replied. 'And thanks for inviting me.'

Just before she climbed into the van, Laoise grabbed Dylan's wrist and, using an eyeliner pencil, wrote a phone number on his upturned palm. Diarmuid pretended not to see. The van reversed out, and as Dylan walked up the street in the direction of the hotel, it slowed briefly and he heard Laoise's voice ring out. 'Hey, Dylan! Don't be a stranger!'

Dylan walked back to the hotel having had the best night of his life. Ever.

CHAPTER 15

*A*t breakfast the next morning, Conor announced, 'Well, folks, today you leave the nest. I know some of you have plans and some are just going to take it easy, but whatever you do today, just enjoy yourselves. We leave early tomorrow morning, so I want everyone tucked up in bed by ten tonight, do you hear me?' Conor wagged his finger as the group chuckled. 'Seriously, folks, have a great day, and my mobile is on if you need any help. But the petty cash fund won't stretch to bail, so try to stay on the right side of the law, OK?'

Dorothy Crane threw her eyes to the heavens and muttered, 'Must he continue with these inane attempts at humour? It really is most tiresome.'

If any of the group heard this particular aside of hers, they pretended not to.

Bert planned a quiet day reading the *Wall Street Journal* and the *Washington Post*. It was time he started thinking about his new project. He had been having a blast up to this point, and while his fellow passengers were a motley crew for sure, most of them were getting on very well together. It was always hard to blend in with this type of situation, but he was very adept at coming across as open and friendly without giving away too much. He never told lies; he just never told the whole truth. Whenever he set about choosing a new project, or a new location, one of his priorities was to ensure his own invisibility.

He had seen a documentary about Ireland and was impressed. They had real get-up-and-go; they tried to fix things themselves rather than wait for handouts. Whenever he thought about the welfare situation in the US, it nearly drove him crazy. The Irish, on the other hand, were not a nation of whiners. They had faced such adversity in their long and turbulent past, but yet the world over, they had a reputation for being fun-loving and friendly. Sure, one had to be wary of some of them, especially in the construction business, but overall he liked them. Bert was retired now, and his son ran the company very efficiently, so he didn't have to worry about that any more.

Whenever he was asked what criteria he used for choosing a project location, Bert always gave the same answer: He had to like the people in general. Aside from that, he just arrived in a location, blended in as much as possible and took it from there. The thing was to watch and listen. The next steps always evolved over time, requiring no great effort on his part.

He decided to take a stroll. He *loved* this climate. In Texas, buildings were either sweltering hot or air-conditioned. He had tried installing a top-of-the-range climate control system in his property. It was supposed to make the building feel cool yet not air-conditioned, but he wasn't happy with it. He'd lived all his life in Texas, so it surprised people how much he disliked the weather there.

Returning from his walk, he spotted Ellen dealing with something at the front desk. He really liked her company; plus she wasn't trying to hit on him. He thought that perhaps Ellen would like to do something today.

'Hello, Bert. What have you planned to do today?'

'Well, Miss Ellen, I was just going to ask you the same question. It seems a pity to waste the day sitting around a hotel, though I have been known to take protracted snooze periods. Gee, I'm turning into a real old-timer, ain't I?'

'Well,' Ellen replied, 'I will totally understand if you don't want to, but today I am going to try to find the house where I was born, and I wondered if you would like to come with me.'

Bert looked into the eyes of the woman he had known for such a short time but to whom he felt a close connection. 'Miss Ellen, it would be an honour.'

* * *

PATRICK GAZED out the window of the public bus serving the route from Killarney to Cork. He felt a combination of excitement and trepidation. Was he about to make a complete fool of himself? He had called Cynthia last night and had suggested meeting for lunch in Cork. She seemed happy to hear from him, but maybe he wasn't reading the signals right. He never had much luck with women back in the States. He always seemed to say the wrong thing. With Cynthia, however, things were different. True, he didn't have a clue what she was talking about most of the time, and she looked a little bit crazy if the truth be told, but he just couldn't shake the feeling that if he didn't do something, say something, the opportunity would pass and he would regret it forever.

He thought about his old man, an alcoholic dreamer who always was just on the brink of a fortune that never quite materialised. One of his many pieces of advice to his son was, 'The opportunity of a lifetime must be taken in the lifetime of that opportunity.' While from an early age, Patrick O'Neill had vowed always to do the complete opposite of anything his father suggested, on this one occasion, old Patsy O'Neill's advice might be exactly right.

* * *

CORLENE WONDERED how on earth things had turned out this way. She had it all – looks, personality, charm, wit – and yet she was drawing blanks everywhere. She had been so sure the tour would deliver the answer to her prayers; instead it had proved to be a total washout. Her credit card was maxed out, she'd had an email from the landlord citing non-payment of rent for three consecutive months as the reason for her eviction, and now here she was, miles from anywhere, penniless and alone and, it seemed, homeless to boot.

With a deep breath, she lifted the phone and dialled a number. A recorded message instructed her to dial the code next to the advertiser's name and listen to the message. Following the instructions to the letter, she heard the advertiser's gruff voice say, 'Strong farmer, mature, WLTM woman, aged twenty to sixty, with a view to marriage. Must be interested in farming. Killarney area only.'

He was her last hope – none of the others had replied to her messages. Time was of the essence, and this guy seemed as anxious as she was to cut to the chase and get hitched. At least she wouldn't have to invest months in him only to discover that he had some 'commitment issues' as had happened too often in the past. No, this sounded perfect – a big landowner who wanted to marry, who wasn't fussy about age and all that. Not, of course, that Corlene looked anything like her age; it was just that for some men these days, it seemed nothing less than a teenager would do.

'Well, hi there,' she began. 'My name is Corlene, and I am...well, let's just say I'm not twenty-one. I thought your ad sounded really intriguing, and I am definitely an outdoor kinda girl. I prefer to do almost everything outside.' She giggled suggestively. 'Call me on 064 6671300, Room 104, if you would like to chat some more.'

Twenty minutes later, the phone on the bedside locker rang. 'Hello, Corlene here,' she simpered.

'Right, Caroline. Come down to Pajo's pub on New Street at seven o'clock this evening till I get a look at you. Maybe we can do business,' a gruff, heavily accented voice muttered.

Corlene only caught about one word in three, so she decided the safest thing was to agree. 'Why, certainly,' she replied. 'Mr...?'

'Just ask for Pa,' growled the voice, then the man hung up.

* * *

DYLAN WOKE to the sound of the phone ringing. 'Hello,' he said groggily.

'Hey, Dylan, it's Laoise. Howyadoin'?'

Dylan sat bolt upright in the bed. 'Laoise! Hi! Uh...good to hear from you...' He paused. He was completely tongue-tied.

'Listen, I'm in Killarney, so I was wondering if you wanted to, like, hang out or something? My mam had to do some shopping, so I came down with her. She's supposed to be teaching me to drive, but she's got so nervous all of a sudden, she now says she won't allow me to drive us back home later after all. I dunno. What's her problem? I'm a brilliant driver. Dad had to stand in at some music committee thing in Cork today. He told me what it was, but I wasn't listening.'

Dylan swallowed. He couldn't believe his luck. Was he dreaming? 'Sure...great...yeah, that would be totally awesome. Just gimme a few minutes to get ready and I'll...' he stammered. Then he was struck dumb yet again.

'Hey, Dylan, are you still there? Don't worry, dude, I'm not coming up to molest you or anything,' she said, giving a cute chuckle. 'I'll give you ten minutes to make yourself decent, and then I'm coming up, OK? So what's the room number?'

'Uh...it's 105,' replied Dylan, who was amazed, delighted and terrified all at the same time.

He dashed into the shower; there was no time for make-up, no time to fix his hair. There was a knock on the door. He ran to open it.

'Hey, Dylan. Wow, you look different without the goth make-up and the mad punk hair. Cool room! Where's your mam?'

Dylan smiled at Laoise and admired the confident breezy way she approached life. 'Dunno, don't care. Probably still face down after a night in the bar,' he replied with a grin. 'Hey, it's so cool to see you again. We don't have to do the tourist thing today. I got a day off to do whatever, so...' His voice trailed off. *Jesus*, he thought. He was trying to sound cool, but so far it wasn't working. He never let *anyone* see him without his hair and make-up done, and without those props, he felt kind of naked.

Laoise said she was starving and suggested they get some breakfast.

'Breakfast is included here, so let's just go downstairs,' he suggested.

'Cool,' she replied.

As he made for the bathroom again, Laoise said, 'Hey, the goth thing is cool, don't get me wrong, but you look fine without it too, y'know? Let's just go, yeah? I'd eat a nun's arse through a convent gate.'

Dylan exploded laughing. 'Jesus! You are something else! OK, bossy boots, let's go get some of this cholesterol-laden, pig-fat breakfast you all love so much here.'

As they ate, Laoise told Dylan some more about the music course she wanted to do now that she was finished with school. Her mam, Siobhán, wanted her to go to college and get a proper degree. It wasn't because she had anything against music, Laoise explained, it was just that she had spent her whole life around musicians. She knew how tough it could be to make a living, and she wanted an easier life for her daughter.

'My older sister, Éadaoin, is in London, and she's doing great. She's just got a job in the West End in a musical,' Laoise explained through a mouthful of toast and sausages. 'And my brother, Cathal, is a bass player with Unprecedented Incompetence.'

Dylan looked puzzled.

'Never heard of them? Jeez, do you live under a stone or what? They're really big here, and in England too, so he's never at home. My mam is scared he'll get into drugs, but I keep telling her he's too stingy to pay for them. I know she gives out, but someone has to be the sensible one. If it wasn't for her, we'd probably have the electricity cut off. My dad is a bit of a dreamer, y'see. He loves piping and it kinda, like, takes over his life. That's why he took to you, I think. Like, none of us wants to play the pipes. So anyone at all who shows interest, he jumps on them.'

Dylan felt he could listen to Laoise forever. Her accent was so cool, and even though he didn't understand a lot of what she said, he knew he was in love. 'I think the pipes are awesome. I dunno what it is about them – they make me feel sad and happy and excited all at once.' Dylan realised Laoise was looking at him quizzically and trying to suppress a smile as he spoke. He felt a deep blush begin to rise up his neck.

'Jaysus.' She laughed. 'You have it bad all right. Why don't you learn them so, if you are, like, that into it? Hey! Why don't you do a piping course here? I think it's not too late to apply. Dad has loads of practice sets you could borrow.'

It seemed like the most logical thing in the world to do, the way Laoise described it. Suddenly, Dylan felt like he had at last found somewhere he belonged. The logistics involved in moving to Ireland, aged seventeen, and with no visible means of support didn't occur to him. He just knew two things for sure. He really, *really* wanted to play the pipes, and he never, ever, *ever* wanted to leave Laoise.

* * *

Concentrating hard, Dylan waited for someone to answer the phone. 'Fees and Grants. How can I help?'

'Er...I...I am...and uh...I want to, like, to stay and maybe do a course here – I mean at your school – and I was wondering if it's, like, very expensive or if you have to be, like, Irish or something?' Dylan's palms were sweaty, and he realised he wasn't making any sense.

'OK,' said a woman with an accent that sounded a bit like Conor's. 'Let me get this straight. You are an American who wants to study at this institute, and you want to know how to apply. Is that correct?'

'Um, yes, ma'am. That's exactly what I want to know,' Dylan replied, greatly relieved at being understood.

'And what instrument did you have in mind?'

'Um, the uilleann pipes,' Dylan replied, feeling really stupid. Laoise was staring expectantly at him, so he put the phone on speaker.

'Right,' said the woman. 'There's a beginner's piping course starting next week, and there are still one or two places available. You're lucky because this particular pipe master is in great demand.'

'Awesome,' replied Dylan, finding it hard to believe that this was actually happening.

'Indeed,' the woman said, with humour in her voice. 'Well, firstly, you print off an application form from the college website, which you submit to the assessment committee. We don't require any previous qualifications, but knowledge of an instrument and previous performance experience would be an advantage. The normal procedure is that if you qualify, you will be invited for an interview, and if that goes well, you will be offered a place. In terms of fees, the course is 6,000 euros per year for non-Irish students.' The woman, while brisk and businesslike, seemed friendly.

'When is the closing date for applications?' Dylan asked, beginning to feel an excitement that he had not allowed himself to feel up to this point.

'One moment, I'll just check that. I'm not sure exactly, as each course has a different closing date.'

Dylan heard a series of clicks, followed by, 'Oh dear, the closing date was last Tuesday and interviews are being held today.'

'Oh,' said Dylan, crestfallen. 'I guess I'm too late?'

'Well, yes, I'm afraid so...'

Suddenly, Laoise grabbed the phone from Dylan. 'Hi,' she said. 'Sorry for butting in like this, and I know you have to stick to the rules and all that, but honestly he really, *really* wants to play the pipes. If he doesn't get this chance, he'll have to go back to America, and no one there has ever even heard of the pipes, not where he lives anyway, and he would be, like, a totally *awesome* piper. Can he please come for an interview? We can be there in, like...' – she looked at her phone to check the time – 'an hour and a half. Please?' Laoise crossed her fingers as the woman on the other end deliberated.

'I'm afraid this is a very heavily subscribed course. I'm sorry, but what you are asking is impossible for this year. I mean, we don't even have an application form or any paperwork as yet. We would require evidence of education to date and so on.'

'I know,' said Laoise, 'but if you give him this chance, we will arrive with all the forms sorted and everything. It will be, like, perfect, I swear.'

'Does this young man actually live here? It's not just a simple matter of enrolling in a course, you know. He would have to sort out his visa, and have someone here who would vouch for him...'

'Totally!' interrupted Laoise. 'My mam and dad are going to sign for him or whatever.'

'And their names are?' asked the woman in a weary tone.

When Laoise told the woman who her father was, suddenly everything changed. The interview was arranged for that afternoon, and all they had to do was download the forms and fill them in.

'You are totally *awesome*. Thank you, thank you, *thank you...*' Laoise said, and she hung up. 'OK, sunshine,' she announced. 'Let's rock. We have to be in Cork by one.' She pulled a car key out of her pocket. 'My mam will murder me if I take the car, but needs must, this is, like, totally an emergency.'

'Are you serious? Oh my God! You are amazing. Do you think this might actually work? The fees, though, Laoise – they're 6,000 dollars or euros or whatever. I don't have that kind of money.'

Laoise smiled. 'Look, don't worry about that yet. Parents always say they're broke, but they come up with it in the end. I'm sure you can convince your mam as soon as she sees how much it means to you.'

Dylan fixed his new friend with a wistful look. 'You don't know my mother. She doesn't give a rat's ass what happens to me just so long as she hooks a new rich husband. She never has. My grandma is the only one who ever cared about me. Maybe she'd help me out with the cash to do this course if I explain to her how much it means to me. I know she'd try anyway.'

'Well,' said Laoise, 'it looks like you are about to become the first goth uilleann piper in Ireland. Deadly!'

CHAPTER 16

There was a sharp knock on Juliet's door. As she looked through the spyhole fitted in the centre of the door, Juliet sighed deeply. She supposed it would have been too good to be true to enjoy a whole day without Dorothy. Reluctantly, she opened the door.

'Oh, hi, Dorothy. How is your suite?' she asked in as breezy a tone as she could muster. She'd managed to avoid her all day yesterday by making sure she was in conversation with the other passengers every time there was a break, and sitting on a single seat on the bus.

'Adequate, considering the country we're in,' Dorothy replied. 'Though how these European hoteliers have the audacity to call these tiny spaces suites, I'll never know. I'm sure the company wanted the best for me, but the managing director will be hearing from me the minute I get back, and when he does, I don't imagine this hotel will be on their itinerary in the future.'

Juliet winced as Dorothy marched into the room, leaving the door wide open behind her.

'Now, Juliet, I've decided that today we should take a long walk around the National Park. I took some fruit and yoghurt from the breakfast bar – I assume you did the same – and I got a free map in the lobby showing an extensive walking route through the park and into some bogland. I've been looking for samples to put into my fungi collection but have not had the opportunity until now.'

She looked critically at Juliet's outfit and continued as if to a five-year-old. 'Those sneakers won't do at all. And that top is entirely unsuitable. Change into the boots I helped you buy before we left. And get your Gore-Tex jacket. The forecasters said it might rain.'

Juliet felt the familiar lump rise in her throat, but she forced herself to speak. 'Actually, Dorothy, if you don't mind, I was hoping to do a little shopping today. I would like to buy a few gifts and –'

Juliet's hesitant excuses were met by Dorothy's barking. 'Oh, for goodness' sake, Juliet! Whom do you have to buy gifts for? It's not like you have children or anything. Don't be ridiculous. Get your things and let's go before the first shower comes. There's a sign in reception saying there'll be complimentary finger food in the bar this evening. There's some kind of sports event on, so I want to be back in time for that.'

Something snapped inside Juliet. Perhaps it was the callous way in which Dorothy had referred to her childlessness, the only tragedy in her long marriage to Larry, or possibly it was the way Dorothy constantly spoke down to her. Whatever the trigger, it had the effect of rendering Juliet uncharacteristically articulate all of a sudden.

'Dorothy, listen to me carefully, as I'm only going to say this once. You are a mean, miserly old harridan, and I cannot stand you. I never wanted to take this trip, but I am actually enjoying it – in spite of you, not because of you, I hasten to add.'

Juliet gulped and then continued. 'I may not be as well educated as you or as well travelled as you, but I have great friends and a great life. I miss Larry desperately, but when I get sad, I think how much worse it would have been never to have known love like that. Much better that I had him all those years and lost him than to have lived a life like yours – without love or friendship. I don't know what makes you happy, Dorothy. I doubt that anything does. But you will not bring me down with you for one more second. You are a cantankerous old woman, and I have never met anyone who liked you. You bully me and harass me and put me down constantly. So from now on, count me out of any plans you might have. From now on, I don't want to have anything to do with you. Now, if you will excuse me, I am going shopping to buy gifts for my real friends, something *you* wouldn't know anything about!'

As Juliet swept past Dorothy and walked out the door into the corridor, she practically collided with Conor as he emerged from his room. He had clearly heard most of the exchange. He grabbed her hand and drew her into the safety of his room and out of the path of Dorothy, who was storming down the corridor.

'Did I just do that?' she asked shakily.

'She had it coming. Don't worry, she just needs to cool down,' he said, putting his arm around the trembling Juliet.

* * *

ANNA RETURNED to her room after breakfast. Elliot was standing at the end of the bed. A surge of joy rushed through her. He must have come to his senses, she thought, finally realised just how horrible he had been, wanted to sort it all out. He turned to face her as she entered. It was only then that she noticed he was filling his suitcase, which lay open on the bed.

'Elliot! What…what are you doing?' she stammered.

'What does it look like? I'm packing,' he answered coldly as he carefully folded his handmade silk shirts and Armani trousers into the case.

'But I thought…'

'More thinking, Anna? Just like when you *thought* you'd trick me into marrying you, you *thought* you'd con me into having a baby with you, *thought* you'd get me to move back to Hicksville to live with your moronic family? Well, guess what? You thought *wrong*. I don't know why the hell I've been wasting my time with someone like you. You're pathetic,' he spat as he headed to the bathroom to retrieve his Louis Vuitton grooming kit.

Heart pounding in her ears, she finally saw Elliot not as she *wanted* him to be, but as he *actually* was – a horrible, spoiled, vindictive man.

He cared nothing for people, only for possessions. He loved his clothes and shoes more than he loved her, or *anyone*. Years of hurt and sadness bubbled to the surface. Strangely, she didn't feel the need to weep, rather the need to lash out, to hurt him like he had hurt her. She spotted the bottle of merlot on the table. She had bought it to bring to Patrick's next cocktail hour. She grabbed it and was relieved to see it had a screw cap. Miraculously, it opened quickly, and she took great delight in watching Elliot's horrified expression as he emerged from the bathroom to find her pouring the entire contents of the bottle all over his carefully folded clothes.

'What are you doing, you crazy bitch!' he screamed. 'Those garments are worth thousands! What the fuck...'

'I *thought* you loved me. I *thought* I meant something to you other than just an unpaid PA! Elliot, you are an asshole of such proportions it's hard to articulate. My *parents* hate you, my *sisters* hate you, my *friends* hate you...hell, *your* friends hate you! Do you know that, Elliot? Everyone who has the misfortune to meet you hates you! And do you know why? I'll tell you why – because you are a miserable, bitter, boring, money-grabbing little *dwarf*!'

All colour drained from Elliot's face. 'I'm not staying here to listen to this. You're crazy, you know that? No one will ever hire you in New York again. I'll make sure of it. You were a nobody with crooked teeth and a fat ass when I took you on, but I fixed you. I made you fit into civilised society. And this is how you repay me?'

'Oh no, Elliot, it's *you* who'll be paying *me*! I'm carrying your baby, though considering the size of that dwarf dick of yours, it's amazing you were ever able to father a child at all! So *yes*, you will be hearing from me. My baby is going to have the best of everything, and *you will pay*. I just thought you should know that! Now get out before I throw you out. Which I could, *easily*!'

Incensed, he stormed out, slamming the hotel door and leaving his sodden suitcase on the bed. Anna immediately stuffed the rest of his belongings into it and zipped it shut. She then dragged it over to the window, which was directly above the entrance to the hotel. As Elliot emerged, she heaved the suitcase out the window. Knocked to the ground by the weight of the direct hit, he lay winded and speechless on the gravel, gazing up in shock at the source of the missile.

Anna called down, 'Maybe Snow White can get the red-wine stains out when she's doing the laundry for the other six *dwarves!*'

For the next half hour, Anna lay on the bed staring at the ceiling. She couldn't believe what she had done. She had never in her whole life spoken to anyone like that. *It felt good, though.* She chuckled to herself. *Thank God it happened here and not at home.* She was glad it had only been witnessed by strangers. She would have to explain to the hotel about the wine stains on the bed and pay for the damage, but it was worth it.

She had always imagined herself as a career-driven person, and working for Elliot had not left her time for much else. Plus she had never factored a baby into her plans. She supposed she believed that she would have a family someday, but it was in a vague, abstract kind of way. She admitted to herself that she had never raised the topic with Elliot because deep down she knew what his reaction was likely to be. The longer she was apart from him, the clearer she could picture her husband. He wasn't damaged or just overworked, or any of the other excuses she had made for him. He was a selfish, spoiled man who cared for no one but himself. He had no real friends of his own, and none of her friends had ever been enthusiastic about him. *It's amazing really what a person can kid themselves into believing even when the truth is staring them in the face.*

She spoke to her baby aloud. 'Well, little one.' She sighed. 'I've really done it now. Your father hates me, and unless he undergoes a major change of heart, he probably hates you too. That's not a bad thing, though, because you really are better off without him. If Ellen's dad could take care of a baby in a strange country with no money and no contacts, I'm sure I can look after you. We are going to be just fine, you and me. Maybe we will go back to Kansas. You have a grandma and a grandpa there and lots of cousins and aunts and uncles who'll be delighted to meet you.'

As the sun shone through the open window, Anna fell into a peaceful sleep for the first time in days.

CHAPTER 17

*P*atrick felt nervous as the Bus Éireann coach drove along the River Lee in the direction of the station in Parnell Place. He was trying to work out a conversation in his head that would not make him sound crazy or like a stalker.

Jesus, he thought to himself. *You're not fifteen years old. What's the matter with you?*

He admitted to himself that the reason he felt such anxiety was because no woman he had ever met before had had such an impact on him. If he had met Cynthia back home, maybe they would have gone out a few times, seen how things went, taken it easy. But the fact that he only had a few more days left in Ireland meant he would have to act fast. Not, he thought ruefully, his strongest suit.

'Why can't you be like the McLoughlin boys down the street?' He heard his mother's voice echo down through the years. 'They joined the force same time as you, and Jimmy is a sergeant already. It's so embarrassing when I meet Maureen at Mass, everyone asking what you are doing now. Still a beat cop after all these years. I don't know, Patrick, really I don't. Are you trying not to get promoted?'

Patrick knew his shortcomings only too well. In the force, nowadays they wanted guys who had done computer courses, fellas who were pushy and would step on their buddies to get ahead. Patrick wished sometimes he could be like them as he watched guys much, *much* younger than him become his superiors. But the ambition for a big desk job just wasn't in him. The Boston Police Department didn't think knowing the name of every old lady and teenager on your beat was important in modern policing. That didn't deter Patrick, who walked his beat anyway, always had a word for the storekeepers and kept some candy for certain kids in his pockets, even though that wasn't actually allowed any more. Plus the kids these days were scared of everyone and no one. The Boston he knew was disappearing day by day.

He thought about the chief's words again. Maybe he should take the early retirement package they were offering him. 'Go now and take the cash or be pushed anyway,' was how the thirty-six-year-old station chief officer had put it. Harsh maybe, but true. Patrick had rejected the offer without even considering it. What would he do? He was a cop, nothing more, nothing less. He didn't have kids, his buddies were in the force, and his social life revolved around the Boston Police Social Club. His job was more than a job – it was his life.

His reverie was interrupted by the swearing of the bus driver. Someone had abandoned their car right in the middle of the bus loading bay in front of the station. Muttering expletives, the driver opened the door, through which Patrick could hear a familiar voice ringing out. 'Oh, hello, my dear! So sorry, no parking in this dratted city any more... I know it's dreadful, isn't it? I am going to write a strongly worded letter, I can tell you. Pardon me...oh, righty-ho, you want to park here? Oh, certainly, jolly good spot too. Happy to hand it over in just a mo. I'm actually looking for a friend of mine, Patrick, an American chap... Have you seen him?'

The driver couldn't get a word in as Cynthia continued prattling away while simultaneously scouring the area in front of the bus station for a sign of her American chap. As Patrick descended the steps of the bus, she swivelled back to the driver and trilled, 'Oh, not to worry, my dear. No need to look any further! I've found my friend. Patrick! Woo-hoo!' she screeched loudly, even though Patrick stood less than four feet away from her.

'Right, missus,' said the driver with an exasperated sigh. 'Now do you think you could move that...eh...car...from the forecourt of the bus station?'

'Of course, of course!' Cynthia yelled. 'No harm done, eh? Patrick! How simply champion to see you again.'

As Cynthia ground the gears and jerked the vehicle out into the traffic, Patrick guffawed. 'Jeez, pull a stunt like that in Boston and you'd get arrested.'

Cynthia smiled but looked puzzled. 'A stunt like what, my dear?'

* * *

PATRICK AND CYNTHIA were sitting at a table in the courtyard of Fota House Café when a man came to take their order.

'Cynthia!' he exclaimed. 'Why didn't you tell us you were coming up to town? Roger will be devastated to have missed you. He's in Ballydehob having his aura cleansed.' The man's expression clearly showed just how ridiculous such an outing was in his opinion.

'Now, Charlie dear, don't be ghastly,' Cynthia chided. 'Roge probably just needed some "downtime", as the Americans say. Speaking of which, I would like you to meet a friend of mine. Charlie, this is Patrick O'Neill, from Boston. Patrick, this is my cousin and dear friend Charlie Langtree.'

Patrick stood up, smiled and shook the man's hand. 'Nice to meet you.' At last he was getting to meet real Irish people.

'Roger and I went to the Pride Parade in New York a few years ago,' Charlie volunteered. 'What a city! I think we got about five hours' sleep the whole time we were there. It was amazing! I had to take poor old Roge home after four days. I mean, honestly, he would have gained fifty pounds if I'd let him stay!'

Patrick didn't know how to respond. He'd never imagined there were gay people in Ireland. This trip was getting weirder by the day. He debated raising the contentious case in the 1990s when South Boston became the focus of a Supreme Court case on the rights of gay and lesbian groups to participate in the St Patrick's Day festivities. The case was decided in favour of the parade's sponsors, with the United States Supreme Court supporting the South Boston Allied War Veterans' right to determine who could participate in the St Patrick's Day parade. Patrick had, at the time, been against letting gay people march, but something told him that such opinions wouldn't go down too well in this company. Cynthia was watching him carefully, checking out his reaction to Charlie; he could feel it.

'I don't get to the Big Apple that often, but I know you're right. It's not called the city that never sleeps for nothing, that's for sure,' Patrick said.

Cynthia smiled. Patrick had passed the test. 'So, my dear, what do you fancy?' she asked.

They ordered seafood chowder and roast beef sandwiches and sat in easy companionship in the afternoon sun. Charlie brought out the most wonderful soup Patrick had ever tasted, and as they ate and chatted, it emerged that Cynthia was not nearly as crazy as she appeared. She actually had quite a good business going, breeding horses.

'So, my dear,' Cynthia enquired, 'what does one do in Boston when one is not fighting crime?'

'Well,' replied Patrick, 'not much, to be honest. I'm just a cop. I guess I should have progressed through the ranks by now – my mother certainly thought so – but I suppose I'm not that smart, and the job I was trained for doesn't seem to exist any more.'

As the afternoon wore on, Patrick found himself telling Cynthia about his life, his numerous shortcomings and the offer he had been made by the Boston PD. She, in turn, told him about the man she had once loved, who it turned out was married all along and everyone knew it except her, how she was the pity of her family and friends for years afterwards, and how after that experience, she wasn't overly inclined to go down the relationship road again.

As the sun set on the courtyard of Fota House, Cynthia and Patrick both speculated on the fact that it had been a long time since either of them had spoken to anyone so honestly or in such detail about their lives, their hopes or their expectations.

CHAPTER 18

*C*onor eased the coach out of the hotel car park, with Ellen and Bert as his only passengers.

'All in a day's work, eh, Conor?' said Bert.

'Sure I love this,' Conor replied. 'It breaks things up a bit, and anyway, I'm very interested in genealogy. The trouble with all this family tree research is that a lot of it is down to luck. I have known people over the years who have nearly bankrupted themselves trying to find their people. And I've known others who, with very little time or effort, strike it lucky and find out a huge amount. It doesn't seem fair when that happens, but it's how it is.'

'I guess we Americans must seem a bit crazy to you, obsessing about people we have never even met,' Ellen said.

'No, I can't say I ever felt like that about it. I think every person needs to know where they came from, and that need gets stronger as we get older. I think when we're young, we never think of dying or the generations before or after us, but that changes as life goes on, and we all realise we are part of something bigger. Here in Ireland we're lucky. We take our heritage for granted. Most people can easily go back at least two or three generations. But I can't imagine what it would feel like not to know, not to have any inkling of what your grandparents or great-grandparents were like. Maybe not even know their names. So no, I don't think it's mad at all. In fact, what I can't understand is why so many people *don't* want to know. I'm amazed all forty-four million Americans who claim to be of Irish descent don't come back here *desperate* to find out where they originated from!'

'Well, my story is something I've been thinking about for a long time,' said Ellen slowly. 'I always wanted to come back, but my father never showed any interest in returning, so I suppose I took my lead from him. I think, like a lot of Irishmen, he wasn't too comfortable talking about his feelings,' she added with a smile.

'Well, I don't think that's just a problem with Irishmen,' Bert joked. 'My wife regularly used to tell me that she got more emotional talk from our old skinny cat than she did from me. Maybe it's something to do with working on the land. It's a kinda quiet job, so you don't get too good at all that jibber-jabber talk. Most American men are not like Dr Phil, you know.'

All three of them laughed.

Around noon, they stopped for a break near Glengarriff. As they sat and chatted over coffee and walnut cake, Ellen thought Conor seemed quite distracted. He was constantly checking his BlackBerry, something she'd never seen him do before.

'Conor, I don't mean to pry, but if there's something you need to do or deal with, please don't let us stop you. I really hope I haven't put you out by dragging you away today.'

Conor shook his head. 'Ah no, Ellen, it's nothing like that. I'm sorry. I know I'm like a teenager today, glued to the phone.' He decided to do something he rarely did, on the basis that Ellen and Bert seemed like very genuine people and maybe they could advise him. 'I just have a bit of a situation going on, and I'm not too sure how to deal with it.'

'Well, between myself and Bert here, we have a combined age of about two hundred years, so we might be able to help if you want to tell us,' Ellen said encouragingly.

'The thing is, I'm in the middle of a bit of a dilemma at the moment,' Conor said. 'You see, there's this woman. She and I were friends years ago, and I really thought back then that it might have turned into something. But anyway, it didn't. I think she knew how I felt about her, but she was dazzled by my younger brother, Gerry. I can't blame her. All the girls were mad about Gerry.'

He paused and sipped his coffee as the atmosphere filled with a slight tension. Ellen wondered what kind of girl would turn down the very handsome and also kind and charming Conor. Bert was wondering what revelation was coming next.

'Anyway, they took off for the States, and I stayed. I never said anything to her or to anyone else. I thought maybe she would be good for Gerry, settle him down a bit. My father left us when we were kids, and my mother died when he was twelve and I was sixteen. So I kind of took over the rearing of him. He was always too restless, and he got into trouble a lot. I might as well be honest – it broke my heart to let her go and I nearly said something, but in the end she made her choice. The thing is, she got back in touch the other day, and she wants to meet up with me again. She has a child now – well, he's a teenager – and she has cancer herself, and I'm all she has in the world it seems. I did write a few times over the years but they never replied, so it's all news to me now. I just got this email from her a few minutes ago.'

Conor handed his phone to Ellen.

Hi Conor,

It's so great to talk to you again. It feels like nothing has changed really, does it? I could always tell you anything. I remember that about you. I wonder what you look like now. I'm a bit scared about you seeing me, to be honest. This bloody cancer is playing havoc with my looks. Seriously, though, it's such a relief to me to know that Conor Jr will have someone when I'm gone. I'm so looking forward to reconnecting, as they say here. I hope I won't sound like one of those returned Yanks! Remember that guy who used to come back to Passage West when we were kids and how we laughed at him with his faucets and highways? Anyway, I'll be arriving Friday into Shannon, and I was thinking I could check into the hotel you stay at? I can't wait to see you.

All my love xx

Bert observed Conor as Ellen questioned him about the woman.

He had seen him leave the hotel in Clare a few nights earlier with another young woman, and it looked to him like they were a couple. The way the young woman looked up at him seemed to indicate it was definitely more than a friendship, so he was surprised to hear about this new woman. Conor struck him as a very honest guy who wouldn't mess people around. He hoped this woman from the past wasn't trying to take advantage of Conor's kind nature.

'But why now? Do you think she wants you to take over rearing her son? That's a big ask from someone you haven't seen for twenty years,' Ellen said.

'That's the thing, Ellen. I don't know. Maybe she has become too sick to take care of him, or herself. Or maybe she just has had enough of waiting for Gerry to turn up and has decided to come home.'

'Do you think she is coming back for you?' Ellen asked him pointedly.

Conor winced. He wasn't used to answering such questions about his personal life. 'That is something else I don't know,' he admitted ruefully.

'It's not my business, I know,' interjected Bert, 'but I happened to see you the other night with a woman leaving the hotel. I assumed you and she were together? Where does she fit into all of this?'

'Ah no, that's just Anastasia. She's my friend. In fact, she's the only other person I've talked to about this whole thing.'

'And what does she think?' asked Ellen.

'She didn't know what I should do either. Though she has been kind of strange lately anyway. I think she might have relationship troubles of her own.' Conor sighed. 'I'm grand at fixing other people's problems but not so great when it comes to fixing my own.'

'Well,' said Ellen quietly, 'for what it's worth, I think you should tread very carefully with Sinead. I don't know her, of course, but she did let you down once before, and in my experience, people rarely change.'

'Ah, Ellen, maybe you're right, but it wasn't really like that. I mean, if you met my brother, you'd understand. Anyway, enough about me.

I'm sure it will all work out – it always does. Now let's get you going on your adventure, shall we?'

As Conor turned the key in the ignition, he said, 'I think the best place to start is in the village of Inchigeelagh and see if we can locate the exact house – that is, of course, assuming it still exists. You say your father had two brothers, one older and one younger, who stayed in Ireland, so there's a good chance that one or both of them may have stayed in the Inchigeelagh area and may even have family there. The brothers on your mother's side are worth checking too. Let's just go there and see what we can turn up.'

Ellen smiled. 'My father was born in 1898. Even the great genes of the O'Donovans didn't last beyond a century. In fact, my grandmother died soon after he left, and my grandfather died sometime during the Second World War, as I recall. My father's younger brother, Sean, wrote to tell us.'

'Did your uncle tell you anything else about the family in those letters?' asked Bert.

'Not really. He married and had children. There was a photo. Remember those old square ones with the scalloped edges? Well, we got one of those in a Christmas card one year, and I think the people in the photograph may have been Sean's family. He became a school-teacher, and I think that's perhaps why he was better at writing letters than anyone else in the family. I'm not even sure my grandfather could read and write. My father's oldest brother, Michael, worked the family farm, but I don't think he ever got in touch, or at least if he did, those letters don't exist today…'

Ellen's voice trailed off as she lapsed into a reverie about all the questions she wished she had asked her father before he died.

'Can you remember when that photo arrived?' Conor asked. 'You see, if we knew or if we could guess the ages of his children then, we might be able to find some birth records in the parish record books. But you would need a rough idea of the date to look under. Other-wise, it's like searching for a needle in a haystack.'

Ellen paused and tried to remember. 'Well, the date on the back of the photo is 1942,' she said, drawing the photograph out of her handbag.

Bert leaned over. 'Can I see?'

'Sure,' she replied, handing it to him. 'The funny thing about it is I think one of the girls in that picture looks just like a picture my dad took of me when I was that age.'

'Have you any clue why they lost touch?' Bert asked. 'A dispute of some kind maybe?'

'I don't know, but I don't think so. My dad just wasn't much for writing letters. Even when I moved away from home, I only got the occasional postcard from him. I don't think anything happened between him and Sean, just that he was never that good at staying in touch. I guess Sean died, and that was that. I know everyone says this, but I wish I could turn back the clock and just ask my dad so many things about Ireland and what happened here all those years ago. I don't know what it is I expect to find in the village of Inchigeelagh. All I know is that I've wanted to go there for so many years. You are both so kind. I mean, this is probably a wild goose chase.'

As they saw a signpost for Macroom, Ellen recalled her father mentioning the town on one of the rare occasions that he spoke about his life in Ireland. 'It was here that he got a job in a big store, I think. He said there was a big army barracks here?' She struggled with her memory.

'Well,' Conor offered, 'this is where the Crown forces would have had their headquarters. And I suppose any IRA activity in the surrounding townlands would have been monitored from here. It seems hard to imagine now, but Ireland in the 1920s was a dangerous, violent place. People were living in fear of the British, especially the Black and Tans and the Auxies, as they were called.'

Ellen nodded in agreement, but Bert looked confused. 'Y'see, Bert,' Conor explained, 'by that time, around 1920, the War of Independence was in full flow and the British forces here were stretched to the breaking point. That and the First World War nearly finished them, so they had to recruit men specifically in order to keep on top of things over here. The people had no love for the regular British soldiers – there's no doubt about that. At least they had a kind of code of behaviour, and for the most part, they observed that code. But the Tans and the Auxies, well, they were a different story altogether. A law unto themselves. Most of them were recruited from demobbed ranks after the First World War. A fair share of them were so damaged by what they had witnessed – or had been involved in – over there that they were never right in the head again. Half-mad, a lot of them. Heavy drinkers and very unpredictable. People were really scared of them because it seemed they just did anything they felt like.'

'Tough times then,' Bert interjected. 'Tell me, Conor, why were they called Black and Tans and Auxies and not just British soldiers?'

'Well, I suppose they were different to the ordinary Tommies who were just part of the regular army. It seems there was no love lost between the army and the Tans, that's for sure. The British officers generally had control over their men. So for the local people, if you kept your head down and you didn't cause any trouble, they left you alone. But the Auxies and the Tans could just pick a fella off the street or in a pub and rough him up for no reason. You never knew where you stood with them. The Black and Tans were called that because they had a kind of mismatched uniform, not a proper kit at all, bits of police and army and whatever else was going spare.'

Conor paused for a few seconds, wondering whether his impromptu history lesson was sufficiently impartial. He was always wary of presenting the case of Irish history with too much of a republican slant. Deciding his account was objective, he continued. 'The word Auxie is short for Auxiliary, and they were a different kettle of fish altogether from the Tans. They were a highly trained force of commissioned officers who had all seen significant action in the First World War. They were considered an elite kind of a force. They arrived in July 1920, and their job was to deal with the growing support for the IRA. They occupied the barracks in Macroom Castle. The Auxies and the Tans between them terrorised the local population, especially with their arbitrary reprisals for any subversive activities. Their idea was to scare people into denouncing the IRA by burning houses and carrying out beatings and even killings. Only a week before the famous ambush at Kilmichael, they opened fire on a crowd at a Dublin-Tipperary football match in Croke Park in Dublin, killing fourteen civilians, one of them a player on the pitch. The leadership of the IRA in West Cork felt that people were losing heart for the fight because the IRA hadn't made any significant strike against these Auxies, no matter what atrocities they had committed. Since open combat was never going to be effective against them, it was decided that a series of ambushes on British troops as they moved around the countryside would have the best chance of success to raise the profile of the IRA and give people hope.'

Ellen was familiar with the history, but Bert was fascinated, hanging on Conor's every word. The history of this island was becoming more and more real to him – all the more so because today they found themselves travelling the very same roads that many of the people Conor was describing had done eighty years earlier.

CHAPTER 19

*E*llen and Bert sat outside the petrol station while Conor made enquiries about directions. Bert leaned over and squeezed her hand. 'How are you doing?'

'I don't really know. It's sort of strange, realising your dreams. I don't know what to expect. I really don't.'

Climbing into the driver's seat, Conor announced, 'We're on the right track anyhow. The girl in the shop is only a young one, but she said that there's a man living up the road here, a local historian, and he might be able to help us.' He turned to face Ellen. 'Are you ready?'

'As I'll ever be,' she replied.

The house they were directed to was a modern bungalow with manicured lawns. The door was answered by a woman Conor judged to be in her fifties.

'Oh, hello,' Conor began. 'I wonder would Eamonn be around at all?'

She hesitated, eyeing Conor a bit suspiciously. He noticed her glancing at the coach – no doubt making a mental note of the registration and wondering why this stranger needed to speak to Eamonn. Conor could feel her discomfort and thought he had better elaborate.

'You see, the girl in the shop told us he was a local historian and that he might be able to help us. Myself and my two American friends here are trying to find out about a family who lived around here, and we thought maybe Eamonn could help.'

'Come in, let ye for a minute,' said the woman, visibly relieved now that she knew the purpose of the visit. 'He's up the yard at the moment, but I can give him a ring.' She ushered the three of them into a sitting room featuring an array of photographs arranged across two walls. Among the pictures of weddings, graduations, children and babies, three poster-sized framed photographs stood out: a triumvirate of Pope John Paul II, President John F. Kennedy and General Michael Collins.

As the woman disappeared to phone her husband, Bert whispered, 'Hey, I guess I've seen it all now. An enormous photograph of an American president in the living room of a house up the side of a mountain in Ireland. Why do they have him on their wall, do you think?'

Both Conor and Ellen smiled.

'Well, Bert,' Conor answered, 'there are only a few people who make it into the Hall of Fame in certain Irish women's living rooms. Jack Kennedy was a great favourite of the Irish, and he was well loved here. He visited Ireland just before he was assassinated, and he's always remembered in this country with great fondness, especially by the ladies, it must be said.'

'He sure did have an eye for women, and I guess he was a handsome devil, but I am surprised that such a Catholic country would overlook his colourful love life.' Bert chuckled.

'Ah sure, don't you know the women always turn a blind eye whenever it suits them,' Conor said, giving Bert a sideways wink. 'Anyway, he's safe up there beside the pope and the Big Fella.' Conor nodded in the direction of the Michael Collins portrait. 'You can tell the politics of a household by whom they have on the wall of the living room or kitchen. This is a Fine Gael house, no question.'

Bert looked totally baffled.

Conor explained. 'After the War of Independence, Michael Collins and others went to London to negotiate a peace treaty with the British. As Ellen will know, the outcome of those negotiations caused a deep divide in the country. What was decided was that the twenty-six counties in the south of the country, now known as the Irish Republic, would become a free state, and the six counties of Down, Derry, Antrim, Armagh, Fermanagh and Tyrone would remain part of the United Kingdom. Those who had fought in the War of Independence were deeply divided, with Éamon de Valera on one side and Michael Collins on the other. The rift resulted in the formation of two major political parties, Fianna Fáil on the de Valera side, and Fine Gael on the Collins side.'

Just as Conor was finishing his brief history lesson, the woman returned. 'He won't be long now. He just has to bring the cattle in, and he'll be down to ye then. Ye'll have a cup of tea while ye're waiting?'

Ellen and Bert were just about to refuse, not wishing to put the woman to any trouble, but Conor got in there before them. 'That would be lovely. Thanks very much.'

'Grand so, I'll just put the kettle on,' she said, and she was off again.

'It's considered rude not to have a cup of tea when it's offered,' Conor whispered conspiratorially. 'It kind of relaxes an atmosphere, and it's what we do here. Don't worry, it's no trouble. In most Irish houses, the teapot rarely goes cold.'

A door on the other side of the house slammed, and that noise was quickly followed by the sound of approaching footsteps. Turning, they saw who they assumed was Eamonn, a short, thin man, standing in the doorway. It was difficult to guess his age; it could have been anywhere between sixty and ninety. Out of the pockets of his ancient-looking waxed jacket peeped newspaper cuttings, raggedy brown envelopes and various bits of paper. Both his corduroy trousers and navy woollen jumper looked like they had seen better days. He had a big shock of iron-grey hair and hand-knitted socks on his feet, presumably having just removed his wellington boots. 'Eamonn O'Riordan is the name. You're all very welcome. Julia tells me you're looking for some information about a family that lived around here.'

Ellen felt that she should speak first. 'Yes, please. I don't know if you can help, but my name is Ellen O'Donovan, and I was born in the village of Inchigeelagh on December 18, 1920. My father was named Thomas O'Donovan, and he had an older brother, Michael, and a younger brother, Sean. My mother's name was Bridget, and she died when I was born, I believe. My father took me to America when I was a baby, and I haven't been back here since then.'

Eamonn's face broke into a smile. He crossed the room purposefully, and clasping Ellen's two hands warmly, he said, 'So you came back to us at last. They always said you would. Welcome home, Ellen.'

As Julia served tea and scones, Eamonn spoke at length. 'When I was growing up, I remember the older people around here would often speculate about what happened to Tom O'Donovan and his baby girl. Michael O'Donovan was a quiet man, kept himself to himself, and of course, in those days, feelings ran very deep about all the trouble that had gone on. The War of Independence, the Civil War and all that. So most people felt that what was done was done, and was best left alone.'

Ellen looked stunned. This man actually *knew* people who knew her father. What on earth was he going to come out with next?

Eamonn noted the flabbergasted expression on Ellen's face and decided to continue anyway. 'Let me think now. Your father was older than me and was a long time gone to America before I was born. But I grew up here, and everyone for miles around knows your Uncle Sean. He's quite a character,' Eamonn said, registering a new expression on Ellen's face, this time one of shock. 'Were you expecting that you would have been forgotten?' He smiled gently. 'The thing is, Ellen, nothing gets forgotten around here. That's sometimes a virtue, but other times it's not. Your father was a young man when he left, and the circumstances were difficult, God knows, but his family stayed on in the parish. In fact, you have quite a few relatives not two miles from this house. As you sit there now, I can see the look of Mary O'Donovan about you.'

Ellen gaped at him, completely nonplussed.

'Mary is one of Sean's daughters, married to a Casey man back the road here. Their farm adjoins mine. A grand woman altogether. She would be a first cousin to you.'

Ellen's eyes filled with tears. 'I'm sorry, Eamonn,' she said. 'I just never thought for a second that there might be someone... I thought maybe a grave or something...but I didn't dare to hope. It's so long ago, you see.'

Bert squeezed Ellen's hand.

'I'm overwhelmed,' she stated simply. 'I'm sorry, Eamonn, please continue.'

'I would have to research my papers, but as far as I understand it, your grandparents were farmers who had a few cattle, and your grandmother kept geese and hens. They supplied all the turkeys for Christmas too. Or so I believe anyway. They were blessed with three sons who were grand lads. Michael, the eldest, who got the farm of course, and Tom, your father, and Sean, the youngest. He was a bit of a surprise, I'd say. He was a good bit younger than the others. Again, I'm not too sure by how much, but the census will tell us all that. The family weren't political as such. At least I never heard that they were. But your mother's family, they certainly were. There were mixed feelings at the time about the IRA. A lot of the local people around here supported them wholeheartedly, but there were quite a few others who felt that they were only making a bad situation worse. It led to a lot of bad feeling, I can tell you, especially in such a small community where people relied so much on their neighbours. Not like the way it is nowadays.'

Eamonn seemed to hesitate at this point, noting her look of confusion. 'How much do you know about your father, Ellen?' he asked gently.

'Just that he took me to America when I was a baby, and that my mother died. What's all this about trouble?' she asked.

A shadow of concern crossed Eamonn's face. 'I'm sorry, Ellen. I don't know what I'm blathering on about. Anyway, 'tis your Uncle Sean who'll tell you anything you want to know. He's getting on in years, though he wouldn't admit that in a fit. He's as sharp as a tack. C'mon, let you, and I'll bring you up to meet him.'

Ellen began to tremble, her cup rattling audibly on the china saucer. 'Sean is still alive?' she asked incredulously.

'Oh yes,' replied Eamonn. 'I thought you knew that. Though now that I come to think of it, if you did know that already, you'd have come looking for him, not me. Anyway, yes, your Uncle Sean is still very much alive and completely with it. He lives with Mary just over the road there.'

Ellen suddenly felt quite weak. 'I'm so sorry, but do you think I could just go outside for a moment? I need some air,' she said, standing and moving in the direction of the door.

Bert instinctively followed her and didn't say a word until they reached a secluded corner of the garden.

'I had no idea...never dreamed Sean was alive. But to discover this... Bert...what should I do?' The usually composed Ellen looked at him with real fear in her eyes.

Bert turned her to face him, resting his hands on her shoulders. 'What is it that you're afraid of, Ellen?' he asked quietly.

'I...don't know,' she said, searching for words. 'I suppose this story was always in the past, and so I could imagine it as I wanted it to be. I think that is why I feel more fear than excitement. I mean, what if I don't like these people? Or what if they don't like me? What if the reason my father didn't keep in touch was because of something terrible that someone did? What if there's more to this story than meets the eye? What if the reason he never told me was to protect me from some horrible truth?' Panic was evident in her voice.

'Ellen, no one is going to force you to do anything you're uncomfortable with, but I'll say this and I hope you won't mind. We are neither of us getting any younger, and you don't know if you will ever get this opportunity again. You know how it is. There comes a time when long-distance travel just isn't an option any more. You can walk away now, get into that fancy coach over there, and we can forget this ever happened. But I think it would be a mistake. You're a gutsy lady, and Lord knows this must be an emotional roller-coaster, but I think you didn't come all this way to turn back now. So I'm going to go back inside now, and you take your time. Decide what you want to do, and whatever that is, I will accept it and be there for you one hundred percent. You're right, though – once you open this door, it will be tough to close it again. If there are things you'd rather not know about, it might be best to leave now. So just relax on the seat there and let your intuition decide. You know what's best for you. Try to focus on what your heart is telling you to do.'

Eamonn seemed upset when Bert arrived back into the room. 'I'm very sorry if I gave Ellen a terrible fright. I just assumed she knew Sean was alive. I should have been a bit more sensitive. The way I just blurted it out... I don't know what kind of an eejit she must think I am.'

Bert smiled and placed a hand on Eamonn's shoulder. 'Don't worry about it – you've been great. She just needs to decide what she wants to do next. I think we all imagine the past and how it was, but she's having to face the reality of it all for the first time. I guess she's just a bit wary of what's about to be revealed. If you know what I mean.'

The three men stirred nervously as Ellen entered the room.

'Let's go,' she said. 'I want to meet my uncle.'

'Maybe we should give them a ring first,' Conor suggested, 'rather than land in on top of them unannounced. What do you think?'

'Of course,' said Ellen. 'I hadn't thought of that. Perhaps it won't suit them to have us visit today.'

Eamonn smiled. 'Don't worry. Julia has that in hand. You can be sure she'll have phoned Mary the minute you arrived. I'd bet the farm on it.' He winked and then added in a whisper, 'A mad one for the gossip is my Julia, and herself and Mary are thick as thieves. I guarantee the good skirt is being dragged on and the good china is being dusted off up there as we speak. Baby Ellen O'Donovan back after all these years? Sure you'll be the talk of the parish for years.'

As he headed for the Land Rover parked around the side of the house, Eamonn muttered, 'The state of me from the cows. I'd only destroy the seats of your lovely bus. I had to have strong words with a particularly recalcitrant heifer that was refusing to go into the stall this morning. Let's just say she didn't hold back in showing me what she thought of her new accommodation. Give me ten cranky men over one cranky cow any day. I'll take the Land Rover. Let you just drive behind me. Is that all right?'

Ellen settled herself into the coach for the short journey up the hill, a whirlwind of emotions engulfing her. Not only was she in fear and trepidation at the prospect of meeting her family, and possibly finding out something unsavoury about the circumstances surrounding her father's departure to America, she was also feeling a little foolish about her reaction to the news that Sean was alive. She had never been one for big scenes, and she had very little patience for those who did. She mulled over the information Eamonn had revealed. What exactly was he driving at? Her father had never given her the impression he had been involved in anything political, but Eamonn seemed to be hinting – *more than hinting*, in fact – at something like that. Tom O'Donovan had never been a chatty man, but neither had he ever given her the impression that he was hiding some big secret.

Eamonn's Land Rover turned into a long lane leading to a remarkably clean farmyard with newish-looking machinery and pieces of equipment visible here and there. The farmhouse, while obviously very old, possibly Georgian, Ellen thought, was beautifully maintained, with hanging baskets and window boxes bursting with trailing begonias and geraniums, all apparently trying to outdo the other in terms of colour display and profusion. Just as Conor pulled up to the front door, a woman who looked to be about seventy appeared. Small and slight, she was smartly dressed in a navy wool skirt and cerise linen blouse, her white hair swept up in a stylish chignon. Ellen took a deep breath and walked slowly and as steadily as she could down the steps of the coach.

The two women stood looking at each other for what seemed like a long time before breaking into broad smiles. Mary O'Donovan made the first move. Arms outstretched, she embraced Ellen as if it were the most natural thing in the world.

Bert wanted to say something but was feeling too choked up to speak.

Sensing this, Conor said, 'It's uncanny, isn't it? They could be sisters, they're so alike. Same hair, same build, same look around the eyes. It's just remarkable.'

Bert nodded in response. It was true. Mary and Ellen were as alike as any two people he had ever seen. The snow-white hair, the way they moved with virtually identical grace and elegance.

Ellen was the first to speak. 'I never met anyone who looked like me before,' she said with quiet wonder. 'I had no idea what it felt like to have someone say, "You have your mother's eyes or your aunt's hands", or anything like that.'

Mary beamed with delight. 'Well,' she said in a soft voice, 'I have loads of relations all over the place, but not one of them looks like you, so it's an unusual feeling for me too, I can tell you. I remember my father talking about Tom and his little girl over the years, but we never could find out what became of you at all. I think Daddy said the last time he heard from Tom was back in the fifties sometime. We assumed he died, although we never got any notification of it or anything. Those were different times, of course. It's not like now with computers and mobile phones and all those things, where we can talk to everyone no matter where they are in the world. Anyway, Ellen, you are very welcome here. Even if it's nearly eighty years since you left. Daddy is inside, so I'd better take you in to him, not be keeping you out here in the yard.'

Ellen glanced back to the coach where Conor and Bert stood, looking nonplussed, unsure of what she wanted them to do. Ellen beckoned them over. But before she had a chance to introduce them, Mary exclaimed, 'Lord, what must you think of me at all? I'm so sorry. You are very welcome too. I was just so overwhelmed to see Ellen that I forgot to introduce myself. Come in, let you, and we'll have a cup of tea and we can all relax.'

'Tea! Tea, she says!' A voice could be heard booming through the open door. 'There's no way I am greeting my niece home from

America with a watery auld cup of imported leaves. She'll sit here by the fire, and we'll have a glass of whiskey together at long last.'

Mary ushered them into the kitchen and introduced them to the owner of the booming voice, who was sitting in an easy chair in front of a glowing turf fire.

'So you came home at last. Somehow, I always thought you would. Mind you, I was starting to worry. Thought I'd be gone by the time you got around to it. How old are you now?'

Smart and all as he was, it never entered Sean O'Donovan's head that this was a rude question to ask any lady, and particularly a lady of Ellen's years. 'Stand into the light there, so's I can have a look at you,' he almost barked, without giving her time to answer his original question. 'By God, hah? You're the head cut off my Mary here. Isn't she, Eamonn?' he asked his neighbour.

'She is indeed, Sean.'

'When did Tom die?' the old man enquired. 'I wrote to him all right, back years ago, but after a while the letters got sent back with a note on them saying "not known at this address". I could never understand that. I mean surely to God even if he was moved or something, the neighbours would have known where he'd gone to.'

Ellen smiled at the very idea. Things didn't work like that in the apartment in the big old house that she and her father had shared. She recalled the Polish couple downstairs, who never even said hello, and the Jewish widow upstairs, Mrs Greenberg, who had designs on her father – as a result he avoided her like the plague. *No*, Ellen thought, *when we moved house, none of the neighbours would have had a clue where we had gone to.*

While Ellen was only too delighted to embrace her cousin Mary, she felt no such need in the case of her Uncle Sean. She was fascinated by him, certainly, but she felt more comfortable viewing him from a distance. That seemed to suit him too, and as Mary bustled around directing the others to chairs at the large pine kitchen table, Sean didn't budge, preferring to remain in his usual spot beside the fire.

Ignoring the two men, he shouted, 'You'll have a drop of whiskey.'

Ellen wasn't sure if this was a question or a statement, so she made a non-committal gesture. 'Well, I don't drink that much, to be honest. Usually –'

'Usually I don't either,' Sean interrupted her, 'but this is no usual day. So put away the teapot and bring out the glasses, Mary, like a good girl.'

CHAPTER 20

'What can I do for you today?' the young hairdresser asked Corlene as she sat in front of the mirror. Corlene had chosen this salon purely on the basis of a conversation she had overheard in a store earlier that morning: two women discussing their mutual hairdresser who was having problems with her credit card machine – a problem with the phone link to the Visa centre in Dublin, or something like that.

This particular morning, Corlene had begun to really despair of her situation. She was flat broke, her credit cards completely maxed out. The food and accommodation costs of the tour were already paid for, but after that, she didn't even have the fare to get her and Dylan from the airport to their apartment. Come to think of it, she soon wouldn't even have an apartment, now that the landlord had served her with an eviction order.

There was nothing for it but to try to find a man here in Ireland willing to engage in a whirlwind romance and a speedy marriage, and hopefully she would be soon back on easy street. There was one problem with this master plan, she thought ruefully: Her hairline was dominated by two inches of black – well, OK, to be honest, *greyish-black* – roots. Worse, she had managed to dye her fingers and her ears orange as she attempted to apply cheap fake tan the previous night. She was going to seed and she knew it. Her only defence against the tide of time was to throw cash at it, quickly and in vast quantities.

During her last marriage, she had maintained a glamorous look with the help of twice-weekly hair appointments and regular manicures, pedicures, waxing and spray tans. Recently, however, without the wherewithal for this cosmetic commando regimen, things had been going downhill, and fast. The news that she could at least get a hairdo and use her useless credit card in this salon in Killarney gave her hope.

Corlene looked up at the young girl. 'Are you Aisling?'

'I am indeed. What can I do for you?' replied the effortlessly gorgeous twenty-five-year-old.

'I would like my colour touched up, and a cut and a blow-dry please,' Corlene said, trying to sound nonchalant. 'I've been travelling now for a few months, and I just haven't had a chance to get my roots done. I was going to wait until I got home. Usually I go to Gigi on Rodeo Drive – that's in Beverly Hills – but this morning I just decided I couldn't look at it one more minute. I have a big event in London tonight, a charity thing – you know, the usual, black tie – so I've just got to get it done.'

'Er, right,' said Aisling. 'Well, we can't claim to be Beverly Hills, but we'll do our best for you anyway. The colour you have at the ends here is a bit brassy. Probably been bleached by the sun. Were you travelling somewhere hot? It's just the combination of the chlorine and the sun can do that desperate damage to your hair.' She looked critically at Corlene's dry, split and corn-yellow ends. 'I'll have to chop a fair bit off it to get rid of these straggly bits, and anyway, there comes a time when long hair just doesn't really work on someone of a certain age. Maybe we'll tone down the colour a bit too? What do you think? I have some lovely caramel and ash tones that I put on my aunt's hair for her fiftieth wedding anniversary last weekend, and it was lovely.' She smiled at Corlene with innocent blue eyes.

Corlene was raging. *What is wrong with young people in this stupid country? First that kid of a barman and now this child.* Comparisons with people's elderly relatives were really taking their toll on Corlene's confidence. The rejection by Bert was a blow, but she consoled herself with the knowledge that he was too old for her anyway. On the other hand, constantly being addressed as if she were an elderly person by all these people in Kerry was simply ridiculous. With all the dignity she could muster, she replied coldly, 'I just need my natural blond touched up. Please do the roots only, as you're quite right – the sun *has* taken its toll.' She somehow managed a frosty smile.

'Righty-ho, whatever you say,' said Aisling innocuously, but a few minutes later, Corlene was convinced she heard her mutter to her colleague as she was mixing the colour, 'Yeah, right, love, the sun makes you go grey. Natural blond, me arse. That one hasn't been blond since God was a child.'

Corlene was on the way to being restored to the blond bombshell she knew herself to be. Her mood gradually began to lift. Everyone *needs a little help now and then*, she thought to herself. Her recent run of bad luck was just due to a little bit of slippage in the maintenance department. New hair colour and a chic cut and all would be well.

She passed a pleasant few hours in the salon, enjoying the free coffee and the magazines and eavesdropping on the conversations of the stylists, which, to Corlene's ears, were like most conversations with the Irish, utterly bewildering but, in this case at least, very entertaining. Aisling was regaling the salon with a tale of her farmer boyfriend's new bull that seemed to be showing very little interest in the cows but that did seem to enjoy staring at Aisling herself as she tried to get dressed each morning.

'Do you know what, Aisling?' one elderly woman said between roars of laughter. 'If they could bottle you, there'd be no need for antidepressants.'

As the junior stylist was putting the finishing touches to Corlene's do, Corlene overheard Aisling say, 'I think they have the credit card machine working now. They said they're just running another check on the system. Should be up and running in about ten minutes.'

Corlene was horrified. Her Visa card had maxed out a week ago, and she was relying on the fact that the salon would just take an imprint to be redeemed at the bank long after Corlene had left town.

Corlene shot up out of the chair. 'Oh my God! Is that the time? I need to go, this second. I should be on my way to the airport by now. I swore to my husband I'd be back by four at the latest. We're meeting Elton John and Tom Jones this evening,' she couldn't help herself adding as she grabbed her handbag.

'Well,' Aisling said, 'if you could just hold on for a minute – they promised me this machine would be working. Unless you have cash?'

'No, I'm afraid all I have are rand and Aussie dollars. We have been travelling so much lately, I never seem to get to a bank. I'm afraid I really must dash – I'm under terrible time pressure.'

'If you're in that much of a rush, we'll have to use this old one then,' said Aisling, producing a manual machine from underneath the counter. 'The money probably won't come out of your account for a few days, though, OK?'

Corlene had lied and cheated all her life. Wearing her most convincing expression, she replied as she scribbled her name on the imprint, 'Oh, I never look at those things anyway. My husband's accountant takes care of all that.' With a tinkly laugh, she dropped the counterfoil into the gaping maw of her handbag and fled the salon as fast as her scuffed five-inch heels would carry her.

Once safely back in her hotel room, she assessed her wardrobe critically. Tonight was going to be a resounding success, she convinced herself. All she had to do was dress to kill and exude confidence, and this big land-owning Irishman would be in the bag. The advertisement stated that he was a farmer. Surely a few thousand acres anyway, she reckoned as she chose her reliable leave-nothing-to-the-imagination leopard-print wraparound dress once again.

She wasn't an outdoor kind of girl as such, but she could do the big house and the four-wheel-drive-cars bit no problem. She wouldn't have to actually *see* the animals or the crops or whatever. No, this guy was going to be so blown away for having punched so far above his weight that she just knew she'd be able to get him to hand over whatever she wanted. *Hey, maybe he has a place in Dublin too. I mean, most of those land-owning types have a city pad for nights out and so on, right?*

Humming tunelessly, she imagined herself featured on the society pages of those glossy Irish magazines she had spent the morning browsing through in the salon. She had been quite taken aback at how glamorous the Irish could be, and she was happy to see lots of photos taken at race meetings. As the wife of a wealthy landowner, breaking into the horse racing set shouldn't be a problem.

By the time she finally managed to wriggle into the maximum-control body shaper – which held all her lumps and bumps in place – she was red-faced and sweating. *The big problem with these industrial-strength undergarments,* she thought ruefully, *is taking them off.* The image of a sexy man whispering in her ear as he seductively undid her wraparound dress to reveal the cappuccino-coloured silk lingerie irresistibly caressing her curves was blown out of the water by the reality – a greyish-beige body shaper with inch-wide straps and a reinforced gusset that resembled a 1950s swimsuit.

Oh well, she thought. A quick trip to the ladies and a change from greyish-beige to a cappuccino silk slip had worked in the past, so it would have to work again. Hopefully, the candlelight and champagne would distract him from the red weals caused by the tourniquet-tight undergarment.

In normal circumstances, Corlene would have planned to hold out on the physical end of things – well, at least for a few weeks – in order to build up her victim's sense of anticipation. Unfortunately, however, on this occasion, time was of the essence. It meant she would have to give this Pa a night he would never forget and ensure he believed he couldn't last one more day without her. The false eyelashes were once again pressed into commission, along with several layers of make-up. By the time she was finished, she had to admit she looked ravishing.

Her feet once more squeezed into the five-inch heels, she teetered out the door and headed for the lift. Crossing the lobby, she couldn't help but notice the glances from the young girls on reception. *No doubt about it – I still have it,* she said to herself.

CHAPTER 21

*D*orothy Crane tramped around the National Park. Even she had to admit that it was an area of exceptional beauty. Once one got away from the car park a little bit, there was a real sense of peace and tranquillity. The lake water lapped gently on the rocks surrounding the shoreline, and every so often she could hear the sound of animals or birds or something or other rustling in the woodland. Despite the lovely surroundings, however, she couldn't enjoy herself. She was so annoyed at the way Juliet had spoken to her.

Juliet. That little mouse. If it weren't for Dorothy, she'd still be in Des Moines playing bridge and growing flowers in her little suburban garden. Dorothy recalled one occasion when she had eavesdropped on a conversation at a church social about how, years ago, Juliet had been accused of stealing a baby. It turned out she hadn't actually succeeded in stealing the child, but nonetheless.

Had Dorothy ever raised the subject of Juliet's shameful past with the rest of the tour group? No, she had not. They wouldn't think much of her if they knew the truth now, would they? *That ungrateful, stupid woman*, Dorothy raged. Dorothy had given her experiences she would never otherwise have had, taken her to see sights so far beyond the imagination of an Iowan housewife, and what did she get for it by way of thanks?

She had never been spoken to in that way by anyone in her entire life. She knew that Juliet was in awe of her, what with her academic record and vast life experience, but instead of benefiting from such a friendship, learning from it, she did the total opposite and attacked her. And as for the rest of them, they were just like all the other groups she had met over the years – morons!

Dorothy had never considered herself a tourist; she was a traveller, whose experience had led her to develop what she regarded as a quirky cynicism about the world. She had seen so many amazing places and had so many amazing experiences, she really felt embarrassed by gauche people who gazed in wide-eyed wonder at things. These people were to be pitied and, if possible, educated.

She thought back to the conversation in the corridor. Imagine Juliet saying that Dorothy had no friends, that no one liked her, that she was a bully and a snob. Good Lord, the woman must be unhinged. That was the only conclusion she could come to. Since they had left Des Moines the previous week, she had made such efforts with Juliet, knowing she wasn't well off, trying to save her money. Juliet was so foolish and trusting, she would hand over her cash to any charlatan who spun her a line, and Ireland seemed to have more than its fair share of such individuals.

Dorothy remembered a previous trip she had taken to the former Yugoslavia. The guide was asked how the children's education in Bosnia had been affected by the war there. By way of response, she offered to take the group to see a school. Dorothy knew right away it was a scam, but the rest of the group were taken in by the young woman. Both she and her husband were volunteer teachers, the guide said. They worked whenever they had some free time. She had some sob story about the fact that many of the children were orphaned during the war and needed both an education and somewhere to live. Apparently, the economy was in bad shape, and voluntary programmes like theirs depended entirely on charity. Dorothy was very sceptical, as it seemed highly unlikely that a country would be unable to provide education for its people through taxes and so on.

She recalled her fellow travellers' tears as the children told their stories of dispersed families and destroyed homes. Dorothy was in no doubt that these urchins had been coached to recount such tales in order to generate maximum donations. At the end of the tour, the children sang for the guests and the director of the school made some speech about the children being the future. It was a lot of emotional blackmail. These ridiculous Catholics, Muslims and Serbs had got themselves into this mess, and once more, they were expecting the Americans to solve their problems for them. Earlier on, the guide had bored them to death with stories of the humanitarian awards the school's director had received. She then proceeded to give undoubtedly false assurances that all monies raised for the school went directly to the school itself. The result of this elaborate begging was foolish, gullible Americans opening their wallets. Dorothy still remembered the sense of satisfaction she felt in the knowledge that she was the only one of the thirty members of the group with the good sense not to contribute. She had explained to her fellow travellers later that evening that simply by being in these wretched countries, they were helping the economy. Any additional financial help and these backwards people would never learn to fend for themselves.

That particular group was remarkably stupid and gullible, she remembered. A number of them had argued against her, so she avoided their company after that.

In the case of her difficulties with Juliet, she reckoned that the best thing to do would be to put the stupid woman out of her mind. There were some people in life one simply could do nothing to help, and Juliet was one of them. She had spent her life with the boring Larry, living in a boring house in a boring suburb doing a boring job. The height of her ambition was to retire to Florida for God's sake!

Dorothy knew she should employ some calming techniques, but her anger was bubbling inside her; she could think of nothing else. She recalled venomously the psychologist who had facilitated the anger management course she had been forced to attend by the university after an unfortunate incident with a student two years ago. She had apparently screamed at him that he was obviously deranged and threw a metal ruler at him – causing him to need several stitches to his head – in front of 200 undergraduates. She did not actually recall the exact details of the event, but unfortunately all of her classes were being recorded. The head of the department had insisted upon it, claiming there had been several complaints against her. He stated firmly that the only options she had were to attend therapy or to terminate her tenure.

But try as she might, her anger would not subside. Juliet would *have to* apologise for the way she had spoken to her. No, she just *wasn't* going to let her get away with it. Dorothy turned around and headed back to the hotel. There was no way she was going to be spoken to like that by *anyone*.

* * *

ANNA CLOSED her bedroom door and headed down the corridor. She had fully expected to feel devastated after the horrible encounter with Elliot, but now she actually felt liberated. She had slept for a while and was refreshed. Enough was enough. She had wasted so much of her life on that jerk already. She wasn't going to waste one more minute.

She decided to call on Juliet to see if she would like to go shopping. They had drifted together often during scheduled stops on the tour, sharing a love of the luxurious Irish tweeds and linens. Juliet reminded Anna of her mother. She was kind and interested and was so excited for her about the baby. Yesterday they had stopped at a café and gift store and Juliet had bought the most darling little sleep suit with 'The Leprechauns Made Me Do It' written across the front as a gift for Anna's new baby. Anna had been so touched.

She tapped gently on Juliet's door.

'Anna. Wow! You look much better. Did you sleep?' Juliet asked with concern.

'Hi,' said Anna cheerfully. 'Oh, I finally gave that awful husband of mine the bullet – I can't actually believe I did it, to be honest. He came back this morning, and he was just so vile.' Anna surprised herself by opening up to Juliet this way. Normally, she was much more reserved.

'Well, I did hear a bit of the dialogue, I have to admit. There must be something in the water in this hotel because I finally told Dorothy what I thought of her this morning too,' said Juliet with a nervous giggle. 'She was not happy, to put it mildly.'

'Really? I'd have loved to have witnessed *that*. Oh God, do you think everyone heard me screaming at Elliot like a lunatic? How embarrassing. He had it coming, though. You should see the bedroom. Red wine everywhere. I'm going to have to replace the whole thing, I'd say.'

'Wine? What did you do?' Juliet asked.

'Come in and I'll show you.' Anna led Juliet to the room to survey the damage. There were red-wine stains on the bed, as well as several on the carpet.

'Oh my God! Well, it's done now,' Juliet said with a giggle as she stood in the doorway. 'I'm sure if you explain to the manager and offer to pay, he'll be fine about it. What a pity Conor isn't around. He's great for sorting things out. Forget the room. Do you have plans for today? It's just that since we're both free of other *encumbrances*, I was going to do a bit of shopping and maybe have a bite in town, if you would like to join me. We can call to reception on our way, and you can fess up to the damage. I'll come with you for moral support if you like.'

'That's exactly what I was coming to suggest to you. Sounds great,' Anna replied. Looking out the window, she added, 'I think it looks like rain – let me just grab a coat.'

* * *

As Dorothy marched indignantly down the corridor, she spotted Juliet standing in the doorway of Anna's room. She heard her name being mentioned. The two of them were *laughing* at her! She approached the two women, rage surging through her.

'Oh, so this is what you're doing, Juliet,' she spat. 'Skulking around the hotel, afraid to go out. You're to be pitied. How dare you speak to me the way you did this morning?'

Juliet paled. 'Dorothy, I just want to be left alone, all right?' she said, backing into the bedroom.

Dorothy's face was now almost purple with rage. 'You just want to be left alone,' she mimicked cruelly. 'Oh, don't worry, Juliet, you'll be left alone all right. The only sensible thing your stupid husband ever did was die in order to get away from your stupid mousey little self.'

Anna interrupted. 'Dorothy, I think Juliet told you already how she feels, so maybe you should just –'

Dorothy's eyes glittered with malice. 'Well, if it isn't our little deserted mommy here to rescue mousey Juliet. Bet she didn't tell you what she really is, though, did she? Maybe when you know the truth about her, you won't feel so inclined to have her as your new best friend! Oh yes, I know about the two of you with your cosy and cute little friendship. But did she tell you she's a baby thief?'

Juliet looked stricken. 'Dorothy! No!'

'What's the problem, Juliet? Oh, have you not mentioned that you stole a child? That you had to be sent to a mental hospital for the criminally insane? Oh yes, Anna, I'd be very careful about leaving her anywhere near your baby. In fact, it's probably the only reason she wants to befriend you.'

Juliet started to shake. 'Dorothy, how could you? Do you really hate me that much? You must be so sad to have so much hate in you.'

'How *dare* you pity *me*!' Dorothy screeched.

New waves of rage seemed to wash over her as she shoved Juliet against the bathroom door. As Juliet stumbled backwards into the bathroom, Dorothy shoved her again.

'Dorothy! Stop it! Just leave her alone. She's told you how she feels,' Anna said assertively.

Dorothy pushed Anna aside violently, sending her flying against the bed. 'You pathetic imbecile, Juliet! I'm the one who should pity *you*! Boring anyone who will listen to tales of the saintly Larry! He was a fat, self-satisfied lump, and you deserved each other. Thank

God you couldn't breed because heaven knows what kind of moron you and he would have produced!'

With another vicious push, Dorothy propelled the stunned Juliet backwards, in the process causing her to knock her head against the corner of the bath.

Anna rushed forward and saw with horror Juliet lying unconscious on the bathroom floor, blood oozing from a cut on her head. She screamed at Dorothy. 'Stop it! You've really hurt her! Call an ambulance quickly!'

Dorothy just stood there, immobile, as Juliet lay on the white-tiled bathroom floor, blood forming a small pool around her head.

'Oh, for God's sake, get out of my way!' Anna barged past Dorothy and dialled reception. 'Yes, quickly, an ambulance to Room 106, and the police. There's been an assault!'

Anna returned to Juliet, sat on the floor and cradled Juliet's head in her lap, talking to her the whole time as they waited for the ambulance. Hotel staff milled around, trying to calm other guests who had been disturbed by the screaming. Within ten minutes, an ambulance crew appeared.

'What's her name?' the paramedic asked Anna.

'Juliet.'

'OK, Juliet, we're going to put you into this back brace now, so just relax and leave it all to us. You're going to be fine,' the paramedic announced to the still unconscious Juliet.

'Can I come with her?' Anna asked. 'I'm not family, just a friend.'

'Of course,' he replied. 'What's your name?'

'Anna.'

'Juliet, Anna is coming with us to the hospital,' the paramedic said as they wheeled Juliet on a stretcher past Dorothy, who remained expressionless.

* * *

ANNA SAT beside the hospital bed. Juliet had come around in the ambulance, and the gash on her head had been stitched as soon as she was admitted. The consultant said he was fairly sure there was no other injury but they'd have to keep her in overnight for observation.

'Will I stay or do you want to rest?' Anna asked Juliet.

'I'd like you to stay if you could,' Juliet replied weakly. 'It wasn't like she said, you know, Anna. I would never...'

'Of course not,' Anna replied, patting Juliet's hand. 'I don't believe a word of it. She's really scary crazy, you know. The look on her face! She was like...she was out of control.'

'I know,' said Juliet. 'She really frightened me.'

'Why did you agree to travel with her? Could you not have refused?'

Juliet sighed. 'I know I should have, ages ago. She never asked if I wanted to go or not. She intimidated me, I suppose. That probably sounds pathetic, but since my husband died, I just don't seem to be able to deal with things as well as I used to.'

Anna sipped her tea. 'What made today different?'

Juliet didn't respond.

'I'm sorry, Juliet. It's none of my business. Forget I asked.'

Tears were now streaming from Juliet's eyes, but she managed to say, 'I was married for thirty-seven years to a wonderful man. Larry. We were so happy together. I won't say we never had a cross word. Of course we did. But we were best friends. Larry died suddenly fifteen months ago, and to be honest, I don't think I'm over it. Sometimes I forget that he's dead and I find myself buying two steaks in the super-market or throwing his shaving soap in the trolley, and then it hits me again. I think my local supermarket manager thinks I'm a bit of a nutcase.' She gave Anna a watery smile. 'I just never imagined living without him, you see. I always thought I'd be the one to go first.'

She paused again, momentarily lost in thought, before continuing. 'The only thing that made us sad was the fact that we never had chil-dren. I guess nowadays there are things you can do, but back then it wasn't talked about. We tried for ages, and nothing seemed to be happening. Eventually I had some tests, and it seems my ovaries never really worked the way they should. I was more or less told to go home and get a dog.'

Anna smiled and squeezed Juliet's hand.

'It drove me crazy for a long time. It seemed everywhere I looked, there were babies. People stopped making references to the pitter-patter of tiny feet and all that after a few years. I guess they knew there was a problem. Larry was so good to me then, telling me that I was enough for him and how we had more going on in our relationship to make us happy than most people did. What he never realised was how he, no matter how wonderful he was, wasn't enough for me. I ached for a baby. I pleaded with God. I took all sorts of crazy potions that were advertised for fertility, but nothing worked. Over time, I began to get really depressed.' She looked directly at Anna. 'I did something terrible.'

Anna didn't react, so Juliet carried on. 'You see, Dorothy wasn't lying. One day, I was in a store. I don't know what came over me, honestly I don't. But there was a woman trying shoes on her little boy, who was about four years old. She had a baby in a pram beside her, but she was giving all her attention to the boy, who didn't want to try on the new shoes. I just walked up and pushed the pram away.'

Her voice was barely a whisper now. 'I rushed out the door and ran to my car. As I was putting the baby on the back seat, she began to cry, and I lifted her out again, trying to soothe her. Just then, the security men came out of the store and spotted me. They shouted, and people all around stopped and stared at me. The woman, the baby's mother, was beside herself with grief and dragged her baby from my arms. The police were called and I was arrested. Larry came down to the police station looking so sad and worried. They kept me there for two days, and then they released me after the woman said she wouldn't press charges. Larry never admitted it, but I think he asked our pastor to go and speak to her, plead my case about how I was messed up because of the infertility. The police let me go. That was so kind of her...'

Anna stood up and put her arms around Juliet. 'You poor thing. The whole experience must have been awful.'

Juliet nodded. 'Yes, it was a bad time. I couldn't have managed without Larry being so supportive, so understanding. I went to stay at a small psychiatric facility after that, and I had a lot of counselling to try to come to terms with everything. Larry visited me every day. We walked in the garden and talked about the fact that we would never have a family. We thought about adopting, but we were too old by the time we found out we couldn't have any children of our own. I think the relief of being able to talk about it with Larry without trying to pretend everything was OK was as useful as the therapy. Eventually I decided we had to make our lives as good as we could and accept the fact that it was going to be just the two of us. Maybe if we'd had children, I wouldn't have taken his death as such a blow. It just wasn't to be so...' Juliet looked as if she had just shed a huge weight. 'You must think I'm crazy,' she said.

'Not at all,' Anna replied. 'I think it must have been a terrible sadness to you to discover that you wouldn't be able to do what it seemed everyone else could do.'

'Yes, that was the thing. You asked me earlier what Dorothy had said to make me flip out at her like that. Well, she hit a raw nerve. I told her I wanted to spend the day browsing around the stores, maybe buying a few gifts, when she snapped that I didn't have anyone to buy gifts for. "It's not even as if you have children," she said. It stung me, even after all these years, and I just lost control.'

Anna smiled. 'What you said to her this morning was nothing more than she deserved. And for her to come back hours later and attack you like that! She could have killed you. You know something, Juliet, I'm starting to think there is strong karma operating in this country. So many things have happened in such a short space of time to turn my life upside down and inside out. But then I meet people like you and Ellen, who help me to see things so clearly. There you were, so sad because you couldn't have a baby although you had a fantastic husband, and here's me with a baby but no one to share it with.'

'Don't you have family?' Juliet asked.

'Oh yes, and they will be great eventually, I know. It's just that...it's just that they – my parents and my sisters, I mean – they did everything the right way round. Married nice reliable husbands, made a beautiful home and then had children. They may not understand my choices, and they really disliked Elliot on the one occasion they met him. I know they would accept my child, but the problem is I really don't relish the idea of living in a small town again. When I was growing up, I found the town so claustrophobic. Everyone having opinions on everyone else's business, always the same people around – I can't imagine much has changed in the intervening years. I couldn't wait to get out. I became Elliot's PA, and actually I was very good at it. I don't know what on earth I'm going to do now, though. He was my only employer, and it's unlikely he will give me a great reference after all this.' She shrugged. 'I know it might seem a bit of a mystery why I put up with him and his selfish ways, but he was so cosmopolitan, *so New York*. I *loved* the life. We knew lots of people, went to lots of events. We were even photographed for the society pages a few times. It all seems so stupid and trite now, but at the time, I really felt I had shaken off my small-town roots and was a genuine career-driven city girl.'

'Well, I'm not exactly in a position to ask you why you put up with Elliot considering the way I allowed Dorothy to treat me. Sometimes it's not until you are out of a situation that you appreciate just how bad it was. It seems we have more in common than we first thought, Anna.'

Anna smiled and nodded.

'The thing is, what now for Anna and the baby? Is going back to your parents the only option?'

'I think so, but I wish it weren't. I mean, I've no home, no job and only a small amount of savings. I have some investments that have come good but not enough to start again. I don't think Elliot is going to offer to support either me or the baby, so I'll have to sue him for it, which could take forever. And he can hire better lawyers than I can.'

'Hmm,' mused Juliet. 'I know how you feel, but he does have legal responsibilities – for you *and* the baby. From what you're telling me, the only thing he cares about is his bank balance, so why not make him feel a bit of pain? It will make your life a whole lot easier and maybe make him sit up and think about the way he's living his. My advice would be not to do anything hasty. He has enough money, and he is obliged to support his child. The courts will see it that way too, I know.'

'You're right, Juliet,' Anna conceded. 'I just want nothing more to do with him.'

'Well, my dear,' Juliet said, 'that's what lawyers are for. You need never speak to him again if you don't want to. Larry's brother is a family law attorney. He lives in Florida. If you like, I can call him and get some advice. Or maybe you have your own lawyer?'

Anna and Juliet continued talking for hours, covering every topic under the sun – from how much they both loved interior decorating to how they both disliked the cold. As the dawn began to creep across the sky, Juliet said, 'Anna, this might sound like the craziest idea you've ever heard. But I wonder, would you think about moving to Florida? I have the down payment in the bank for a small condo in Sarasota. Larry and I had planned to retire down there. Originally, we were going to buy a place with a garden and a small pool. But the way the prices in that development that we liked have gone, I'm afraid a small two-bedroom condo is all that I can afford now. It's a really lovely place, Anna – I'll show you the website. I have some friends there, and if you want to, maybe we could go down and have a look at it together. You could stay with me for as long as you want, at least until you get a settlement from Elliot and enough money to pay for a more suitable place for you and the baby. In the meantime, you could make a fresh start, and if you want to work or retrain as something else, I would just love to take care of the baby for you. I guess I'm offering to be a surrogate grandma.'

Juliet's look of anticipation mixed with fear touched Anna deeply. 'Juliet, that is an incredibly kind offer. I...I don't know what to say.'

'It's OK, Anna,' Juliet interjected, assuming the younger woman was trying to find a way of refusing without causing offence. 'It's all a bit sudden. And you don't have to say anything. I'd probably feel the same way if I were you.' She smiled, feeling foolish at her suggestion. This young woman barely knew her. She was probably afraid Juliet would try to steal her baby.

'No! I just can't believe you would make such a generous offer. I mean, you hardly know me. But if you really mean it...'

It suddenly dawned on Juliet that Anna was seriously considering her proposal. 'Well, all I am offering is a roof over your head for a while, and someone to help out with the baby. I'd enjoy the company. Believe me, Anna, the prospect of being a grandma, even a stand-in one, would make me very happy.'

Maybe there is a master plan for humanity after all, Anna thought. No question, Juliet would be a much better influence in her child's life than Elliot ever could have been. The prospect of Sarasota sounded enticing – sunshine and beaches for the baby to enjoy, and Florida had a vibrant economy, so there was bound to be work available. And with Juliet's support, she could still have a life and be able to earn money.

Suddenly, she had a brainwave. 'Hey, Juliet, I have a better idea. That place you mentioned, with the pool and the garden...well, how about we buy a place together? It could be all done legally, and we would own it fifty-fifty. If either one of us wanted out at any time, we could just sell up. Property doesn't really lose value down there if it's in a good location. Somewhere with a garden would be just lovely for the baby, and we would both have a bit more room in a bigger place. We would be like roommates, but with the grandma bit thrown in. I couldn't afford anything like that on my own, and not many people want to share with a single mom, so it might suit us both. I have some contacts in a publishing house in Miami. Maybe they could get me some freelance, home-based work. And if you would help with child-care, even part time...' Anna's eyes positively glittered with excitement.

Juliet stuck out her hand, and Anna gripped it. 'Deal,' they said in unison.

As the rumble of an approaching breakfast catering cart grew closer, Anna rose quietly from the bedside chair, leaving the now sleepy-eyed Juliet to get some badly needed rest.

'Thanks, Larry,' Juliet whispered gently before drifting off into a deep slumber.

CHAPTER 22

*D*orothy heard a key being turned in the lock. About time. She had been kept waiting for hours. The same detective who had arrested her earlier that day beckoned to her to follow him down the corridor to Interview Room 1. The chair that he invited her to sit on was bolted to the floor, she noticed. As if that weren't embarrassing enough, on the desk opposite her stood a camcorder aimed directly at her face.

'I'm putting in a new tape to record our interview,' he said, stating the blindingly obvious. A green light appeared. 'Interview with Dorothy Crane, 27th of July 2000 at...3:44 p.m. Detective John O'Keeffe present.'

Taking off his watch and placing it on the table in front of him, he said, 'This is a preliminary statement regarding the events leading up to your arrest today. As I mentioned, you don't have to say anything. Neither do you have to speak to me without a solicitor present. If you have a solicitor, we can call him or her for you. If you cannot afford a solicitor, the state will provide one for you. Do you understand?'

Dorothy made a quick mental calculation. He seemed to be young, maybe early thirties, and was dressed in civilian clothes – navy trousers and a blue-striped shirt. She imagined he probably wasn't paid very much. She cleared her throat. 'Well, officer. I...um...I have some money. I can get access to it quickly if that's necessary. Possibly even used notes? I'm sure you and I can come to an...arrangement? Then we can forget any of this silliness.' She gave what she hoped was a charming smile.

The detective gazed at her, expressionless. Dorothy mistook his gaze for one of interest and continued blithely. 'I'm sure the government doesn't pay you enough at all. It must be a terrible job dealing with all those terrorists and so on. I would be happy to offer you something for your trouble. I know you don't believe I am guilty of anything. But to save all that paperwork, it would be much easier if we came to an arrangement, and I could leave here and you could treat yourself and your wife or girlfriend to a nice holiday...'

The detective cleared his throat. 'Ms Crane, I think it would be in your best interest to avail yourself of the services of a solicitor. In addition to a charge of aggravated assault, you have now added another charge – attempting to bribe a member of the Garda Síochána. A charge, I must warn you, that is taken most seriously by the courts. Interview terminated, 3:48 p.m.'

He busied himself with removing the cassette from the camcorder, wrote something on a label and summoned the uniformed Garda at the desk. 'Please accompany Ms Crane back to her cell.'

The gravity of her situation had rendered Dorothy temporarily speechless, so she meekly followed the young Garda down the corridor.

'Do you want us to call a solicitor for you, or will I put you on the list for a state solicitor?' he asked.

'I...don't know any solicitors here. Do you mean an attorney? I have an attorney back in the States, but I don't know anyone here...' Her voice trailed off.

The Garda waited at the door of the cell.

'When can I go?' Dorothy asked.

The Garda looked at her as if she were senile. 'You've been arrested. The next thing that will happen is that you will be formally charged at a sitting of the District Court. Then the case will be put on a list for hearing. If you have a solicitor at that stage, he or she will most likely apply for bail for you. And if the judge doesn't see you as a flight risk, he or she might grant it. It's hard to know. They're usually inclined to remand foreign nationals in custody. Almost certainly, the judge will confiscate your passport and notify your embassy.'

Dorothy felt weak. This situation was so horrific it caused the haughty air that usually enveloped her to evaporate completely. She barely recognised her own voice as she handed a piece of paper to the Garda. 'Could you call this number for me, please? The man's name is Conor O'Shea. He might be able to help me. Can I have a visitor?'

The guard looked down and saw that the piece of paper contained an Irish mobile number. 'I must warn you, Ms Crane, you may not contact friends or associates. The only person you will be allowed to see is a solicitor. And the sooner you get yourself one of those, the better, I'd say.'

Regaining some of her composure, Dorothy replied, 'This man I am asking you to contact is a bus driver. He is not now, nor has he ever been, an associate of mine. I hold a doctorate from the Radcliffe Institute for Advanced Study at Harvard University, and I am currently here on vacation. This man, Conor O'Shea, is responsible for the group with whom I am travelling. I want you to contact him so that he can secure the services of an attorney for me. If you will not permit me to speak to him personally, perhaps you could relay my request?'

Suppressing a smile at her stuck-up notions, the guard took the number and agreed to phone Conor.

* * *

CONOR WAS SITTING on the bed reading his emails on his laptop, having recently returned with Bert from Inchigeelagh.

Dear Conor,

Great to hear from you. We arrive in on Friday at 8:00 a.m. We can't wait to see you. It will be just like old times.

Lots of love, Sinead

It had been a very long day, and he was exhausted. Taking Ellen to the house she was born in was something he would remember until the day he died. But God, he wished there wasn't so much else going on as well at the same time. His mobile rang. Glancing at the screen, he saw it was Anastasia.

'How's my favourite communist?'

'Hi, Conor. I am fine, thank you. And you?'

'Ah, fine. Tired, you know yourself.'

'You don't sound so happy. Are you OK?'

'Ah, no, I'm grand. I just have a lot on at the moment.'

'Oh, OK. Did you hear more email from the woman in America?'

'As a matter of fact, I'm reading an email from her now as we speak. She'll be in Shannon at the weekend. I suppose we'll meet up then.'

'Oh. Yes, if she had coming all of this long way to see you. What do you think will happen?'

'Who knows, Anastasia, who knows. Anyway, how about you? Did you sort out your love life?'

'What?'

'Remember? The other night you were saying about your heart and your head and all that. I assumed it was over some fella. Well, it's none of my business, but you tell him from me he'd be a madman not to grab you with both hands and never let you go.'

'Oh yes. Him. He is bit difficult, I think. I dunno.'

'Well, if he can't see what a fabulous girl you are, then he's not worth bothering about.'

'Oh, he is worth it, but, well, it's complicated.'

'Sure, isn't everything complicated? Maybe things will turn out grand for the two of us soon, eh? The girl I loved twenty years ago is coming back, and all you have to do is sort out this complicated fella of yours, and we're both sorted!'

'Yes, I suppose. I better go. Bye, Conor.'

Conor was surprised at how abruptly she ended the call. She didn't even wait for him to say goodbye. *She must be really cut up about this fella. He has to be a right eejit to pass up on Anastasia.*

Conor was just about to order something to eat from room service when his mobile rang again.

'Hello. Could I speak to Conor O'Shea, please?'

'Speaking.'

'Hello. This is Garda Paul Healy, Killarney Garda Station. I've been trying to reach you all afternoon.'

Conor felt sudden panic. What the hell had happened now? He lived in fear for his groups as they navigated the Irish streets. No matter how often he reminded them, there was always someone who forgot that cars drove on the left-hand side of the road in Ireland. More than once, he'd had to haul someone of his group back onto the pavement as a truck came whizzing by.

'I'm sorry. I was in West Cork, and my mobile was out of coverage for most of the afternoon. What's happened?' Conor asked.

'We have here in custody a Ms Dorothy Crane. She has been arrested and is currently being held under Section 4 of the Non-Fatal Offences against the Person Act 1997. I understand you are responsible for her.'

Conor almost laughed out loud. 'I'm sorry, Guard, but I'd say you have the wrong woman there. She is travelling with me on a tour, and we are staying here in the Hotel Killarney, but I don't think you have the right lady. She is some kind of a college professor and –'

'That is a matter for the court to decide,' the Garda interrupted, 'but in the meantime, she asked that you organise a solicitor for her. Is that something you are willing to do?'

Conor was totally taken aback. 'Er, well, yes. I suppose I can do that. Will I come down there?'

The Garda sighed. 'Mr O'Shea, as I have already said, the suspect is under arrest awaiting hearing. She cannot have visitors, but she does need a solicitor. Can I tell her you will organise one, or will I notify the Chief State Solicitor's Office and ask them to appoint someone?'

'I'll sort it. Tell her I'm on it. Thanks, Guard.'

As he hung up, all thoughts of Sinead and Anastasia disappeared. *Dorothy Crane assaulted someone?* That was the craziest thing he had ever heard in his life. A cantankerous old wagon who was never done

161

moaning, for certain – but physical violence? *Surely not. There must be some mistake.* Conor thought back to his remarks to the group that morning about not having enough cash to bail them out of jail. He had heard Dorothy's muttered comment about his lame jokes, and naturally he had chosen to ignore it. And now, here she was, needing a solicitor of all things!

Conor left his room in search of Juliet. He was sure Dorothy had sufficient funds to pay a solicitor, but he decided he had better check all the same. She was such a skinflint, so maybe she would prefer to go for the state solicitor option. On the other hand, given that she had asked him to organise someone, presumably that meant a private one. Conor didn't know any solicitors in Killarney. On the few occasions he had required legal services, he had used a big Dublin firm. Maybe Juliet would have some ideas about what Dorothy was likely to want him to do. He walked down to reception to see if anyone there might know what had happened and what this Garda arrest was all about.

'Conor, at last!' the hotel manager greeted him.

'God, John, not you too. What the hell has been going on? My phone was out of coverage on and off this afternoon.' Conor followed the manager into his office. Dumbfounded, he listened to the details of the attack.

'Sweet Jesus,' he said when the manager finished. 'And you're sure Juliet is OK? Just stitches?'

'Yes. Her friend Anna Heller, the one who destroyed Room 106 with a bottle of red wine and then nearly hospitalised the porter when she threw a suitcase from the first floor at her departing ex-husband, assures me she will be fine.'

'Jesus, John, I'm so sorry –' Conor began.

John Maylor interrupted him with a wide grin. 'In thirty-six years of managing this hotel, I've never had such an eventful day. Mrs Heller offered to pay all expenses for cleaning the carpets and the bed, and she also asked me to pass on a voucher for Gaby's restaurant for the porter with her apologies. So that's all fine. She seems nice despite her volatile nature. Hell hath no fury, eh? That other one, the Dorothy Crane person, is, it seems, in the Garda station for assaulting Juliet

Steele, who will be released from the hospital tomorrow. It's hardly your fault, Conor, but don't take any more days off, OK?'

Several phone calls later, Conor finally managed to make contact with a local solicitor who had come highly recommended by the hotel manager. John Maylor assured Conor that Lucinda McAuliffe was both efficient and discreet, and when Conor briefed her on the background to the incident, she promised to visit Dorothy later that evening.

* * *

DOROTHY, meanwhile, was progressing rapidly from fear to blind panic. She recalled watching a movie some years previously, called *Mission Express* or *Midnight Express* or something like that, about a young American who had tried to get through customs in some country like Turkey or Iraq or France or somewhere...with packets of drugs taped to his body. He ended up spending years and years in a horrible jail, never shaving or cutting his hair. Dorothy ran her hands over her short haircut. She hated long hair.

She looked up, startled, as the door opened. A different uniformed officer, a young woman this time, announced, 'Your solicitor is here. Follow me.'

Dorothy walked down the corridor to Interview Room 1 and, once more, sat into the chair that was bolted to the floor. A woman of about forty sat opposite her. She seemed very efficient and spoke in a clear, concise way.

'Ms Crane,' she began, 'my name is Lucinda McAuliffe, and I have been engaged on your behalf by a Mr Conor O'Shea. The sergeant on duty told me that you were arrested today on a charge of assault causing grievous bodily harm to a Ms Juliet Steele. Is that correct?'

'Yes,' Dorothy replied, barely audible.

'OK, can you tell me what happened in your own words? Take your time now and try to be as detailed as possible.' She smiled kindly at Dorothy.

'I...I...was in the park. And I was looking for fungi. I collect them, you see, and dry them. I have lots of display cases at home with examples of rare fungi from around the world.'

If Lucinda McAuliffe thought this was an unusual pastime, she gave no indication of it.

'I'd had an argument with my roommate earlier this morning. Something silly. So when I was walking in the woods, I decided to go back and make amends. Well, I went back to the hotel to find Juliet... and I saw her go into Anna's room – that's another one of the group. Anyhow, we had words and she fell and banged her head.'

Lucinda looked impassively at her client. 'OK, Ms Crane. The thing is, there's a witness to say you assaulted Mrs Steele, and that it was your repeated and forceful pushing, while screaming at her in anger, that caused her to fall backwards and hit her head on the bath, as a result of which she was rendered unconscious. The emergency services were then called, and she was taken to the hospital, where she is recovering from her injuries, *thankfully*,' she added pointedly.

Dorothy stared insolently at her solicitor.

'Is that what happened, Ms Crane?'

'Well, Anna Heller would say that, wouldn't she? She and Juliet are thick as thieves,' Dorothy snapped.

'I must advise you that to offer a plea of not guilty when there is consistent and compelling evidence to the contrary will not serve you well in court, Ms Crane. Now, do you want me to represent you or not? Because if you do, I suggest you begin by telling me the truth.'

Dorothy felt trapped.

'Now, if you could begin again and tell me in as much detail as you can what happened exactly. Please begin by giving me some background to your relationship with Mrs Steele. I understand she is to be discharged from the hospital tomorrow and, therefore, may be called to give evidence at the hearing. Generally, a case like this could take some time to get to court, but I think the judge may wish to hear it sooner rather than later, given that you are all on vacation and Mrs Steele and Mrs Heller will want to fly back to the United States as scheduled.'

'As indeed will I,' spluttered Dorothy. 'Well, simply put, what happened was this. Juliet has been behaving irrationally since we left the United States. She is obsessed with her dead husband and talks about him incessantly. She verbally assaulted me this morning for no reason whatsoever – I can only assume she is unhinged. I did not react to her outburst but simply left for the National Park. As I walked, I was becoming increasingly concerned about Juliet in her distressed mental state, and so I decided to return to the hotel to ensure she was all right. There is no telling what that idiotic woman would do. I saw her and Anna Heller in Anna's room, and I approached her. Again she became almost hysterical, and as I was trying to calm her down, she was walking backwards into the bathroom and fell and bumped her head slightly against the bath.'

Lucinda held her client's gaze. 'Your repatriation is entirely dependent on the outcome of the hearing, so what happens next remains to be seen, Ms Crane. Assault is taken very seriously in the Irish courts, so it would be foolish to underestimate the severity of the situation. Now, I will be in touch as soon as I get a time for court tomorrow.' Lucinda began to gather her papers and put them in her briefcase.

'Um, there is one other thing,' Dorothy began.

Lucinda raised her eyebrows.

'You see, I may, inadvertently, have given the detective the impression that I...um...that I...'

'That you what?'

'That I was offering him a bribe.'

Lucinda sat down again. 'How exactly could the detective have got that impression?' she asked in a measured tone.

'I may have said something along the lines of an arrangement...for money...and used notes...'

Lucinda's tone was icy. 'Ms Crane, tell me honestly. Did you or did you not offer a financial bribe to a member of the Gardaí?'

'I think I did,' Dorothy replied in a small voice.

'Well then, Ms Crane, that certainly puts a different complexion on your situation. Bribing, or attempting to bribe, a member of An Garda Síochána brings with it a criminal conviction, often a custodial sentence, and a very hefty fine. That was a very foolish move on your part, Ms Crane.'

Dorothy did not like the woman's tone. Furthermore, the pressure of the situation was now beginning to overwhelm her. 'Well, you hear of it, don't you, in countries like this?' she spat. 'Where the police are corrupt. How was I to know he wouldn't take it? I mean, I thought it was probably common practice here.'

Lucinda prided herself on her professionalism in dealing with even the most unsavoury of characters, but she was rapidly losing patience with Dorothy Crane. 'Evidently, your opinions of the Irish people and of our justice system leave quite a bit to be desired. I would, however, caution you to resist the urge to display such attitudes tomorrow, or you may well risk adding contempt of court to your list of problems. In the meantime, I will file a defence and request bail. You will have to surrender your passport to the court if – and it is by no means a guarantee – they grant bail. I must warn you, Ms Crane. The judiciary in this country takes a very dim view of those who feel they are above the system, so the best attitude to adopt is one of humble apology. Unfounded and unsupportable assertions that the system is corrupt will do nothing to help your cause. Good night.'

Dorothy was left sitting on the bolted-down chair as she watched the retreating back of her one and only hope of rescue from this horrendous situation. The female police officer took her back to the cell and handed her a single blanket and a sheet. As the door of the cell slammed behind her, the young woman said, 'I'll be turning the light out in ten minutes, so better get organised.'

And so Dorothy Crane, PhD, arranged the sheet on the bunk, which was secured to the wall, and lay down to spend her first night in custody.

CHAPTER 23

*B*ert sat in his room and kicked off his shoes. What a day! What an eye-opener it had been to learn all about the history of this island. He'd been so distracted and enthralled by all of it, he'd barely had time to think about the real reason he was in Ireland in the first place. The tour had never been anything other than a cover for his real plans. Now, however, the entire project had been catapulted into the back seat as a result of all this other stuff going on. Insofar as he'd had time to give it much attention, he had come to the conclusion that no one individual in the tour group had emerged as a candidate just yet, but he wasn't unduly concerned about that. There was still time to spare. He badly needed a nap but decided instead to power up his laptop in order to check in with the others for a few minutes and see how things were going. Smiling as he keyed in his password – CAERUS, after the ancient Greek spirit of opportunity, – he checked who was online: Chin Li, Harry and Ibrahim. *Good*, he thought.

Status report? Bert typed.

In process, replied Harry.

Delivered. Awaiting next, responded Ibrahim.

Nothing yet, replied Chin Li.

Bert turned off the laptop and was asleep in less than two minutes.

CHAPTER 24

*E*llen O'Donovan sat in the small parlour off the kitchen as she and Sean pored over piles of old photos. In her hand she held a small black-and-white photo of a young woman smiling at the camera. It was her mother. Ellen knew how fortunate she was to have such a precious thing, given that cameras had been a rare enough commodity in Ireland at the time. This particular photograph carried the name of a photographic studio in Cork on the reverse side.

'I always knew you'd come back, y'know,' Sean said. 'I don't know why exactly, but I just had a feeling that somehow you weren't finished with us.'

'I don't have very much information really. All my father told me was that my mother died and that shortly after that he brought me to the States. When he died, I found some letters that you had written to him. That's how I knew to come to Inchigeelagh. I'd like to know more about my father, about what happened, if you're prepared to tell me.'

Sean settled back into his easy chair and fixed Ellen with a penetrating gaze. 'Of course my memory isn't what it used to be,' he said, 'and God knows it was all a long time ago now. I was a child when the two of you left, but I'll do my best to give you the full story. Inasmuch as I know it anyhow.'

He paused, staring into the fire for a few moments, before continuing. 'Tom was involved with the IRA. The old IRA, I mean, not that shower of criminals – the Continuity IRA and the rest of them – that exist nowadays. Well, I suppose Mammy and Daddy were like most people around here at that time. They didn't like the British being here. They didn't like the way they treated the people. But they thought the best thing to do was to try to stay out of that whole business as much as they could. "Keep your head down, work hard and mind your own business." That's what they always used to say. Michael was the eldest of us three boys, and 'twas acknowledged that he would be getting the farm. I suppose it wasn't fair, looking back on it, but that was how things were done around here for hundreds of years. So we just accepted it.

'As I'm sure you know, the tradition in a lot of Irish families at that time was that one brother would be sent for the priesthood. I think maybe Mammy harboured some notions in that direction for Tom, but if she did, she got nowhere with them because Tom had no interest in the Church at all. I mean, he went to Mass and all that, the same as everyone else, but he didn't show any signs of interest in the priesthood anyway.

'At the time, we all worked on the farm together – children, women and all. There was no machinery much really, so almost everything had to be done by hand. Tom was great with the animals – strong as a horse. Tom and Michael never really hit it off, though – they were too different, I suppose. Michael was like my father in temperament, quiet and kept himself to himself, whereas Tom was always mad for a bit of action. As a young fella, he'd do anything for a laugh. He was great craic, always in trouble in school for all the pranks he played on the master, Badger Buckley. Even though he was a right divil, people liked Tom. He had a good heart.' Sean paused again and looked down at the photographs as if considering where to go next with his account.

'After Tom had left for America, you wouldn't believe the number of people who called up to the house with stories about all the fun they'd had with him. The old people in the parish had the best yarns. Tom loved old people, and he used to spend hours listening to their stories about the old days. He had great respect for them. But be that as it may, the big problem was that himself and Michael rubbed each other up the wrong way. Michael believed in hard work and not much else, and while there was no denying that Tom did work hard on the farm, Michael always thought he was too giddy, always thinking of mischief, mad for the bit of divilment. Anyway, one night there was a bit of a row between the two of them, the way brothers can have a go at each other sometimes. In the finish, it was decided that Tom would be better off working somewhere else.

'Mammy was mortified, of course, to see one of her boys going looking for work and there a fine farm at home. But there was nothing to be done about it. After the fight with Michael, Tom was determined to go. Mammy was always worried about what the neighbours would think – sure what woman isn't? Tom got a job in Kiely's shop in Macroom, pulling and dragging stock mostly. They were delighted with him because he was a big strong lad and well used to hard work. He loved it, meeting everyone coming in and out of the shop and hearing all the news, and it seemed after a while that the new arrangement suited everyone.

'Now at that time, even though we're only fourteen miles from Macroom, most people only went to town once a month, if even that, so all the carry-on with the Auxies wasn't that obvious to us. Tom saw a lot more of it, of course, because he was working in town. He passed them every day. He used to come home with stories about how they would push old people off the footpath, how rude they were to everyone. I remember one night he could hardly eat his dinner, he was so vexed. The story was that there was an old man who used to come in from Coachford direction to town, selling eggs. He was a harmless auld fella, God help us, just trying to keep going, the same as ourselves, and he had a word for everyone. Well, one day he had to go into the shop for a bit of twine to put around his bag because it had burst, and he was afraid he'd drop the eggs. He left the bags of eggs outside the shop – everything was safe in those days, nothing would be robbed from you – and he got the bit of twine from Tom. Anyway, they had a bit of a chat, and when the poor man went out, he was fierce upset. Some soldier had stood on all the eggs and was laughing at the poor old man trying to save them. You might think that in the grand scheme of things that wasn't much, but for Tom it was the thing that turned him. He couldn't bear to see the way good, hardworking people were humiliated by the British, and so that night he joined the IRA.'

Ellen sat, mesmerised. The image of her father as an IRA man was very difficult to reconcile, but she was in no position to contradict her uncle's story. Though she sometimes had trouble understanding his West Cork accent, she hung on his every word.

'Mammy and Daddy had no idea about Tom's activities at first. And if they had, they'd have tried to put a stop to it for definite. Anyway, after a few weeks, they must have copped on that something was up. The thing they noticed was that Tom had started hanging around with the O'Driscoll boys, and everyone knew they were up to their necks in the IRA. Their father had been put in jail for anti-British activity, and they were following in his footsteps. They were from town, and I suppose 'twas them that recruited Tom really. He spent a lot of time with them and came home later and later in the evenings, sometimes even in the early hours of the morning. Daddy was very upset, but as usual, it was Mammy who was left to deal with it.

'Daddy was like Michael – he didn't say much. I remember her begging and pleading with Tom not to stay out late. "You're only looking for trouble," she'd say to him. But she might as well have been talking to that wall over there for all the good it did. Michael got stuck in him then, when he wouldn't do as Mammy asked. But he wouldn't listen to Michael either, so in the end, Michael said that Tom would just have to move out, and that was that. He said he didn't want his family drawn into anything just because Tom wanted to be a hero and play soldiers. I remember that night so well. I was only a child, sitting at the top of the stairs listening to this fight going on. I was crying because I didn't want Tom to leave. He was great to me, always playing football with me or bringing me sweets on payday. That happened in July 1919, I suppose.

'Well, he left anyway, but before he did, he promised me he'd take me to the mart on the next big fair day. I loved going in to see all the cattle being sold, and Tom would get me a bottle of lemonade and sweets, and we'd stay out all day. He went to stay with the O'Driscolls in town, and while he was there, I suppose he took a shine to Bridget. She was the only daughter of the house. I thought she was lovely. She had a great big, gutsy laugh that everyone around here used to find kind of infectious. That's my strongest memory of her, always laughing and joking and everyone around her smiling. I suppose that's why herself and Tom got along so well. She was small and dark, with curly hair, and a bit wild from having only brothers around her. Her mother died when she was young, so she wasn't brought up too lady-like, if you know what I mean. She wasn't rough or anything – no, no, no, nothing like that. She was just a bit of a tomboy, I suppose. She used to play with me whenever they would collect me and take me on days out. Tom and Bridget were very good to me, so they were, the two of them.'

Sean stopped to take a sip of tea. 'I suppose you must be thinking, "Will he ever get to the point of the story?"' He smiled.

'I can never express how much hearing all of this means to me,' Ellen responded. 'I want to try and remember every detail, every word. You can't imagine how often I've dreamed of this moment. Actually, that's not really true. Because I never dared to believe anyone would be able to tell me anything after so long. I really thought finding a headstone in a graveyard would be the highlight of my trip. So please, Sean, if you're not too tired, go on – tell me more.'

'OK so,' Sean began again. 'Well, next thing we knew, things started getting much worse with the British. They seemed to feel more threatened by the IRA, so they took out their frustrations on the people around here even more than they had done before. It was decided by the IRA that a guerrilla-style campaign was to be used against them, and so the British started suffering small losses. By that time, they were rounding up anyone they even suspected of IRA involvement, so some of the lads had to take to the outdoors. Because it wasn't safe for them to be found in one place, the best thing they could do was live on the run, like.

'By then Mammy and Daddy had accepted that Tom was going to do what he wanted, although they never said it, mind you. Do you know, I think they were secretly kind of proud of him? I remember the night of our cousin Ann Creedon's wedding, when the soldiers came in and hit Donal Creedon, Ann's father, with the butt of a rifle. God, that was a terrible night altogether. They took loads of fellas away that night and roughed them up very bad. After that, anyone involved with the IRA had no choice but to go on the run – Tom included. They organised themselves into small fighting forces called flying columns, and no one really knew where they could be found. 'Twas safer for everyone that way.

'Bridget would cycle out from Macroom to visit us every few weeks to see if we had any news of Tom, or to let us know if she had spoken to him or had received a letter from him. Tom and Bridget weren't engaged or anything like that, but they had an "understanding", as it was called. I'd say Tom would have loved to have asked her to marry him at that stage – he was mad about her – but if the British thought she was connected to him, it would have put her in terrible danger. So the pair of them left that end of things alone.

'Anyway, they did their best to keep in touch with each other, but Tom knew he had to stay away, from their home places especially, for the safety of their families. I couldn't tell you the number of times the British came to the farm looking for him, shouting and roaring and making an awful mess, being destructive just because they could, like. One time, a young soldier, only about eighteen or so, put me up against the milking parlour wall and threatened to shoot me if Mammy didn't tell them where Tom was. She was great that day. She stood up straight – she was only five foot one – and said, "I don't know where Tom is. I wish I did. Now kindly let go of my boy. I'm sure your mother didn't bring you up to threaten women and children."

'Her tone was so cutting, and the way she spoke so dignified, he did let me go. 'Twas frightening all the same, though.' Sean took another sip of tea.

His reticence to continue was palpable, Ellen thought, his mind debating how he would go about telling her the next bit. Reading his mind, she said, 'Sean, please don't worry. Just tell me the story as it is. I'm not as fragile as I look.'

Sean smiled sadly. 'You are a perceptive woman, Ellen O'Donovan, but then again you didn't lick that off a stone. Your mother was the same. Well, the next big memory I have of Tom was a night out in the barn over beyond. Bridget and Tom were there, and Michael and Mammy and Daddy of course, as well as the two O'Driscoll boys. I wondered why everyone was out in the barn, but I suppose they didn't want anyone to see them from the road. Tom was a wanted man, and so were the O'Driscolls, so they were taking a huge risk coming out into the open, especially all together.'

Taking a deep breath, he said, 'You see, the thing was, Ellen, the long and the short of it was that your mother was expecting, and they were all trying to decide what to do about it. In those days, it was a terrible scandal, and the girls who found themselves in that position were locked away in terrible places, their babies adopted in America. Usually the priest would get involved but not in this case. You see, the parish priest here at the time had spoken out against the IRA – he had family in the British Army during the Great War, I think – and so he was very unpopular in the parish as a result.

'Mammy was crying and so was Bridget. Michael was giving out yards to Tom, asking him over and over if there was no end to the disgrace he wanted to pile onto his family. Then he called Bridget... well, not a very nice name – I won't repeat it – and her brothers and Tom had to be pulled off Michael by Mammy and Daddy. It was a terrible scene. It seemed that Tom and Bridget desperately wanted to marry, but it was just too dangerous. The priest couldn't be trusted, and Tom's situation meant that he had to stick with his flying column for fear of arrest. The problem was that leaving poor Bridget to cope on her own, having a baby out of wedlock, was a terrible fate too. In those days, a single mother was something that was unheard of. Not only would the mother be shunned from society, but the child would be too. God love them, it was an awful dilemma.

'After going around and around in circles for ages, it seemed that only one solution was possible. Bridget would have to marry to give the child a name, and if she couldn't marry Tom, then the only other option was to marry Michael.

'And so that's what happened. I know it must sound strange, especially what with Michael being the way he was, but he had to accept that was the only way out of it. Michael and Bridget got married, and if anyone thought it strange, then they had the good sense not to comment. I'm sure your arrival seven and a half months after the wedding caused a few raised eyebrows too, but conservative and all as people were, they looked after their own.

'And so you were born, Ellen Margaret O'Donovan, daughter of Michael and Bridget.'

Sean leaned over and took Ellen's hand as the tears coursed down her cheeks. 'I know this must come as a terrible shock to you,' he said kindly. 'But you should know this. Your father adored you. He took massive risks to see Bridget throughout her pregnancy, and on the night you were born, he sat outside in the barn, even though there was a price on his head, just to hear your first cry. Mammy was upstairs with Bridget and the midwife, and I was out in the barn with Tom. When we heard your little voice through the open window, your father cried like a baby and made me promise that I would look after you until he could do it himself. That is why, darling Ellen, you have made me the happiest man in the world by coming home. I can die happy now, knowing I did right by you and that I told you how much your parents loved you.' The normally gruff Sean choked with emotion.

For the next few minutes, Ellen and Sean sat in silence, holding hands and gazing into the fire, each lost in their own thoughts.

Finally, Sean broke the silence. 'I suppose you know the rest, but I might as well finish it now...'

Ellen nodded at him through her tears, indicating that he should continue.

'The next day, we were all around the little crib, admiring you. Even Michael seemed delighted with you, picking you up and cuddling you. We were amazed. Nobody who knew Michael could ever have pictured him so soft. But he was mad about you, even if he was still mad as hell at your father. Neighbours came and went, bringing little presents, and all in all, it was a great day. I remember that night hearing pebbles being thrown at my window. I opened up, and there was Tom in the back garden whispering to me to come to the back door. I crept down the stairs and let him in. He had a big bunch of wild flowers and a homemade dolly that he told me someone had given him "for his little niece". I went up and woke Bridget. She slept alone. I don't think she and Michael ever – well, anyway, she was alone. I told her she had a visitor, and then Tom walked into the room. I never saw two people so happy to see each other. You stirred in the crib, and Tom took you out and held you in his arms. I stood in the doorway, and I'll never forget that moment. He looked down at you and said, "Welcome, little Ellen. I'm your daddy, and you must stay here with your beautiful mammy until I get rid of these cursed Englishmen so you can grow up a happy little Irish girl. I won't be long, I hope, but they're being a bit stubborn! Don't worry, though, my little angel, your daddy is on the job. So it will be sorted out soon."

'He kissed your head and handed you to Bridget. He stood there for a few minutes with his arms around the two of you. He told her he loved her more than life itself and that he'd be back to see you both as soon as he could. With that he was gone. He never saw her again.'

'How old was I then?' Ellen asked, finding it hard to get the words out, tears streaming down her face.

'Let me see. I suppose you were only about two or three days old at that stage. Of course, all hell had broken loose after the Kilmichael ambush the previous month, and everyone knew the English were jumpy and even more dangerous than before. They were like cornered rats by then. I don't know if someone saw Tom leave that night or what it was, but when the Auxies turned up again in search of Tom, this time there was no messing. They dragged my father and Michael and me out into the yard and put us facing the wall, roaring at us that we'd better find Tom or we'd all be dead. Mammy was screaming and telling them we knew nothing when one of them hit her across the head with the butt of his rifle. Daddy went to help her, but they rounded on him and gave him an awful beating. The poor man was never the same again after that. Luckily, Mammy was a tough old bird, and she got over her injuries fine.

'Bridget was in bed nursing you when they broke down the bedroom door. I heard her screaming, "Please don't hurt my baby!" Next thing we knew, a young soldier came downstairs and handed you to Kitty O'Dwyer, a neighbour who was visiting at the time. We could hear them roaring at Bridget to tell them where Tom was. She kept saying she hadn't seen him in months, that she thought he was gone to England. They must have lost patience with her or something because next thing we heard was the sound of gunshots, then silence.

'Later that night, Tom arrived and told us he was going to America. It was too dangerous to stay, he said. It was like someone had turned off a light inside him. He was distraught over Bridget, but there was no time for tears or funerals. Mammy and Daddy, and even Michael, begged him to leave you with us. America was so far away and Tom knew nothing at all about babies, but he wasn't for turning. His daughter was going with him, and nothing anyone could say would change his mind. And so we wrapped you up warm. I remember Michael gave you –'

'His coat,' Ellen interrupted. 'I still have it. My father always told me my Uncle Michael gave me that coat to keep me warm on the boat.'

'Yes, that's exactly what he said. Michael loved you too, but he couldn't say it any other way. Some bottles were found for you and a few napkins, and away you went into the night. We were all nearly demented with worry those first few weeks, not knowing if you were all right or not. One day we got a letter. It was in code, of course, in case the British intercepted it. It was from our Aunt Florence in Boston saying she had just got a new puppy, and even though it was her first puppy, he seemed to be managing fine. She did mention that she had no idea taking care of a puppy was such hard work. Mammy and Daddy were so relieved, and even Michael smiled. We had letters over the years, but when Mammy and Daddy died, and then Michael died, we just lost touch. I'm glad Tom had a good life, and that he was a good father to you.'

Sean's voice had become virtually inaudible, and Ellen became acutely aware that telling the story had taken its toll on him – physically and emotionally. She stood up, leaned over and kissed him on a wizened cheek. 'Thank you, Sean,' she said quietly.

In the kitchen, the main light was switched off and Mary was sitting by the fire, reading. The light was fading outside, and stillness had descended on the house.

Mary stood up. 'Are you all right, Ellen?'

'I'm fine. It's been an incredible day, though.'

'Conor and Bert went back to the hotel. I told them you'd be staying here tonight. I'll drive you back tomorrow morning. There's tea in the pot and a few sandwiches. You must be hungry. I've made up the bed for you, and your electric blanket is on so you won't freeze. I know 'tis summer, but the nights can be chilly all the same, especially if you're not used to it. I'll just help Daddy up to bed, and then I'll be down to show you where to go. 'Tis great to have you home, Ellen. I hope you'll come again.'

Ellen sat eating the sandwiches and looking at the photographs that were dotted around the large room. Arriving back, Mary said, 'The room I had planned for you to sleep in is across the corridor there, but Daddy says you might like to sleep upstairs. Say it now if you would rather not, but it's your mother's room, and it's the bed you were born in.'

Ellen felt her eyes well up for what seemed the hundredth time that day. 'This was my father's house?' she asked. 'I just assumed it was your husband's place.'

Mary laughed. 'Oh, Lord save us, no, not at all. Daddy wouldn't live anywhere else, so we moved in here with him a few years ago.

Our farm is further back the road, but we live here in the O'Donovan's home place.'

Ellen looked up at the ceiling. 'The house where my mother died.'

She followed Mary up the stairs and into a room with a big double bed covered in a deep-red brocade quilt. A great sense of peace and love washed over her. She hugged Mary good night and settled into the bed she had last occupied eighty years earlier.

CHAPTER 25

'*R*elax, they're not going to eat you.'
Laoise poked Dylan in the ribs as they sat on plastic chairs outside the room where the interviews were being held. Dylan wished he was anywhere else but there at that moment. He just knew they were going to laugh him out of the interview. Sitting either side of himself and Laoise were a teenage girl and a guy that Dylan reckoned was in his twenties. The girl had a violin case on her lap, and he knew, just by looking at her, that she had probably first learned the instrument as a baby and had been playing it ever since. The guy sitting beside her was dressed in scruffy jeans, a grandfather shirt and a battered, brown leather jacket. On the floor beside him was what looked like a banjo case, but Dylan couldn't be sure. Even if he had brought his guitar to Ireland, he would have been too embarrassed to play at this interview, he thought. What had he been thinking of, allowing Laoise to talk him into coming here? He was about to make a terrible fool of himself, he was certain.

Laoise's mobile rang, and she ran down the stairs shouting, 'Ah, Mam…just calm down, will ya? I had an emergency…'

Dylan strained to hear the next bit, but Laoise had disappeared out the front door of the building. The whole thing was insane. He looked down at the application form in his hand. He wasn't going to be able to do this. His stomach was in knots. He decided to head after Laoise, tell her the whole crazy plan was off, he wasn't going through with it.

A nearby door opened, and a woman's voice rang out. 'Dylan Holbrooke?'

'Er…yeah…that's me,' Dylan said, barely audibly.

'Please come in,' she said, smiling. 'Did you bring an instrument?'

'An instrument? Oh…er, um…no…no instrument…just…'

'Just yourself then,' she answered as she ushered him into the room.

He stood looking at a long table, two men sitting on either side. The woman sat down at the top of the table.

'Dylan, please take a seat,' said the younger of the two men.

As he pulled the chair in towards the table, Dylan had a good look at the two men. The blood drained from his face when he recognised Laoise's father. He began to tremble so violently he could barely manage to hand the woman his application form. Seeing his obvious nervousness, she tried to put him at ease.

'Dylan, my name is Sheila O'Mahony, and I'm the head of administration at the college. This is Kieran Cassidy,' she said, nodding at the younger of the two men. 'Head of first year and dean of the faculty. And this is Diarmuid Lynch, the well-known piper who gives guest lectures and demonstrations to our piping students. Diarmuid doesn't usually sit on these interview panels, but due to the illness of another staff member, he has kindly agreed to stand in today. So, Kieran, would you like to begin?'

Dylan managed to croak out answers to Kieran's general background questions. Throughout, Diarmuid looked kindly at him but displayed no hint of recognition.

When Kieran finished going through his list of questions, Sheila O'Mahony took over. 'Well, I can see you have all the necessary forms filled out correctly and so on. I will look at them in detail later on. But for now, we would like to know why you feel we should award you a place on this course.'

Diarmuid gave him an almost imperceptible wink and nodded to him encouragingly.

'Well,' Dylan began, 'I only arrived in Ireland recently, and I happened to overhear some music that was being played in a church. I went in and discovered that what had drawn me in was the sound of uilleann pipes. The piper was nice enough to answer my questions. Up to that point, I had never even heard of uilleann pipes. The truth is they kinda got into my soul.'

He blushed with embarrassment at the very idea of using such language, but at the same time, he knew that if he was to stand any chance at all, he had to convince these people the music meant so much to him. 'No instrument has ever had such an effect on me. I was in a band back in the States, doing metal and that kind of stuff, but the music I heard that day in the church was so different. Since that first day, I've done nothing else except travel to gigs and listen to as much traditional music as I can. It's amazing, and I...well, I love it. It's like I hear it with my heart, not just with my ears. The fast tunes give you a kind of rush to the head and make you want to, like, jump around or something. Like, nothing matters, only keeping the music going. And the slow ones, the slow airs, it's like you can feel the sadness of the person who wrote the piece. It's like the pipes are joining in the loneliness.'

The three interviewers looked at him and smiled. Kieran Cassidy was the first to respond. 'Well, thank you, Dylan. We'll let you know, but I must tell you that this course is very heavily subscribed, and most, if not all, applicants have at least a background in traditional music. So it would be wrong of me to send you away without giving you a true picture of the situation here. If you are not successful this time, might I suggest that you take up another, perhaps less challenging instrument and reapply next year?'

Sensing he had not made a good enough pitch, Dylan said, 'Look, I know there are loads of people applying for this course. And they probably all have more experience than me. But I swear to you, if you give me a chance, I'll work so hard. Those other people probably come from families where traditional music is played all the time, and so they'll get a chance to learn in lots of different ways. But for me, this is my only shot. If I don't get this, I guess I'll just go back to the States, but I can't imagine anyone there could teach me the pipes...not in the kind of world that I live in anyhow. If you let me in this course, you'd be doing much more than giving an American kid a chance to play the pipes. I'm kinda alone, so you'd be kinda saving my life.' He felt his ears burning red. He had never spoken so candidly to anyone in his entire life.

'And if we were to offer you a place, are you in a financial position to pay your fees, upkeep and so on?'

Dylan shifted uneasily in the chair. He knew that his mother would probably refuse. *Although, hell*, he thought, *surely she can't be as broke as she makes out. She's divorced four rich guys, for God's sake. That's a lot of alimony.* 'Er...yes, ma'am. My mother will pay the fees. She's very supportive of my music.'

Laoise looked up from her mobile as Dylan emerged from the interview room. She said nothing, just stood up and walked down the stairs behind him. As they got into the car, he spoke his first words. 'Did your mom freak out about the car?'

'Ah, don't mind her,' replied Laoise breezily. 'She'll eventually cool down. She had to get the bus back from Killarney, though, and she went to the Garda 'cause she thought it was robbed, but she'll be grand.'

Dylan watched her as she reversed the car erratically out of the parking space. She had more confidence in her little finger than he had in his whole body. He wondered if that was how kids who grew up with two loving parents turned out. Suddenly, he heard himself saying, 'Hey, Laoise, you know who was in there, right?'

'Yeah, Mam said it when she rang me. I had seventeen missed calls from her, so she was kinda pissed off by the time I answered. She only told me when I admitted to her where we were.'

Dylan winced as the wing mirror on his side of the car tipped the wing mirrors of at least a dozen cars parked along the street. 'Your dad never said he knew me or anything. He just asked me questions like everything was normal. Do you think he's angry or what?'

Laoise laughed. 'Nah, he's cool. It's my mam who has forty fits a day. He loves the pipes, and he knows you genuinely want to play them, so he would encourage you. He won't rat us out. I'm in enough trouble already. I know he'll try to calm her down. It's always been like this since I was a kid. The pair of them, with their good cop, bad cop routine.'

Dylan looked out the window as a dog narrowly missed being flattened as a result of Laoise's inexpert driving. 'Y'know, I'm always saying it, but seriously, you are so lucky. I wish I had folks like yours.'

'You won't be saying that when my mam tries to beat seven kinds of shit out of you for making me rob her car.' Laoise laughed.

'What?' Dylan exploded. 'It was *your idea*! Jesus, Laoise! Don't tell me you said I made you take the car.'

'Relax, will ya?' Laoise said with a cackling laugh. 'She has a wicked temper, but it blows over quickly. All you have to do is just, like, chill, man. You worry too much!'

As Laoise eased the car into the driveway of her house, Dylan felt sick for the third time that day. He had made her stop at a store to buy Siobhán some flowers to apologise. He knew Laoise wasn't bothered about her parents' reaction, but he was a stranger and that was a different story.

'C'mon.' Laoise nudged him gently. 'She'll be grand, honestly.'

'Well?' demanded Siobhán as she stood at the front door. 'What have the pair of you to say for yourselves?'

Before Laoise could open her mouth, Dylan said, 'Siobhán, we are really, *really* sorry. I guess we just got carried away 'cause the lady on the phone said we only had an hour to get to the interview. I never should have allowed Laoise to drive me there. And I'm so sorry about you having to get the bus, and going to the police and everything. It's totally my fault, and I just got you these flowers to say how sorry I am. I...um...well, I'm just really sorry I guess,' he finished lamely.

'Yes, well, thank you, Dylan. Actually, it's not your fault. Laoise knows she's not supposed to drive on her own. You could both have been killed! Not to mention that I could get done for wasting Garda time trying to convince them my car was stolen. Honestly, Laoise' –

she turned to her daughter – 'when are you going to grow up? I don't know what your father is going to say when he hears about this latest stunt. After the tattoo, you promised no more crazy behaviour, and then you go and do *this!*'

Laoise knew that once her mam threatened her with 'when your father gets home', she was pretty much home and dry. Her dad never managed to stay cross with her for long. Often, after her mother had banished Laoise to her room for her behaviour, she would follow this by dispatching Diarmuid to the room to reprimand his youngest daughter. The conversation always went along the lines of, 'Don't be upsetting your mother, and when she asks, tell her that I nearly killed you.'

Laoise always looked suitably chastened after the encounter with her father and somehow managed to make her mother feel that she had suffered some consequences after all. The exasperated nuns at St Angela's told Siobhán that Laoise was the school's 'enfant terrible', the total opposite of her much-better-behaved older sister, Éadaoin. Diarmuid and Siobhán often wondered if the fact that Laoise was the youngest and that they had spoiled her was the reason she was so incorrigible. But no matter how bad her behaviour was at times, she always managed to make them laugh.

Laoise and Dylan were sitting at the counter in the kitchen eating toasted cheese sandwiches when they heard the key turning in the front door. Dylan paled, and the piece of sandwich he was eating stuck in his throat.

'How's everyone?' Diarmuid asked pleasantly as he gave Siobhán a kiss on the cheek and pulled Laoise's hair playfully.

'Grand,' said Laoise innocently. 'How was your day? Meet anyone interesting?'

Diarmuid sat in his favourite chair and raised his eyebrows. 'Now, miss, I hear that you've been driving your poor mother insane again with your antics. And you think I'm going to buy you a harp? Now get upstairs and clean Cathal's room.'

'What? It's not even my stuff in there!' she protested. 'It's all yours and Cathal's and Éadaoin's, and anyway, it would take hours – it's like a skip in there.'

Diarmuid smiled. 'Which is precisely why you need to tidy it, my dear.'

Laoise was outraged. 'You're only making me do it 'cause if I don't, you'll have to do it yourself! That's, like, so unfair. It's all pipes rubbish and bits of paper. I wouldn't know what to do with all of it. I'd probably wind up throwing out something really valuable.'

'I'll chance it. Don't forget who's forking out for a harp for you. If you asked nicely, I'm sure a certain young American gentleman would help you, given that I am apparently offering my services as his sponsor. And if he is going to study here, then he needs a bedroom. And since the only one not in use is full of stuff, then it would be in his interest, as well as yours, to tidy it up.'

For a second, Laoise and Dylan just gaped at each other. Did Diarmuid just say that Dylan had got the place and that he could stay in their house? Surely he was imagining things.

Laoise launched herself on her father. 'You're not messing now, are you? Did he get it? Can he stay?' she screeched with excitement.

Diarmuid's smile told them everything they wanted to hear. 'Yes, he got it, and yes, he can stay here, under certain terms and conditions, mind you,' he replied, his words barely audible over Laoise's screams.

Dylan eventually found his voice. 'I...I don't know what to say. I... Are you sure? I won't be in the way?'

'God almighty, child, will you calm down!' Diarmuid rebuked his daughter. 'Go out and help your mother. I want to talk to Dylan.'

Reluctantly, Laoise left the kitchen.

'I just don't know how to thank you –' Dylan began.

'Hang on now one minute,' Diarmuid interrupted. 'Before we finalise anything, I need to explain the terms and conditions of this arrangement. So listen carefully. Firstly, myself and Siobhán need to meet your mother to make sure this is OK with her. So we will go down to Kerry tomorrow and hopefully meet up with her and make all the arrangements. Secondly, while you are under my roof, you have your room and my daughter has hers. I don't know what's going on with the pair of you, and up to a point, I don't mind. But she is my baby girl and I won't stand for any messing. She can be a bit of a divil sometimes, so I'm relying on you to be a bit more sensible. No more stunts like today, d'you hear me? Are we clear?'

Dylan nodded. 'Crystal.'

'And finally,' Diarmuid continued, 'you are coming here to learn to play the pipes. I want you to work hard at it. It won't be easy, and there'll be days when you'll be sick of it. But I took a chance on you today, so don't make me look like an eejit, right?'

Diarmuid took a tin whistle out of his coat pocket and handed it to Dylan. 'Right, start with that,' he said. 'You have a week until the course begins. Let me see if you can make any fist of the whistle before we go any further.' Taking one of his own whistles out of a drawer, he gave a quick demonstration.

After a few false starts, Dylan made a reasonable attempt at a simple tune. Delighted with his progress, he grinned broadly and said, 'Thanks, Diarmuid. This is awesome. I'm gonna practise every day, I swear.'

'You'll be grand. It just takes perseverance and willpower and plenty of practice. You have the makings of a piper.'

'Diarmuid, I don't know how to thank you and Siobhán. I mean, no one has ever taken this much interest in me before. Sure you can meet my mother, but I gotta tell you, she doesn't care what I do or where I live so long as I don't come looking to her for anything. I don't know who my father is, so that's no problem. My grandma will lend me the money for my rent and all that, I know she will, and maybe I could get a part-time job in between my music studies to pay you back. I know my mother will bitch about paying the fees for the college, but she'll be so glad to see the back of me, she'll pay in the end.'

'Well, the fees are expensive, and eventually you'll have to buy a set of pipes – I'll lend you a set in the meantime. But if you can pay your tuition, we will put you up. We won't be taking any money from you. You can eat and sleep here and just chip in with the housework and cutting the grass, putting out the bins and all that. Don't worry, Siobhán will come up with plenty of jobs for you to do.'

Dylan opened his mouth to object, but Diarmuid got in ahead of him. 'Look, Dylan, I benefited from good people helping me when I was starting out playing music. I hadn't a bob, and I used to land up at various houses and I got fed. Pipe masters taught me for nothing and even lent me pipes until I could afford my own. I'm just paying it back into the system with you. You seem like a nice young lad, especially now that I've seen you without all that muck on your head. So if it's a chance you want, here it is.'

Dylan beamed. 'Look, about the Laoise thing... She is incredible and funny and so talented and...well, gorgeous. But this is your home, and I won't do anything that would let you down. I'll try my best to learn quickly, and I won't be a burden. I promise.'

Diarmuid returned to his favourite chair and opened the newspaper. 'Good man. Stick on the kettle, will you? I'd love a cup of tea.'

CHAPTER 26

*C*orlene took a deep breath as she read the name of the small establishment. She wasn't at all sure she had the right place as it seemed to be half bar and half some kind of store, if she was to judge by the stuff in one of the front windows. It contained a large sign bearing the slogan 'Guinness Is Good for You' and a graphic of a man pulling what looked like an old-fashioned cart. One of the other windows contained a display of what seemed to be a random collection of objects and what she presumed were grocery products with very faded packaging. Corlene noted a box of Kellogg's Corn Flakes, a large card with several pairs of what appeared to be shoelaces attached, a box of what looked like mousetraps, a bar of soap called Sunlight and several cans of fruit, dog food and beans. Perhaps it was one of those mock retro bars that were becoming so popular at home, she thought.

The voice on the phone had been quite indistinct, but she was sure the man had said 'Pajo's'. She looked again. Yes, that was definitely the name inscribed on the frosted glass in front of her. As she pushed the door, an overhead bell rang loudly. The room was almost pitch dark, and it took a while for her eyes to become accustomed to her surroundings.

A pungent odour assailed her senses. As best she could tell, the various components of the smell encompassed manure, sour milk, beer and cigarette smoke. By now she could make out a long counter running down the side of the room, and in front of it a few timber bar stools. On a shelf above the counter sat a variety of products, presumably for sale. Below the shelf, piled against the back wall, lay large sacks of what appeared to be grain or potatoes or something.

This is like a movie set, she thought, running her eyes over her surroundings one more time. As she returned her gaze to behind the counter, she spotted a woman, stooped with old age, cleaning a glass with a rag. She looked like a witch, with wild grey hair and a face so creased and lined it was almost impossible to see her eyes.

'Arrooolosht?' the woman said.

'Excuse me?' replied Corlene, having no clue whatsoever as to what the old woman had just said.

'Aar oooh losht?' the woman repeated again.

Perhaps she was speaking Irish, thought Corlene. 'I – am – looking – for – Pajo's – bar,' Corlene enunciated slowly.

'Ooh, found it,' replied the woman with a sinister cackle.

Corlene was bewildered and by now feeling a little nervous. Desperation forced her to try again. 'I – am – looking – for – Pajo's – bar.'

The woman observed her for a second or two and then put down the glass she had succeeded in making even filthier as a result of her rag-wiping efforts. 'Shtay there letchoo, till I call him,' she mumbled as she shuffled off.

Corlene wasn't sure if the woman had understood her or not but decided it was best to wait. She considered sitting down but then thought the better of it. Not just because every surface in the place seemed to be filthy, but also because she presented a shapelier figure standing up. A third but equally important reason for remaining standing was that her ultra-strong underwear was putting up a tough fight against her tummy bulge. She knew from experience that her underwear lost the fight whenever she sat down. So for these reasons, Corlene stayed where she was, standing in the middle of the floor.

The silence was broken by the sound of the woman returning, this time accompanied by a small, fat man whose girth seemed to take up the full width of the doorway. He stood looking Corlene up and down without uttering a word. From what she could make out, he was almost entirely bald except for a rim of hair that grew in wisps over his collar. His face was adorned by a pair of glasses with lenses so thick they could have been made from the bottoms of jam jars, and worse, what appeared to be his last two or three remaining teeth were an alarming shade of yellow. The sleeves of his horrible, hairy suit jacket were so shiny Corlene would have bet money, if she'd had any money, that neither jacket nor sleeves had ever been within a mile of a dry cleaner. Under his hideous jacket he wore an equally hideous mustard polyester shirt with a long pointed collar in a style that may have been popular in the early 1970s. His trousers, which appeared to be on the short side, were held up by a piece of yellow string. On his feet he wore manure-encrusted wellington boots.

Calm down, calm down, Corlene told herself silently. *This is nothing more than a misunderstanding. I will leave here, go down the street to the other Pajo's bar, where a sophisticated, casually dressed man will be anxiously checking his watch while sipping a martini and helping himself to the olives supplied by the young waiter.* How she and the sophisticated, casually dressed man would laugh their heads off when she regaled him with the story of the old crone and this...this leech-like nightmare of a creature standing in front of her, assessing her as if she were nothing more than a piece of meat.

She had almost reached a state of calm at the prospect of meeting her real date when she became aware that the creature was walking around her in circles. Before she could react, he gave her a massive whack on her rear end – much in the style of a farmer at a cattle fair – and growled, 'You'll do.' Wheeling around towards the old crone, he wheezed, 'She's grand, eh, Mam? No spring chicken like, but she'll do.'

Oh God, Corlene thought, *this is the right pub after all. There will be no casually dressed landowner, no martini and no olives.* This was it. This was what she was reduced to. As she looked into the eyes of this hideous creature and the old woman who was presumably his mother, the true depths of her situation struck her. Even she could do nothing with this guy. He was beyond all help.

With as much dignity as she could muster, she looked the pair of them in the eye and said, 'I'm afraid there's been a terrible mistake. Now, if you'll excuse me, I have to go.'

Turning on her heel, she half limped, half ran out the door and didn't stop until she found a park bench, where she collapsed and slowly came to terms with the fact that she had burned her last bridge.

Corlene Holbrooke decided that for the first time in her life, as terrible and all as that prospect was, she had no other option. She would simply have to get a job.

She hobbled back to the hotel. Rounding a street corner, she almost tripped over Dylan, who had just got off the bus from Cork.

'Hey, Mom. Something amazing just happened. I must find Ellen and Conor to tell them.'

'How 'bout you tell me instead?' Corlene responded coolly.

Dylan looked at her, clearly taken aback. 'Well, I don't think it's really your thing, but OK, sure. I went for an interview today to a music college here – well, not here exactly, in Cork. That's where Laoise is from. You know my friend I told you about…' He blushed as the words tumbled out. 'Anyway, they said I could enrol and learn to play the uilleann pipes. That's the instrument I was talking about at dinner the other night. Laoise's dad, Diarmuid, he plays them. They're just so cool. Anyway, they said they'd help me, Diarmuid and Siobhán – that's Laoise's parents. So they're gonna help me to get set up and all that, and I'm gonna stay here and study music.'

Corlene was temporarily speechless. The fact that her son didn't feel the need to ask her permission to stay on in this country hit her like a truck. Here was the only person in her life who would notice if she dropped dead, and yet she was such a crap mother it had never occurred to him that certain choices he made would impact her. He most likely thought she would be delighted to get rid of him. Suddenly, an emotional dam burst inside her. She was his mother – she couldn't let him go. He was only seventeen, and he'd never lived away from her. Surely he didn't mean it. All her years of neglect came into sharp focus, and she finally realised that he had made a sacrifice to leave his friends and his band and come to Ireland with her in order to prevent her from doing something stupid yet again. All his life she had dragged him from place to place, from school to school, never once taking into consideration how he felt about it.

The accumulation of the day's troubling events were by now taking their toll. Corlene had often heard that in order to make a better life for themselves eventually, alcoholics and addicts often had to first go through the experience of hitting rock bottom. Stealing from that young hairdresser, the encounter with the dreadful Pa and his crone of a mother and now the prospect of losing Dylan had achieved precisely that for Corlene. She had sunk lower than ever before. Enough was enough.

'Hey, Dylan, I think it's time we talked – properly, I mean,' Corlene said. 'Let's go up to my room and order some food.'

While they waited for room service, Corlene began to explain the details of her dire financial situation. She apologised for being such a lousy mother, admitted to the credit card scam with the hairdresser and described the full horror of the Pajo's bar encounter and everything that had led up to it. Hard and all as it might be for him to believe, she added, she loved him and was proud of him. She, on the other hand, had run out of cash and had no skills to fall back on. All they could do was go home and stay with her mother for a while. Maybe she could do a computer course or something. It broke her heart to say it, she added tearfully, but there was no way she could afford 6,000 euros to let Dylan stay on in Ireland.

Dylan was bitterly disappointed but tried his best to hide it. It was comforting to hear his mom say she loved him, and he felt enormously relieved that she was giving up man hunting and was going to get a real job. But what about him? All this meant that he had to leave Ireland, abandon the prospect of proper music training and, worst of all, abandon Laoise. He felt like a flash of a new, better life had been offered to him and then quickly snatched away again.

Grandma didn't have the kind of cash he needed, Corlene told him gently. Even if Diarmuid and Siobhán allowed him to stay in their house, there would be college fees, books and materials as well as transport to pay for. Reluctantly, he had to agree she was right. His mother was being honest and kind for the first time in her life, and he believed her when she said that if there was a way she could help him financially, she would do it, but unfortunately, there wasn't. He resolved to not make her feel bad about it. Maybe he could go home, get a job and reapply next year.

CHAPTER 27

*P*atrick lay on his back contemplating the peeling ceiling, feeling a contentment the likes of which he had never previously experienced. *This house sure is in need of some attention*, he thought. His apartment in Boston was built in the 1970s and was looked after by a maintenance company, so he rarely got a chance to do much DIY. As a kid he had enjoyed helping neighbours fix things up, but that was in the days when people actually fixed things rather than threw them away and bought new stuff.

The sound of Cynthia stirring brought him back to the present. He looked down at this extraordinary woman nestling on his shoulder. She moved closer to him, sighed and then fell back asleep. She was exhausted because they had stayed awake most of the night discussing their future. He knew things were happening fast, but he had no doubts.

Patrick had never previously understood why women wanted to call sex making love, but now he completely understood. He also knew he had finally come home in every sense of the word. He decided to tender his resignation that very day, and apart from a quick trip back to Boston to sell his apartment and tie up some loose ends, he was moving to Ireland.

They would get married here and live out their days together in this beautiful place, his homeland. Cynthia had told him that she had inherited her late uncle's house, so maybe they could fix it up and live here? His pension would be enough to allow them to live comfortably, and maybe they could invest the money from the sale of his apartment in her horse-breeding business. Cynthia certainly seemed to know what she was about in that department, and Patrick was excited at the thought of learning something completely new.

Never in a million years had he envisaged anything like this happening. The way he had imagined Ireland had been all wrong. He found no kindred political spirits, no sense of outrage at the years of British oppression. Instead, he had found something profoundly better. For many years, he had harboured hopes of meeting someone, settling down and all that, but as the decades passed, such a possibility seemed less and less likely. He never knew why exactly, and he finally accepted that he was just not the kind of guy women wanted.

Sitting with Cynthia in the courtyard café yesterday, he felt like he was living a whole lifetime in one day. They had talked about work, friends, God, crime and punishment, Irishness and anything else that occurred to them. Never before had he felt so uninhibited with anyone.

Sure, everyone saw Patrick as the big, loud Irish American, but underneath all the bluster, he knew he was a shy man, especially when it came to the opposite sex. He had been burned in the past, and his self-confidence in relation to matters romantic was zero. His sexual experiences had been a catalogue of disasters. He recalled some truly horrendous dates that had ended in embarrassment, with women saying not to worry, it was common, it happened to lots of guys. But Patrick knew they didn't mean it and that he wouldn't be hearing from them again. He got so nervous he just couldn't perform, and most women took it personally. The result was he avoided the entire sex thing altogether.

That was the thing about Cynthia, though; it was as if she weren't a woman – well, obviously she was a woman, but she wasn't like any other woman he had ever met before. He could talk to her.

As the afternoon turned to evening, she fixed him with a stare. 'Must you go back to the tour tonight?'

Patrick didn't dare think what he half hoped and half dreaded she was suggesting. 'I'm on vacation.' He smiled. 'I can do what I want.'

With that she seemed to take a deep breath and said, 'I hope you won't imagine me forward, Patrick, my dear. I'm afraid I've rather lost the touch of wooing, as it were. Not sure I ever had it actually. How and ever, I want to say this. I have never met anyone like you, and although I've only known you a very short time, I feel, well, rather taken with you actually. Normally I don't speak like this. Well, normally I don't meet anyone with whom I feel any desire to speak like this. But what I am trying, albeit rather clumsily, to say is that I like you, Patrick, quite a bit in fact, and I don't want you to walk out of my life now, just when we are getting to know each other. So perhaps do you think you could, or would like to...possibly...stay? Here? Well, not exactly here in this café, but here in Ireland. With me. For a while or...?'

Patrick's life, suddenly, for the first time in fifty-six years, made sense. He knew why he had been put on this earth. Never before in his dealings with women had he been confident to take the initiative, but this was different. He stood up and took Cynthia's hand and led her over to the sunny side of the old house. As they walked, he slipped his sovereign ring off his little finger and put it in his pocket. Then he stopped, and looking deep into Cynthia's eyes, he said, 'Cynthia, I don't know what's happened to me, but today is the best day of my life so far, bar none. You think you're bad at this romantic stuff? Well, let me tell you, I am a whole lot worse. I have never managed to keep a relationship going longer than three dates, but with you it feels so different. I don't know what you are talking about most of the time, and you kinda mystify me, but I know one thing – I love you. And now that I know you, I can't ever imagine being away from you, even for a second. I always thought that love at first sight was a crazy thing made up by people who wrote dime-store novels and schmaltzy movies, but it's not. It's happening to me, and to you too, I hope. So I can't think of any reason why we should waste one more second of this life apart. I don't have much, but what I have is yours. You are beautiful, amazing, funny and kinda crazy, and I love you so much I can't even tell you.'

He took her hand and dropped onto one knee. Taking his ring from his pocket, he said, 'Cynthia, will you marry me?'

Cynthia's eyes filled with tears, and as she put the huge ring on her finger, she said, 'Yes, I will. Right now if possible.'

There have been many great kisses in history, but everyone who stood in the courtyard that day and cheered for the happy couple was sure that Patrick and Cynthia's embrace was the most passionate they had ever seen.

They left the café, having drunk the bottle of champagne that Charlie had insisted on opening, and they headed for Cynthia's uncle's house near Kinsale. As they walked into the large, dusty hallway, an ominous scurrying could be heard as the rodent population made way for the guests.

Cynthia put her arms around Patrick's waist and looked him in the eye, which she could easily do as she was almost as tall as him. 'Patrick, is this really happening? I am having to pinch myself to believe it. You see, I invited you here but...I must admit to you now that I didn't really have a plan when I did. The thing is, you see, that I...' Cynthia blushed a deep red. 'I suppose one had better be honest. I did have a rather misguided affair many years ago, as I told you, but it was never, well, properly...consummated, as it were. I have never been with, well, a man...before. Well, I mean, I have been with men, in their company as it were, but not in the...in the sort of, well, bed sense...if you understand me, and so I am not sure what – if indeed anything – one is actually supposed to do. Oh Lord, you must think me ridiculous,' she finished in a state of acute embarrassment.

Patrick, for the first time in his life, felt no anxiety. 'Cynthia, sweetheart, I am so honoured that you would consider me at all. Let me tell you something. I've spent the past forty years or so terrified of girls. I was scared that I couldn't live up to their standards and have them screaming with multiple orgasms or whatever it is guys are supposed to do. Hell, I even bought a couple of women's magazines over the years to try to figure out what they wanted from me. The results were nothing less than disastrous, I gotta tell you. In the end, I just gave up. It seemed I either came too soon or else couldn't get it up at all. I was a mess. So the last time I was in a potentially intimate situation with a woman was sometime in the 1980s, and after that terrible experience, I swore off sex for good. So here we are. You may not be any Mata Hari, but guess what? I'm no Casanova either. But it's just us here. Nobody's taking notes or making comparisons. So what do you say we just go upstairs and relax and talk and see what happens? No pressure, OK?'

The lines of worry that had creased Cynthia's face disappeared as she took Patrick's hand and they climbed the stairs.

CHAPTER 28

*C*onor leaned over to silence the persistent trilling of his mobile phone alarm clock on the bedside locker. He had slept badly, for what had seemed like only a few minutes. Now it was time to get his tour group on the road once again. Running through the itinerary for the day, he squirmed at the prospect of the most immediate drama to be dealt with, and all the logistical and other complications associated with it – Dorothy's court appearance.

He had spoken to her solicitor, who seemed to think that the charges against her were serious. She couldn't go into any detail without her client's permission, but she needed him to know that Juliet and Anna could be called as witnesses and there would be a preliminary and possibly even a full hearing of the case that day. *By God, this has turned into a right fiasco*, he thought as he stood under the shower.

And that wasn't the only fiasco on his hands. There was the whole Sinead situation to contend with. In her latest email she was going on as if they were already a couple, and he wasn't at all sure how he felt about that. Ellen, Bert and Anastasia did not seem overly enthusiastic about it either; to a person, they reckoned she was an opportunist. And then there was this whole business about the cancer. She had mentioned in one of her early emails that it wasn't looking good, but despite him asking her repeatedly how she was doing and if she was having treatment, she just ignored the questions. *Maybe she just doesn't want to talk about it,* he thought. *But moving countries in the middle of cancer treatment surely cannot be advisable. On the other hand, maybe it's too late...maybe she's coming home to die.*

This realisation struck him forcefully. God almighty, how was he supposed to deal with that? Not to mention deal with the young lad. Conor wasn't at all sure he was the right person to take this boy on. Sure, they were related, but he'd only found out his nephew existed last week!

If she was coming home to die, she wouldn't be writing emails hinting at coupledom. Would she? Conor thought his head would explode with the worry of it all.

In the meantime, he had no option but to head to the dining room, round up as many of his charges as he could find and take it from there. As he put on his jacket, he heard his mobile beep with an incoming text message. It was from Anastasia.

Have a good day! :) X

Well, at least she was still talking to him. She had obviously put their somewhat strange conversation of the previous day behind her. Maybe she had patched things up with her boyfriend. Conor wondered who he was; he couldn't remember ever seeing her with anyone. Well, he was a lucky man whoever he was anyhow.

You too x, he replied.

At least that was one less thing to worry about. He sighed as he gathered up his wallet, keys and phone. It was going to be a long day, and he groaned inwardly.

As he walked into the small private dining room reserved for his tour group, his eyes alighted on Cynthia. She was chatting away animatedly to Patrick. *Aha, so that's what's been going on,* Conor thought. *That's where Patrick disappeared to on his free day!*

Anna and Juliet appeared in the doorway behind him.

'Juliet!' Conor said. 'How are you doing? God love you, you must have got a terrible fright altogether. I'm so sorry I wasn't here to help, but I was driving Ellen over to West Cork to see where her ancestors came from. I feel terrible for abandoning you.'

Juliet smiled. 'Conor, don't be silly. I'm fine. A bit battered and bruised, but I'll live. You...nobody could have predicted what happened. Have you heard any news of Dorothy?'

'Only from her solicitor. Spoke to her last night. She said Dorothy is in serious trouble. There's a court hearing this morning. They don't usually deal with things this quickly, but I suppose it's because you're all here for such a short time. Anna, I'm afraid both you and Juliet are to be called as witnesses. The solicitor asked me to tell you to be in court at 10:00 a.m. this morning. Lord save us, I can't believe how things have turned out.'

Anna put her hand on his shoulder. 'Conor, please stop blaming yourself. None of this is your fault. Dorothy just flipped. We should be grateful that Juliet needed nothing more than a few stitches. It could have been so much worse.'

'What about the tour?' Juliet asked. 'I don't want everyone else put out because of this.'

'I think the best thing to do is to get everyone together and have a chat about it. If the hearing is this morning, who knows, maybe it will be all over by lunchtime and then we can carry on. I suggest we just see how things go this morning, and we'll make a decision at lunchtime when we know more.'

BERT FINISHED his breakfast and observed Corlene as she sat, staring into her coffee despondently. She looked different. She was wearing a sweatshirt and jeans, and her face was devoid of make-up. Her hair was scraped back into a clip of some kind. Bert thought she looked much nicer that way, although she probably wouldn't have believed him if he told her. He strolled over to her table. 'Well, good morning, Miss Corlene. Do you mind if I join you?'

'Sure.' She sighed, all trace of the coquettish charm gone.

'No Dylan today?' asked Bert kindly.

'He's upstairs I guess.'

'Is everything OK?'

Corlene sat back, weighing up whether or not she should confide in this man. 'We had a big talk last night. First one in, oh, I don't know, maybe *ever*. It seems he has decided that he wants to stay here and learn to play some unpronounceable Irish musical instrument. It's strange really. I'm the one who came to Ireland looking for something, but he's the one who's actually found it.'

'He's a nice kid. I must admit, however, that when I first saw him, I thought he looked like something from a scary movie. But over the past few days, I've gotten to know him a little bit. Ellen gets on so well with him, so I just kinda tagged along. He's really fired up about this music, you know. You can hear it in his voice when he talks about it.'

'Yes, I know. The thing about it is this, Bert. You see…uh…I haven't been a great mom to him and that's the truth. He's been the one taking care of me, if I'm honest with you. He only came on this trip to try to stop me doing something dumb like finding a rich new husband.'

'Well, maybe a husband isn't what you need.'

'Ain't that the truth. It's just that I've never done anything remotely useful, so it's hard to know where to start. Having Dylan was an accident, and as I said, I've been a pretty crap role model. I want to let him stay here, but he's so young. I know he's got more sense in his little finger than I do in my whole stupid body, but I still can't let him stay in a foreign country on his own, even if I had the money for the fees and everything, which I don't.'

'Well, I don't know much about your situation, Miss Corlene, but maybe you could stay here with him?'

'And live on what? Fresh air?' She smiled. 'Nah, that is most definitely not an option. It's a pity, though. I would have liked to have done something good for him for a change.'

Dylan approached the table. 'Hi, Mom. Hi, Bert.'

Bert couldn't get over the transformation. Gone were the tattoos and the scary spikes on one side of his head. Dylan's hair was now cut short all over. Like his mother, he was devoid of make-up, and he was wearing a normal-looking T-shirt and jeans. 'Wow, Dylan, you look so...so different!' Bert exclaimed.

'Yeah, I went to a hair place this morning to get it cut. They were open extra early because of a wedding or something. At first, the lady didn't want to take me, but then she said she would be doing the whole world a favour if she got rid of the spikes. My God, she was funny. Oh, Mom, I left the envelope in there like you asked, but I don't think I spelled the name right. Ashlynn, I think I wrote. Anyway, she was the one who cut my hair. She asked me who the envelope was from. I said I didn't know, and she opened it and took out the money.'

Bert noticed the glance Corlene gave her son, one that suggested he shut up.

'What about those tattoos? Surely you didn't get them removed overnight too?' Bert asked jokingly.

'Nah, they were just temporary. I might put them back on again sometime, but I just felt like a change of image. Laoise – she's my friend – she's got a little tattoo of a treble clef on her neck, and it's like totally awesome. So I might get something like that.' Dylan then began to wolf his breakfast.

As he exchanged a shared smile with Corlene over Dylan's bent head, Bert's eyes were drawn to the door. Ellen walked in looking bright and happy. He was relieved. He knew she wouldn't be cross that he had returned to Killarney without her. But at the same time, he would have hated her to feel that he had deserted her. He walked over and gave her a hug.

'Hello, Bert. Well, here I am. In one piece. Mary very kindly drove me back this morning. I have so much to tell you. Such an incredible day.'

Their chat was interrupted by Conor addressing them all. 'Well, folks, I have a few things to tell you. I must say, this has been the most eventful trip I've ever had. I'll cut to the chase. There was an incident yesterday involving an assault. I'm sorry to say that it seems Dorothy attacked Juliet, who spent last night in hospital.'

The group looked shocked and gathered round Juliet, asking if she was OK.

'I'm fine,' she assured them. 'Just a few stitches. I'm right as rain.'

Conor continued. 'Elliot Heller has left the tour and won't be rejoining us.'

Anna smiled gratefully as Juliet squeezed her hand and Patrick patted her on the back.

'In addition to that, Dorothy Crane is in the local Garda station awaiting a court hearing, which is due to take place this morning. So if no one else has any big news, I was going to suggest that we wait until lunchtime to move on with the tour. Anna and Juliet are both to be called as witnesses for the court hearing. If Dorothy's case is called first, then we can base our next move on the outcome of the court case. Is that OK with everyone?'

General murmurs of agreement emanated from the group, most of whom were stunned at the news of Dorothy's situation.

As Conor turned to leave, Patrick approached him. 'Everything OK, Patrick? I see you went back to Cork yesterday,' he added with a smile.

Patrick struggled to find the words. 'Uh, yeah. I sure did. Conor...I was wondering if – now, it may not be allowed...and I totally understand – but uh...would it be OK if Cynthia joined us for the end of the tour? I will pay, of course. It's just that I'd like to...' Patrick blushed beetroot red with embarrassment.

Conor resisted the urge to tease him. 'Well, Patrick, I'm only insured to carry the originally booked members of the tour with me, but so much off-the-wall stuff has gone on on this tour, I can probably bend the rules a bit since it's only for two more nights. Anyway, the departure of Elliot Heller means that we now have one free space. On the money front, don't worry about it. I won't say anything if you don't. On the hotel thing, well, if you need another room, I'm sure the Dunshane can oblige. Just pay for any extra meals. I'll square it with the manager.'

Patrick's wide grin almost cracked his face in two. 'That's great, Conor, really great! Thanks, buddy!' he said, giving Conor a high five.

CHAPTER 29

*D*iarmuid, Laoise and Siobhán arrived into the dining room just as everyone was about to leave. They spotted Dylan's table and waved.

'Oh, hi, guys,' Dylan said, introducing them to Corlene and Bert. 'These are my friends from Cork who offered to help me with the music college,' he said by way of explanation. 'I'm so sorry to have to say this, and I'm really, *really* grateful. It's totally amazing that you would offer to help me like that. But I spoke to my mom last night, and it's just not gonna be doable. I really do want to learn the pipes and stay here, but even if I stayed with you guys, we don't have the money for the fees or to buy books or anything. But I was thinking maybe I could get a job back in the States for a year or two and save hard and then come back and try to get in again.'

'What? Ah no!' cried Laoise. 'Surely you can find the money somehow?'

'No, Laoise. Mom and I talked about it all night. There's just no way. Believe me, no one is sorrier about this than me,' he said, visibly upset.

'But –' Laoise began.

Siobhán interrupted her. 'Laoise, it's really not our business. Well,

Dylan, the offer is there. I do understand it's a lot of money, and I'm not sure I'd allow Laoise to go and live in America if the situation were reversed, so it's Corlene and Dylan's decision.'

Corlene gazed at this extraordinary Irish woman. She was dressed like a yoga teacher, she thought, floor-length skirt and a tie-dyed T-shirt that Corlene wouldn't be seen dead in, but she seemed nice, trustworthy.

'Can I get you a coffee?' Corlene asked her. 'We all have to wait around here in the hotel until lunchtime, for a reason that I just couldn't begin to explain. So you might as well.'

Dylan and Laoise looked at each other. 'Er, we might just go for a walk, OK?' Laoise announced, and without waiting for an answer, grabbed Dylan by the hand and dragged him away.

Diarmuid's mobile rang and he moved out to the corridor to take his call.

Corlene continued her assessment of the woman sitting opposite her. She had lived her entire life in a world where nobody gave anybody anything for nothing. She wondered what was in it for this Irish family. This woman, 'Shove-on' or whatever she was called, struck her as someone who liked straight-talking. 'I hope this won't come across as rude or ungrateful,' she said, 'but why did you offer to help my son? I mean, you barely know him. And let's face it, anyone can see he is crazy about your daughter. So why are you offering to bring this stranger who has designs on your youngest child into your home? I'm failing to see the angle here.'

Siobhán held up her hands. 'It's a fair question. One I would be asking in your position too. So no, I don't think you're rude. You're being a mother. You're looking out for your child. We told Dylan that everything hung on your agreement. OK, we made the offer for two reasons. Firstly, Diarmuid is totally incapable of denying Laoise anything, and she wants Dylan to stay in Ireland. Secondly, though, and this is the bigger reason, Diarmuid really loves the pipes and lots of people helped him when he was young. None of his family was particularly into traditional music, so he was dependent on the kindness of strangers, who shared their love of the instrument and talent with him in order to help him get to where he is today.

'He has been fairly successful, and we have built a good life for ourselves and our kids, largely funded by music. If nobody had helped him when he was young, then none of that could have happened and he would probably have spent his life working in a bank or on a building site instead of doing what he loves. He has passed his talent on to our kids, and they all are stuck in the music world. I suppose with Dylan, Diarmuid sees it as his chance to pay something back. Does that make sense?

'I know Dylan is mad about Laoise, but I can tell you she's more than able to stand up for herself. If I were to be worried about anyone, I have to say it's Dylan I'd be worried about, to be honest. My husband is a very easy-going man, but when it comes to his daughters, he wouldn't stand for any carry-on from boys. He's made that abundantly clear to Dylan.'

Corlene laughed. 'I would have liked to be able to do this for him. I'm his mother, but I guess I haven't always been a great role model. It's not an excuse, I know, but I was a single mom and I spent all my time trying to find the perfect marriage. Not everyone is as lucky as you, you know!'

Siobhán gave a throaty chuckle and said, 'Are you joking or what? We don't have a perfect relationship, I can assure you. Diarmuid and I *do have* an understanding, though. I don't give in to every notion he takes, and he doesn't give in to every one of mine. But if one of us says that something is important, then the other tends to accept it. It's worked for the past twenty-five years, so we'll probably stick with that strategy.'

'Sounds like a good plan,' Corlene agreed. 'When I said a few minutes ago that I wasn't always a great role model, that was to understate the case. I'm sure Dylan told you I was a lousy mom. We had a big, long talk about everything last night – probably the first time I've ever had a proper conversation with him. I know how much this music study thing means to him – studying that pipe thing that I can't pronounce – and I *really* do wish there was some way I could help him to make this happen, but I'm flat broke. It's just impossible.' Eyes brimming with tears, she added, 'I do love him, you know.'

Siobhán handed her a tissue. 'Of course you do. Being a mother isn't an easy road for anyone, despite how it appears to an outsider. I can tell you there have been times when I've been fit to murder all of mine – mostly Laoise, it must be said. But at the end of the day, they're your kids and you'd do anything for them. It's as simple as that.'

Corlene smiled gratefully. At last, someone who didn't judge her.

'Look, I completely understand if you don't want Dylan to stay with us, even if you had the money. I mean, as I said, I wouldn't probably allow it if the situation were reversed. I can barely manage Laoise when I have her in my sights, let alone if she was left to her own devices. God alone knows what she'd get up to. But our offer stands, and maybe he can work for a while in the States and make the fees and then come back.'

Corlene trusted this 'Shove-on' person. God, why couldn't she be called something simple like Mary? At least she'd be able to pronounce that. The woman was honest and sincere. Dylan would be safe with her and her husband, safer probably than he would be with Corlene herself if she were to be honest. 'Maybe he could get a job. But he doesn't have any skills, so I think it would take a long time to save up for the fees. But it's such a shame. Music is all he ever talks about. I've never achieved that much in my own life, and I've spent all my time trying. I would like to think that Dylan will be different.'

Siobhán thought for a moment. 'Well, my husband seems to think he has great potential. So that's good enough for me. He's very rarely wrong on anything to do with music, and he's a great judge of character. Pity I can't say the same for his housekeeping or organisational skills. But I suppose you can't have it all.'

Both women laughed knowingly, and Corlene felt a pang of envy. From the easy way Siobhán spoke about her husband, it was obvious that they really loved each other. Not in the way that Corlene had always dreamed about – expensive presents and romantic gestures – but something deeper, more solid. Dylan would really benefit from living with these people, get to see what a real family was like, how they lived, how they handled life.

'Thank you, Shove-on. I was suspicious when Dylan told me about your offer, but now that I've met you and Diarmuid, I can see you are good people. I really would love for Dylan to get this chance. But unfortunately, it's a chance that I just can't give him,' Corlene said with an audible sigh.

'What will the two of you do now? When you go back to the States?'

'Well, right now I guess we don't have a plan. The tour is paid for, so we have somewhere to sleep for the next two nights. Then we fly home. But after that? Who knows. Don't worry about us, though. Something will turn up – it always does,' she added with a confidence she didn't feel.

Siobhán resisted the urge to offer suggestions. She was always being teased by her family for being a fixer. It was unusual that on this occasion Diarmuid was the one who was behind the plan to help Dylan. Corlene needed to sort herself out, Siobhán thought, and she sincerely hoped for everyone's sake it wouldn't be in the shape of husband number five.

As the two women walked down the corridor to the hotel lobby, Siobhán took out her phone and started writing a text message to her husband. Just as she pressed 'send', she looked up to see a small crowd gathered near the reception desk. An impromptu concert seemed to be underway. Laoise was singing a melody and Dylan was trying to accompany her on the whistle. The pair of them were sprawled on a sofa, blissfully unaware of their audience. Eventually, Dylan spotted Siobhán and his mother, and his face suffused with worry.

'It's OK, Dylan,' Corlene reassured him. 'I didn't say anything embarrassing.'

He stood up smiling as Siobhán approached and drew him into a hug. 'Well, I suppose it's goodbye, Dylan, at least for now. I'm so sorry things didn't work out for you. As I told your mam, the offer is open-ended, and so if you're ever thinking of coming back to Ireland for any reason at all, just let us know.'

Diarmuid lifted his head out of the book he had been engrossed in and stood up. 'We'll see you again, Dylan. Don't forget there's a set of pipes there for you to borrow any time at all. You've been bitten by the bug now, so you won't shake it off that easily. There are a few fine players over in America too, you know, who could teach you. I'll send you some names in an email. Don't give up on it anyway – now sure you won't?'

Dylan followed them out to the car park, gripping Laoise's hand all the way. Corlene, Siobhán and Diarmuid made small talk about the hotel landscaping as the two young people clung to each other.

'I thought you could stay. It would have been so cool,' Laoise said, tears rolling down her cheeks.

'I'll come back, Laoise. I promise. I don't know how, but I'll try my very best. You are the coolest girl on the planet, and I can't believe you could like someone like me,' he said, gripping her hand even tighter.

As Diarmuid drove out of the hotel grounds, Corlene stood with her arm around her son, wishing with all her heart that things could have worked out differently.

From a bedroom window upstairs, Bert Cooper watched, drinking in every detail.

CHAPTER 30

*D*orothy Crane did her best to freshen up at the small stainless steel sink in the corner of her cell. She was due to meet her solicitor at the courthouse and would be driven the short distance from the Garda station to the courthouse in a squad car. The prospect of what lay ahead made her cringe. The humiliation of it! Thank God nobody out there in the real world was remotely interested in what went on in this little bog hole of a country, she thought viciously. At least she would be able to get this nonsense over with today, then go home and forget about it. Apart from Juliet, no one needed to know a thing about it. She would swear Juliet to secrecy somehow. What had happened to that woman? She was normally such a little mouse, and had always struck Dorothy as a bit fragile mentally. No doubt Juliet was now crippled with guilt over her harsh and totally unnecessary words to Dorothy. Well, she'd have to do some grovelling if she wanted Dorothy Crane to take her on a trip ever again!

These and similar thoughts had gone around and around in her head all night long as sleep evaded her. The possibility of being held on remand while awaiting trial, or some other worst-case scenario, she simply refused to entertain. This whole situation she found herself in was a complete farce. Juliet had just slipped and banged her head. It was as simple as that. Bungling, small-minded provincial cops playing at being proper policemen, with all their stupid unpronounceable Irish names – really it was laughable. They probably didn't have more than one second-rate university in this entire country. They couldn't even begin to understand how inappropriate it was that a person of her academic standing would find herself in this ridiculous position.

She wondered if she should check out whether this Lucinda McAuliffe woman was even a proper attorney. It was quite likely that the same standards of legal training didn't apply in this backwater. Hadn't Conor told them that often in Ireland the local storekeeper was also the undertaker and the congressman or whatever? This little nugget of information had raised a big laugh from those simpletons on the tour, but now she wondered what a person actually needed in order to qualify to practise law here. Perhaps her fate was now in the hands of a woman who doubled up as a hairdresser for God's sake!

She looked up as the observation panel on the door was moved to the side. The young uniformed man from yesterday addressed her, although his accent was so impenetrable, she couldn't make out what he was saying.

'OK, Ms Crane. It's time to go. Your solicitor will meet you in court. There's a big case being heard today, so be prepared for a wait.'

Dorothy threw him one of the looks she reserved for undergraduates she considered too stupid to take her course. The young Garda made polite conversation as they made their way to the squad car. 'What part of America do you come from?'

'Iowa,' she snapped, indicating clearly that she was in no humour for small talk.

'Oh, right,' said the Garda. 'I was never there.'

'No,' said Dorothy, dripping with sarcasm, 'I wouldn't have imagined you were.'

'No, I never went that far west. I did my master's in ethnic conflict at NYU after I qualified with a law degree here. I really enjoyed it. It was interesting to see the difference in approaches to crime prevention between the States and Ireland. There's much bigger ethnic diversity in the States obviously, compared with here in Ireland, so it was a great place to learn first-hand about various world cultures and how conflict between them can be tackled.'

Dorothy gaped incredulously at the young Garda. 'Are you telling me you have a degree and you are working as a police officer?'

The Garda seemed amused by her question. 'Well, most of the younger generation of Garda Síochána have third-level qualifications. I am actually studying for a PhD in Islamic studies at the moment. I think problems between Irish nationals and those with Muslim belief systems – racism in various forms, if you like – will be a source of major conflict in this country in years to come. We as law enforcers need to understand as much as possible about these cultural practices and belief systems in order to deal with potential conflicts efficiently and sympathetically.'

Before Dorothy had time to respond sarcastically to his mini-tutorial, the squad car pulled up in front of a large, grey limestone building. As the car door opened, Dorothy noticed to her horror two television cameramen and several photographers lined up to her right. Surely to God her case didn't warrant this amount of media attention? As she emerged from the car and headed for the courthouse, the media scrum moved back when they saw that she wasn't the person they were waiting for after all.

'I mentioned to you that there was a high-profile case being heard today. Big drugs seizure off the coast. It was a joint operation between ourselves and Interpol. There'll be lots of international press here too,' the Garda said as he ushered her into the building through a side door. 'This entrance leads directly to the cells, so I'll leave you there, and you'll be called when they're ready to hear your case. I wouldn't be holding my breath if I were you, though.'

Dorothy sat seething on a plastic chair – literally the only furniture in the cell apart from a scarred and battered table – as she awaited the arrival of her attorney, who, for some ridiculous reason, was called a solicitor in this country.

'Good morning, Ms Crane,' said her solicitor as she was ushered in by a female Garda. 'I hope your night wasn't too unpleasant.'

'It was dreadful. I never slept a wink. And now apparently I must wait until some big drug case is heard before I can even get into court. Really, this is *intolerable*. Can't you do anything? I mean you are *supposed* to be my attorney,' Dorothy snapped.

Lucinda McAuliffe withdrew a file from her briefcase and sat down. In calm, measured tones, she said, 'Ms Crane, it seems to me that you are failing to grasp the gravity of your situation. You are charged with a serious assault. On top of that, you made efforts to bribe a member of An Garda Síochána. These two acts show a lack of respect for the law and for law enforcement in this country. I think we should focus our efforts on how best to defend you, spend less of our time grumbling, shall we? Now, as I see it, the testimony of the two witnesses for the state, Mrs...em...' she said, flicking through the file to find her notes. 'Mrs Juliet Steele and Mrs Anna Heller will be pivotal. If they are damning in their evidence, then I'm afraid things may go very poorly indeed. Can you give me any indication of how you think they will present the story to the court?'

The extent of the trouble she was in had finally become apparent to Dorothy. 'I'm sure they will tell the truth,' she said quietly.

'Well, then,' Lucinda McAuliffe replied, 'we'll just have to wait and see. In the meantime, you should know I have requested that your case be heard first – before the drugs case – as that is likely to go on for some time. We should expect to be called any moment. It is important that you speak civilly and respectfully to the judge, whom you should address as "Judge". Judge Condon is sitting today, and let me assure you, she takes no prisoners, if you pardon the unfortunate pun.'

Dorothy just stared at her, unwilling and unable to react to her incarceration-based humour.

'Judge Condon has a reputation for being sharp and will not spare you if she feels you are holding her or the court in contempt. Answer any questions you are asked honestly and clearly and try to ensure that you do not display even the slightest hint of derision in anything you say. Believe me, you are in no position to display anything but abject and true remorse.

'I will argue that you did not intend to harm Mrs Steele and that you are genuinely sorry for any pain you have caused her. As regards the bribery issue, I will simply plead that, having never been in any trouble before, you panicked and had a momentary lapse of judgement for which you are extremely sorry. You will then, if given the opportunity, apologise to the court and to Detective O'Keeffe for casting aspersions on his integrity. Whether or not the case is dismissed, or whether you are sent forward for trial, will depend to a large extent on Mrs Steele's testimony. However, I must warn you that it will also depend on your demeanour. For your own sake, I hope you can manage to come across as very, *very* contrite. Now do you have any questions before we go?'

Dorothy reflected on her earlier idea of questioning this McAuliffe woman's credentials but thought better of it. It appeared that right now she was Dorothy's only possible hope of an escape from this nightmare situation, so she probably shouldn't take the risk of antagonising her. 'I just have one question,' she said quietly. 'Based on your experience, what would you say are my chances of having the charges dropped?'

Lucinda McAuliffe noticed the change in attitude in her client and decided to take pity on her and err on the side of optimism. 'About fifty-fifty, I'd say. Are you ready?'

* * *

CONOR, Bert, Ellen, Patrick and Cynthia sat together in the public gallery watching the seemingly endless comings and goings of Gardaí, solicitors and bewigged barristers. Anna and Juliet had been ushered off to a separate area by a court official.

'It sure is nice to be in a courtroom gallery for a change,' Patrick whispered to Cynthia with a suppressed giggle.

'Why? Are you often in the dock? Perhaps I should have investigated your background a little more thoroughly before agreeing to hitch my wagon to yours, as you Yanks would say.'

Their conversation was interrupted by the clanging of a large wooden door behind the ornate mahogany bench, signalling the arrival of the clerk of the court.

'All rise,' the clerk announced as a tiny woman sporting half-moon spectacles emerged from her chambers and took her seat in the middle of the bench.

'She looks just like Judge Judy!' Anna whispered to Juliet.

The clerk spoke loudly. 'First case on the list, the Director of Public Prosecutions versus Dorothy Crane.'

Conor and the others watched as Dorothy was led out. Juliet and Anna exchanged glances. In the twenty-four hours since they had laid eyes on Dorothy Crane, incredibly, the woman seemed to have shrunk in height.

Detective O'Keeffe was sworn in and began his testimony, detailing the events leading up to, and following, Dorothy's arrest.

Juliet was called next. As she was being sworn in, she could feel Dorothy's eyes boring into her.

'Please state your name,' ordered the official.

'Juliet Steele.'

The judge took off her glasses. 'Now, Mrs Steele, could you please tell the court in your own words what happened at eleven thirty on the morning of the twenty-seventh of July in the Hotel Killarney.'

Juliet had made a decision. Her life was going to be bearable for the first time since Larry died. Clearing her throat, she began. 'Dorothy and I had an argument. We are friends, and it was about something silly. I wanted to go shopping, and she wanted to go hiking. I went to Mrs Heller's room to ask her to come shopping with me. While we were standing in the doorway of Mrs Heller's room, Dorothy came down the corridor. We had words, and I said I was going to spend the day with Anna. I must have been in a bit of a temper because I wasn't looking where I was going, and I slipped and fell. I banged my head off the side of the bath. It was an accident.'

The judge consulted the papers on her desk. 'I'm looking at the

Garda report, and it states that Mrs Anna Heller said to the Gardaí who were called to the scene that Dorothy Crane pushed you. Is that not true?'

Juliet looked over at Anna. 'No, that's what it looked like from where Anna was standing because she was in the bedroom while Dorothy and I were in the bathroom. Dorothy had her back to Anna, you see. Anna saw Dorothy with her hands outstretched, and from where she was standing, it could well have looked like she pushed me, but in fact she saw I was falling and tried to grab me, I think.'

The judge nodded. 'Thank you, Mrs Steele. I wish you a speedy recovery. Now can we have Mrs Anna Heller to the stand, please?'

Anna passed Juliet and gave her a barely discernible nod. After Anna was sworn in, the judge said, 'Mrs Heller, in your opinion, did Dorothy Crane push Mrs Steele, causing her to injure herself?'

Anna stared directly at Dorothy. 'Initially, that is what I thought I saw, but as Juliet stated, I could only see Dorothy's back and I couldn't see Juliet at all, as I was in the bedroom and Juliet in the bathroom. Dorothy was standing in the bathroom doorway, so my view of the bathroom was blocked. It was only when I heard the crash and saw Juliet on the floor with blood pumping out of her head that I assumed she had been pushed. So no, to answer your question, I did not see what happened before Juliet fell.'

'Thank you, Mrs Heller. You may step down. Now I understand that there is a second element to this case. Ms Crane is also charged with attempting to pervert the course of justice and with bribing a member of the Garda Síochána. Is that correct?' The judge looked directly at Dorothy.

'That is correct, Judge,' the court clerk responded.

* * *

DOROTHY FELT NAUSEATED. Half an hour had passed since she had first taken the stand. During this time, her solicitor had presented her defence, speaking eloquently and persuasively in favour of dropping the charges. The judge seemed to be wavering and eventually asked

Dorothy if she had anything to say. Dorothy Crane had never felt so out of control of anything in her entire life. Looking around the court, she could see familiar faces in the gallery. Giving them a weak smile, which she hoped would indicate that she appreciated their support, she began addressing the court. 'I wish to take this opportunity to apologise most sincerely to my friend Juliet Steele and to the court.'

A look of relief spread across Conor's face.

'As regards the matter of the bribe I offered Detective O'Keeffe, I would like to say how incredibly sorry I am. The detective was at all times courteous and professional in his dealings with me, and he certainly never gave me any indication whatsoever that such a possibility for corruption existed. I admit to having had an ignorant attitude in terms of my dealings with the law enforcement services in Ireland, and for that, I am embarrassed and truly ashamed of myself. I would like to take this opportunity to personally apologise to Detective O'Keeffe.'

The detective gave her a slight nod, indicating that her apology had been accepted.

Juliet couldn't believe her ears. Was this the same Dorothy who looked down on everyone and everything? If it was, the transformation was nothing short of miraculous.

When Dorothy had finished speaking, the judge removed her glasses and gazed directly at her. 'Ms Crane, I understand from your file that you are an academic professor of applied physics' – she checked her file – 'at a prestigious university in the United States, which should, one would assume, mean that you are not an unintelligent woman. Yet your behaviour is not that of an intelligent, rational woman, or indeed that of a friend. However, I do accept both your and Mrs Steele's version of events. I think if Mrs Steele can let it go, then so should we, given that the nature of her injuries is relatively minor. However, I would caution you to keep your temper in check, as next time the consequences of your intemperate behaviour could be much more serious. If in the future a friend expresses a wish to go shopping, I suggest you comply with their wishes.'

A ripple of laughter spread around the courtroom. Dorothy's eyes remained fixed on the judge's face.

'In relation to the bribe, I regard this as altogether more serious because it indicates to me that you regard Ireland as in some way backwards and corrupt. Ms Crane, may I remind you that this country is a very ancient and cultured one. Indeed, it predates your own civilisation by several millennia. Prior to English rule, Ireland had its own system of law dating from Celtic times, the Brehon laws, a system that survived until the seventeenth century. The members of An Garda Síochána in this country are exemplary in carrying out their duties, and your ill-judged offer to Detective O'Keeffe showed not only an extraordinary level of ignorance but also a considerable measure of arrogance.'

The judge paused and consulted her notes for what seemed like an eternity. Eventually, she raised her head and said, 'I do, however, believe your protestations of regret, and I believe that you have learned a valuable lesson. If you travel abroad in the future, I suggest you leave aside your attitude of superiority and try to read up in advance on the country you are visiting. You never know, Ms Crane – you might actually learn something. Now I don't believe a criminal conviction would serve anybody well at this juncture, so I'm sure, Ms Crane, you would like to express your regret by making a donation to the court poor box? This fund is donated to a variety of registered charities at Christmas. Shall we say 500 euro?' The judge looked at Dorothy with raised eyebrows and waited.

Realising that she should respond appropriately and quickly, Dorothy said, 'Of course, Judge. I would be happy to agree to that.'

'Fine, Ms Crane. Go speak to my clerk now and make arrangements straight away. Case dismissed.' She banged her gavel.

Dorothy couldn't believe her ears. It was all over! She could go back to the group and forget that this nightmare had ever happened.

As Dorothy emerged in front of the courthouse, she caught sight of Lucinda McAuliffe in conversation with a barrister. She stood some distance away, waiting for them to finish.

'Well done in there,' Lucinda said pleasantly. 'You *sounded* as if you meant it anyway, so congratulations – you are free to go.'

'I would like to say something to you, if I may,' Dorothy said awkwardly. 'Firstly, I would like to thank you most sincerely for your help. I have no doubt that had it not been for your eloquent argument, I would now be in a very worrying situation indeed. Secondly, I want to apologise for how I behaved towards you and towards the Irish people generally. The past twenty-four hours have given me ample opportunity to reflect on many things. I came to this country with a preconceived idea of what it would be like, and I refused to waver from that position, despite seeing significant evidence to the contrary. I realise now that Judge Condon was right. I was arrogant and felt that I, and indeed my country, was in some way superior to you. I have been treated with a courtesy and professionalism in Ireland that was far beyond what I deserved or expected, and for that I will remain eternally grateful. Because I will be returning to the US in a few days, thanks to your powers of persuasion, I would like to settle my bill with you now.'

Lucinda considered herself a good judge of character, and though not in any way cynical, she was sceptical about how much a person could really change in a short space of time. Perhaps Dorothy Crane was putting on an act, but her instincts told her otherwise.

'Thank you for saying that,' she began. 'I appreciate it. On the subject of the bill, I wonder if you would mind calling into my office? It's just down the street there, a few minutes' walk at the most. Sarah, my secretary, will be there, and she'll be able to prepare a bill for you. I have to stay in court to meet with another client. Otherwise I would walk down with you.'

Dorothy extended her hand. 'Of course I will, and thank you again.'

As Dorothy turned, she noticed the small group from the tour standing inside the courthouse door. They seemed unsure whether or not they should approach her. Juliet, in particular, looked worried. Dorothy gathered her backpack and belongings from the clerk's office and walked over to them.

'Thank you all for coming this morning,' she began.

The group seemed to heave a collective sigh of relief, clearly thanking God she wasn't going to make a scene or say something acerbic.

'I assumed you would continue with the tour. I can't tell you how pleased I am that you didn't, not least because it gave me a great boost to see a few friendly faces in the gallery.'

She turned to Juliet and Anna, who had now rejoined the group. 'Juliet, I am so sorry. Thank you for what you said in there just now. I know I don't deserve your friendship, but I hugely appreciate what you did for me.'

Juliet smiled. 'A long time ago someone showed me kindness when I really didn't deserve it, so I guess the wheel is always turning.'

Conor was the first to recover his composure at the sight of this new and definitely improved Dorothy. 'Well, Dorothy,' he said, 'we had arranged to leave Killarney at lunchtime, but it's still only eleven, so we have plenty of time to get organised before we set off.'

Dorothy smiled a genuine smile, the first the group had seen since the tour began. 'OK then,' she said, 'but first I must go up the street to settle my account with my law – I mean, my solicitor. Since we have a bit of time to spare, how about we all have coffee and cake in that nice café across the street? I promised myself that if things went well today, I would treat myself, and of course, treat all of you too. How about we head there now?'

Patrick glanced at Anna and Juliet. Dorothy offering to pay for something? *What?* This tour really was turning out to be an amazing experience. Taking a risk he wouldn't have even considered a few days earlier, Patrick put his big arm around Dorothy's shoulder. Instead of flinching or looking like she'd just caught fleas, she beamed up at the enormous cop.

'That sounds like a really good plan to me, Dorothy,' Patrick said gallantly. 'I'm starving. And can I add that we're all glad this has ended well for you.'

While the group took their seats and ordered a selection of coffees and cakes, Dorothy spoke quietly to the waitress. 'I'll be paying for everything. Can you please give my friends whatever they would like? Would this cover it?' she asked, proffering a fifty-euro note.

'Of course!' The young waitress laughed. 'Crikey, things are dear, but they're not that dear! Twenty would be fine, I'd say.'

'Well, keep the change,' Dorothy whispered conspiratorially, shaking her head at the girl's protestations. 'Please, take it.'

Approaching the table where the group were seated, she announced, 'I must just pop out and pay my bill. I'll be back in a few minutes. Please order whatever you would like. The lady at the desk knows it's all covered.' She walked out of the café, the stunned group gaping at her departing back.

Dorothy entered the solicitor's office and approached the receptionist. 'Good morning, I would like to speak to Sarah. I want to settle my account with Ms McAuliffe. She defended me in court this morning.'

'No problem, Ms Crane. I'm Sarah. She phoned to tell me you might pop in, so I have it all ready for you here.'

Dorothy glanced at the amount on the invoice and began peeling off a wad of notes. Handing them to the receptionist, she said, 'I wonder if you would be kind enough to help me with something?'

'Certainly…if I can.'

'I would like to make a donation to a charity connected with the Garda Síochána. Could you suggest one?'

Sarah thought for a moment. 'Well, I know the Gardaí do lots of charity things, and I think they have a few different charities that they support all around the country. So any of the big ones – the Irish Cancer Society, the Irish Heart Foundation, that kind of thing – they'd have had support from the Gardaí over the years. On the other hand, there's something going on here this weekend that you might be interested in. The local Gardaí and some friends are doing a charity cycle to raise money for the children's oncology ward in Our Lady's

Children's Hospital in Dublin. I'm actually taking part myself because one of our local detectives here, his little daughter has leukaemia. It's being heavily supported locally. They need fifty thousand to upgrade one of the wards, so they're hoping to get the ball rolling with the charity cycle. John O'Keeffe, that's the detective, was a school friend of my husband's.'

Dorothy nodded. 'Well, that certainly sounds like a great cause. If I send you a donation of fifty thousand dollars, will you see that it gets to the right people? I would, if possible, like to remain anonymous,' she added.

Sarah looked at her, gobsmacked, and eventually squeaked, 'Of course I will. I'd be happy to. And I won't say a word to anyone about the source.'

'Thank you. I'll make the necessary arrangements when I contact my lawyers in Des Moines today,' Dorothy said, gathering up her backpack.

CHAPTER 31

onor watched in despair as Patrick once again loaded the cases into the boot of the coach in a haphazard fashion. Conor had given up trying to dissuade him, so now he just resigned himself to rearranging them once he had managed to get Patrick on board and out of the way. In the meantime, he decided to use this gift of time to check his BlackBerry for emails. Sinead was due to fly in that morning. He had already told her he wouldn't be able to collect her as he was still in Kerry with the group, and they had arranged to meet in the bar of Dunshane Castle later that afternoon.

While Patrick continued his packing efforts, the remaining members of the group loitered in the sunshine outside the hotel. Ellen was deep in conversation with Anna, Juliet and Dorothy, describing the incredible events in Inchigeelagh. Dylan was telling Bert all about the music course and how he was going to get a job back in the States to fund his studies. Cynthia and Corlene stood slightly apart from the rest.

'I say,' Cynthia addressed Corlene. 'I hope you don't think me frightfully rude, but your hair really is a most wonderful colour. Is it natural?'

Corlene chuckled. 'No, Cynthia, there ain't nothing natural about me. I'm fake, head to toe. Bleach, tan, make-up, boobs – it's all an illusion.'

Cynthia gushed, 'Well, you look simply marvellous nonetheless. I don't really wear make-up. Well, I did try some years ago for a hunt ball, but I ended up looking rather like a dog's dinner. I never had any sisters, you see, and Mummy only wears powder and rouge, which does make her somewhat cadaver-like,' she added, giving her trademark tinkly laugh.

Corlene had never in her life met anyone like Cynthia. The woman dressed like a hobo and never brushed her hair. In normal circumstances, Corlene would have felt nothing but bewilderment and revulsion at such neglect and lack of femininity, but for some reason that she didn't quite understand, these sentiments did not apply in the case of Cynthia. She heard herself say, 'Hey! How about a makeover? You're staying with the group now, right? How about when we get to the next hotel, you come to my room and I'll do your hair and make-up. I'll tell ya, Patrick won't know what hit him!'

Cynthia gazed at her in amazement. 'Well, Corlene, I don't know what to say. I would love it. I feel so dowdy sometimes, and while I absolutely *love* colourful clothes and so on, sometimes I'm not really sure I'm quite "á la mode". Mind you, I do admit to loving *this*,' she added, indicating her blouse. 'And it's really the only thing I have that goes with this skirt.'

Corlene scrutinised the collection of garments that made up what Cynthia claimed was her favourite ensemble. Her assessment began at Cynthia's feet, which were clad in a pair of wide, flat sandals that may at some time in the past have been a kind of khaki colour. It was hard to tell. Under the sandals, she wore purple woollen socks of the kind mainly favoured by hill walkers. The exposed expanse of white hairy legs between the end of her skirt and the top of her socks almost caused Corlene to convulse. Both the band of the denim encircling Cynthia's waist and the hem of the skirt were embroidered with daisy-like flowers. The skirt itself seemed to billow around her like a sail, making her seem far wider than she actually was. The peach polyester blouse featuring a floppy bow at the neck was, however, undoubtedly the worst aspect of this horrendous outfit. Combined with the bird's nest of hair held together with an assortment of pins, it served to make Cynthia look mentally unhinged and possibly homeless.

'Hmm,' Corlene said, wearing the most inscrutable expression she could manage.

'I wish I could be there for the transformation,' Bert interjected, having overheard bits of their conversation. 'If Corlene can teach you how to use make-up as well as she taught her son here, you'll be in safe hands.'

Dylan laughed. 'Seriously, Cynthia, you should let her. She's good at all that kinda stuff.'

Corlene blushed with pride. She had never heard Dylan say anything nice about her to anyone.

Cynthia was so excited at the prospect, she began to giggle. 'I never had many girlfriends, you know. Tended to veer more towards the stables and the chaps, I suppose. There was a dreadful old crone when we were at school who taught decorum or deportment or some other such useless nonsense – I never took too much notice. Patrick mentioned that there was going to be a dinner to celebrate the last night of the tour. How wonderful if I managed to look a bit more... well...a bit more glamorous.' She seemed embarrassed.

Corlene had never experienced the joy of giving without a motive before. She was wondering what on earth had come over her when she heard herself say, 'Don't worry about a thing. By the time I'm finished with you, you'll look like a million dollars.'

Cynthia looked doubtful.

'It's easy when you know how, Cynthia. Not a word to Patrick, promise? We want to *wow* him.'

* * *

CONOR PULLED A VERY miserable-looking Dylan aside. 'You know we're having a bit of a farewell dinner tomorrow night in the hotel. I was thinking, why don't you ask Laoise and her parents to come along too? It's only about two hours to Ennis from Cork. I'll organise rooms for them in the hotel.'

'Are you serious? Oh, Conor, man...that would be –'

'I know, I know – *awesome*. I'm like totally...awesome!' Conor chuckled, slapping Dylan on the back.

* * *

DOROTHY HUNG BACK as the group boarded the coach and then took the only remaining single seat without a word. Patrick and Cynthia cuddled up on the back seat, Corlene sitting beside them chatting animatedly. Ellen and Bert sat side by side and interjected every now and again in the various conversations going on around them.

Is there anything as weird as the dynamics of group travel? Conor thought to himself, not for the first time. *At this point, these people probably know more about each other than do their nearest and dearest back at home, and despite protestations to the contrary, only one or two of them will keep in touch once they leave.*

* * *

BERT WATCHED AND LISTENED, as he always did. The project had been decided. This was his favourite bit, he thought as he sat back with satisfaction. When he retired from his company, his family and friends were worried about him, thinking he would go crazy sitting around the house all day. None of them had a clue that he was embarking on a new, much more interesting career. None of them were aware that he had been involved in a small way for many years with another organisation that had nothing whatsoever to do with his construction business. Now that he was retired, he had the freedom to assume the role of coordinator of the organisation's global operations, involving people of many different races, cultures and religions, including people he had never, nor would ever, meet in person. These people had only one thing in common: membership in CAERUS.

CHAPTER 32

*T*he coach pulled into the now familiar grounds of the Dunshane Castle Hotel.

'Hey, Conor, is it really only a week since we were here? It seems like a year ago,' Bert said.

'Gee, Conor, I hope all your tours aren't as interesting as this one,' Juliet piped up.

'No indeed,' Conor agreed. 'This is one I don't think I'll ever forget. Little did I realise when I picked you up at the airport that morning what dramas lay ahead.'

Everyone laughed.

'Well, Conor, if you'd known the trouble I was going to cause, you would have left me in the arrivals hall,' Dorothy said with a rueful grin.

'And miss all that excitement and courtroom drama? Not for all the tea in China.' Conor chuckled.

'Dorothy, you'll be the highlight of the trip when I tell the story to my buddies,' Patrick joked.

Everyone sat on the edge of their seats, holding their breath in anticipation of Dorothy's response. They had all witnessed her remarkable transformation, but wariness still prevailed.

'Well, I'd better be good-looking in the retelling, Officer O'Neill,' she said good-humouredly as the group guffawed in unison.

Conor hopped off the coach and headed for reception to get the rooming list. As he waited, he scanned the lobby for signs of Sinead and young Conor. He felt uncharacteristically nervous, anxious to get the group settled into their rooms so that he could deal with this monumental milestone in his life.

Returning to the coach, he took the microphone. 'Righty-ho, everyone. Tonight you're free to eat out or eat in the hotel. Maybe take in a bit of traditional music in the pubs in Ennis. I'll give you a list of some of the really good spots. On the other hand, some of you may just need to rest after all the excitement of the past few days.' He surveyed the exhausted faces of Patrick, Ellen and Bert. 'I know from experience the quality of the room service is very good. So I can certainly recommend that option if you'd rather eat in your rooms.'

Several heads nodded in agreement.

'Tomorrow we visit Bunratty Castle and the Folk Park, which I know you'll enjoy, and you'll also get a chance to do a bit of last-minute gift shopping. Tomorrow night, we have a very special dinner planned in a private dining room here in Dunshane Castle, so make sure you don't eat too much for lunch. By the way, Dylan's friend Laoise and her parents, Siobhán and Diarmuid, will be joining us also. They are wonderful musicians, so you'd all better prepare a party piece.'

Corlene mouthed a silent 'thank you' to Conor as he continued.

'Now, folks, for the last time on this completely amazing tour, let me give you your room keys...'

After they had all departed, he took a few minutes to tidy up the coach. As he threw newspapers and empty water bottles into a refuse sack, he heard a tap on the window. He pressed the button to release the door.

'Ah, Anastasia,' he said, giving her a hug. 'How's everything? How's your mam?'

'She's much better. I think maybe she will come back from hospital in few more days. She must take it easy now, but she will stay with my brother and his family for some weeks until she is again strong, so I am glad.'

'That's fantastic news. I'm delighted.' He deliberated about mentioning their awkward phone call and then decided it was better to take the bull by the horns. 'Listen, Anastasia,' he began, 'I hope you didn't think I was being rude the other day on the phone. It's just that I'm not much for chatting on those yokes. It's much more for your generation, I think…' he added with a rueful grin.

'I'm not so much younger than you, you know,' she said, looking serious. 'Always you say I am young, but I look younger than I am. I am twenty-five and you forty-five, not so much. Only twenty years.'

Conor grinned. 'Ah yes, Anastasia, my darling, but a lifetime can happen in twenty years.'

'Oh God, there is Mr Manner!' she squeaked. The manager was peering out the door, scanning the car park. 'I supposed to be working. I just come to say welcome home to you. I better go,' she said, before dashing into the hotel through the service entrance.

Conor walked into the hotel with trepidation. As he approached reception, Katherine O'Brien came out from behind the desk to meet him, something he had never seen her do before.

'Conor, can I have a word?' she said, motioning towards the manager's office. She closed the door behind them.

'Is everything all right, Katherine?'

'I don't know, Conor,' she replied, without a trace of her customary frostiness. 'It's none of my business, but I just wanted to tell you that a woman checked in today, with a boy, and she asked… She said she was… Well, the words she used – I'm paraphrasing, Conor – she said she was with you. Now you never said anything to us about it, so I wasn't sure what we should do. I gave her the room adjoining yours. I hope that was the right thing to do.'

Conor sat down and sighed heavily.

'Is anything the matter, Conor?' Katherine asked with genuine concern.

'Have you a spare ten minutes, Katherine? I could do with a bit of advice.'

'Of course,' she said as she too sat down.

'Well...you know I'm not like the other fellas, different women every night of the week, so I'm a bit clueless when it comes to this stuff. That woman, Sinead, is an old friend of mine. One time, almost twenty years ago, I'd hoped that maybe she'd be my girlfriend or whatever, but anyway, she left Ireland with my brother, and that lad with her is my nephew.

'I never declared myself at the time, but I think – in fact I'm fairly certain – she knew how I felt about her. When she and my brother left, it tore the heart out of me. I swear, I thought I'd never get over it. I never thought I'd see her again, but then she wrote to me. That was the letter you gave me last week. In it she said she'd been trying to track me down for ages. Anyway, here she is, and I just don't know what to do. She's sick – she has cancer – and I don't know, maybe she's come home to die or something. But the thing is, she's been talking like we're getting together. Like it's a given. I was absolutely mad about her back then. I'd have done anything to have her, but I think now maybe it's too late.'

'She has cancer? That's strange you should mention that, because I overheard her talking to another guest while she was waiting to check in. The complimentary newspapers were on the desk, and the front-page story on *The Irish Times* was about that poor woman in Roscommon whose breast cancer was misdiagnosed. She died as a result, and her husband and children got a big settlement in court yesterday. Anyway, this other guest said to your friend how awful that was, and she replied that she'd had a brush with cancer last year but after she finished her radiotherapy treatment, she'd been given the all-clear. I wonder why she would have said that if she still had cancer,' Katherine said pointedly.

'I don't know. Maybe it's come back? It all seems so overwhelming, Katherine. I did love her...maybe I still do – I don't know. It could be that I'll meet her and it'll be just like old times.' Noting the sceptical look on Katherine's face, he added, 'I suppose you think I'm a right clown to even consider it. Sure, maybe I'm reading it all wrong. If she didn't want me years ago, she surely wouldn't want me now. Look at me, hiding in here instead of going up to face her. I'm a right eejit, I know.'

'Oh, Conor, I think you *are* reading it right. I'm not claiming to know *her*, but I do know *you*. I think she definitely does want you. But do you want *her*? This is something you'll never hear me repeat again, so listen carefully. You are a lovely, charming and, dare I say it, handsome man. You have a big heart, and you deserve to be happy. Tread very carefully, Conor. That boy is not your responsibility and neither is his mother. Don't do anything foolish.' She got up from the chair.

'I've discussed this with Anastasia too, and she didn't seem to think it was such a good idea, but then she doesn't know Sinead either.'

'You get on well with Anastasia, don't you?'

'Ah sure, she's a lovely girl. She was a bit upset last week actually, boyfriend trouble, I think. Is she going out with someone from here? I don't like to ask her in case she thinks I'm prying into her business. But I hate to see her so down, and I know you know everything that goes on in this hotel.'

Katherine gave Conor a funny look. 'No, Conor, she's not going out with anyone, not from here or from anywhere else. She's in love with a man, but he can't see it. If he doesn't wake up soon, though, I'd say she'll be going back to the Ukraine.'

Conor stood up. 'Well, I'd better go and face my fate, whatever it's to be. I suppose I'll just know when I meet her whether we still have feelings for each other. I think when it comes to stuff like that, you kind of know instinctively, don't you?'

Katherine suppressed a smile. 'Oh yes, Conor, I'd say you are a very perceptive man. Just be careful, all right?'

Conor decided to get a coffee in the bar and call Sinead from there. She had given him her mobile number in her last email. The hotel bar was a beautiful old room, and Conor noticed with relief it wasn't busy. He would ask her to come down. He wanted to meet her on neutral ground. Maybe in a public place he wouldn't make such an eejit of himself. He took a seat at the bar. As he was about to ring her mobile, he spotted Anastasia taking an order from someone in the corner.

He could hear a woman with a brash American accent saying, 'Oh, for heaven's sake! All I want is a Colombian roast coffee with almond milk. This is supposed to be a five-star hotel. Even my local Starbucks has that. Are you sure you understand right? Maybe you could send someone who speaks better English?'

Anastasia spotted Conor rolling his eyes to the heavens in solidarity with her plight in having to deal with this nightmare of a woman. 'Madam, I know exactly what it is that you want,' she said, 'but I am sorry, we don't have almond milk here. Can I get you regular latte? Or a latte with soya milk? Low-fat milk? Also we have cappuccino, espresso, Americano.'

'Gee! I just want what I want, OK? Is Ireland still back in the dark ages? No almond milk? Perhaps you should check with someone more senior? Oh, look, just forget it. Clearly I'm wasting my time here. Just bring me a gin and tonic, and I don't want lemon – it must be lime, organic and unwaxed. Have you got that?'

'There's always one, eh?' Conor whispered sympathetically to Anastasia as she went behind the bar to get the order.

'She is terrible,' Anastasia murmured back. 'I don't think she is on tour – she comes alone, I think. Not surprise she had no one to come to holidays with her. Do you know she order lunch earlier, eat all of it except for one tiny piece, and then she say to Timmy, food is disgusting and she won't pay! Anyway, what you like?'

'Just a coffee when you get a chance. No rush. I'm meeting the woman I told you about. I'm just about to call her now. Wish me luck!'

'Oh,' said Anastasia, looking surprised and turning her back.

Maybe she didn't hear me, thought Conor. *Or maybe she is upset at the carry-on of that old cow in the corner.* He took out his phone and punched in the number, his heart thumping in his chest. In the corner of the bar, a mobile phone started to ring.

'Hello?' a woman with an American accent answered. 'Hello, Conor? Is that you?'

Anastasia watched as the colour drained from Conor's face, the realisation dawning on him.

He walked across to where the woman sat. 'Hello, Sinead,' he said.

* * *

'Are you having dinner here tonight?' Anastasia asked Conor two hours later when they almost collided in the lobby.

'No, not tonight. The farewell dinner is tomorrow night, so the group are on their own tonight. Doing their own thing.'

'Ah yes, I am working in Burren dining room tomorrow night – is for your group, yes? So now I am off tonight,' she said hesitantly. 'Maybe you are very tired or have something to do with your friend from America, but if not, perhaps we can go to eat something...?'

Conor looked at the elfin face of his young Ukrainian friend. He knew he should go inside, do some paperwork and get ready to wind up the tour. Today felt like it had been the longest day of his life. He knew he just couldn't face paperwork tonight of all nights. The thought of an easy relaxed evening with Anastasia, a nice dinner and a glass of wine was so tempting.

'Do you know what, Anastasia? That's the best offer I've had all week. Where will we go?'

'Well, how about I will cook for you at my house? My housemate is gone back to visit family in Lithuania. I have apartment all by myself this week.'

'Ah no, love, sure you must be wrecked after your day. No, I'll take you out somewhere. You decide.'

'You are feared I poison you? Or make you eat something from Ukraine, like *varenyky*?' Anastasia teased. 'Really, I would like it, and I think maybe you get sick from so much restaurant food. I like to cook. I just do something simple.'

Conor was touched. After the disastrous conversation with Sinead and all the drama and carrying on of the tour group over the previous day or so, a relaxed evening with Anastasia was exactly what he needed. Anastasia was everything that Sinead was not. She was kind and funny and thoughtful, and she seemed to want nothing from him but his company.

'Well, Anastasia, that sounds absolutely lovely. And I love *vark...var...*'

'*Varenyky*,' she prompted. 'It's dumplings with different fillings. It's very good, I promise.'

'A home-cooked meal is something I dream about when I'm on the road. And after the day I've had, well, you couldn't make it up. Let me just go up and get a quick shower and change, and I'll be down in ten minutes, OK?'

'Sure, I sit outside. It is not so much sunny here, so I want to enjoy when sun comes out.'

As Anastasia skipped out the door, Katherine O'Brien shot him a knowing look.

'You were right,' Conor said. 'There's absolutely no future for Sinead and me. She isn't the person I remember. Or maybe she is, and I just didn't remember her correctly. I didn't get to meet my nephew, unfortunately, and I hope I will if she stays around. But no, she's definitely not the one for me.'

'Well, I'm really sorry if it didn't work out as you wanted it to. Can I get you anything? Have you eaten?'

'No thank you, Katherine. That's very kind of you. Anastasia's cooking me dinner. I think she feels sorry for me. She had a bit of a lash of Sinead's tongue earlier, so now she knows what she's like. Poor Anastasia – she doesn't know what she's in for. I'm probably not the best company tonight,' he added ruefully.

'I'm sure you'll have a lovely time. Forget about all this now and take it easy. You look tired.' Katherine returned to her paperwork.

At the lift, Conor ran into Patrick.

'Hi, Conor. I'm just going out to get some things for Cynthia at the store. We were gonna get something to eat later in the bar if you'd like to join us.'

'Thanks, Patrick,' Conor replied with a grin. 'You're very good, but I'm going out.'

'Someone sure has cheered up your evening – you got a date?'

'Ah, nothing like that. I'll leave all that romancing to yourself, Patrick. No, I'm just having dinner with a friend.'

'Well, judging by the happy look on your face, this friend sure is better looking than me. Have a great night, buddy. You deserve it after all you've done for us this last week.' He gave Conor a playful thump on the back.

Anastasia was sitting outside the hotel in the early evening sun waiting for Conor to emerge. He crept up behind her and put his hands over her eyes. 'Right so, Ms Wonderchef, are we off?' he asked cheerfully.

'Hey, Conor, how about we take a taxi to my house, then you can have a drink and not worry about driving.'

Good idea, he thought as he spotted a taxi dropping off a passenger near the hotel. He grabbed Anastasia by the hand, and they ran across the car park to hail it.

Anastasia's place, a two-bedroom apartment in a converted warehouse complex, seemed eerily quiet as they let themselves in through the security gates.

'Where is everyone?'

'Most of the people who live here have two jobs. It's a bit more expensive than other places, but I like it. It's quiet. In other places where is lots of Polish or Ukrainian, there is many boys in big groups living together. They can be a bit noisy, lots of vodka, you know?'

'Don't I know well.' Conor nodded. 'So you live here with Svetlana?'

'Yes, we are very good together here. She work often different shift to me, so many days I don't even see her. But now she gone back in home to her father's birthday. She is very happy to go back to her family. She gets lonely.'

Conor took the glass of wine proffered. 'And what about you, Anastasia? Don't you get lonely for home?'

Anastasia thought for a while. 'Yes, of course, sometimes I get sad, especially if it's birthdays or something, when I know all my family will be together. But I like it here also.'

'What about the job offer? You were trying to make up your mind about it last week,' he said, trying to sound casual as he gazed out the living room window.

'I still am not sure. It depends on some things.'

Conor wandered away from the window to look at the books

crammed into a small wall-mounted bookcase, and they fell into an easy silence. Anastasia observed him as she peeled and chopped, remarking to herself how much younger he looked in his off-duty gear, dark jeans and a pale-blue cotton shirt open at the neck, his hair swept back and still a bit damp from his shower earlier on.

As he removed a copy of *The Oxford English Dictionary and Thesaurus*, the entire wall-mounted bookcase unit collapsed and dozens of books crashed to the floor.

'Oh feck it, Anastasia! I'm so sorry. I'm having a really bad day,' Conor said, looking aghast.

'Don't worry.' She giggled. 'Always this happens. Svetlana and I have many books, and this bookshelf is not made properly. We buy it when we come in Ireland, and the instructions was in English, so I think we make it wrong. When we finish, we have many more pieces of wood and nails and things not used.'

Conor chuckled. 'Well, in my experience these flat-pack people only give you barely the right amount. I'd say there could be some technical problem there, right enough. I don't suppose you kept the extra wood and things?'

Anastasia opened the drawer and extracted a small plastic bag containing screws and a screwdriver. 'Here is it, I think. Svetlana, she keep everything. The other pieces of wood are behind the TV.'

Conor laid out all the bits and pieces on the sofa and stood staring at them for a few minutes as he tried to figure out what fitted where. Then slowly he began reassembling the bookcase properly.

'You don't have to do that!' Anastasia protested. 'It's supposed to be your night off.'

'No problem, Anastasia. Listen, I couldn't have had it on my conscience that you were at risk of being killed by an avalanche of hard-looking Russian books. I wouldn't be able to sleep at night, worrying about it.'

As they chatted over dinner, it struck Conor yet again just how easy it was to be in Anastasia's company. She was interesting, funny and lovely – particularly so at that very moment as she sat at the table, sipping wine, her pretty little face and urchin-cut hair bathed in candlelight.

'You don't have to tell me if you don't want to, but how was the meeting with your old friend?' she asked shyly.

Conor sat back and let out a big, heavy sigh. 'No, not at all. I don't mind talking about it. Well...for a start...eh...she's different. I mean she's not as I remember her anyway. But you saw for yourself what she's like, didn't you? She wants to come back to Ireland. Said it was my fault that she left with Gerry. I should have stopped her apparently. If I'd told her how I felt about her back then, she would have stayed. She seemed to think that she could just show up and I'd be waiting for her.'

'And is she right? Not...are you waiting for her. I mean...do you feel the same about her as you did all those years ago?'

Conor shook his head slowly. 'No. I just sat there, I listened, and I felt...well, kind of nothing, kind of numb. I don't think she really has cancer. She might have had it last year, but it's cleared up now, thank God. I'll tell you how I know that another time. On the other hand, the whole cancer thing might have been a bit of a ploy on her part. Who knows? Her son I can't tell you anything about. I didn't get to meet him. But I will meet him, and I'd like to get to know him if they stay here in Ireland. But as for her and me? No. To be honest, I thought I'd feel sad, or regretful at least, for what might have been, but I feel nothing for her. So tell me, Anastasia, since we're all heart-to-heart, did you sort out that fella of yours?'

'Conor, I don't have boyfriend. Not anyone since I come in Ireland.'

'But...but I thought you said –'

'Conor, I want to say something to you.'

He sat back in the chair. 'Sounds serious,' he said with a grin.

'Many things about Ireland is different from Ukraine. There we are more straight and just say things with no...em...no joking. I think it's something to do with communists,' she added with a weak smile. 'So here for me is difficult sometimes. I don't know when there is joking or serious, you know? OK, I have now got to be honest.'

She took a deep shaky breath. 'I know you think I am young and you are so much older than me, but...I really like you, Conor. Not just for friends. I like you like...like a woman likes a man. Last week I feel so stupid after calling you and you talk about this woman, and then I sending you that text, but Svetlana say to me to just tell you how I feel. I think she is getting sick from me talking about you.'

Anastasia looked at him closely, trying to decide if she should continue. His face was hard to read. It was worth the risk, she thought. 'It's difficult because even though we are friends, I don't know so much about you. When I tell you about job offer back in Ukraine, I suppose...I hope you say, don't go. But I can't go back and not say what I feel. It's too hard. So now I am saying it. I like you. OK...I more than like you. I think maybe I love you, and I want to... well, I want to know if you feel something for me.'

Conor was too shocked to speak.

'I'm sorry...' she said, her voice now barely audible. 'I should not do this to you, but if there is nothing, you feel nothing, then just say it and I go back in Ukraine. There is nothing else keeping me in Ireland. I have only stayed for this long because I hope...'

Conor looked at this gorgeous little creature whose eyes were now filling with tears. He had never allowed any previous relationship with a woman to develop to this point. He often wondered why that was. He'd gone out with some really great women over the years, but the spectre of Sinead had hung heavy over them all.

He remained silent for only about a minute, but to Anastasia it felt like an hour. 'OK, Conor,' she said. 'You don't have to say it. I'm sorry. I should not have put you in this position. It's not fair. You never give me reason to think, to hope that you liked me in that way, so...'

Conor reached across and clasped her two hands. 'Anastasia, this is very new territory for me. I had no idea you felt anything for me other than friendship, and even then, I was a bit mystified. I mean, any man would be delighted to have you paying him attention, let alone someone of my age. I... Well...you know more about me than most people. It's hard for me to do this kind of thing. You're way ahead of me with this, and I won't lie to you. My initial reaction is to say no, but that's because, well, that's what I do. But…if I'm honest, I do think about you. A lot. I just never let myself think of you as anything other than a friend. An incredibly gorgeous friend, I should add.' He smiled, then paused again, for what seemed like another hour.

Struggling to find what he hoped was the right formula of words, he said, 'God, Anastasia, are you sure? I mean, I don't have much to offer you. I… What am I saying here? I really like you. I think you're so… Well, you're not like anyone I've ever met. You're so honest and brave. I don't think I would ever have got the guts to say to you what you just said to me. I just don't know what you see in me. Honest to God, I don't. If I were your father – and I'm almost old enough to be – and you brought the likes of me home, I'd… Well, I wouldn't be exactly thrilled, put it that way.'

Anastasia looked confused. 'So is that a yes or a no? If you worried about my family, my parents are nice. Also, my father is twenty years older than my mother and they are very happy. So I don't think they would mind.' She sighed and looked at him with hope in her eyes.

He hesitated, terrified of saying the wrong thing while trying simultaneously to process what was happening.

Anastasia looked at him and then turned away. She stood up, walked towards the window and gazed out over the Irish countryside, which was now enveloped in the late evening twilight. Conor remained at the table, gradually understanding that this might be his chance, his one and only hope of long-term happiness. He allowed himself to visualise life with Anastasia by his side. Living together, going on holidays, spending Christmas together, perhaps even having a family. Maybe it wasn't too late; maybe he wasn't destined to spend his life alone.

He looked across at this incredible girl and realised how much she meant to him. Her silhouette was framed in the fading evening light, and he felt a huge rush of affection and a need to protect her – emotions he hadn't experienced in many, many years. Not since Sinead.

He crossed the room to where she stood and put his arms around her. Gently, he turned her around to face him. Using his thumbs, he wiped the tears, which by now were coursing down her cheeks.

'I want you too...' he began, 'but I'm afraid, Anastasia, for loads of reasons. As I said, you're much braver than me. But I do have feelings for you. I suppose I never even realised it because it would have been like imagining a white blackbird or a steaming-hot Christmas Day in Connemara or something equally ridiculous. But if you're serious and I'm what you want, then I'd love to try. I don't know where this is going to take us, and I'll need time to get my head around the fact that this amazingly beautiful, smart, funny woman wants me in her life. But if you're willing to give it a go, then so am I.'

Anastasia's face lit up like a child who had just received the best birthday present ever. She put her arms around Conor's neck and drew his face towards hers. He held her as tightly as he dared, terrified that his enormous bulk would crush her diminutive frame. As they kissed, Conor felt as if he had finally come home.

* * *

As CONOR OPENED his eyes the next morning, the events of the night before came flooding back. He rolled over to the other side of the bed, but there was no sign of Anastasia. Panic gripped him momentarily, but then he heard the sound of rattling cups and plates emanating from the kitchen. He sat up just as Anastasia appeared in the doorway carrying a tray and wearing his shirt, which completely swamped her.

'Good morning,' she said shyly. 'I make you some breakfast.'

Conor glanced at his phone on the bedside table. Luckily, he had told the group they wouldn't be hitting the road until 10:30 a.m. It was only 8:30 a.m., he noted with relief.

'Am I dreaming?' he asked her as she placed the tray on the locker and cuddled up to him.

'No.' She smiled enigmatically. 'Not dreaming. Is all real.' She leaned in on one elbow and looked directly into his eyes. 'No regrets, I hope?'

'Em, now, let me see... I wake up to the sexiest communist on earth, who claims to love me, though for what reason I can't imagine. The same communist is attending to my every need, and all it's costing me is the rent of my shirt. I'd have to say now, in all fairness, eh...no regrets.' He pulled her into his arms.

'Your coffee is getting cold,' she whispered.

'True.' He smiled. 'But I can have coffee anytime...'

* * *

'GOD, I'D BETTER GET GOING,' he said an hour later. 'Though I would much rather stay here with you.'

Anastasia's head nestled on his chest. 'I must also go. If I'm late, Mr Manner will probably make me cut grass with nail scissors or something.'

'Listen, *you* are gorgeous. *He*, on the other hand, is not. That's his problem. Now I really, *really* wish I didn't have to work tonight, but I do. I know I'll see you in the hotel during the day, but can we meet up after dinner?'

Anastasia just looked at him.

'Sorry, am I coming on a bit strong?' he said, looking worried. 'Maybe you have plans.'

'No, I'm just so happy. I felt like it was all me, and now for you to want to see me, well, it's...my dream come true. Of course I will see you after work.'

As Conor was getting dressed, he had an idea. 'Anastasia, have you got some holidays that you could take?'

'Yes. I was going to go home for a week soon, but flights in summer are very expensive, so probably I will wait until September when children go back in school and flights are cheaper. Why?'

'It's just that when I drop this tour tomorrow, I have a few days off. I don't pick up again until Friday. So I was thinking maybe we could go off somewhere, the two of us, like. What d'ya think? I have a small little place in Spain – we could go there.'

'Oh, Conor, that would be so lovely, like a real couple. But...' She hesitated. 'I am kind of broke at the moment. I had big phone bill after calling home so much when my mother was sick, so I can't really afford to go anywhere right now. Maybe in a few weeks. I know you will say no, that you will pay, but I can't have relationship with you like that. I must pay my part also...'

Conor looked at her. 'I know what you're thinking, and it stops now, OK? I love you, and you and I are going to work out just fine. I know it. And so what I have I will share with you with an open heart. What else is money for?'

Anastasia whispered, 'You love me? Really?'

'Sure. Isn't that what I've been trying to tell you for months?' he said with a big laugh.

Anastasia punched him on the shoulder.

'I'll book you a ticket today, OK? Just pack your bikini – or better still, don't bother.' He gave her a big wink. 'I'll drop the tour to the airport in the morning, park up the coach and all that, and we leave tomorrow at lunchtime.'

She looked doubtful.

'Don't worry about Carlos. I'll sort that now when I go in, all right?'

'OK, boss,' she said with a giggle.

CHAPTER 33

*W*hile the group shopped till they dropped, Conor spent the day sitting in the coach doing his paperwork. He attacked this chore somewhat more enthusiastically than usual because getting it over and done with now meant that he could buy extra time with Anastasia before the next tour group landed in on top of him.

As the day wore on, he almost had to pinch himself several times to believe his luck. He knew he'd be in for a right slagging from everyone once the word got out. In the meantime, he didn't care; he felt like a teenager. In between sorting out diesel receipts and other tour expenses, he mused about some of the challenges that lay ahead and would have to be met head-on. On the plus side, it was reassuring that there was such a big age gap between her own parents. Maybe they'd organise a trip to the Ukraine at the end of the season, which would give him a chance to learn a bit of the language so he wouldn't look like a total eejit when he met her family. God, it was strange the way life worked out sometimes. There he was, just a week ago, envisioning yet another winter on the Spanish coast, playing golf and reading. And now look at him, only a couple of days later, planning to go to a part of the world he could barely find on a map, much less somewhere he had ever planned to visit.

Conor was not so naive as to think that every romance had a happy ending; he had enough personal experience to know that this wasn't true. But he had a good feeling about Anastasia and himself. She was honest, sincere and kind, and he believed her when she said she loved him. For now, what they had was enough, and his instinct was to seize this chance at happiness while he had the opportunity.

In between checking invoices and receipts, he looked at his phone every few minutes in case he had missed a text message from her. 'Ah, for God's sake, would you ever cop on,' he berated himself. 'What are you like?'

Almost on cue, his phone beeped. *I miss you xxx.*

Conor felt ridiculously happy. He rang the travel agent he always used and booked two seats to Málaga for the following day. This task completed, he popped by reception to see Katherine O'Brien and tell her the good news. Simultaneously, the restaurant manager appeared out of nowhere.

'Carlos! How are you?' Conor said jovially.

Carlos Manner managed to look extremely put out at being interrupted on his inspection tour. 'I am well, thank you, Conor,' he replied in his usual clipped tone. 'Busy,' he added pointedly.

'I won't keep you long. I just wanted to ask a favour. I was hoping to take Anastasia away for a few days, leaving tomorrow. Would that be OK, do you think?'

Carlos looked puzzled. 'Do you mean Anastasia Petrenko?'

Conor's cheerful tone did not betray his mounting irritation. 'The very one. Is there more than one Anastasia working here?'

'No, at least I don't think so,' Carlos replied. 'But excuse me, Conor, are you telling me she will not be covering her shifts as normal? Miss Petrenko knows the procedures regarding annual leave. All requests must be submitted in writing at least three weeks in advance, and then I make a decision depending on what is going on in the hotel at the requested time. I'm afraid it is completely out of the question for any staff member to take leave at such short notice.

Also...to ask someone else to approach me on her behalf, well...to be frank, I am shocked that she would. I'm sorry, did you say *you* are taking Anastasia on a holiday? I don't understand.'

Conor lowered his voice almost to a whisper. 'Carlos, Anastasia is my girlfriend. I want to take her away for a few days as a surprise. She's had a tough few weeks, what with her mother being sick and everything...'

Carlos gave a disdainful snort. 'Anastasia Petrenko is your *girlfriend?*'

'Yes, Carlos, she is.'

Katherine O'Brien, having overheard most of the exchange between the two men, left the reception desk and marched over. Standing beside Conor, she said in a tone that brooked no argument, 'I'm sure we can organise that, can't we, Carlos? I mean, after all, given the business that Conor brings to this hotel, it would be our pleasure to do something for him in return. Anastasia must be entitled to holidays by now anyway. I'm sure the other girls will be glad of the few extra shifts.'

Carlos knew better than to argue with the formidable Ms O'Brien. 'I'm sure we can arrange something,' he said through gritted teeth. 'Have a nice time.'

As he turned on his polished heels, Conor and Katherine exchanged a conspiratorial wink.

* * *

CYNTHIA KNOCKED TENTATIVELY on Corlene's door. Immediately, the other woman opened it.

'Cynthia! Come in, come in. We don't have much time.'

Cynthia crept into the room as if she were on some kind of a secret mission. 'I've told Patrick I needed an hour to make some telephone calls about the stables, so he's gone out for a walk. I'm meeting him in the bar at seven o'clock. I must say, Corlene, this really is awfully good of you.'

'It's a pleasure, honey. Now, what have you brought?'

Corlene emptied the plastic bag Cynthia was carrying and laid out the contents on the bed. Each piece of clothing was worse than the next. Nothing matched. This was going to require ingenuity and improvisation on a grand scale. She weighed up the various options, mentally measuring Cynthia as she went. Hmm, she was taller than Corlene, no question, but in terms of dress size there probably wasn't a whole lot between them.

'Oh dear, it is rather hopeless, isn't it? I'm afraid I don't usually worry too much about clothes, you see,' Cynthia said quietly, suddenly feeling very young and insecure.

'Don't worry, Cynthia. I mean, some of that stuff' – Corlene gestured at the mishmash of a pile on the bed – 'would be nice out around a farm or something. But for a dinner party, I think we need to go for something a little more elegant. How about you borrow this?' She hauled a remarkably classy black cocktail dress out of the wardrobe. 'It's too long for me, and it strains a bit on the bust, but I think it will look amazing on you. Go try it on.'

Cynthia stroked the fine wool fabric. 'Good God, I couldn't possibly borrow this, Corlene! Really you are *too kind*, but –'

'Well, you sure as hell ain't going out to dinner in anything you brought here, so less talk and more dressing...*now!*' she ordered.

The dress was a triumph, flattering Cynthia's figure beautifully. On Corlene's instructions, she removed it and took herself off to the bathroom to wash her hair and shave her legs. She returned wrapped in one of the hotel bathrobes and sat in front of the mirror. Soundlessly and purposefully, Corlene began her reconstruction work, liberally applying a hair-straightening solution and dragging a comb through the wet, nest-like heap on top of Cynthia's head. It took herculean effort, but Corlene finally managed to tame the mess and produce quite a good imitation of a sleek, blow-dried bob.

Cynthia's ample facial hair was next on the list. Ignoring Cynthia's yelps of protest, she began plucking stray hairs from her eyebrows, upper lip and chin. A thorough cleanse, tone and moisturise routine followed next, and after that, the application of foundation. Corlene expertly gave Cynthia's eyes a smoky look and slicked on a coral lip gloss. Mostly it was Corlene who did the talking, regaling Cynthia with the sordid details of her many marriages.

'But why on earth do you keep getting married, my dear? It clearly doesn't suit you. Why not set up on your own instead? You are simply marvellous at this sort of thing,' Cynthia said, indicating in the direction of the cosmetics covering every inch of the dressing table. 'Clothes and hair and such. I know lots of ladies would love someone like you to come in and sort them out. Especially as one approaches a certain age, one needs to maintain standards in order to prevent the chaps straying too far from the home turf, if you know what I mean. Several of the gals in our set have had their rather silly old chaps *whipped* from under their noses by brash, busty types...' She suddenly realised the implication of what she had just said and got totally flustered. 'Of course, I'm not suggesting you were... I mean, a totally different...'

Corlene laughed out loud. 'You know, Cynthia, I think you might be onto something there. I was "the other woman" for so long. Maybe I could teach wives a thing or two about holding on to their men when they get the urge to wander. Hmm...interesting idea.'

Cynthia seemed relieved that she had not taken offence.

As Cynthia wrestled with sheer tights, Corlene began to think that there was something in what her new friend had just said. It had never occurred to her before that she had any talent. She used her cosmetics ability skilfully to trap men, nothing more. If she could use those same skills to show wives how to stop their husbands being trapped by women like her – and to be honest, there were plenty of women like her out there – surely this was a service that wives would be willing to pay for? It was certainly a business idea worth developing, she thought.

Slowly and painfully, Cynthia squeezed into a pair of Corlene's impossibly high leopard-print stilettos. 'Oh, my dear,' Cynthia began. 'I simply can't wear these, but I must say they are absolutely lovely. You see, I have only ever worn flat shoes, and I rather do believe these shoes are also a size too small.'

Corlene sighed. 'Cynthia,' she explained as if to a child, 'pain is a small price to pay for beauty. Think of the look on Patrick's face when he sees you – trust me, you will forget that you have sore feet. Just walk around for a while and you'll get used to them, I promise. One thing, though, and this is really important – *do not* take them off until the end of the night. If you do...'

'I'll turn into a pumpkin?' Cynthia suggested, wincing with pain.

'No. Much worse than that. You'll never get your feet back into them,' Corlene said, shaking her head forlornly.

'OK,' said Cynthia as she began her first lap of the bedroom.

After the tenth lap, she was walking almost normally. Throughout, Corlene forbade her to look in the mirror. As she finished lap number eleven, Corlene instructed her to close her eyes. Taking her by the hand, she led an unsteady Cynthia into the bathroom where she positioned her in front of the full-length mirror on the back of the door.

'OK,' said Corlene with a dramatic flourish. 'Now open your eyes.'

Cynthia stared in amazement at the stranger in the mirror. Who was this woman with shiny, sleek hair, beautifully styled, subtle make-up that somehow managed to accentuate her dark-blue eyes and full mouth while at the same time seeming to camouflage her unquestionably long nose? The dress clung seductively to her tall, willowy figure, while the leopard-print stilettos served to create an aura of elegance that she never in a thousand years could have imagined was possible.

Corlene was delighted with the overall effect. *A job well done*, she said so herself.

A single tear threatened to begin trickling down Cynthia's cheek.

'Don't you dare!' Corlene said mock sternly. 'You'll ruin your make-up! No blubbering *under any circumstances*. You look like a million dollars. Now go downstairs and knock out that cop of yours!'

Cynthia quickly recovered her composure. 'Corlene, I hardly know you, but I must just say...nobody in my life, except possibly Patrick, of course, has *ever* made me feel so good about myself. I look...well, I look...almost pretty, and I can assure you that has *never* happened before.'

Corlene smiled with satisfaction as Cynthia continued. 'Now, I want you to have this,' she said, giving the American woman an envelope. 'I don't want any argument. You have done an incredible thing this evening, and I can never thank you enough. I was not being in any way facetious when I suggested that you could develop a business out of this, you know. I can get you at least four or five clients to begin with, and once the word spreads about the miracles you can perform, well, I think your financial problems may be behind you. Without,' she added with a huge grin, 'the need for another husband.'

Corlene took the envelope and hugged Cynthia. 'My pleasure,' she said.

CHAPTER 34

*E*veryone had dressed up for the occasion, even Dorothy, who had been prevailed upon by Anna to buy a dress during their shopping spree earlier that day. Patrick was at the bar insisting on buying everyone a drink when a hush descended. Cynthia had just walked in, and as she did, the entire group stopped and stared in amazement.

As she walked towards the group, she became suddenly very self-conscious, and had it not been for a nudge in the back from Corlene, she might well have fled there and then.

Patrick was almost rendered incapable of speech, but finally managed a strangulated, 'Cynthia, you look...incredible. What did you do? I'm...I'm...I'm stunned.'

'Corlene did it. She's simply amazing.'

Bert sidled up beside Corlene and whispered, 'You sure have a talent there, Miss Corlene. Can I get you a drink?'

Corlene looked at Bert and smiled. 'A dry white wine would be lovely. Thank you, Bert. But I must tell you, it's gotta be a no-strings thing, OK? I'm not really interested in a relationship right now.'

'Well, ma'am, I can't pretend I'm not devastated, but I guess if you've made up your mind...' He grinned.

'I have,' she replied.

Bert returned with Corlene's drink just as Dylan joined the group. He looked so much better these days, Bert thought – and it wasn't just that he had ditched the goth look.

'Dylan!' he called. 'Come and join your mom and me. Sit down there, the two of you. I want to tell you something.'

Dylan and Corlene made themselves comfortable on the sofa as Bert addressed them. 'You two sure have come a long way in a week, haven't you?' he said.

'We certainly have,' Corlene replied. 'I just wish I had arrived at this point sooner. I've wasted so many years – his whole childhood and all of his adolescent years.'

'It wasn't that bad, Mom,' Dylan said with a sigh. 'I told you, I'm good. Sure, I wish I could stay here in Ireland, but I can't, and that's how it has to be. I'm gonna work really hard and call Laoise every day, and hopefully I'll get back here and she won't have forgotten me.'

'Well,' said Bert, 'that's what I want to talk to you about. I'm a member of an organisation called CAERUS. It's not a secret society or anything, but we like to keep a low profile. There are members all over the world doing what I do. I've not been entirely honest with you. I came on this tour because once a year I travel somewhere, usually somewhere I've read about or admire, and I look for someone who needs help. I don't help people who ask for it, only those I consider deserving.

'Miss Corlene, when I met you and young Dylan here, I thought you were two of the scariest human beings I had come across in my whole life. But as the days went on, I came to like you both very much. That's why I'm giving you this.'

Corlene and Dylan sat dumbfounded, trying to take in what he was saying. In his extended hand was an envelope. 'Take it,' he said.

Dylan took the envelope and opened it. Inside was a personal cheque.

'Five hundred thousand dollars! Bert, are you crazy? Is this some kind of joke?' Dylan asked.

'No, son, not crazy, and it's no joke. It's for you and your mother to start a new life here. Maybe a beauty business, Corlene, maybe buy a house. And you can go do your music course.'

'Bert, that's so kind of you,' Corlene said, 'but we can't take this money from you. I know you did well in your business, but that's for your children and grandchildren. Please don't think we don't appreciate it, because we do – *really we do* – but we can't take it.'

Bert laughed. 'The old Corlene would have bitten my hand off. I can't force you, but I am asking you to *please* take the money. I mentioned this organisation – well, that's what we do. All over the world, there are people like me who go out and find worthwhile causes and give them money. It's as simple as that. No fuss, no fanfare. Sometimes we recommend causes to each other, and other times we consult with each other about how much to give and so on. We come from all walks of life and with many different skill sets. The only thing we have in common is that we are all millionaires many times over. You are not depriving anyone of anything, Miss Corlene. I am a very wealthy man. I just want to help you and your son, so please let me do that.'

Corlene and Dylan looked at each other.

'Well, if you're sure... I...I just can't believe this,' Corlene stuttered.

'Believe it,' said Bert.

* * *

ELLEN LISTENED HAPPILY to Juliet and Anna as they outlined their plans for the move to Florida. They both seemed so excited at the prospect. Their enthusiasm was infectious, and even Dorothy was making suggestions about study courses and potential career ideas for Anna.

Juliet seemed touched but surprised. 'I didn't know you knew so much about Florida, Dorothy. I didn't think you'd ever been there,' she said.

'Oh no,' said Dorothy. 'I've actually been down there several times for conferences. Our faculty has links with the University of Tampa. I go down two or three times a year to give guest lectures and so on. Plus my father lived there until he died.'

What a turn-up for the books. With each passing day, Dorothy was becoming more and more human. Juliet heard herself say, 'Well, maybe when you come down, if we had a place, maybe you could stop by, meet the baby.'

Anna smiled and added, 'And do a bit of babysitting...'

Dorothy seemed taken aback at the offer. 'Well, if it would be convenient... I mean...I would love to come visit with you. Thank you.'

Juliet and Dorothy smiled a smile of genuine friendship for the first time.

* * *

As dessert was being served, Dylan and Laoise regaled the group with stories of their plans for the coming term. Nobody could figure it out exactly, but it seemed that something had been sorted out about Dylan's tuition fees. He and Corlene were going to stay on in Ireland.

The chatter subsided as Conor tapped a glass. 'It's customary for me to stand up at this stage of a tour and say a few words,' he began. 'Usually, it goes something along the lines of, "You've been a great group. I hope you enjoyed yourselves and come back to see us again sometime."'

A ripple of laughter ran around the room.

'However' – he paused for dramatic effect – 'this tour has been so eventful and such a unique experience for me that I think it warrants a bit more than the standard farewell speech. I was thinking earlier about what I was going to say, and if you don't mind indulging me, I would like to address each of you individually, and in no particular order.

'I'll begin with Dylan here. As we all know, he arrived at Shannon Airport looking less than thrilled to be here. I was particularly struck by his unique take on clothes and hair. Indeed, I've heard mutterings that Bert there might be thinking of copying some of his style tips.

Now, while he was here, Dylan met some interesting people. He developed a real love of traditional Irish music, and as of tonight, he is planning to stay on here to study. I have a feeling there will come a time in the not-too-distant future when the name Dylan Holbrooke will be well known in music circles in Ireland and perhaps even further afield. So, Dylan, from all your friends in this room, I want to wish you the very, *very* best of luck.'

The group clapped, and a voice at the far end of the table shouted, 'Hear, hear.'

Dylan beamed.

'That leads me neatly to Dylan's mam. Corlene, while your choice of footwear sometimes caused me to fear for your life, I can honestly say I have never before seen anyone anywhere traverse a bog so gracefully while wearing five-inch heels. It was quite a sight to behold. But gracefulness is not your only talent. You are truly a woman of many surprises, Corlene. Until now, nobody here would have guessed your skill as a make-up artist. Cynthia's amazing new look is a fitting testimony to that talent. I also hope that this tour enabled you to find what you were looking for.'

'Y'know, I think I just might have,' Corlene said, as right on cue, Dylan put his arm protectively around her shoulders.

'Ellen O'Donovan,' Conor went on, 'your story is truly one of the most wonderful and heart-warming I have ever heard. I know Ellen has shared her story with you all at various times, but I can't tell you how moved I was, Ellen, when you gave me the honour of asking me to join you on your voyage of discovery. The image of you sleeping in the bed you were born in, all these years later, will stay with me until the day I die.'

Conor walked down and gave Ellen a huge bear hug. Once again, the table erupted in applause, and a few tears were shed.

'Bert,' he continued, 'if I could, I would make sure that every tour had someone like you on it. Your constant good cheer and courtesy to everyone lifted our spirits. I know that the support and strength you gave to Ellen were invaluable, and only you could have done it so well.'

'Hear, hear,' concurred Ellen as Bert took her hand. At the end of the table, Corlene raised her glass in a silent salute. Much and all as she would have loved to tell everyone her good news, she had been sworn to secrecy by her benefactor.

'Anna and Juliet, I understand that you two are off on another adventure to the sunny state of Florida. Sarasota, I believe. A very beautiful spot, by all accounts. Well, again, I know I speak for everyone when I wish you both the absolute best of luck. Sometimes triumph born out of adversity is all the sweeter for that. I know both of you have experienced loss, but I think in each other you have found true friendship. If the members of this group have in some way been instrumental in some aspect of that process, then we are proud and honoured. Good luck with the baby, Anna. With Juliet by your side, we are all very confident that you and the baby are in safe hands.'

'How do you feel about him or her having us all as godparents?' shouted Patrick as everyone cheered.

'Well, if it's a boy, I think we'd better name him Conor,' Anna said, to the accompaniment of further loud cheers and much clinking of glasses.

'Well, with a mother like you, I can tell you he's bound to be better looking than his namesake standing here in front of you. Now, a bit of order, please. Next to our seasoned traveller...'

Everyone laughed. Dorothy smiled and managed to look pleased and sheepish at the same time.

'I hope you enjoyed your trip to Ireland and that it has produced memories that you will cherish in the years to come.'

The group gave Dorothy a big round of applause. Hesitantly and somewhat unsteadily, Dorothy rose from her chair. 'I...well...I would just like to thank you all for your support. I realise I have been difficult, and well, I apologise, and I... Well...it's been a lovely trip. The best I've ever taken, so thank you.'

'And last, but of course by no means least, our friend Patrick,' Conor continued. 'You came here, like so many Irish Americans have done before you, expecting to find something that I don't think exists on this island. The culture of Irish America is definitely born here, but that culture has grown and gained strength in your country. Though it is *of* Ireland, it *isn't* Ireland.

'I have observed over the years that some people find this painful or disappointing. But not you, Patrick. You came with one idea, and you will leave here with something far, *far better*. You have found a wonderful person in Cynthia here, and we are all delighted for you both. You are willing to see this country with new eyes and appreciate all that it has to offer. I feel very sure that we will all continue our friendship in the future. So to Patrick O'Neill, whose people came from this old country, it is my pleasure to say – welcome home.'

As Conor sat down, the group rose to their feet and gave him a standing ovation. Anastasia and the other waitresses who were standing off to the side joined in. When the applause eventually subsided, Bert stood up.

'Now it's our turn,' he began in a mock-menacing tone. 'The group asked me today to be the one to say a few words tonight, and I was delighted to oblige. I think we all agree that for each of us, in very individual ways, this week has been life-changing. When we book a vacation, we don't know what to expect. We all know you are taking a chance by going on a tour. What if the people are awful? What if the guide is terrible? But no one could have predicted this. We all learned something valuable here about ourselves in this beautiful country, and there is only one common denominator.

'Conor O'Shea, you are a remarkable man, and you are a credit to your country. Your knowledge, kindness, common sense and sense of humour succeeded in uniting a bunch of very different people and creating what I am sure will be many lifelong friendships. For that alone, we can never thank you enough. You have gone so far beyond the call of duty for each of us, and we will never forget your kindness. I know I speak for each member of the group when I say our doors are always open to you if you ever come to the United States.'

Though Conor made such speeches and listened to such speeches virtually on a weekly basis, he had to admit that on this occasion he was finding it hard to keep his emotions in check. So much had happened in just a few days. Events had taken so many twists and turns – good and bad. Despite all the drama, here they all were, gathered together in a room positively brimming with camaraderie and friendship. He looked across the room, past all the smiling faces exchanging email addresses and phone numbers, and his gaze met that of the woman he loved. He gestured to her to come and join him.

As she walked across the room wearing a radiant smile, he knew, with more certainty than he could possibly express, that he wanted Anastasia beside him. Then and always.

The End

I SINCERELY HOPE you enjoyed this book. The next book in the Tour Series is called *Safe at the Edge of the World* and can be purchased by clicking this link:

https://geni.us/SafeAtTheEdgeAL

Did you know that tours are an excellent place to hide? There's no paper trail, as reservations are made for groups, not individuals. So if someone was desperate not to be found, then a tour of the Emerald Isle might be just the thing....

Here's a sneak preview!

Safe at the Edge of the World
Chapter 1

Ireland

Declan and Lucia held hands as the luxury tour bus trundled and bounced along the narrow, winding Irish roads. Declan glanced around as she laid her head on his shoulder, still a little uncomfortable with this type of public display of affection. Beside him, seemingly lost in her own world, Lucia gazed out the window. She was such a sweet girl, not at all the spoiled princess she could have been given her background. He felt such a strong surge of love and sense of needing to protect her. Sitting here, the sun shining in the window of the bus as the green fields sped by beside them, he almost found it hard to believe that they were in danger, but they were, and to forget it, even for a second, would be a very grave mistake.

The past forty-eight hours kept running around in his head. It was inconceivable to him how much his life had changed, and yet here he was, on a bus tour of Ireland, sitting beside Lucia, thousands of miles away from home and, well, everything. He wondered if they looked like a normal couple on vacation. He hoped so. This was difficult enough without anyone on the tour asking awkward questions. It felt right, the two of them together, but in so many ways and for a myriad of reasons, it was wrong. His head hurt from trying to analyse the whole situation.

The tour guide and bus driver, Conor, was a highly entertaining guy, and if Declan weren't so caught up in his own thoughts, he knew he'd enjoy the commentary. The atmosphere on the bus was jovial, and everyone seemed to be having a good time. He laughed when they did, though he'd missed the joke, and even took pictures when told to, but the land of his ancestors was passing him by in a blur.

As he'd told Lucia several times since they left the States, worrying solved nothing, so he tried to focus on the endless emerald fields and stony farms of the Irish countryside.

His reflection in the glass showed the face of a man who had aged so much in just a few short months. His black hair was grey at the temples and his face had become thinner. He was six foot two and couldn't really afford to lose weight, but the stress of recent weeks meant he just couldn't eat. Despite his best efforts to blend in as a happy-go-lucky tourist, his piercing green eyes seemed to him to betray him; he thought he looked hunted. He wondered if people noticed. One or two of the ladies on the coach had been friendly, maybe a little too friendly for an initial meeting, but he was used to that. Lucia often teased him about the admiring glances he received from the ladies of the parish every Sunday, but he explained it was because they didn't see him as a man as such; that's why they confided in him and sought him out. She wasn't convinced, though, pointing out that old Father Orstello, who was in his eighties and had very bad rheumatoid arthritis, didn't get the same treatment.

He smiled. All these feelings were so new – to have a woman love him as Lucia did and to find him attractive, for him to reciprocate. It was all so amazing, and under any other circumstances but these, it would be wonderful.

If times were normal, and this were a normal vacation, it would have been just fantastic, though possibly they would book into a little hotel somewhere and explore on their own. But a bus tour was safer. Someone had confessed to him a few years ago that he was having an affair and that he had taken his mistress on a bus tour simply because there was no paper trail. You didn't need to rent a car or check into a hotel using your details. You just booked the tour and the tour company made all the reservations for you, so it was much more difficult to be caught out. At the time, Declan had been appalled at such duplicitous behaviour, but the information had proved useful. They'd had to get out immediately and with a minimum of fuss, and a bus tour was the first thing he thought of. Ironically, this one was called Irish Escape. That's precisely what he and Lucia needed, so he made the reservation in New York at 10 p.m. and flew to Ireland at 7 a.m. the next morning. Thank goodness for lastminute.com.

He'd always wanted to visit Ireland; he knew he'd love it. He planned to one day visit the places his great-grandparents came from, maybe even find a cousin or two. But they certainly weren't there to relax and take in the gorgeous scenery.

He had been surprised to notice how Irish he looked, now that he was here. He'd expected there to be lots of red-haired people, but Conor had explained that the more typical Irish look was exactly Declan's combination of colouring: pale skin, dark hair and blue or green eyes. Lucia looked so Italian by comparison. Declan's skin never tanned, while she was olive-skinned, with dark-brown hair that fell over her shoulders and eyes the colour of melted chocolate. He felt his stomach lurch as he thought of her beauty. No woman had ever had the effect on him that she did. She didn't dress provocatively, quite the opposite, and unlike the other female members of her family, she wasn't one for tons of make-up. She had a natural beauty that was breathtaking. He was unsure about so many things, but his feelings for her were never in doubt. He loved her, heart and soul, and no matter what happened next, he would be by her side, protecting her.

Lucia had told him that she was sure their fellow passengers thought she was a little unhinged, as she was so jumpy and nervous, but Declan assured her that nobody on the tour thought anything about them. They were just folks on vacation who wanted to see Ireland, drink a pint of Guinness and take some pictures. He told her she was being paranoid. She had sighed, replying that maybe he was right, but she questioned how on earth they were supposed to just act normal. He asked himself the same question, but he had to make Lucia feel like he was in control, that she was safe, so he kept his concerns to himself.

'Fake it till you make it,' Declan repeated to himself several times a day, so he stood in for pictures and acted like the enthusiastic tourist as best he could. It was torture initially, but as the hours went by, he began to let the sense of tranquillity on the island seep into his bones and take in the splendour and peacefulness of the land. He felt curiously at home, even though it was his first trip to Ireland. It felt like nothing bad could happen there. It didn't stop him scanning every newspaper headline and checking the news channels the moment they got back to the room, but as the sun shone through the glass of the bus window, warming his face, he took a deep breath. Maybe it was all going to work out OK. He just had to keep it together for a bit longer; he could do that.

He thought about his ancestors who came from Ireland, who left their home and everything they knew and understood for the excitement and uncertainty of life in the United States. If they could show such resilience, then so could he. He had Sullivan blood in his veins, and Sullivans were made of tough stuff.

A cousin of Declan's, Patti, was into genealogy, and she had presented each branch of the clan with a beautiful family tree a few Christmases ago, showing how Daniel and Hannah O'Sullivan, both aged seventeen, got married in the church at Cobh, County Cork, a mere two hours before sailing from the dock there for Ellis Island. They came into the United States through the new immigrant inspection station in 1938. Declan recalled his grandmother telling him about the trauma of getting to the States. They sailed by the Statue of Liberty and saw the Manhattan skyline, tantalizingly close, but the immigration station had to be endured first. The inspection officers boarded the ships and processed first- and second-class passengers there and then, allowing them off the boats almost immediately. But Dan and Annie, as they were known, were in third class and had to wait on the ship for two days because so many immigrants were awaiting processing. Declan would hang on his granny's every word as she told him about the buttonhook, which the doctors used to check under eyelids for some awful disease; he couldn't quite remember now what it was. But his grandma was determined that both she and Dan would be found in perfect health. They exercised on the ship every day and only drank rainwater, and they brought their own food and doled it out daily. They were determined from the start to pass any inspection, get into the United States and make a new life.

When Declan was a student, he'd visited the museum on Ellis Island and was moved to tears as he thought about brave young Dan and Annie standing in separate lines in that huge hall, every language of the world ringing in their ears, their hearts filled with trepidation and hope. Annie had some dollars sewn into her skirt, sent by her older brother – Declan was named after him – who was killed on the railroad two weeks before Dan and Annie landed. Annie loved him and often talked of her first days in New York when a neighbour and friend from home had to break the news to her. She was tough, though, and with Dan forged ahead. She said she considered for one minute the possibility of going back home, so heartbroken was she, but she realised that the fare and the few dollars were Declan's legacy to her; to return would be to dishonour him, so they stayed. They settled first in Hell's Kitchen, where they had some contacts, but they were quick learners and hard workers. Dan soon got his foot on the ladder of a building firm and worked his way up, eventually setting up his own firm in Brooklyn.

They lived to see Declan grow up, and he had lots of memories of them surrounded by the extended family. Dan and Annie went home to God within months of each other, both well into their eighties, and their send-offs were fitting tributes to two brave, hardworking, kind people who took on the world and won. They died surrounded by their children, grandchildren, and even a few great-grandchildren.

The extended Sullivan family were deeply proud of their Irish heritage. They took all the things about Ireland they liked, admired and could identify with and celebrated their culture with gusto. Declan smiled at the memory of his dad, Dan and Annie's youngest son, singing 'Mother Mo Chroí' every St. Patrick's Day, and his rendition of 'Danny Boy' at the funerals of their many friends and relations left few eyes dry. His mother, Bridget, a good Irish Catholic girl herself, played her part when the family kept the tradition first started by Annie, entertaining the neighbourhood each March 17 with music, songs and enough corned beef and cabbage to feed a nation.

Declan thought about his parents. How they'd have loved it here. It was hard to believe they were gone too, killed instantly together in a car accident five years ago. They had planned to visit Ireland for the first time the summer after they were killed. His dad had been so excited at the prospect of visiting Ireland; he'd been researching the trip for months, working out where they could visit to establish the link between his generation and those that went before.

Declan fought back the stinging tears as he gazed out the window. He missed his parents desperately, but at least their untimely death meant they didn't have to endure the last few months. He couldn't begin to imagine how they would have felt at seeing everything they worked so hard for destroyed. It had embarrassed him as a young man how proud they were of him.

For fourteen years it looked like they would be childless, when out of the blue Bridget and Tom Sullivan found out they were going to have a baby. His mom was delighted, if a little embarrassed she later confided to him; it wasn't seemly to be pregnant so late in life. But he was born fit and healthy and the whole family was thrilled. Tom wanted to name his son after his mother's brother, the reason they were all in the States. Declan remembered vividly his mother recounting the first time he, as a baby, was placed in Annie's arms; she said the connection between them was instant and so strong it was palpable. She and Dan were proud of all their grandchildren, but Declan had a special place in Annie's heart. He used to love visiting his granny and granda (though all the other kids in his class had different names for their grandparents, his were called what grandparents were called back in Ireland). They loved his visits as well and always had treats for him. He was an only child but never lonely, as he had many cousins and aunts and uncles around. It was all one big happy family, and his childhood was punctuated by birthdays, communions, confirmations and weddings. Those carefree days seemed like a lifetime ago now.

His parents worked hard so that he could be well educated, sending him off to the Jesuits when he was seven. Looking back, he probably seemed like a deeply thoughtful child, and he was always very devout. All his life, God was not just a notion, someone to be kept in a church, but more a real living presence in his life. He remembered the day he told his parents he was going to the seminary. They were so happy he had a vocation. He'd always known, since he was a little boy, that he wanted to be a priest, and they couldn't have been more pleased. Annie and Dan sat in the front pew of the cathedral beside Tom and Bridget, and even though his grandparents were elderly and very frail, Declan remembered thinking the four of them might burst with pride. They were good Catholics who went to Mass every Sunday without fail and observed feast days, Lent and Advent. To have a priest in the family was a dream many Irish Catholic families harboured but few realised. They weren't the kind of family to be boastful – they worked hard for everything they had – but that day, well, it was a high point and he knew it.

Once ordained, he baptised the babies, married the couples and buried the dead of the Sullivan family. He loved New York and New Jersey and felt he was at his best there. Bishop Rameros and he were good friends, and Declan always made a great case for staying. He visited his parents in Brooklyn often; it was only a short drive from where he lived in Hoboken, New Jersey.

So many of his fellow priests had to deal with the care of elderly or infirm parents, but he was lucky – Tom and Bridget were fit and healthy and really enjoying their retirement. They loved to travel all over the East Coast in their RV. Declan used to joke that he needed to make an appointment to see his parents. After the accident, he fell apart for a while. He just missed them so much, and not having any siblings, he found it hard to explain just how huge their loss was for him.

One of the first real conversations he'd ever had with Lucia was about them. He didn't usually let his parishioners into his personal life, but she was different, in every way imaginable. The only time he'd ever cried for his mother and father with another person was with her. He'd spoken about it at the time to Father Orstello, with whom he ran the parish, and the other priest was kind and understanding, although it was clear he felt bad that his illness prevented him from being much help to young Father Sullivan, especially when he was grieving. Father Orstello had a large extended family, lots of nieces and nephews, and was very close to them, so he rarely needed to confide in Declan. Though the two men were fond of each other, they weren't that close.

Declan was very raw for a long time, frequently picking up the phone to call his mother, only to realise she was gone. He didn't need mothering, but his childhood home was gone, and with it a large part of him. Slowly, he came to terms with the loss and life resumed.

Lucia watched the Irish landscape go by. She knew she should be enjoying the scenery, but all she could do was concentrate on not vomiting. Declan's idea to go on a bus tour – something about being less detectable – seemed like a good idea at the time, when her whole world was crashing around her, but now, as the little coach lurched over the impossibly bumpy roads, she just tried to focus on the horizon and control the nausea. She was a bad traveller at the best of times, but this was torture. She'd hardly eaten a thing – she'd barely even drank any water – but still she swallowed constantly, praying she didn't get sick.

Declan had been amazing, and it was entirely her fault that they were in this mess. She squeezed his hand and gave him a gentle smile. She could be in a much worse position now if he hadn't acted so decisively, so bravely. He squeezed hers back as she tried to focus on what the driver was saying.

Conor was telling a very interesting story from Irish mythology about a woman whose husband was always drinking too much and then bragging about her abilities, which were of course, supernatural. She was happy to perform amazing feats for him but in return she asked that he keep quiet about her abilities. But he wasn't capable of keeping his mouth shut, and insisted at a party one night, that she could run faster than the chieftain's horse. She had to make good on his assertion as to make a public declaration in that culture and not be able to back it up was a grievous offence, so the woman ran the race, pregnant. She easily beat the horse in the race, but the effort brought on labour and she had to give birth there and then at the finish line. The men stood around, useless and appalled and she was so annoyed at them all for their bravado and stupidity she placed a curse on them, that each month for a day or two they would be laid low with cramps in their stomachs. This curse was to last for the rest of their lives. She defended this action when her husband complained bitterly by saying that women endured it, why shouldn't they?

Lucia and Declan managed a smile. Everyone on the bus was giggling as they got off to take a photo of the breathtaking vistas of green patchwork fields bordered by tiny stone walls.

They were in County Clare on the west coast of Ireland, and the expanse of the crashing Atlantic was laid out before them, a glittering azure blue. Huge seabirds circled and cawed overhead as they went back and forth to their nests on the high cliffs, the pounding surf relentless below.

This was the second day of the tour, and though Lucia was still jumpy, the gentle Irish landscape soothed her troubled mind. Last night she'd slept in Declan's arms for the entire night for the very first time. They'd been together before, but never for a whole night, and to wake up to him beside her was such a lovely feeling. At least until the nausea set in, that was. He'd never seen it before and had no idea what to do as she retched and retched and eventually crawled back into bed. She had to explain to him that it was normal, that in fact it was the sign of a perfectly healthy pregnancy and that he needn't worry.

Today was Saturday. If she'd not run away, if she had stayed and done what was expected of her, she'd be married now. She thought about Antonio and wondered how he was. She felt awful, such crushing guilt, at humiliating him and breaking his heart. He wasn't at fault at all, but she couldn't lie any more. Declan was the one for her, he always had been, and to marry Antonio would have been a terrible lie. She knew that if she'd gone ahead with it, she would have ended up hurting everyone in the end, but still it felt so horribly cruel. Her father's face replaced Antonio's in her mind. Where was he now? What was he thinking?

I HOPE that's whet your appetite to come back to Ireland with Conor and the gang.

Click here to keep reading
https://geni.us/SafeAtTheEdgeAL

ACKNOWLEDGMENTS

To my parents, John and Hilda, who each in their own unique way gave all of us roots and wings at the same time. To Rob, Barb, D-daw, and Ais, my best friends. For all my ladies who share their lives with me. I am so lucky to have such wonderfully funny, strong, and inspirational women friends – thanks for the tea, the wine, and the laughter. I am truly blessed. To all the Beechinors, for helping me to learn how to have my voice heard. No one could have a better gang. To Gran and Granda, for giving us all another place to call home. For all the wonderful people I worked with on tours over the years – visitors, drivers, and guides. The craic was mighty, and I loved every minute. To the band, Natural Gas, who I shamelessly used in writing this book. For Don and Johnny. For the staff and students of De La Salle College, Macroom, Co. Cork, a very happy place to be. I would like to extend a special thank you to the wonderful professionals whose expertise and attention to detail have turned this from a dream into a book. For Conor, Sórcha, Éadaoin, and Siobhán – thank you for all the joy you put in my life. I love each of you with all my heart.

And finally, for my lovely husband, Diarmuid, without whose constant love, support, and help I would never have finished this book. Because of you, I believe in true love.

ABOUT THE AUTHOR

Jean Grainger is a USA Today bestselling Irish author. She writes historical and contemporary Irish fiction and her work has very flatteringly been compared to the late great Maeve Binchy.

She lives in a stone cottage in Cork with her husband Diarmuid and the youngest two of her four children. The older two show up occasionally with laundry and to raid the fridge. There are a variety of animals there too, all led by two cute but clueless micro-dogs called Scrappy and Scoobi.

ALSO BY JEAN GRAINGER

To get a free novel and to join my readers club (100% free and always will be)

Go to www.jeangrainger.com

The Tour Series

The Tour

Safe at the Edge of the World

The Story of Grenville King

The Homecoming of Bubbles O'Leary

Finding Billie Romano

Kayla's Trick

The Carmel Sheehan Story

Letters of Freedom

The Future's Not Ours To See

What Will Be

The Robinswood Story

What Once Was True

Return To Robinswood

Trials and Tribulations

The Star and the Shamrock Series

The Star and the Shamrock

The Emerald Horizon

The Hard Way Home

The World Starts Anew

The Queenstown Series

Last Port of Call

The West's Awake

The Harp and the Rose

Roaring Liberty

Standalone Books

So Much Owed

Shadow of a Century

Under Heaven's Shining Stars

Catriona's War

Sisters of the Southern Cross

Printed in the USA
CPSIA information can be obtained
at www.ICGtesting.com
LVHW040721300424
778778LV00003B/195